D0462918

The East Indian

A Novel

BRINDA CHARRY

SCRIBNER

NEW YORK   LONDON   TORONTO   SYDNEY   NEW DELHI

Scribner
An Imprint of Simon & Schuster, Inc.
1230 Avenue of the Americas
New York, NY 10020

This book is a work of fiction. Any references to historical events, real people, or real places are used fictitiously. Other names, characters, places, and events are products of the author's imagination, and any resemblance to actual events or places or persons, living or dead, is entirely coincidental.

Copyright © 2023 by Brinda Charry

All rights reserved, including the right to reproduce this book or portions thereof in any form whatsoever. For information, address Scribner Subsidiary Rights Department, 1230 Avenue of the Americas, New York, NY 10020.

First Scribner hardcover edition May 2023

SCRIBNER and design are registered trademarks of The Gale Group, Inc., used under license by Simon & Schuster, Inc., the publisher of this work.

For information about special discounts for bulk purchases, please contact Simon & Schuster Special Sales at 1-866-506-1949 or business@simonandschuster.com.

The Simon & Schuster Speakers Bureau can bring authors to your live event. For more information or to book an event, contact the Simon & Schuster Speakers Bureau at 1-866-248-3049 or visit our website at www.simonspeakers.com.

Interior design by Kathryn A Kenney-Peterson

Manufactured in the United States of America

1   3   5   7   9   10   8   6   4   2

Library of Congress Cataloging-in-Publication Data is available.

ISBN 978-1-6680-0452-4
ISBN 978-1-6680-0454-8 (ebook)

To V. Shankar Charry and Malathy Charry

A lovely boy, stolen from an Indian king . . .

William Shakespeare,
A Midsummer Night's Dream

Every town our hometown,
Every man a kinsman . . .
Our lives, however dear,
follow their own course.
Rafts drifting
in the rapids of a great river . . .

Kaniyan Pūṅkunṟaṉ
Puṟanāṉūṟu 192
       translated from the Tamil
       by A. K. Ramanujan

The East Indian

PROLOGUE

A witch was hanged from the yardarm of the ship on the fourth week of my voyage to America. Some days before, we had stopped at the isles called the Azores to load wood and fresh water and were well on our way to the New World. They hanged the witch just before dusk. I was among those who gathered to watch as she was led up by two sailors, one on either side of her, her legs in chains although she could not have gone far even if she had tried to flee. Her name was Ann Brady. It was May, and the winds that filled our sails and blew the *God's Gift* towards Virginia were still chilly, but the waters were quite tranquil.

Captain Coxe had conducted Mistress Brady's trial and had been judge and all the jury. He had set up court on the deck with an eager crowd of sailors and Virginia voyagers pressing around him. Being among the youngest, Little Sammy Mason, Dick Hughes, and I were at the back of the crowd, straining to see and hear. The three of us were of the same age, or thereabouts—between ten and fifteen, with Sammy being the youngest, Dick being a bit older than I was. Sammy was a slight fellow, smaller even than me, and I was said to be small for my age. His eyes were the lightest I had seen, bluish gray, like the sky on a certain kind of day, his hair was a thatch of gold, and his face that of a girl. Sammy suffered from ulcers in his mouth through the journey. I recommended some of the medicinal powder I had filched from a London apothecary, but Sammy looked doubtful, and would sit with his mouth hanging open—just to air out the insides, he said, and Dick and I would keel over with laughter at how foolish he looked. We were boys and, in spite of our unfortunate lot, we could laugh at just about anything. Dick, for his part, was tall and gangly with brown hair and green eyes, his face sorely afflicted with spots—he was good at doing things the sailors asked him to do, things with ropes and such, and one of them said he should consider working on a ship. And then there was myself—the brown-skinned boy, the East Indian who went by the name of Tony.

"Where you hail from, lad?" the sailors asked me curiously.

"Where your moor friend from?" they asked Sammy and Dick.

"Tony is an Indian from East India, sir," they explained.

The sailors always looked surprised at that. "East India is a long way off, even further than America," one of them remarked.

It was dawn on that occasion. The ship, which never fully slept, was stirring to renewed life. The distant horizon silently bled red and pink.

"It is somewhere that-a-way, I think," I said, pointing eastwards. "Somewhere there."

Dick and Sammy squinted at the sky, trying to catch a glimpse of the land from where I had started.

"An East Indian . . ." the boatswain remarked, looking at me speculatively. "You are the first East Indian sailing to America, lad. Do not know of any who have gone before you."

Not knowing whether to be proud at that or dismayed, I smiled uncertainly.

"What is Virginia like, sir?" Dick asked. He was not interested in talking about me.

"Wood and water," the man replied. "Water and wood."

And I imagined green forest and winding river, balanced on the outer edge of the world.

A man who had known Mistress Brady in England stepped up at the trial and told of how her presence had stopped the milk from creaming in the churn, how chickens had died after she visited a farmstead—first one or two and then by the dozens. The crowd sighed and murmured as if they had been there and seen it all with their own eyes—that unyielding cream, that souring milk, those dying fowl, that village.

I gathered that they were not trying her for ill deeds in England, but rather for the spells she had worked on the *God's Gift*: one of the women on the ship had developed sores on her dugs—a slight chortle at that from us boys, quickly silenced by Captain Coxe. The sores had burst and yielded white pus that stank like rotten fish. The woman was now so sick that she was worn to the bone and could hardly walk. It was doubtless the doing of Mistress Brady, who had got into a quarrel with her, a petty dispute that had ended with Mistress Brady spitting and cursing.

The ailing woman was brought forward. She looked very ill indeed, with her weary, hollow face and gaunt frame. The sores had started on her breasts like small, ugly fruit, she claimed, a mere week after the quarrel. The captain had already had her examined by his wife, who had testified to the eruptions on her.

"And who else has had an encounter with the witch?" he asked. He had already judged her to be a witch, *knew* she was one.

There were also confused accounts of how a child had caused Mistress Brady offense, how he had perished after a bout of fever and vomiting, how his skin had turned a bright yellow, a sure sign of a witch's malignance, how he had refused all food. There were several ill children on the ship. It was unclear to me which one they were describing.

"What have ye to say to this, mistress?" Captain Coxe asked, turning to her solemnly. She did not say a word, she did not raise her eyes. We waited.

"Nothing?"

It appeared that the captain had had enough. His hot grog awaited him in his cabin. It would be best to hang her and be done with it.

The *God's Gift* was a small ship with just some hundred-odd souls in her, crew and migrants. There was a fair chance of meeting the other passengers at least once in the course of the crossing. Sometimes even the two gentlemen on the ship, Master Warburton and Master Marlow, stopped us boys for a chat as we scampered across the deck doing chores for the sailors. They were elegant young men with pointed beards, falling lace collars, and slashed sleeves, although they were not as wealthy as they looked, so some of the sailors told us, being merely second sons. They were out to make their fortune in the New World. They too were curious about me.

"From where do you hail, you little tawny ape?" Master Marlow asked.

"He is a gypsy, I warrant, just like that woman—the witch," Master

Warburton ventured. "The kind they used to call Egyptians. One of those who roam the countryside telling fortunes and swindling the folk, and such."

"No, sire," I said hastily. "I am no gypsy." And I explained, once again, that I was an Indian from East India.

Master Warburton then wistfully said he should have gone to East India instead of to Virginia, which was all swamp and sickness, from what he had heard. In India, he would have sailed to Soorat, met the mighty Moghol, and earned fat rubies just for paying his respects. I had no idea what he was talking about but feigned I did.

The witch and I had exchanged a few words one afternoon while on deck. The passengers were allowed to take the open air once every day or two in small groups, but no one wanted to be in Mistress Brady's company, so she walked alone. I had been by myself too, looking over at the water, listening to the creak of the ropes, the groan of the wood, and the sound of the wind slapping against the sails. Mistress Brady had come to stand by my side. She had spoken first and asked me my name. I had told her that it was Tony.

Her gaze was unwavering. "What was it before that?" she had asked. "What did your mother call you, lad?"

But I would not tell her. I had lost that name somewhere on my earlier journey, the one that took me across two oceans to England. When she saw that a sullen silence was the only response she was going to get, she had not pressed me further. She had placed her hand beside where mine rested on the rail and I saw that it was nearly as dark as mine, the skin of it rough from labor. I had looked up at her countenance and seen that her eyes were a deep brown—also almost the color of my own. There were some streaks of gray on her dark head, but there was yet a look of youth about her. At that moment, a sailor had come up and roughly told her to shove off downstairs. She had thrust a piece of salted pork into my hand and ruffled my curls as if I were still a very small child, and then she was gone.

So, a witch was hanged four weeks into our voyage to Virginia. After it was over, they hauled the body down and flung it into the water. Captain Coxe trundled back to his cabin, and they shooed us down to the hold, which stank of stale food, sweat, and vomit, but which was at least rid of the witch's envy and spite. We went on our way, breasting the gray-white waves, the ship moaning like a living beast, the winds pushing us briskly westwards.

It has been many years now since that crossing. But in my mind, she still stands there, forever looking out at the waters, forever asking me my name, forever failing to reach her journey's end. And I, forever poised at the start of my own voyage.

It was the year of our Lord 1635, and I, Tony, the East Indian, was the first of my kind, so they say, to reach America.

I

BLACK WATERS

ONE

The earliest memories I have of my birthplace feature salt—acres of it in translucent flats that glistened in the sun and gleamed in the moonlight, silver mountains of it harvested and brought to the warehouses, and smaller mounds piled in bullock-drawn carts. The only whiter thing I was to see in my life was snow. Even the air was saturated with salt, and the townspeople sweated saltier than any other people in the world.

The journey that led me to the *God's Gift* commenced in that salty place, the small port of Armagon in East India, where I was born to my mother, a Tamil woman who had migrated from further south and who was reputed among the townspeople for her beauty. My father could have been one of the many men who worked in the salt pans in the sizzling heat, or he could have been a local merchant, or he could have been a landlord, or a Brahmin priest. In fact, he could have been anyone at all, although my mother insisted that he was a well-known medicine man and astrologer from another town who had lost his heart to my mother till his wife firmly reclaimed it. I got accustomed to the many men who came to see my mother in the evenings after the lamps were lit and after she adorned her hair with jasmine and patted scented waters on her skin. Every man in the town wanted to claim that he had been with her. She was lovely even in the harsh white light of day, and in the softness of twilight she was transformed into a goddess. We lived with an older woman who I called my grandmother, though she might or not have been related to us. A man I knew as my uncle lounged on the veranda, a wooden club always by his side.

In truth, you could say that my story was set into motion well before my birth, when the English East India Company traders came, dreaming of ventures bigger than anything the world had yet seen. Armagon is on what the white men called the Coromandel, the long, low, scrubby coastline punctuated by the deltas of many broad rivers and the rich alluvial soils they leave behind. For as long as I could remember, there had been light-complexioned foreigners living in the factory they had constructed on the seashore.

"Who are they, Amma?" I asked.

"Just Company men," she said, distracted.

"Why are they pale like that?"

"For the same reason you are dark—the gods decided."

Unlike some other people, my mother kept track of the passage of days and years, perhaps because she knew that her days in her profession were numbered. That was why she could tell me that it was about five years after I was born that the Englishmen had first come and asked our local chieftain for land to erect a factory. They could transform our sleepy, salty town into a thriving trading post, they had promised—men and money would flow in from all corners of the world. Taking off their hats, in a gesture our chieftain had come to recognize as respectful, they had reminded him how prosperous Pulicat, just a two-day journey south of us, was under the Dutch traders who had arrived there decades ago. They would make sure our town would benefit from the trade, there would be wealth as never before . . .

However, the chieftain had heard enough stories about how the Dutch had filled their ships with local young men and taken them across the ocean to the Spice Islands. Their families had waited for their return till they gave up waiting. The rumor was that they had become slaves at plantations of clove and cinnamon. When the raja had questioned the English about that, they said no, the Dutch were the Dutch, but they were the English, Englishmen of the *English* East India Company—they would do nothing like that. And they had given their word on that and many more things.

Eventually, the Englishmen were granted land enough to erect their factory and changed the name of our town to Armagon in honor of the local landlord who had advocated with the raja on their behalf. He was called *Aru-mugam*—the "six-faced one," named for the god Murugan—but the white men got it slightly wrong, and it became *Armagon*. Armagon, the city by the sea, the city of salt, the city with the Company fort.

The factory was a lonely place and we, the people of the town, had very little to do with it. Its stone walls were two stories high and its wooden gates were soon eaten away by the salt-laden winds that blew in from the sea. None of the Company men stayed very long, and as I grew into boyhood, I noticed new faces reddened by the sun replacing the previous ones every now and again. Trade was dull and the riches we had been promised by the Englishmen never came to transform Armagon. The winds that arrived late in the year made it the devil of a harbor, they complained, impossible to dock in. And they cursed their bad fortune in Armagon, in the Coromandel, in East India.

As I think about it all these years later from the other side of the round earth, with New World sky above my head and New World dust under my feet, Armagon is a place visited in a dream, one remembered in fragments: the scented jasmine clambering up the walls of our small house; the salt beds glimmering in the light of the moon; the surf rolling onto the sandy shores; the weeds that grew around the walls of the East India Company factory bursting into bloom after the rains; the river flowing at the bottom of the hill on which the factory was built; and, at night, the white stars wheeling silently over all of it—the factory, the salt, the sea—surely still there, making giant arcs against the inky sky.

Perhaps, in a few years and if my mother had lived longer, I would have learned to blush at being the son of a courtesan. But at that time all seemed well. My mother earned enough to keep us in comfort, she was of lower caste perhaps, but not of the lowest; she was deemed very touchable even by the highest caste men, her presence did not pollute. With her by my side and my paternity obscure, I was one of those few children who floated in the unnamed space between castes.

I was adored by my only parent, who insisted that with my large, watchful eyes and thick, wavy locks of hair, I was the loveliest child in Armagon. Of course, she would say that, but others said it too, showering me with compliments, comparing my looks with this deity's and that one's. Their admiration first pleased me and then made me embarrassed, because were boys not supposed to be strong rather than lovely?

One distinct memory lingers: a snake, gray-gold in hue, slithered into the house on a warm afternoon and was scooped up on the end of a stick and carried out by my uncle with a stern warning from my grandmother not to kill it. Snakes were wise sages in their previous lives, she said.

"And what were the wise sages in *their* previous lives?" I asked.

She did not know. All she knew was birth followed death, one life followed another, and every birth was not only a continuation of the previous, but also an awakening, a renewal.

"You must have been a prince in your previous life, my darling," Amma crooned, taking me in her arms.

"And what were you, Amma?"

"I do not know, but I would like to be a bird in the next one—a forest-dwelling one, colorful, swift-winged."

My grandmother snorted from her corner. *Nonsense—a bird, indeed.*

But the old lady was not always so cynical. I could practically see her heart soar when she told me the ancient legends of the gods—the dozens of them who populated our town, and the country beyond, slipping unannounced in and out of mortal lives, some colossal, some diminutive, some with the countenances of men and women, some animal-featured, most of them multilimbed, all beautiful and terrible and grand—the red-skinned, warlike Murugan, whom she particularly revered, the lion-faced Narasimha, the noble Rama, the mischievous Krishna, the fiery Siva, and the even fiercer Yellamma, goddess of smallpox and sacrifice. My grandmother filled my head with their stories—their epic adventures, their acts of honor and deceit, their amorous exploits, their divinity, their humanity. I devoured her tales with greedy ear, as did Amma and even my uncle. They were the most enduring of the old lady's gifts to me, and in later years, in America, even when I had largely discarded them, I was to be visited every now and then by those deities of my early days.

One evening, shortly after the lamp was lit, my uncle brought home a white man. As soon as the stranger stepped in, my amma put on the expression that I had learnt was reserved for her patrons, demure, yet bold and flirtatious, her eyes making promises she would not put into words. Sir Francis Day was a slender young man, probably in his twenties. His eyes were blue as the seas he had sailed across, his mouth was small and thin-lipped, his jaw sharp and long. He wore the tight breeches all Company men wore, a coat, a ruffled blouse, and a feathered hat that I coveted right away. His fair, fine hair was slightly limp in the heat and tied back with a ribbon. My uncle brought him to the chamber where my mother sat, as he did all visitors; my grandmother came in from the back room to scrutinize him, as was her habit with all men. I announced my name to him, provoking a tight smile. He probably had not expected to meet a child in this house. My mother was all large, lovely eyes, scented shoulders, and lustrous locks. She knew all about the fleeting nature of men's desire and how she must snare it while it lasted, and reel it to land.

And then I was ushered away into the backyard, as I always was when my mother had her patrons visiting, and the rest of the evening was no different than one of the many evenings of my childhood—a touch of lamplight, my grandmother's tuneless crooning, and, beyond our walls, the sound of the sea. Master Day might have come several times before, and certainly came many times after, but it is that day that remains in my memories—the white man hesitating momentarily at our threshold, my mother, welcoming and curious.

Master Day, who we learnt was factor of the Company's fort in Masulipatnam, a little further north on the coast, seemed to admire my amma. There was nothing new in that; after all she *was* famed for her beauty. And she did have regular customers who gifted her with jewelry and other fine things. The only difference was that Master Day was her only English patron. Others might have looked down on her for consorting with a white stranger—I do not know. White men were considered unclean meat eaters by the higher-caste people in Armagon, and they would not have anything to do with them. But perhaps my mother was not subject to the same expectations. I could not tell then and certainly cannot now, after all these years. A gambler and adventurer with a flashy smile and sudden shouts of laughter, Master Day was also a most sensible, hard-nosed trader who pored over his books filled with figures in black ink. When he was in Armagon, he would spend his days at the lonely factory supervising the loading and unloading of goods to and from the Company's ships. In the evenings he would usually come back to us, unless business kept him away.

"White man here," my uncle would announce, although he knew our visitor's name, and although Master Day was less white than exceeding red in the heat, which bothered him terribly. I do not know what my mother felt about her Englishman, but she always welcomed him graciously and smiled as he took her hand in his to kiss, a gesture my grandmother thought was not becoming because it was performed in public.

I now wonder what they spoke about to each other and in what language they communicated. Those details evade me. But I do know that it was from Master Day that I learned English. I had a shrewd wit and a good ear, he said, and very soon I could patter away in his tongue to the wonder of the towns-people. He even wrote down the English alphabet for me and gave me printed books which I would study in the lamplight to my grandmother's exaspera-tion. She said I would go blind if I read in the dark, that learning the white man's tongue served no earthly purpose. Soon my mother, who, I suppose, was beginning to tire of her trade, stopped accepting other visitors; we furnished our house with finer things; and my uncle spent his days smoking hemp or napping on the front porch, his wooden club lying half-forgotten by his side.

Master Day's main business was in Masulipatnam and he would be ab-sent for weeks. By the time I was approaching my eleventh birthday, my mother allowed me to sail in his vessel to his factory up north or on his other voyages up and down the Coromandel. She thought it would allay my grow-ing restlessness at home, a trait she did not know how to deal with. Often Master Day's superior, one Master Andrew Cogan, another Company factor, came with us. I served Master Day and Master Cogan their drinks, fetched them their meals, and cleaned their shoes. We docked at small shallow ports, some of them filled with bustling crowds and marketplaces, others deserted except for the sea lapping against the shore and a few stray jackals that scamp-ered into the scrub at our approach. Master Day and Master Cogan desired to found a new factory, the biggest on the Coromandel, unrivaled in the whole of the East Indies, to and from which ships would sail, carrying commodi-ties between England and the Indies, bringing the Company riches beyond its grandest dreams. To this end, the two Englishmen tirelessly explored the coast. I enjoyed these brief voyages, learning to speak their tongue like they did and learning also to eat their foods, including certain forbidden ones my mother never found out about.

Around that time, my grandmother died of a brief, fierce illness. Master Day had by then determined that Armagon had sadly proved a complete failure, so he convinced my mother, who was grieving the loss of her older companion, that she had little to keep her in the town and promised to settle her in a fine dwelling further south in a place he planned to visit more fre-quently in the course of his trade.

So, my mother, my uncle, and I packed our possessions and bade fare-well to Armagon and that forlorn fort looking over the foamy white Bay of

Bengal, the second factory set up by the English East India Company on the southern Coromandel, the place that the Company men now said was best forgotten, better lost than found. We uneventfully sailed some fifteen sea leagues south and came to the house Master Day had found for us near the Portuguese port settlement of São Tomé. It was concealed by dense shrubbery and fruit trees near a town called Mylapore—the Place of Peacocks. Through the day and sometimes at night the air was punctured by the big birds' harsh, penetrating cries.

Once upon a time, there was an apostle of Christ who struggled between doubt and belief.

It was Master Day who recounted his tale to me. Thomas, *Doubting Thomas,* had insisted on seeing the resurrected Christ's wounds and on handling the soft dampness of torn skin and flesh before he accepted that the Master had indeed returned from the dead.

Except I shall see on his hands the print of the nails, and put my finger into the print of the nails, and thrust my hand into his side, I will not believe, he had declared stubbornly. But after Thomas had examined Christ's body for himself, as a physician does a patient, clinically rather than reverentially, feeling the spongy wounds, some yet leaking blood, others starting to crust over with growth, after he had finished, he had marveled. *My Lord and my God . . .* he had declared in a simple affirmation of faith. *My God and my Lord.*

Master Day told me this when I questioned him about the gods worshipped by the Portuguese in their temple—the one not far from our new home. They had called their settlement São Tomé after the doubting saint, and it was the base from which they explored the Coromandel looking for the riches that trade would bring.

My mother was content, I believe, in the year or thereabouts we spent near São Tomé, the year that turned out to be her very last. Master Day sailed north to Armagon and further up the coast, to solicit the paramount ruler of the kingdom, a sultan, for trading permissions. We waited for him to return to us, watching the tides rise and fall, the crabs scuttle on the sandy shores, the fishermen set out on their long, narrow catamarans, singing plaintive airs.

I wished to go with Master Day, but he never took me on these longer journeys. However, I was allowed to accompany him to the Portuguese temple, which he instructed me to call a church—an imposing white structure standing tall in the burning sun. Like Master Day, Saint Thomas, I learnt, was destined to be a wanderer. He had been reluctant at first, this time caught between belief and doubt in his own ability to confront the unknown. But he could not ignore the insistent voice that whispered to him night after night: *Fear not, Thomas . . . Go away to India and proclaim the Word, for my grace shall be with you.*

Hence, Doubting Thomas had come to East India to tell people about his One God. He had eventually perished on a hillock some leagues from São Tomé, pierced in his side with lances by heathens (which was another word for people like me). I heard that the soil of the hillock was still red with the apostle's spilt blood. His body was moved to the seashore and interred. Centuries later, the Portuguese traders had built the church over his tomb, which was revered by them, as well as by some of the Muslims who lived in Mylapore.

Master Day was not a man given to enmity, but he disliked the Portuguese. He told my mother and me that they were godless idol worshippers, which bewildered me, because I thought that they worshipped the same gods as the English. But no, Master Day firmly insisted, the Portuguese were papists, thugs, and boors to boot. I suspect the main reason behind Master Day's aversion was the success of the Portuguese merchants, who had grown rich on the trade in fine chintzes, pepper, and indigo, who had managed to arrive at profitable agreements with the local chieftains, who built large houses with balconies overhung with whispering trees, who were brash and arrogant, and who scorned the plodding English. Sometimes he and I would walk through the fortified Portuguese settlement together—tall white man, perspiring in his finery, and young Tamil boy, wearing little more than a piece of plain cloth wrapped around his waist and a gold stud adorning each earlobe. I would hold up a palm leaf umbrella to shelter Master Day from the sun. A few of my people strolled about the streets, but most of the people I saw were Portuguese. I remember passing men conversing outside a drinking house.

"What are they saying?" I whispered to Master Day.

He shrugged, and I realized for the first time that all white men do not speak the same tongue. We visited Dom Castalino, whom Master Day knew fairly well because he had an English mother and had dwelt in England for some years. A young woman came out and served the two men wine and gave me a drink made of mango pulp.

"Yours?" the merchant asked, raising an eyebrow and gesturing towards me.

"No, sir," Master Day said stiffly.

"The local ladies are sooty of hue but yet fiery hot, my friend, like the chili and pepper they eat with their victuals . . ." Dom Castalino said, smirking and winking meaningfully, and although I was but a boy, I knew exactly what he was talking about. "I would not hold it against you if he were yours, my dear sir," the Portuguese gentleman added.

Master Day changed the subject. He was not of the mood to discuss romances with Tamil ladies.

"One day the English Company too would like to establish a trading factory hereabouts . . ." he said. "I must say this is as incommodious a place as any on this dratted coast, but better than some others. Andrew Cogan and I have been working on getting the necessary permissions."

I was surprised he was confiding in Dom Castalino, but perhaps he had his reasons. The gentleman smiled and listened till the afternoon heat and the wine made him lethargic, at which point Master Day signaled that we should leave. As we walked out of the dwelling I glanced up and saw the maiden who had served us drinks draped over the balcony. I realized she was neither white nor brown-skinned but both. I could not tell if she was Dom Castalino's lover or his daughter.

São Tomé bustled with rambunctious life. The narrow streets were filled with Portuguese gentlemen dressed very elegantly, their mustaches and beards combed, and their hair in dark brown curls. A quarrel erupted outside a wine shop. *Corno,* one man cried out to the other. *Filho da mãe,* spat another—and neither Master Day nor I had any idea what they were saying. A group of women with lips and cheeks stained red, clad in European dresses and bonnets, tumbled noisily out of a house. I noticed that some of them were neither black nor white, just like the damsel in Dom Castalino's house. They turned the corner, shrieking with laughter.

I was ready to return home to my mother, but Master Day had one more stop to make. Once we got past the cool, dark entryway of the house, we saw an old Portuguese dame dressed all in black, sitting at a table with a small heap of delicate bones by her side. A young man lounging on a chair jumped up when we entered.

"Dona Mascarenhas, the famed fortune-teller, at your service," he said with great aplomb, bowing low and speaking English in the manner that Portuguese men who knew the tongue did.

"Pleased to meet you, Dona. I am Francis Day, English East India Company factor," Master Day replied drily, as if he were there against his will. We had fortunes told by Dona Mascarenhas that day. She did not read the bones, as I'd hoped she would, instead she took Master Day's hand in her own, like any palmist at the marketplace would. Her many rings gleamed in the light of the candle, and I noticed scars on her fingers, as if reading other men's fates had marked her own. She smoothed Master Day's red palm as if it were a piece of fabric, and began muttering in Portuguese. The man by her side translated:

"The Dona says you will find a city that has long been waiting to be found."

"What does that signify?" Master Day asked, feigning disinterest. The man asked the dona, who shrugged.

"It will be on a strip of land; it will grow to be the largest one in the Coromandel, and it will be filled with merchant-kings."

Master Day looked doubtful at that and I knew he was regretfully thinking about the little English factory at Armagon, so desolate and so pointless.

She might have spoken to him further—I cannot remember now. But she picked up my hand eventually.

"And you, little heathen boy," the man said, translating for the Dona. "You will cross all the seas in the world and go to the place where the sun sets."

I glanced at Master Day. His face was impassive.

"I do not wish to go anywhere," I said sullenly. "I do not wish to leave my mother."

The man laughed at that. "Foolish child—all boys must fledge and leave their nests," he said.

The Dona continued as if she had not been interrupted: "You will go. But mind you—" she said. "All the roads you travel will eventually bring you home."

She might have divined further, but Master Day stood up. He left her a coin, bowed, and we went to look out into the bright streets and towards a small, clear spring that gushed from the earth near the church.

"The bones of the saint are said to be buried just here," Master Day told me. "That is why the water is of the purest."

I wondered aloud how the saint's remains beneath the red earth would look now.

Master Day was barely listening to me. He had grown very quiet and I wondered if he was praying. But his mood of contemplation lasted only for a short while. On the road back he dwelt on how the old Portuguese dona was a superstitious gypsy.

"So, you will not find that city she was talking about, Master Day?" I asked.

"'Tis doubtful," he said gloomily.

"That means I am not going towards the sunset either," I concluded. "Which is really for the best."

I heard of George Bishop before I met him. The marketplace in Mylapore was filled with vendors, jewelers, street acrobats, workers of charms, dispensers of herbs—all of them engaged in loud conversation. Some of these men talked of the young Tamil man who had voyaged to Master Day's foggy country. Many years ago, when he was but seventeen years of age, George Bishop had been taken under the wing of James Rynd, a Company padre posted in Masulipatnam, who had schooled him in the Bible, English, and Latin, and taken him to England to teach him more. There, he had become a Christian and taken a new name. A few gossipers clicked their tongues in disapproval at his crossing the oceans, the black waters, as some people called them, and so losing caste; at his abandonment of the ancestral gods, but mostly they were indifferent. There were other local Christians, after all—some of them had been converted by Saint Thomas and had been Christians longer even than the English and Portuguese.

I met George one morning when I was out buying medicine made of frankincense and *brahmi* for my uncle. Of late, partly because I had been told that my father might have been a medicine man, I had grown fascinated by the *siddhar* or herbalist's wares of roots, leaves, pastes, and powders. The herbalist claimed to heal headaches and stomach ailments, diseases of the skin and the heart. He also sold a decoction of saffron to make men joyful, though an excess of it could make them too joyous, he warned.

"How much joy is too much?" I inquired. "And who determines the right amount of it?"

But before the herbalist could reply, a short and stout man, about thirty years of age, with a pitch-dark face and large, mournful eyes, came by to purchase something. I lingered, but after the stranger had secured his items the herbalist got busy packing up, so I reluctantly moved away, with the stranger by my side.

He seemed eager to talk. "I have heard of you," he said. "Are you not the boy who speaks the English tongue?"

I nodded. I was proud of my prowess.

He introduced himself: "My name is George."

It sounded odd. Men who looked like him were not supposed to bear English names. But his name, he told me, was conferred upon him by the king himself.

"Which king?" I asked.

"King James of England, Scotland, and Ireland," he said, and I had to laugh because it sounded so pompous and George was so solemn about it.

"Three kings in one?" I cried in amusement.

But George *had* been to England, and the king of that country *had* given him a name. George Bishop, it appears, had seen the One God the same instant he had clapped eyes on Chaplain Rynd. It appears that the good chaplain had seen great promise in him and trained him to be quite the scholar. George could read the Bible, could tell stories of the god who turned water to wine, preached on a mount, and finally (quite inexplicably to me) died on a cross.

"Why did he die if he was a god?" I asked, and George launched into a response so long that I wished I had not asked at all.

I soon learnt that George's tales were dismissed by most people as the ravings of a lunatic, but I still liked whiling away the long days with him. Over the course of several conversations, I learnt that Master Rynd had seen in George an opportunity to bring East Indian heathens to the light, had taken him to London, and eventually christened him at the Saint Dionis Backchurch. Later, when I was in London myself, I visited the neighborhood near Eastcheap and saw the streets filled with merchants and sailors of every complexion. I imagined the curious bystanders watching as the young East Indian man was led up to his christening.

George told me he had dwelt in England for a year after his baptism, continuing his studies under Master Rynd. And then it was time to return home. He had been solemnly charged to carry on the Lord's work in India and put on a ship. The Honorable Company had paid his fare back.

When I asked George how many people he had won over to the Christian faith since his return, he was evasive. He preferred to talk about the sluggish, brown river in London alongside whose banks he had lived, the chill that never left the English air, the short winter days, the long summer ones, the wonder and glory of his baptism. He spent his days doing nothing, in fact, but remembering his time in that place, and living off the wealth his merchant father left him. But he was still the first person I met, other than Master Day, who had been to a country as far as England. My uncle said that George Bishop was a madman and I had better stay out of his way if I did not desire to be abducted and taken to England myself.

"But I would certainly voyage there if I could return in a short while," I said. "And if my amma comes with me."

My uncle chortled. He was in good health and spirits now, having taken the herbalist's prescriptions. "You are not going anywhere," he said, "and your mother certainly is not."

"A Portuguese fortune-teller told me I will travel to where the sun sets," I said defiantly.

"And I tell you that you will be dead in a month. It is damp and disgusting everywhere else in the world but here, and you would starve because there would be no rice to eat."

I knew such trivial things as the weather or a bad diet would not hurt me, but I was not certain if I would venture anywhere without my mother. I was the center of her world and she was of mine—even on those days when boyhood yearnings led me to leave her side and explore the groves of banana and mango or the red hills around São Tomé. I also wondered if all travelers became a bit like George—gabbling on about lands they would never return to and kings who might be real or imagined, a disappointment to his English mentor, forgotten by the other Company officers, dismissed as an eccentric by the locals, forever dispossessed.

One day George disappeared from Mylapore, and no one could tell where he went to.

"Maybe he has traveled back to Masulipatnam, where he came from," said the barber.

"Or to London," guffawed the herbalist, "in order to . . ."

"Become a Christian . . ."

"Or to visit the white men's king . . ." said other men in jeering chorus.

But before he left, George had handed me a cross of wood, which he had said was the idol Christians worshipped, and also conferred on me a new name.

"The world is a big place full of wise people, but they might find the name your mother gave you too difficult to utter," he had said, leaning against the trunk of a tree, watching as I strove to bring down a ripening mango with a stone.

"Do you know of a better name?" I asked, only half-interested.

George thought for a moment. He was taking this seriously. "We will call you *Tony*."

I bit into the mango. It was not quite ready, and the sourness the sun had not yet drawn from its flesh hurt my teeth. I made a face.

"You do not like the name?" George asked anxiously. He was a gentle man who liked to please.

"Not very much."

"I will think of another one," he promised.

"Oh, never mind," I said impatiently. I did not really care.

"Tony!" George called out, as if I was some distance away, and not standing right by him. "Tony . . . !"

And that was the first time someone called me by the name I came to be known by in America.

Before that year drew to an end, an epidemic of cholera took my mother, loveliest woman in the Coromandel and the whole wide world. She was there and then gone, and the silence she left behind was almost unendurable. My uncle had gone before her. At nearly twelve years old, I had no one left in the world but Master Day, who gave me coins enough to buy food, who visited sometimes, but who was mostly away. Sometimes, on the days he was in the house, he looked at me as if uncertain how I had got there and what he would do with me.

A few months passed that way. My grief sat heavy in me, like a stone I could not stir, and when I was not mourning, I was afraid and lonely. Master Day came and went; the December rains came, bringing a little coolness to Mylapore; the peacocks displayed themselves in all their gaudy brilliance as the clouds thickened. One evening, when Master Day was present, I lit lamps in the front chamber of our house so we had light enough to see our hands before our faces.

"On days like this I feel like your mother is back with us," he told me. He seemed genuinely sorrowful and that moved me, although I had heard that he had now taken a lover in the Portuguese settlement, another very beautiful lady, because that is the way Master Day liked women.

"Indeed, I wake up at night and hear her walking about the house," he continued.

I listened, torn between apprehension at the idea of phantoms in the house and resentment that my mother had not shown herself to me first.

"'Tis my fancy," he said, as if guessing my thoughts. "The imaginings brought about by grief that no physic can cure . . . *Doctor, canst thou not minister to a mind diseased, pluck from the memory a rooted sorrow . . . which weighs upon the heart . . . ?*" Master Day murmured, and I was certain that he had had a little too much wine. "You know those lines, boy? They were by this fellow called William Shakespeare, whose plays were all the rage in London when I was there."

"George Bishop has been to London, sir."

"Yes, indeed he has. He is among the first East Indians to be baptized there."

So, George had not been telling untruths after all.

Master Day and I looked at each other in the dim light of the lamp. I realized that I did not know what he thought of me. He had probably resigned himself to my presence only because I was bound to my mother. If he wanted the woman, he must take the boy. Now, with her departed, he could get up and walk into the evening, leaving me entirely alone.

"And what of you, boy? We must do something with you," he said.

"I do not know what is to be done, sir."

He smiled at that. A little sadly, I thought.

"Why don't you go somewhere too? On a great adventure?"

I stayed silent. I was not inclined to agree right away to any plan he might have had. Stories of the men from Armagon who had been shipped to the spice plantations flashed through my mind. But it did not much matter what I said or did not say, because Master Day had decided that something must be done with me. He was not a heartless man, but I was a small piece on the big chessboard of his dreams and I would have to be moved to make place for other, more important things.

Although I did not know it then, that rainy evening in Mylapore, Master Francis Day would go on to make history. Decades later, when I had been in Virginia a long time, an old sailor who had been to the surf-washed Coromandel and seen the bobbing catamarans setting out at dawn told me that Master Day had gone on to found a successful factory just north of São Tomé. Under

him and Master Andrew Cogan, a small fishing village named Madrasapatnam had grown into a bustling trading center that the English called Madras.
Master Day had publicly declared that he had selected the spot for the safe
harbor it afforded East India Company ships, but the common report was that
he was enamored by a lovely lady who dwelt nearby and had chosen that spot
to build the factory so his interviews with her could be more frequent and
uninterrupted.

No, I thought, the loveliest of ladies was long gone by the time Master
Day founded his city. It was the memory of her that kept him there, her shade
that he desired to visit, never mind if he took another woman after her.

So, as it turned out, it was the Englishman, Master Day, who remained in
the Coromandel, in that particular place by the sea where a wandering apostle
of Christ had bled and where peacocks shrieked. I was the one who left.

TWO

London in the earliest dawn. That liquid hour between one day and the next. Fog so deep, so dark, and so ghostly that I could walk in and become one with it.

Master Day had had no distinct ideas for me when he first broached the idea of me going away. It was only when one Sir Miles Davies, another Company official, decided to sail back to London that a plan had fallen into place.

"You are a presentable young fellow," Master Day told me. "You speak the English tongue well. Just the kind of boy that can get into service with Sir Miles."

My long hair, which I tied in a curly knot on the back of my head, was cut to shoulder length on the advice of Master Day, my ear studs were taken away as being too dandyish for a mere servant, and I was presented to Sir Miles. He was a middle-aged, corpulent man who had realized that he was not cut out for life in the scorching Coromandel. It was time to return to his cool, green England, and it would be good to take back a servant to prove to his countrymen that he had indeed been to the East Indies. When Sir Miles asked me my name, I remembered what George Bishop had called me.

"It is Tony, sir," I replied, keeping my voice low and my eyes down.

"Tony what?"

I did not know what he meant. "Just Tony, sir," I answered.

And although Master Day knew my real name, he let it be. My fare was paid and I bundled up my clothes and a small purse of English coins that Master Day presented me (which I later found would not buy me more than a few meals and a coat from a London pawnshop). I was to sail on the *Queene Anne*. I watched Master Day walk down the rough wooden dock to the sandy shore, and almost called out to him to tarry, to take me back with him, but he turned a corner and it was too late. I was never to see him again—Sir Francis Day, Englishman, East India Company factor, founder of the city of Madras, lover of my mother.

So, I arrived in London, about ten months later. But wait, you ask, what about that long, long journey, the one that brought you to England?

It was a blur of sickness brought about by the rocking motion of the ship and then of another fever the ship doctor could not name. Sir Miles complained that Francis Day had saddled him with a lad too-frail.

"I am sorry, sir," I said. "Very sorry." And I meant it. I had so wished to impress him with my diligence.

We sailed so long, it seemed we would never cease. Water covered all the earth. I remembered what my grandmother had told me of *the god of the sea, Varuna: his vehicle, a crocodile; his halo, a storm cloud. He circles the world, embraces it in his watery hold; he separates and unites; he is fluid and powerful, fearsome and magnificent.*

The seas were blue and then green—warm and then cold. We docked to restock at Cabo das Agulhas or the Cape of Needles, the southernmost tip of a great land where the people were as black-skinned as, or even darker than, the darkest of people from the Coromandel; we sailed along a continent where mountains loomed along the coast and whose interiors, the sailors said, had deserts and jungles and waterfalls and the strangest beasts man ever laid eyes on. We stopped at many ports, but rarely ventured to explore. The ships going to the white man's lands sometimes stopped to pick up slaves here, one of the sailors told me.

"Will we be picking up slaves?"

"Nay," he said, "we are not a slave ship."

"Am I a slave?" I wondered aloud, a sudden doubt creeping into my mind.

"No, I think you are not," he reassured me, "though I've heard that twelve of your people were seized and taken on *The Tiger* back in 1599. Whether they were slaves or no, I cannot tell."

"Where are they now?"

He shrugged. "Probably dead."

And I wondered if I would never see land again, if I would give up the ghost as we sailed around Africa and then northwards, always northwards to the land ruled by James, King of England, Scotland, and Ireland, patron of George Bishop, my Christian friend. I mentioned the king to a fellow passenger, to show him that I was acquainted with matters English, and was quite surprised to hear that King James had died some years ago and his son ruled in his stead. I was saddened by that—George had made a great deal of the king, and I had secretly hoped to meet him.

But a deceased king turned out to be the least of my worries because Sir Miles fell terribly ill too, after months of berating me for my ailments. His gums grew black, his teeth loosened and fell off, he stank, a terrible stink. The ship surgeon, Master Williams, said it was the dreaded scurvy.

"His contaminated blood has begun to leak out of his veins," he explained to me, as I stared, horrified and fascinated. He recommended juice of lemons and then *earth bathing,* an operation which involved Sir Miles being covered with the English dirt carried on the ship for the treatment of those afflicted by scurvy. It was thought that the smell and feel of the earth would heal. I helped administer the treatment, and the surgeon complimented me, saying that I had a sure hand. But it was of no avail—in one short month, and just three weeks before reaching his beloved England, Master Davies was hallucinating and developed convulsions that were something awful to see.

And one day, in the midst of such a fit, he exited the world. I wept hard although, in truth, it was more for myself than for Sir Miles, who could be nasty and ill-tempered. Sickness and death had taken so many people and so quickly.

"Does physic ever cure, sir?" I asked Master Williams bitterly. "In my experience it is of little use."

And he replied that some bodies responded to it, for others, the call of death was stronger. "But one has to hope," he concluded. "Medicine is based on good faith, my lad."

But I was so taken down by my own hopelessness that I barely noticed when the *Queene Anne* docked on the Thames, and the dank odor of mud, fish, and urine—the smell of London—reached my nostrils.

Master Williams was the person I had become best acquainted with on the ship, and I asked him for assistance.

"Long way from home for a stranger to be," he said thoughtfully. "And a young lad too."

"Yes, sir. I hope you can aid me."

We had docked in Blackwall, where East India ships converged. Master Williams told me that he knew not what I could do, unless I went home with him as his servant.

"You seem bright enough," he said. "And since I plan to now practice my trade on land, I will soon be looking for an apprentice."

My heart lifted at that. It seemed a good prospect, but as it turned out, it was not to be. Master Williams required an apprentice's fee in turn for learning me his trade for six or seven years, and I did not have the means to pay him. He was regretful, but he could not take me on. In any case, he said, I might be happier in the company of the East Indians who lived in London nigh the docks.

So, guided by Master Williams, I found my way to Peter Mansur, an East Indian who, with his wife, an Englishwoman named Jane Hill, ran a small boardinghouse for East Indian and African sailors. Peter himself had been a sailor on a Company ship and, for reasons he never revealed, stayed on in London. He was a handsome man, with a fine black mustache and aquiline nose—back in my land they would have said he was too handsome for his wife, who was a stout, homely woman, though very kind-hearted. Peter and I had to converse in English since I did not understand his Bengali, and he was not even aware that there was such a tongue as Tamil.

There was much unemployment in the city and even with Peter's help the best I could do was to get a job lifting loads at the docks. It was in London that I came to think of myself as an "East Indian." I had always been a Tamil boy from Armagon, but here in this faraway city, people regarded me the same as Peter—*East Indians* both—although he had his own creed, tongue, king, and homeland, which were quite different from mine. I guessed it was something to do with the color of our skin, a similarity of complexion that put us in the same grouping, although in that too Peter was quite a few shades lighter than me. But it was in London that I became an *East Indian,* and I was to stay one for the rest of my life.

There were others of our kind in London along with Peter and me—mostly seamen who could not find posts on ships and so worked on the docks or begged on the street corners, shivering in the steely rain. There was at least one woman too, a girl they called Mary Bengal, about sixteen years of age, who worked as a nurse to children before she became a midwife's assistant and then a midwife herself. She visited Peter's home once in a while and I got to know her a little. There were other dark-complexioned people as well. In the lane behind ours resided three African men—two of them worked in the wharfs with me and one was a silk weaver by trade. And one morning I saw a stocky, brown-skinned, black-haired man fishing in the Thames. Mistress Jane informed me that he was an Indian of the New World.

"His people are not Mahometan like you," she added. "Back in his native land they worship the sun."

I was not Mahometan. I also remembered the brahmins back home submerged waist-high in water at dawn, bathed in light, facing eastwards.

And, not surprisingly, there were white men everywhere: some of them as fine as Master Day, but many of them ragged vagrants huddled all along the street corners, giving off the stench of unwashed bodies. Peter informed me that an excessive amount of common land in the countryside was being enclosed for private use, depriving the poor of farmland and pastures for their animals. These men had tramped to London over hedgerow and highway to escape want, he said. To me, they did not look any less hungry now that they were in the city, and my heart was filled with pity for them. But one morning I was walking, busy with my thoughts, with just myself for company, when one of them hissed at me.

"Moorish cur . . ." he said, *"little brown shit."*

That was the first time in my life that I was called such things and it filled me with shock. I did not find it in my heart to be sorry for this crew of men any longer. I would have spat in their faces and cursed them with even more hunger, if only I had dared.

On another day I walked with Mistress Jane and her friend, the two women just ahead, when a little boy sidled up to me.

"Good morrow," he said.

I glanced at him warily. He smiled and pressed closer to me. I was glad that he was being friendly.

"What is your name?" I asked.

He smiled yet again, but did not answer. I wondered if he was mute, or feeble-minded. And then I felt a sharp pinch on my thighs where my pocket was and he was gone in a flash of skinny, pale limbs clothed in rags.

"Hey!" I shouted after him. "Hey there . . . !" The women turned around inquiringly.

"The knave took my coin, Mistress Jane!" I cried out. "He *robbed* me!"

Someone laughed from the shadows and soon there was a small chorus of hooting and hissing. I would have cried out to them to hold their tongues, but Mistress Jane hurriedly shushed me and swiftly walked me homewards.

After that I kept my distance from the vagabonds, choosing to walk on the far side of the narrow streets, preferring even the urine-soaked sidewalks to proximity to them.

So that was the London I knew for the eight months I was there—a city of vagrants, cutpurses, foreigners of many hues, and women walking about freely, a sight that surprised me at first. It was a large place, bursting with life, afoul with strong odors, clanging with sound—horses neighing, wheels crunching on gravel and squelching through mud, people calling out. When winter came, the air grew dank and chilly and the cramped tenements and boardinghouses more oppressive. But sometimes, when the sun rose from behind the wooden buildings and steep roofs, the city was tranquil and beauteous.

Mistress Jane was a gentle soul and it saddened me when she said that she was shunned by many of her neighbors because she had taken Peter for her husband.

"But none of the Englishmen in the factory objected when Master Day came to live with my mother," I told her.

She told me that was different. Master Day was a man and a wealthy one too—"And he did not *wed* your mother, you see."

Now that she put it that way, I saw well enough. "Who will wed Mary Bengal when she grows up?" I wondered aloud.

"'haps you will, young Tony," Mistress Jane said with a quick smile. "Handsome fellow like you and dainty thing like her."

"But she is too old for me!" I exclaimed, feeling myself flush. "And besides, Mistress Jane, I am going back home once I find a ship that is sailing to the Coromandel."

"That is what Peter said too, and look what happened!"

"No, mistress," I said firmly. "I must return home. I will find a way."

And I was so sure of my purpose that I did not contemplate the possibility of another destiny. How could I have? How can one imagine a future in a place that one does not even know exists?

I worked on improving my skills in English, just as I had done on the ship, with whatever discarded books and papers I could find. But most of my days were taken up with my work on the docks, work which was hard and monotonous. The few pennies I made, I gave Peter Mansur and Mistress Jane for my keep. One day, Peter generously gave me my day's wages back and suggested that we go see an entertainment on the other side of the river. The money would serve to buy me an entrance. The theater we went to that afternoon was a goodly one, a circular, thatch-roofed structure, crowded with people eating nuts, hawking and spitting all over. The play was ridiculous but very entertaining, about lovers lost in magic woods and little gods they called "fairies" who played tricks with magic potions. And then the fairy king and queen were quarreling over a boy—an *Indian* boy. The king insisted that the boy, the one he called a changeling, was his possession. The queen replied that he could not take the child, that his mother had been her votress, that *in the spiced Indian air, by night, Full often hath she gossip'd by my side* . . . And so, the king and queen bickered.

"What's a changeling?" I whispered impatiently to Peter. "Who is a votress?"

He shrugged in reply, keeping his eyes fixed on the stage. And then he was laughing because a clown had turned into an ass and the fairy queen had fallen in love with him. I wondered why they did not ask the Indian boy if he preferred the king or the queen, or if he would have simply preferred to go home. But at least the Indian boy was desired, I mused on the way out of the theater, by a king and queen no less. For now, all I had was Peter and Mistress Jane, and I knew I could not live with them forever. The high-caste men back in my home would not cross the black waters because they would lose their elevated caste status. I, perhaps, had no distinct caste to lose. But my crossing too had led to loss of a kind that was both intense and indefinable.

"In truth, if you really think about it, the Indian boy did not have a role at all," I told Peter despondently. "Or rather, he did and he did not."

"Yes, little brother," said Peter. "That is like our people who dwell in London—we are a people who live in the shadows."

With that we walked on silently. They were baiting a bear in a pit near the theater. The dogs barked in a frenzy and the people were laughing and shouting, their heads flung back, their mouths red and wide open, nasty, preying beasts themselves. The bear was not bleeding yet, but I knew he would be soon. For now, he stood there chained to the wooden stake like some black, suffering soul.

The play, I discovered, was called *A Midsummer Night's Dream* and it was by Master Shakespeare. The same Shakespeare Master Day had mentioned one time.

I did not first hear of Virginia, I smelt it. Right there by the Blackwall shipyards amidst the reek of human waste and horses and the pervasive odor of the river that hung heavy over all things, a sharp, not unpleasant scent tickled my nostrils—it was the smell of woodsmoke and something else. I saw that it came from a group of my fellow workers who were lounging about, smoking. I asked one of them, an African, what it was he had in his pipe, and he said it was *tobacco*. I did not think much of it till I saw a notice outside an apothecary's shop that proclaimed that tobacco *purgeth superfluous fleame and other gross humours and not onely preserveth the body from obstructions, but also openeth the pores and passages of the body whereby the bodies are notably preserved in health and know not many grievous diseases.*

Being young of body and not afflicted by superfluous phlegm or any obstruction of pore or passage, I had no occasion to buy this strange substance even if I had the means. But I asked Mistress Jane about it later and was told that tobacco was a foul thing. In fact, the old King James had called it a *vile and stinking custom,* she said, with the smoke resembling the fumes from *the bottomless pits of Hell.*

"But the notices said that it was a medicinal purge!" I pointed out.

Mistress Jane opened her mouth to launch into another tirade against the substance, which she had not even tried, when Peter interjected that tobacco grew in the West Indies. "And also in Virginia," he added. And that was the first time I heard that name.

Shortly after, I went into the apothecary's on an errand and saw tobacco for myself. The place was ill-lit and filled with utensils containing all manner of syrups, ointments, and other such stuffs, including a dark, flaky powder labeled as tobacco. I was bending to inhale the substance when the red-haired shop assistant glared at me. "Hey, black fella!" he called out. "Come to buy or steal?"

"To pay good money, sir," I wanted to retort. "For your headache powder, which Mistress Jane takes without feeling one jot better."

But I bit my tongue. Peter had told me that people did not take kindly to impertinent strangers, especially dark-skinned ones. So, I politely announced what I wanted, and while he weighed it out on his miniature scales, I looked around me. The assistant would have told me to stop prowling around, but another customer came in, a pretty young maid, and he turned his full attention to her.

The shop was a magical cavern. Deep in its recesses were dried animal bladders that hung from the ceiling, along with the preserved corpse of a big reptile. Next to a sack of dried leaves labeled *sassafras* was another filled with tobacco, and yet another with a floury, gray substance identified as unicorn-horn powder from India, which could cure rabies, the plague, scorpion bites, and venereal disease. I wondered how I had not come across this miracle cure when I lived on the Coromandel. I glanced at the assistant, now at the front of the store. He was still busy with the maid, and had apparently forgotten all about me. I cannot tell why I did what I did next, perhaps because the shop boy's words still rankled, perhaps because I was envious that he was an apothecary's apprentice and not I, perhaps only because I was no better than a common thief—I scooped some of the unicorn-horn powder into the cloth pouch that I carried and slipped it into my pocket. I did not know it then, but it would come to my aid many years later. I hurried out of the shop, the medicine burning in my pocket.

I was about to flee homewards when a dark, round-faced maid crossed the street and came towards me. I recognized her right away as Mary Bengal. I flushed because of my recent misdemeanor and also because I remembered Mistress Jane saying that I should wed Mary when I grew up, never mind that she was sixteen years of age, and quite a grown-up lady.

"How do you do, Tony?" she asked pleasantly.

"'Tis too cold in this place," I said, not addressing her by her name since that would be discourteous. I did not want to call her "sister" either, in case we *did* end up being wedded. "And everything smells strange."

She smiled. "You will get used to it," she said. "And even if you do not, you will cease complaining."

And Mary told me how she had been brought to the city by a Company official. She lived with him and his wife, cooked, cleaned, and took care of their many children, apart from working as a midwife. In my turn, I told her of the city by the sea and the other dream city still to be founded by Master Day, about Master Day himself, my mother, Sir Miles, who had died on the voyage sans teeth and sans everything, and about Peter and Mistress Jane. How they were good people and kind, but how despondent I was most of the time.

"You are fortunate," I added resentfully. "You have found a place for your-self here. You have steady employment and a home."

I was discomfited by the sudden tears that filled her eyes, turning them into dark pools. She shook her head. "No—no, you do not understand. I want to go home too . . . ."

I wondered if her master and mistress beat her. Because I did not know that worse things than a beating could be inflicted on a young maiden, I did not think beyond those ill treatments. And I quite forgot that I had just cheeked a shop assistant by stealing from under his nose and I too was sud-denly ready to weep.

We met again and yet again. Since she dwelt with English people, Mary knew many things—how the wealthier people used mace, ginger, cloves, and cinnamon from the East Indies in their cakes and cordials, how they boiled ale, ox pith, currant juice, pepper, and nutmeg together and administered them to women who were subject to miscarry, how they gave other spices to women who *wanted* to miscarry, and to women who needed to set their monthly courses right. I remembered *the spiced Indian air* celebrated in the entertainment by Master Shakespeare. Mary was telling me that the English also took tea, coffee, chocolate, and sugar. How they ate the entire world, it seemed, and hungered for more. And because I felt that I too must demonstrate my wisdom, I told her about tobacco. She retorted that she knew all about it. There was nothing Mary was not well acquainted with, it seemed.

"Mistress Jane says that the vapors from it are the fumes from Hell," I said. "She also says it burns up a man's insides. But the notice in the tobacco-nist's shop says it opens up blockages."

Mary shrugged. "Who knows?" she said mysteriously, implying she did.

Since it seemed an appropriate moment, I told her how I could have be-come a physician's apprentice if I had had money for the fee. I would have then learned all there was to know about medicine and such.

"Would you have liked to?" she asked.

"Yes. You see, my father was a medicine man," I said, having quite forgot-ten that that might or might not be true.

By the end of our third meeting, Mary and I had decided that we would find a ship to take us back to our land. We would go to the docks with her small savings, she said, and we would look for a ship. We would beg for a place on it, we would promise to work on board, we would do anything, but we would return. Mary's face glowed with anticipation—I was the one who had to suppress my misgivings and take comfort in the fact that her hope lit up the air around us.

I began to see Virginia mentioned everywhere. At the Saint Dionis Back-church, north of London Bridge, which I was curious to see because it was where George Bishop had been baptized, the priest delivering the homily was moved more by the wonders of Virginia than by the One God who had so touched George's heart. He talked about the beauty of the place, the temperance of its air, the richness of its soil. He urged his countrymen to go there and see these things for themselves, for does not the Scripture teach us that *the Lord had said unto Abram, Get thee out of thy country, and from thy kinard, and from thy father's house, unto a land that I will shew thee . . . ?*

"Why was the preacher so eager that people leave for Virginia?" I asked Peter that evening.

"Because no one wants to go there, little brother."

"Is it not a good place, this Virginia?" I asked. I could not even imagine it, this place poised on the western periphery of the world.

While Peter thought about it, Mistress Jane answered with pursed lips: "People drop dead like flies there. From fevers, or at the hands of Indians. My cousin's brother-in-law was one of those murdered in a dreadful massacre that happened there some ten years ago. They stripped off his scalp even before they cut off his poor head. Who would want to go to a place like that? If you want to starve or die, do it in England, I say."

"Do not frighten the boy with your stories, mistress," Peter murmured mildly. He turned to me. "But it's the truth she tells, Tony."

"Why would I tell a falsehood?" Mistress Jane asked briskly, stirring the pot in which supper cooked. I had long learnt to eat English food, even beef.

After that I looked at every notice expounding the wonders of Virginia— the advertisements distributed around the docks, in churchyards, at beggars' fairs, and on street corners frequented by the vagabonds and immigrants to the city. They entreated all *well affected persons cheerfully to adventure and jointly take in hand this high and acceptable work . . . to goe to the said Plantation to inhabite there . . .* They promised houses to dwell in, farms and orchards, food and clothing, a generous share of the fruits of labor. When I got home one evening, I told Peter that I had learnt that Virginia did not seem so bad.

"Do you want to go there?" he asked.

"No," I said firmly. I pointed west towards the sun setting behind the roofs of the houses. "Virginia is this way, brother, and home is that." I flicked my wrist to point in the other direction.

However, that night I did not dream of home. Instead, I visited well-watered lands abundant with deer and dense woods. I woke up with a start to hear the sounds of Peter's and Mistress Jane's steady breathing and when I slept again I had another dream where I was suspended in a no-place that was like a great bowl of aquamarine light.

What course would things have taken if Mary and I had not decided to see each other one evening? If we had met and gone elsewhere? If we had turned into a different alley, had tarried somewhere just a little longer? Is it possible that such slight decisions have such vast consequences? As it was, Mary met me yet again, having managed to slip away on pretense of an errand. As we walked towards the river, she said she worried she was leaving the house too often, and her master and mistress were getting suspicious. She sounded excited that day, speaking in an uncharacteristically rapid tone, a little breathless, and I noticed that her face was flushed. I cannot remember now why I carried it with me that day, but I had on me my medicinal powder, the same one I had thieved. I considered offering Mary some of it—it might aid her in case she was falling ill. But I knew Mary well enough to know that she would ask all kinds of questions: where I got it, what was in it, and how did I know the appropriate dose.

A loud sound from the direction of the river stopped me in my tracks and I almost bumped into a woman coming towards us. She was middle-aged and inclined to fat. She looked annoyed and I fully expected that she would utter an oath or call us a slur—I was almost curious to see what she would pick: *Neggar,* or *Moor,* or something else. But she did not say a word; instead, she studied the two of us for a minute, and then flashed a sudden smile. One of her teeth was blackened and a few others were missing. I smiled back at her, a little hesitantly, because I was not used to Londoners stopping to be pleasant. She then went on, brushing past us.

I continued my conversation with Mary. "'Tis good you are a servant not a slave," I said. "Servants can leave service when they wish to."

"That is true, but 'tis not as simple as that," she replied.

"It is never going to be simple as long as we do not possess the fare," I pointed out glumly.

She reassured me that she would have it ready. And taking my hand in hers, she squeezed it, and we walked along together. The flesh of her hand was very warm and the skin damp.

I cannot tell now how exactly the events that followed unfolded. A great gust of wind might have blown over the city, picked us up, and taken us along—that is how it felt. I recall that we were passing a ramshackle warehouse when two people—a woman and a man—hurried past, turned around, and took hold of us firmly. The woman held Mary's shoulder and the man grabbed mine. His grip was strong and I remember him by his bruising touch and his smell, which was of beer and smoke—once again, *tobacco*. I recall Mary protesting in a high shrill voice. If I did too, I do not remember. The two strangers were bigger than us and stronger, although we squirmed and kicked (I believe Mary even bit because I heard the woman exclaiming aloud "She's drawn blood, the little cannibal cunt!"). The street must have been empty of passersby because, surely, someone would have noticed what was happening and put a stop to it. Or there might have been a few stragglers, indifferent and not caring.

Our captors pulled us into a building and we were pushed unto a corner of a chamber so black that I could not see my hand nor Mary's countenance, though the faces of the man and woman loomed above me pale, fleshy, and seemingly sans bodies. When the man lit a candle and raised it high, I caught a glimpse of the woman's blackened teeth and recognized her as the heavy woman who had stopped to smile at us on the street earlier. The man addressed her as Mistress Hyde.

What I also noticed in the guttering light of the candle were the stricken faces of other youngsters huddled in the corners of the room. A couple of them called out, and the man strode over and struck out at them with his fists. That made a few others weep aloud and I could tell then that at least one of them was very young, maybe four or five years of age. Sobs echoed through that airless space and soon a child was hiccupping.

"God's teeth!" the woman swore. "Shut up, you lot, won't you?"

I could see that all the children were English. Their pale skin looked grimy even in the dim flame and I could see that they were mostly dressed in ragged clothing. And then, suddenly, without another word, our abductors left, taking the candle with them, and we huddled in the corner clinging together.

"Who are they? Where are we?" I whispered fearfully.

Mary did not respond, but another voice piped up. I could tell it was a boy, a little older than me, a boy whose voice was beginning to acquire the timbre of manhood.

"They're spirits," he said.

"Ghosts of the dead?" I asked in terror.

A short laugh. "No, they spirit young 'uns away to transport them overseas."

And that was the first conversation I had with Dick Hughes, who was to be there with me always, during the crossing and after. He fell into silence after that. And I, because I was really only a young lad, and in the way of youngsters even in the most horrific of circumstances, I slept.

It was dawn when they came in next, the two spirits, with a third, a gangly youth who chewed at a piece of straw. A man's voice and a boot on my ankle woke me up to the dull light and chilly air filtering through the small casement he had opened and to the hunger eating away at my insides. I could see now that there were a dozen children in the chamber, including Mary and myself. As I had estimated, the youngest was just about four—sunken-cheeked and large-eyed, sucking a thumb, his other hand holding the hand of the older boy, who I guessed was the one who had spoken to us the night before. Mary shivered by my side. I felt the heat from her body waft towards me, and I knew she was fevered. They had brought us bread and water and while we ate, grateful for any victuals at all, the woman took a candle and held it to each of our faces as if examining us. She raised an eyebrow when she came before me.

"A blackamoor, eh?" she said, looking interested.

"Yes," I said, and then shook my head: *No.*

"A gypsy then? Or a Turk?" It was not the first time I was being asked the same questions in about the same order.

"An Indian from East India," I said defiantly.

"One of 'em stinkin' Asiatic moors," the man said. "I have seen others before at the docks. All featured like this one 'ere—tawny complexion, big nose, and a lot of hair.

"Sly bastards," he added, as an afterthought.

The woman sniffed, as if Indians must have a peculiar smell too. "He is small, kind of. I hope they take him," was all she said.

She was now standing before Mary. She too must have sensed the fevered heat I felt because she raised her hand and placed it on Mary's forehead. She shook her head.

"No one wants an East Indian girl," she said. "And certainly not one with the ague."

She gestured to the youth, who came forward and peered into Mary's face before he grabbed her by the arm and hauled her up. She cried out softly and reached for me, but the young man was strong and swift. He yanked her towards the door while I shouted and ran after them, calling her by her name. I shouted out in Tamil although my friend could not understand that tongue, and when the man spirit forced me back to my corner, I scratched at him, inviting a blow that made my ears ring and then a sharp kick on my shins. I crumpled in a heap on the floor and wept.

That was the last time I saw Mary Bengal, the girl I might have wedded if we had known each other long enough, if I would ever have learnt to feel older than her and had (miraculously) grown wiser than her, as a husband should be. She was the last of my race that I saw for a long time, that girl from the banks of the Ganges. Now, years later, I often wonder what happened to her after that day. Was she abandoned on the streets and did she make her way back to her master's home to be admonished and beaten for disappearing for a whole night? Was she led to a fate worse than that in the most pestilential and woeful parts of the city?

I like to think that somehow she managed to board an East India Company vessel and made her way first south and then east, that she circled a continent, braved cyclones and sea monsters, sailed towards the rising sun, and finally, at last, reached home.

It was not quite daybreak when we were made to line up and exit the building. I smelt the river ahead. The older man walked before us, the woman behind, and the youth alongside. A light rain fell steadily. The littlest of the lads whined and sniffled softly. His name was Billy. He was among the first to die on the voyage.

"Where are they leading us?" I asked Dick under my breath.

"To a ship," he said. "To America."

I was not going to *America*! It was now or not at all. Moved by fear of what
was to come, fired by my anxiety about Mary, I broke loose from the line and
ran. I heard the other boys yelping in surprise, the men swearing, and the
woman swearing louder. I knew not in what direction I headed. My breath
came out in puffs and my face was numb. My only thought was to get away, to
find Mary, to reach Peter's dwelling. But the straw-chewing youth was upon
me in a trice. He wrestled me to the ground and I felt his hands pressing my
face down in the mud. He held me like that for a minute till I whimpered for
air. He then pulled me up by the collar and clobbered me on the head before
he pushed me ahead of him back to the line of boys, who'd been staring,
mouths agape.

The older man crowed with ugly laughter when he saw my mud-smeared
face. "Look at the moor!" he said "Turd-colored face covered in more of the
same!"

One or two of the captive boys sniggered, but most of them were too
stricken with their own lot to respond to my condition. Only in Dick's face
did I briefly see something like a touch of sympathy for my failure to escape,
for my humiliation. And I was grateful.

We were taken by boat to a place called Gravesend and there loaded onto a
ship, the *God's Gift,* along with the cargo of water, food, pigs, grain, cloth, salt,
pots, pans, kettles, ink, needles, thread, swords, muskets, axes, and sundry
other things, and deposited right away in the hold, which was dark and ful-
some. I did not see Mistress Hyde receiving her payment, but she must have,
as must have been all manner of lords, ladies, and burgers, all of whom were
involved, I later learned, in the profitable trade of spiriting destitute children
to the colonies. Virginia was our destination. With great shouts accompa-
nying the hoisting of sails, the vessel went slowly forward. We stayed in the
hold, but I heard the cacophony overhead, and soon felt the rocking, ducking
rhythm I had become familiar with from before.

I had wiped what mud I could off my face using water from a pail down
in the hold. My limbs were stiff and my ear throbbed from the blow I had
received, but unlike some of the others on board I was not nauseated. My first
long sea voyage had habituated me to the movement of the vessel. I leaned
back, hugging my knees to my chest and pressing my forehead against them,
when I felt something in my pocket. I took it out and saw the pouch of the

unicorn-horn medicine. It was all I possessed apart from the clothes on my back. I quickly put it away when I heard a rustle and a sigh. I looked around and saw a female countenance peering over my shoulder. She appeared to be about forty years of age and, with her pale, drawn face and sunken eyes, she reminded me of some wan goblin stepped out of a tale. Her red hair was shorn so close that parts of her scalp were exposed. The woman reached out, tugged my earlobe, and tittered. I had been through too much that day to be frightened, so I remained where I was and glowered at her.

"What do you want?" I asked impatiently.

She giggled again and then thrust the knuckles of her right hand into her mouth and sucked hard at them.

"Croak not, black angel!" she whispered. "I have nothing for thee."

I heard footsteps and looked to see who was coming—and when I looked back again, she had vanished into the ship's shadows. The next day Captain Coxe was furious because he had not known that we had a lunatic on board. "*Who let her on?*" he thundered. "Who is paying for her passage?"

No one knew. She had perhaps been smuggled on by a relative—someone who had slipped in and out again, leaving behind his burden and his woe. *Mad Marge,* that is what she came to be known as on the ship. Apart from us spirited boys, all of whom ceased struggling and protesting after the first few hours on board, our fellow passengers were dozens of men and women— carpenters, cordwainers, candlemakers, bookbinders, beggars, leatherworkers, minstrels, plowmen, grooms, spinsters, wives, widows, rogues, vagabonds, and other sundry folk—some of whom had been lured on board with food, drink, tobacco, and promises of a better life, some of whom had been bound to masters already settled in Virginia. This latter group had filed aboard clutching their indenture papers after taking an oath acknowledging King Charles as the head of the one true church and swearing allegiance to him for the rest of their lives. There were also a handful of migrants who had paid their own fares and hoped to buy land on arrival, and there were a few gentlemen. There was a perfumer and a jeweler too, and since there could be no earthly use for their trades in Virginia, we guessed that they must be running from the constables or bailiffs. Indeed, a number of the persons on board seemed to be the dregs and scum of their land, the excess and unwanted that England was purging, hoping they would make something of themselves in America. Captain Coxe was mostly in his cups. His wife, who also sailed, was mostly in her cups too, and together they created a great roaring, shrieking, and thumping when they fell into quarrels. One evening there was a mighty to-do because they grabbed coals from the woodstove and flung them at each other and the sailors feared that the ship would be set on fire.

I was the only dark-hued person on the ship, except for Ann Brady, the woman who turned out to be a witch, who was of indeterminate complexion, who might or might not have been a gypsy, who, in fact, might or might not have been a human soul at all. There had been sailors from the Spice Islands on the voyage to London; in London, there had been Peter and others, and of course Mary. On the *God's Gift,* I was alone. At first, I kept to myself in the hold, wrapped in a bristly blanket listening to the groaning of the vessel, to the sounds of people retching and puking, to gruff men talking of the land they'd farm in Virginia, of the money they would earn, the triumphant voyage they would finally make back to London, or Northampton, or Plymouth, or whichever little town or croft they hailed from.

"If we are not killed by the Indians," someone would be sure to say at that point, uncharitably interrupting the course of the others' reveries.

"Aye, that could happen," someone else would add glumly.

"Why are they even called Indians?" I asked Dick.

"Because they are," he said confidently.

"No, they are not."

Dick might have been a little older than me and already playing the man, but he did not understand how vast the world was, how broad the expanse of its waters, how different lands lay on either side, with distinct people dwelling in them.

But perhaps it was Dick's lack of curiosity about things that made it possible for him to be my friend. At first, when we engaged in our boyish tiffs, he'd call me muck-face and other such names and I'd be angry, but he mostly came to simply see me as a lad close to his age, the comrade who had been spirited away with him. To me, he could curse his drunken father, his slatternly mother, his own bad fortune in being trapped. However, as the voyage went on and land was not even a blur on the horizon, Dick glowed with conviction.

"We must make something of it, lads," he urged. "Others have made fortunes in Virginny. Why cannot we?"

We stared at him blankly—not ready to dream, not knowing how to hope. Samuel Mason, nine or ten years of age, had also become part of our little group. Because of his tender years and baby face we called him Sammy or Little Sam. He had not been spirited; his parish had ordered his parents, overburdened with poverty and children, to send him to Virginia on the threat of stopping poor relief.

"It would be a better life for your boy," they promised, and his father and mother had agreed sadly. And the City of London had itself paid three pounds for Sammy's transportation and forty shillings towards his clothing.

And here he was with us, and there we were, with open sea and open sky around and above, ever moving westwards. In addition to the usual seasickness, there were the other afflictions, sores, vomit, and misery of being on a ship—all things not novel to me after my first, even longer, voyage. I offered to help the ship surgeon, informing him that I had assisted the doctor a little on the East India Company vessel, but he dismissed me curtly, and even Dick and Sam laughed at my impertinence in approaching him. Then an infestation of lice broke out, greater than any even the sailors had seen, and soon every man, woman, and child was spotted with bites of the vermin, and even the pigs, cattle, and other beasts on board were scratching frantically. A sailor was flogged for thieving till he was nigh dead; the victuals were depleted in quality and amount. The stars guided us, some nights the moon was ringed with a clear, metallic light. And there was always the sea: giant fish with mighty fins followed us; one man claimed he saw a mermaid beckoning him from the waves, although his careworn wife snorted and snapped back that no woman in her senses—even a half-fishy one—would want to tempt *him*. Four weeks into our voyage, the witch was hanged; seven weeks in, we saw a purple-blue light divide and burn high up on the top of the masts and on the sails—the sailors called it Saint Elmo's fire and said it was caused by sea spirits; four weeks later, we stopped in the Bermudas, which were bewitched isles reported to be inhabited by noisy demons, though I heard no fiendish sounds from the ship; and five days later we set sail again, exhausted and still lice-ridden, north and west in the direction of Jamestown.

II

GANTER'S HOPE

THREE

I sailed into a warm, moist Virginia summer in June 1635. The year before, the colony had been divided into eight counties, and the first Englishmen had arrived at Saint Clements Island to settle the Province of Maryland. The year of my arrival, however, was quite unremarkable.

The weather pleased me, although the gentlemen on board said that it was not a good idea to arrive in the hot season. The *God's Gift* made her way between the two great capes, Henry and Charles, and then sailed up the Chesapeake Bay till she reached the mouth of the James River. It was slow going even with the pilot boat guiding us.

"There's nothing where we are going to," the sailors told us. "Everything in this here vessel will be snatched up in a jiffy."

"Nothing?" Dick asked doubtfully.

"Nothing," the man repeated. "They lack all manner of things here."

That was not what we'd heard in England—Virginia had everything, *was* everything, they had said.

And in addition to all of the stuff needed to sustain life in this desolate place, there were the human souls who had survived the passage—some one hundred of us. Some little 'uns had died early on; the witch was gone, of course; and in spite of the witch's hanging, the other woman with sores on her breasts had perished, and her body had followed the witch into the deep somewhere between England and America.

It was a watery vista that greeted us—the brackish estuary heaving with the evening tide, and the river so broad that there was no sign of its banks and it could well have been the sea. The water was muddy brown, scattered with debris from ships. The air was still, saturated with damp, and I felt the perspiration start up under my arms and on my scalp. Sammy and Dick were somewhere about; by my side was Mad Marge, smiling beatifically, as if we had sailed into paradise and she had been pronounced an angel.

I remembered my mother's game: *What do you want to be in your next life, my darling . . . ?* I did not know it then, but I was being reborn as I sailed up that river—it was an unwilling birth, because which birth is willed? I came into a world where I would be unmade and remade, have to fashion and refashion myself, learn to live anew. A bird cried overhead, and it was the mewling sound of a newborn, hesitant, querulous. I glanced up at the sky to catch its flight, and when I looked out at the river again, I saw the distant green of the forest along the river. Foliage packed tight, to our eyes no more than a green smear on the landscape. Wood and water. Water and wood.

The *God's Gift* anchored at long last, and the passengers were packed into boats that took us to the landing stage. They left Sammy, Dick, myself, and two other boys for the last but one boat, and Mad Marge too, although the captain had been so eager to get rid of her through the journey that we expected daily he would put her in the water. When our boat arrived, I noticed that the oarsman was a young African. He glanced briefly at me, surely noticing how I did not look like the others. But then he looked away, keeping his gaze focused on the water, the shore ahead, and the gathering darkness.

We were not more than a few feet from the shore when Mad Marge stood up with a hiss and lifted her bundle onto her shoulder. The vessel rocked.

"Sit you down, madam!" the boatman barked. But Marge waved her hands and stamped her feet, and we had no idea what had come over her. I tugged at her skirts, Dick got up to hold her by the shoulders and force her down, and the boat swayed and surged ferociously.

"Sit, sirrah!" the boatman cried out, his voice rough with panic.

"Seat yourself this instant, Marge!" Dick said, and I was shocked at the rage in his voice. He was eager to get ashore and could not brook a delay. Mad Marge was deaf to our pleas and curses—she raised her face to the sky and gave out something between a screech and a moan. Sammy put his fingers to his ears and even the boatman flinched.

She has gone mad, I thought, even madder. And Marge lurched forward, trampling over us as if to step out of the boat. In an instant we were in the shallow water, which smelt of brine and mud and fish. Logs of wood and other rubbish floated around us. I put my bundle on my head and waded. Just behind me, I heard the boatman cursing as he held on to the vessel and came ashore. Coughing, sputtering, and soaking wet, I clambered onto land and so, for the first time, set foot in America.

Unlike many of our shipmates we did not have indenture papers. There was no master or agent waiting on the shore to meet us as we staggered forth with our things, getting used to the ground beneath our feet. Where would we sleep? What would we sup on? And where would we go in the morrow? As we stood about uncertainly, I looked around and saw that Mad Marge was no longer with us.

"Where is she?" I asked Sammy and Dick.

Where? Where? And we wheeled around in that first dusk, looking for her. *Where is Marge?* A sizable fort loomed ahead of us and there were houses facing the river. Men dotted the waterfront and the marshy area beyond, some by themselves, others in groups deep in conversation. But there was no sign of Marge, and all we could say was that she had probably drowned.

"That is not possible," Dick reasoned. "The water was not deep enough where the boat tipped."

"Unless she swam back towards the ship and drowned," I said.

Our black boatman only shrugged and made off on his vessel, his body blending with the darkness that was now gathering fast. So, Marge was gone—as if she had been plucked up by an unseen hand that had reached out from that great bowl of sky. Sammy and I were particularly distraught—we had grown fond of Marge, who was harmless and gentle in spite of her madness. I noticed strangers' eyes looking at us and I thought that some of them lingered on me. The last group of our shipmates disappeared; tomorrow they would go further up the river to their new homes, where they would be expected to toil for as long as their contracts bound them. The few others who had come with some money on their own and did not need to bind themselves would also go up the river looking for land, for they had been told that land was riches, riches was land, and nothing else held true—a hoe, a strong back, and a stronger will would do the rest. The gents on board had disappeared into the fort—they were to be guests of the governor himself, so they had bragged. Captain Coxe came on the last boat off the ship—when he disembarked, he was reeling slightly. He and his wife also went into the fort, followed by several sailors.

So, there we were, a huddle of boys, with the dusk falling thick. The gates of the fort shut and lamps began to be lit here and there when a small, plump white man approached us. He carried a lantern, which illuminated his round face. His voice slurring slightly, he addressed us, introduced himself as Parson Blair, and said it had fallen to him to make arrangements for masterless boys like us. Dick and Sammy and the other boys were eager to follow him, but I had my misgivings.

"Why would we be led by you, sir?" I asked, and my voice came out loud and discourteous, although I was really only frightened.

Parson Blair seemed amused rather than angered by my tone. "Perhaps because you have no one else," he replied in a voice that was not unkind.

This was good enough reason, but I hung back even as the four others stepped forward to follow the stranger. I might have stayed behind too, if Sammy had not grabbed my hand and Dick had not looked at me pleadingly. I was reluctant to let them go too—these two English lads were the only friends I had now. I picked up my belongings and, together, we went with the parson.

We stayed with Parson Blair for two days in a wooden dwelling surrounded by a roughly fenced-in garden. He put us to work in the garden, where he raised Indian corn (which I recognized from my own country as *maize*) and pumpkins, which I was also already familiar with, although they seemed new to the other boys. On the dawn of the third day we were loaded into two boats and began sailing downriver. We stayed fairly close to the shore, and in the pearly light the green blur that I had seen from the ship became trees, trees taller than any I had viewed in my life; with their fine leaves and peeling barks they looked like wizened old men scrutinizing us, the newcomers to this very ancient place. I did not know their names, I did not know what birds called out to us from them either, with cries that seemed mournful or mocking. I thought of the mangoes and jackfruit trees of my home with thick, oily leaves of the darkest green and their squat, broad trunks, and of the birds so familiar to me—the crows, the peacocks, and the mynahs; I felt the land's essential alien nature loom out of the silent forest and descend over me like a shadow, and I was afeared of it . . . I did not realize it then, but the English boys were unsettled by the terrain too—even the country lads had never seen such dense forest; such trees, bigger than English oaks; such quantities of land, unbounded by hedgerow or enclosure.

Parson Blair brought Dick, Sammy, and me to a plantation owned by one Master George Menefie. Master Menefie drew up contract papers on the spot, binding us for seven years, and asked us to put our thumbprints on them (he would later claim that it had all been settled in England, that he, George Menefie, had sponsored our voyage and was therefore entitled to land in return). The parson then bade us a brief farewell and went on his way with the remaining boys, who would probably go to another farm or plantation. We were grateful that at least the three of us were together.

Master Menefie was a burly man of few words. He believed in only three things: the value of land, the import of hard work, and the virtues of tobacco, of which he smoked a great deal. He was from Devon and had come on the *Samuell* to Virginia thirteen years before. He had grown to be one of the most prosperous men in the colony, having sponsored many servants, each of whom got him fifty acres of land, just as we had. I learned that, in fact, he had, earlier that selfsame year, brought over a man they said was a Turk, who'd since been sent to work for another planter. Master Menefie looked at me curiously.

"And what manner of moor might you be, boy?" he asked. I'd learnt from Peter Mansur that "moor" signified a person who was dark-complexioned, or non-Christian, or both, which seemed to me to describe many kinds of men.

"Another Turk? But no, too black to be one," speculated his wife, Mistress Elizabeth, an elegant lady if ever there was one. "'haps a blackamoor somewhat lighter hued than his kin."

I was accustomed to this by now—people wondering what manner of person I was and running through all the black peoples they had heard of as being not as black as blackmoors. "An Indian, mistress," I replied. "But not one from there"—I pointed upriver, in the direction of the forests—"one from the East Indies." I might as well have told her that I came from the moon, although her husband seemed to know what I was talking about.

He nodded and proceeded to enter our names in his big register. Since I could read well enough, I noticed that he wrote *Richard Hughes, Samuel Mason,* and then—*Tony East Indian.*

Therefore Dick, Sammy, and I, as able-bodied males, augmented Master Menefie's holdings. Several other servants had come this year alone and seven

Africans were to join us anon. Indeed, they were already on their way. They also would work on the plantation, in Master Menefie's fruit orchard.

The master already had some twenty servants, and unlike other farmers who made do with two or three men and supervised them directly, Master Menefie had hired an overseer. Master Ralph Ganter was a wiry man, with a slight squint in one eye and a patch of red hair on his chest. We quickly discovered that he was prone to fits of rage. He disliked all boys, it seemed, thought they were nothing but trouble, and particularly disliked the three of us only because he thought we were too thick with each other. *Birds of a feather . . .* he would mutter darkly, or *If you lie down with dogs, you get up with fleas* (I suspected that the warning was being issued to Sammy and Dick), or *Tarred with the same brush,* he would say, glowering at us. He thought this last was very apt because of the color of my skin. But Dick and Sammy were pale as the palest of moons and had not yet been blackened in the slightest by association with me, so it did not make good sense, really.

The servants dwelt in little cabins a few hundred yards from the main house. The small wooden shack I was put in with Dick was windowless and insect-ridden. Like everything else in this land, even Master Menefie's dwelling, although it was bigger than most, looked like it had been put together in a hurry and could probably be taken apart in equal haste. I realized that that was because no one here—not the other servants, not Ralph Ganter, not even Master Menefie—thought of Virginia as home. They would come, they would get what they could, they would get rich, and then they would up and return to their crofts and towns in England. This was a halting place, not the end or the beginning, but the midpoint of a longer journey that circled back to another place, which was always home. Perhaps the only people who felt otherwise were the Virginia Indians, and I had not set eyes on one yet, although I had been told that some of them worked on the other plantations. I looked into the forest that began where Master Menefie's land ended and wondered if they were there—concealed behind these unknown trees and bushes, watching and waiting . . . I remembered the swift and elusive demigods that my grandmother had said dwelt in jungles, caves, and water. They came to mind when I thought of the Indians. At the same time these strange people whom I was yet to see somehow brought to my mind Murugan, *the god who is of the hue of the earth, of sunrise, of blood; the god born of fire, the spear bearer, the resplendent yet secretive one; ever youthful, as old as time itself; he who is the chosen god of us, the Tamil people.*

Ralph Ganter never tired of telling us that we should be wary of the Indians.

"Never trust an Indian," he said in his reedy voice, and he would insist on looking at me, although he well knew I was not the kind of Indian he meant. He would tell us horrific stories of the massacre of 1622, how people had been surprised as they ate breakfast, of how this man's head was bashed in with an ax, how that woman was bled like a pig. He seemed to delight in these tales, revel in the gore and terror of them. And so Ganter made the Indians the monsters of nightmare.

"They will never cease trying to murder us and chase us into the sea," Ganter said darkly. "That is why we are erecting yonder Wall. We've learnt our lessons. Nothing is more vital than the Wall."

He was referring to the Great Wall that had been started the year before— a six-mile-long palisade that extended between the James and York rivers about forty miles inland from the bay. When completed, it would enclose 300,000 acres of land and keep the English colony safe from the dangers of the inland—animals, malignant spirits, and above all, Indians. Trees were being chopped down for it and the logs hauled up and arranged behind a six-foot ditch. Older settlers flocked to help with the construction and new ones joined them—a wall meant safety, it would mark territory, a closing in and a shutting out that were vital in this new land where sky and earth were big and intrusive.

"The wall is to keep the Indians out of their own land?" I asked, when Ganter went into the bushes to piss.

Sammy and Dick stared at me goggle-eyed as if I was raving.

"Well, it is our land now—God-given to us," Dick then replied, Dick of the ever-ready tongue and quick wit was remembering the notices and advertisements for Virginia we had seen in London. And then Master Ganter came back wiping his hands on his breeches and gave me such a look that I wondered if he had heard my question. But he must not have, or he would have cuffed me on the ear.

Ganter got himself drunk later that evening and was in an even fouler temper.

"You boys, eh . . . ?" he drawled, revealing his long yellowing teeth in something between a snarl and a smile. "Bunch of bastards, ain't you? Lot of whoresons . . ."

I felt a sudden hot flush of shame at that.

He went on: "Disgusting little creatures—dirty lot, eh, all of you . . . ? Ain't you filthy muck? Filthy like your mums . . . ?"

And we cowered together, not comprehending what he was going on about.

The light lingered later in the sky than I had ever known and the fowl flew over the river and tobacco fields and into the woods, setting up a great clamor. The dark came leisurely, but when it arrived it was heavy and watchful. There were lurid shadows cast on the patch of earth outside the cabin. Dick was elsewhere, and Sammy was asleep in the other cabin, which he shared with some of the men. The older men had gone out after supper. I went indoors, lit a candle, and placed it on a small stool. The glow of it was warm and comforting as I crouched by it. I could at least see my hands in front of me now. The light entered my eyes and illuminated my very heart. I thought of my mother adorning herself in lamplight, placing jasmine in her hair, fastening her nose jewel, getting ready for the night. I barely heard the floorboards creak before I felt a sharp smack on the back of the head.

"Fuckin neggar . . . !" Ganter hissed and punched me again, on the side of my face. I was too startled to move at first, and then I sprang away and around the room, trying to evade him. This only infuriated him all the more—he took off the rope of leather that held his breeches up and lashed out at me. He hit me on the shoulders, back, legs, wherever he could, swinging wildly. The candle guttered and went out, and we leapt about in the pitchy dark. Ganter grunted and breathed heavily. I did not know why he was in such a rage. One particularly stinging lash on my calf brought me to the ground in a heap, and in an instant he was on top of me.

"You little . . . little shit-hue moor," he said. "Never, *never* light a candle before it gets dark. Candles are not here for your taking."

I would have retorted that it *had* been dark, demanded to know why the candle was there if not to be lit. But I stayed still, hoping that not moving, barely breathing would save me from the whip. Suddenly Ganter's breathing grew raspy, and his thighs gripped either side of my hips. He fumbled in the gloom, feeling my face, which was wet with tears and a little blood, and clutched at my curls.

"Pretty boy eh . . . ?" he said, in a tone which was suddenly both enraged and wheedling. "So your brown face is actually pretty . . . eh?"

I did not know what to expect. I only knew the darkness, this man strad-dling me, the weight and smell of him, and the warm airlessness of the room. I felt a hard swelling between his thighs and his grip grew firmer, till he was squeezing my hips. He gripped my hair till it hurt, and forced my head fur-ther back. My heart beating apace, I waited for whatever would transpire.

Suddenly a shaft of moonlight fell on us in a thin, straight line, like an arrow. Someone had opened the door of the cabin. There was the sharp odor of ale and piss.

"G'day," someone gurgled. And I could tell from his voice that he was one of the other menservants. "G'day, Ganter. G'day, lad."

If he was surprised to find us on the floor, he did not express it, or perhaps he was too drunk to note anything. He stumbled about the room asking for a *bloody candle, c'mon, man, give us some light.*

Ganter scrambled off me and cursed. "I'll report you to the master, Matt," he said. "You scurvy sot . . ."

And he left the cabin, without even glancing back at me as I sat up, trem-bling, feeling like I wanted to vomit.

Sammy Mason, quiet and sweet Sam, Little Sam, grew more and more subdued by the day. He missed his ma and pa, he said. And he missed Toby and Susie and Rodger and Molly, Bessie the cow in the little bit of pasture back home, and the wood imps who lived in the willow tree nigh his family's cottage. He had had his cloak stolen just days after we arrived at Master Menefie's farm. He was distraught about that—it was all he had to keep him warm in winter.

"Winter is a long way off, Sammy," Dick and I comforted him, but he said that it was already chilly in the mornings, he needed his cloak, and besides, his ma had given it to him.

"You will go back home, Sammy," I said. "Just bide your time as I am biding mine."

And to cheer him up and, in truth, to impress him with my scholarship, I offered to write a letter on his behalf. There was a bit of parchment, and pen and ink that someone had brought off a ship and left in our cabin. *The victuals here are scant* [I wrote] *I eat nothing but thin gruel made of peas and water, I have not seen a or tasted venison, though they had said that the Virginia deer roamed freely, there are only a few fowls but we are not allowed to catch them, I want a bed, a bit of cheese, and some bread as Christians eat.*

Proud of my penmanship and my skill in composition, I continued:

My only friend is Dick a lad from London and Tony who is an East Indian.

It occurred to me that Sammy's parents might be worried at the thought of their offspring consorting with foreigners, so I carefully blotted out *an East Indian* and wrote in its place *a good lad.*

"Do not forget to tell them about my cloak, Tony," Sammy said anxiously.

I wrote that his cloak had been stolen, that he was nigh clothed in rags. *And I have nothing to gladden my heart, nor is there nothing to be got here but sickness and death. Please write me an Answer, your Answer will be life to me,* I concluded. I found that I was so moved by my own writing that I was weeping a little. I knew that no friend or kin of mine would read this, that no one in that infinitely distant place on the Coromandel would ever know that I was in America, a stranger in this alien earth. I promised Sammy that I would find someone who was passing through on his way to Jamestown to take the missive with him and send it by the next ship.

There were other things to worry about as well. We feared sickness daily, and not only us; Ralph Ganter and Master Menefie feared it too because sickness was expensive—it took away servants who had been brought at great cost; it was a reminder of how dreadful this place could be, how it did not really want us.

"You lads watch out," I told Dick and Sammy, who in truth already looked a little pale and bruised around the mouth. "I will not catch any illness—the weather here is nothing to the summers I have known."

"You are a boastful one, Tony," Dick remarked sourly, and I chuckled.

It was a warm night. I went to bed on the straw, through which beetles scuttled and small mice scampered, and woke up near dawn perspiring profusely—my face and neck were clammy with it. I sensed that I smelt putrid—like the bottom of a decaying pond. As the sun rose, I scurried out into the bushes to defecate, and then I went again and again. Ganter had been sent away on an errand by Master Menefie, and the man in charge was not as much of a brute, but still reluctant to let me rest, in case he got into trouble with the master. I felt faint with exhaustion. Suddenly I heard a cry, and I saw my mother running across the field towards the forest. Her stride was long and lithe. She flew.

"Amma!" I cried. "*Amma!*"

And I dropped my hoe and ran after her. There she was in the branches of a tree, squatting on her haunches, like some monstrously giant bird. She was hideous in my eyes, my own amma. And then she disappeared in a whirl of gray and black that rose towards the sky. *She had wanted to be a bird in her next birth,* I remembered. One that could take wing.

A chalky white road appeared before me and split in two. I hesitated for a moment before taking one branch of it—I meant to return to the main route, but way led on to way and I could not find where I had started. There was a faint murmuring from behind the undergrowth which grew to a titter, which grew louder and louder till it exploded. I whirled around, looking for whence it came. And then the beggars from London streets huddled around me, wild-eyed and rank, and they swirled about and grew into a blur before they transformed into the lepers who crawled through on the streets in Armagon. One of them pushed his big face close and breathed damply on my face. He reached out to touch my face with his damp, fingerless hands, and he was suddenly Ralph Ganter and he was opening his breeches and taking out his giant, red, throbbing cock with one hand and pushing me down with the other, making me kneel before him, forcing my face up, and prizing open my jaw. I screamed, calling for my mother.

"Tony, Tony!"

I opened my eyes. I could feel them crusted and heavy.

"Tony . . . ?"

And it was Little Sammy peering into my face, his own crumpled with worry. I could still feel the perspiration running down my chest and back, and when I tried to sit up, I collapsed back into the straw, and the stink was so awful that I knew I had been shitting liquid right where I lay.

The sickness lasted for two weeks. Dick had caught it too. It was the bloody flux, they said, the summer sickness, the newcomers' disease that migrants got before they became seasoned to the new land. Master Menefie was worried we would die, even as he maintained that the doctors had no cure for the flux, and he was not going to waste tobacco calling one in to see us. I myself—I should have desired death because there was nothing to live for. But I was young and my instinct was to survive and, in any case, my body, moved by energies and yearnings that were distinct from my mind's, fought gamely. I took my pouch of unicorn-horn medicine, which had traveled with me to Virginia, and mixed a pinch of it in water and swallowed it. It might have been that, or it could have been Yellamma—goddess of my place of birth, goddess who caused and cured smallpox and, perhaps, even New World disease—who intervened. And then, in a fortnight or so, I was well again and back in the fields, laboring.

FOUR

Bristol, Edwin, London, Anthony, Cuffee, Jonah, and Francisco arrived the week of my sickness. With them joining us, I was not the only dark-complexioned person in Master Menefie's farm and that gave me a measure of solace. There were other blackmoors in Virginia of course: quite a few worked in Flowerdew Hundred, Bennett's Plantation, Neck o' Land, and several lived in Jamestown. But this was the first group of Africans that Master Menefie brought as servants.

The Africans and I sized each other up cautiously. They must have wondered what manner of man I was. I could not tell if they had heard of East Indians before. I sensed that they would look down on me if I confessed to my gods, because they all had been baptized a long time ago by the Portuguese in their African homeland, and thought themselves very civilized. So, I told them that I had previously been converted by the Company officials in London. A falsehood without doubt but it *could* have happened after all. Master Menefie's Africans were worldly men who were not only Christian but spoke the Portugal tongue and some English.

Like me, the Africans were coastal people, from the western shore of their continent. I was beginning to realize that living on the coast—any coast—was precarious: it did not take much to be picked up and washed away. Bristol and Cuffee—the two I got to know the best—had lived in Barbados for several years before they were brought to Virginia. They were well acquainted with the English tongue, and it was obvious that both the tall, lean, Bristol with his heavy-lidded eyes and inscrutable demeanor, and the broad-chested,

big-shouldered, more loquacious Cuffee with his ready smile were used to
white men and quite at ease with their customs and manners in a way I was
not. I watched them and the others of their crew suspiciously, not getting too
close, torn between envy at their sophistication and relaxed air, and scorn because such black skin sometimes signaled the lowest of castes back in my land.

"Tony," said Cuffee. "You a white boy or black? You want to be with those
white lads all the time, so we assume you're white too, with your face just a
bit dirty."

He was teasing me, but I grew cross and embarrassed and left his side, till
I became lonely and went to find Dick and Sammy.

A couple of months after, Ralph Ganter completed his term with Master Menefie and received freedom dues of a hat, a suit of clothing, a pair of shoes and
stockings, three hoes, one ax, a gun, three barrels of corn and two of tobacco,
and, most important, six acres of land—a great deal more than other servants
got as their dues. Sammy, Dick, and I were jubilant.

"Good riddance to old Ganter!" we said, remembering the casual blows,
the boxes on the ears, the whipping, the never-ending curses, and those other
unnameable things that made us uneasy in his presence. Sammy in particular
lighted up. He had grown very thin and bony, his fingernails were so flecked
that they were all but white, and the ulcers in his mouth had become worse,
leaving him in an agony of misery. But Ganter's upcoming departure cheered
him, and we all dreamt of the day we would finish our indenture too and
played a game of imagining what freedom dues *we* would ask for—a sack of
marbles, a bag of sugar lumps, a satchel of silver pieces . . . fresh cheese, a dog
to take hunting, puddings and custards and fruit pies and gingerbread and
marzipans, all of which we had heard of but never eaten . . . and I, with my
own list of delicacies that were fast fading from memory.

But two days before Ganter—*Master Ganter*—was due to go to his new
lands, which were further down the river, Master Menefie sent word for some
of us. When we arrived at his dwelling, he informed us that he would hand
over Dick, Sammy, and I, along with Bristol and Cuffee, to Ralph Ganter.
The others were simply given on loan; I was the only one to truly become
Ganter's man. I could not believe it—was not my contract with Master Menefie? Later, I found out that it was not unheard of to transfer bonds of servitude
to new masters. What was unusual was for a man of Ganter's status to have

even one servant—and now he had five, albeit four on loan. There was something peculiar there, and we never found out the truth behind it, although we heard reports that Ganter had sufficient knowledge of Master Menefie's many dealings and the master wished to keep him contented. Master Menefie, after promising to give us new breeches and urging us to work hard for our new master, turned away to indicate that the conversation was over. We trudged back to the cabins, so heavy of heart that we could barely utter a word. That evening I saw Little Sam sobbing under a tree.

"We are all downhearted, Sammy," I said, "but at least we are going together. So, cheer up, laddie."

At that he stopped weeping but sat crouched under the tree and was taken by such a fit of shivering that I thought he had caught the ague too.

"Are you ailing?" I asked, alarmed. He shook his head but kept shaking and trembling like a leaf, till I sat down and put my arm around him, and then he gradually stopped.

"We are going together," I repeated because I did not know what else to say. I too was but a boy, barely a few years older than this tearful child; I too felt neither hope nor joy.

"Yes," he said. "I am glad for that, Tony." And then as if a new thought had just occurred to him, he sat up and gasped through snot and tears and all: "My letter!" he said. "My letter! What if Pa gets the parson to write a reply and it makes its way here to Master Menefie's? It will not reach me!"

I did not have the heart to tell him that his letter had probably never crossed the ocean. I had indeed found someone to give it to and requested him to *have it sent to England, sir.* He had taken it from me all right, but later I had overheard him tell another man that he had better things to do than be a messenger for a bloody moor. I remembered what I had written: *your Answer will be life to me.* I had been so proud of my rhetorical flourish then. I was ashamed now for not trying harder to have the letter sent out. I mumbled something about begging Master Menefie to find a way to send on a reply, and Little Sammy, who actually trusted me, stranger though I was, cheered up a little.

Two days later Dick and I boarded one of the two wooden skiffs with Cuffee while Ganter, Sam, and Bristol boarded the other. Ganter's new property—the hoes, ax, corn, and everything else—was distributed between the two vessels. The Africans came to the shore to bid their brethren farewell. Cuffee's large eyes were filled with tears and everyone else looked doleful. Bristol, always a man of few words, said nothing, although his countenance grew very grim. These seven men had seen much and traveled long together and they were now being put asunder without a thought. Once again, I was glad that I was not being parted from Dick and Sammy. Dick and Cuffee rowed our skiff, and I sat there trailing my hand in the water between the two of them, the white boy and the black man. Cuffee's eyes were still wet with tears and, because I had never seen a grown man weep before, I looked away, embarrassed.

The fat, rich lands downriver had all been claimed by wealthier men, like Master Menefie. Although Ganter acted like he was now a squire, his land was deep in the interior. The vegetation grew thick and dense and the river was a glassy green from the reflected foliage. I could see the fish darting below it, and they were so many hues and so bright that they too looked like glass. Glass creatures in a glass river in a fragile glass world. But when I looked up from my dream state, Dick and Cuffee were solid enough flesh, and on the other vessel Ganter was there hunched, hairy, and smirking, also all too, *too* real. The trees on either bank leaned into the river inquiringly, looking for all the world like scraggly giants. An eagle soared overhead and *he was the swift-winged Garuda, King of Birds, the god Vishnu's chariot, sharp-beaked-sharp-taloned killer of serpents, bearer of the nectar of immortality.* It was beauteous around me, and yet I sat in the boat thinking of another place, other trees, another sky.

The other skiff went ahead of us and disappeared down a bend in the river, and it occurred to me that we—Cuffee, Dick, and I—could swerve for the banks, abandon our boat, and make a dash for it through the trees. It would be a bold, mad plan but it would not be impossible. Why not? I shifted and leaned forward to whisper to Dick, and he frowned at the slight rocking I set off.

"Take the oars, Tony," he hissed. "Stop sitting on your bum and admiring the scenery." He gave me the oars and edged over to my spot. As I rowed, I remembered Sammy in the other boat, with Ganter and Bristol. We could not go anywhere and leave Little Sam. So, we went on, and soon the other skiff came into view.

Ganter's newly acquired land needed to be seated before he could claim it as his own—to this end, we built a little house, which was no more than a shack, windowless, in the manner of the cabins we had slept in at Master Menefie's, a fireplace at one end with a cooking pot over it, which Dick and I had charge of. We brought in dry grass to sleep on, although the floor felt damp even in summer on account of the land being swampy. Ganter soon secured a hog, which added to the general squalor, and we built a fence for her close to the cabin. He set us to clear the land, and it was hard work chopping down trees and bushes. Ganter worked alongside us, dreaming of the riches a big tobacco harvest would bring, of more land and yet more, stretching out into what was yet wilderness. He even had a name for his fledgling farm—*Ganter's Hope*. We worked without rest for weeks, and we were soon surrounded by ground that was filled with stumps, rough and uneven looking, but still mostly ready for tobacco planting next May. Till then we grew corn and pumpkins for our feed. Our ears were perpetually bruised with Ganter's foul curses and cuffings. I still felt my old uneasiness and tried to avoid being alone with him and stuck close to Dick, who was suddenly beginning to sprout hair on his upper lip, which we teased him about mercilessly, though we were a little bit envious too. I still looked nothing like a man. Even I had to admit that.

The nearest tavern was a league-long walk through the woods. Ganter mostly went there on Saturdays, but sometimes, when he did not feel like it, he sent us boys to fetch him ale. The Gray Foxe was a rough place, no more than a shack, with cast-off barrels and tree trunks to perch oneself on. A farmer whose tobacco ventures had failed ran the place. The woman who lived with him was stout and quarrelsome, and always looked at me suspiciously, as if she was concerned that I would filch something, or leave without paying, or kill her with a hatchet after I had scalped her husband.

One day Dick, Sammy, and I, on one of our trips to the Gray Foxe, carried a couple of coins we'd saved from our days at Master Menefie's when he would occasionally pay us for extra work like washing the laundry, or trimming his beard or hair. We had decided that we would treat ourselves to cups of ale and the corn cakes that the landlady sometimes kept. Mistress Hodges would fuss a bit because she preferred tobacco in payment, but she would take our coins anyway. Her cakes were mostly stale but they were better than nothing. The ale was not the best either, but it was an improvement on the water, which tasted slightly brackish, although we were far enough from the sea. I had started drinking weak ale in London, although my mother would have disapproved, as she would have of the beef, pork, and all the other unclean victuals I had got used to feeding on. It was that or starvation. And even babes drank ale in England.

It was a fine day when we set out—late summer with the trees just starting to turn yellow in readiness for leaf fall, a time of year I was to witness
for the first time in Virginia. We teased each other on the walk through the
woods, tripping each other up, hiding in the bushes, and mimicking the call
of birds or making farting sounds. I thought I did a fine job of imitating
Ganter scolding: *Ge' on with it, you scum! I do not feed you for nothin . . .* And
although we were being saucy like that only because Ganter was out of earshot, we chuckled with great satisfaction. At least Dick and I did. I do not
remember Little Sammy laughing. Come to think of it, Sammy did not laugh
much those days. To cheer him up I pretended to be an Indian stalking him
through the woods.

"Watch out!" I cried, and jumped on them.

"You do not make a good Indian, Tony!" Dick retorted.

"What do you mean, Master Richard—I do not *make* one?—I *am* one!"

So, we were hot and thirsty when we came to the alehouse. Just outside we
saw two wenches—about eighteen or nineteen years of age—standing about
as if not certain whether to enter. From their apparel we guessed that they
were servants also having the afternoon off. Dick blushed because he was at
that age when women made him uneasy and glad at the same time; Little
Sammy brightened up because women reminded him of his mam and sister;
I did not care. They smiled when they saw us and asked if we would come in
with them—actually they invited Dick and Sammy. Me, they did not seem to
notice, as if I had disappeared into my own squat midday shadow.

"We will be happy to buy you lads a little something to eat and drink,"
the taller one said, and the smaller one ruffled Sammy's golden hair. Dick's
countenance lighted up—I knew he was thinking that there would be nothing
to lose and everything to gain, the everything in question being free drinks
and a pleasant hour with two fine damsels.

"Thank you, mistress," he said very politely, even bowing slightly, and he
and Sammy followed the maids. I hung back, not knowing if I was invited.

The maids walked on, chattering and mincingly holding up their petticoats from the mud just as fine ladies do. Dick looked back inquiringly and
hesitated as if trying to make up his mind whether to offend the ladies by
inviting me, but Sammy spoke up:

"Tony must come too—he is our friend, mistress! He is not a savage if that
is what you are thinking."

Sammy with the hair and heart of gold. The maids looked back and because
it was quite clear that he would not have come without me, they shrugged
and gestured that I join them. I was going to refuse, but I was thirsty. So, I
went in with the lot of them and resolved to have *two* drinks at the expense of
this puffed-up pair. And though Dick smiled and clapped me on the back, it
rankled a bit that he had stopped and considered whether to leave me behind.

The only other pair of drinkers in the tavern was Cuffee and an African
man we did not know. Cuffee glanced at us and the maidens and winked at
Dick, who flushed. I considered whether to join the black men at their table
and leave the others behind, but not only had it become habitual to be with
Sammy and Dick, I was not certain if the Africans would desire my company.
So, I stayed where I was, feeling cantankerous and lonesome. Mistress Hodges
brought us a round of ale and then another. Only Dick and the ladies drank of
the second round. Sammy and I decided that we had had enough. The maidens
were laughing too much and too shrilly, and Dick, who had been awkward and
mumbling for a while, started trying to impress. He said that his father had
run a haberdashery in London, that he had carried a stock of money with him
to Virginia, that no horse could throw him off, that he had shot a wolf last
week, would shoot an Indian if he so much as dared to come within twenty
feet of the farm. The maidens begged for a ballad; he refused politely; and I
guessed that he did not think it manly to break into song. Little Sammy was
nodding off, and I sat there glowering and mum.

"What has eaten your darkie friend?" the smaller of the two damsels
asked. I had not cared to note their names.

"Does not speak English, eh . . . ?" the other one guessed, and they peered
at me curiously. The landlady came in with more drinks and corn cakes at
that moment and the girls got distracted, insisting we eat and drink well,
saying that there was money enough for this round and one more. I nudged
Dick to remind him that we should be getting back with Ganter's drink if we
did not desire a lashing. Cuffee looked like he was getting ready to leave. The
two maidens downed their ale, stood up, simpered, and after signaling they
would be back, stepped out. We guessed it was to piss. Flies buzzed around
the goblets and around our sticky faces. A lizard clucked somewhere. Dick
looked impatient, as if he could not bear the maids to be gone for even two
minutes.

Such a loon, I thought, and swore that I would never be a fool with women.

The maids took their time. It seemed like they were pissing a river out in the bushes. The two minutes became ten and soon we had been waiting for half an hour. It seemed improper to check on urinating maids, so we stayed there and waited for them to come back to pay Mistress Hodges.

We finally sent Sammy to see what had happened. He stumbled out half-asleep and came back saying they were not pissing outside; they were not outside at all. Dick and the landlady rushed out to see for themselves; I refused to budge. Cuffee was looking at our table, grinning widely. When Dick and the stout Mistress Hodges came back, she had him by the ear and was insisting he pay and pay up now.

"The maids . . . they've cozened us . . ." he stuttered. "They said they would buy us drinks!"

"Don't care what they said or did not. I want my money," Mistress Hodges said, and, big as she already was, she seemed to grow and swell further before our eyes. Dick looked like a very small boy in front of her. We hastily put together all the pennies we had, which covered only one round of the drinks, and promised to bring the landlady a few pumpkins and a quarter pound of tobacco, all of which we would have to steal from Ganter. And we looked so panicked and miserable, I suppose, and Little Sammy was so close to tears that Cuffee came up to us all-laughing and added to our little sum of money, so lightening our debt to the unforgiving landlady, who was now certain that the maids were strumpets. She had suspected it right from the time they stepped in, and she would have warned us if we had not been so cheeky and full of ourselves. She glared at me as she said that, as if I was the one to blame for this and all other manner of foolishness and error.

So, we left, bracing ourselves for a lashing from Ganter, who did not brook tardiness. Dick's embarrassment gave way to anger. He would never be taken in like that again, he said, he would never have anything to do with women. And he blathered on in the same vein.

"Do not make promises you cannot keep, Dicky," Cuffee told him. He was still mighty amused, laughing at us.

Cuffee then turned to me. "White boys are easily taken in. Why, pray, were you conned like that, young brown fellow? Because they was two English maids? 'Haps you are spending too much time with these two here, and are becoming soft in the head like them?"

I bit my lip and did not reply. I had felt an aversion to the maids from the start. Dick was the one who had fancied them. As for the other things Cuffee had to say . . . I would not consider them further.

For the rest of the way Cuffee chuckled each time he caught my eye.

It all went as expected: we got a beating to remember from our master. Ganter, he first thrashed Dick a bit, and sent him to the fields to work though the sun was setting. He then slapped Sammy and sent him to his cabin. He lashed me last and it was a slow and methodical lashing—and he cursed throughout, said that he did not know how he had gone and got stuck with a servant from god-knows-where, whose face was the exact color of dirt, who thought he was too big for his boots, who was crafty beyond belief, like a Jew man, because that was the way all East Indians were. I did not dare ask how many East Indians he knew or how many Jew men for that matter. I held my tongue and took the whipping for there was little else I could do. After finishing, Ganter spat in the dust and went towards his cabin. I hoped he was not going to lash Little Sammy. But no sound of wailing emerged, so I supposed that even Ganter was done with beating for the day.

The post that came from Banbury
Riding on a red rocket
Did tidings tell
How Lunsford fell
A child's hand in his pocket.

We would sing that ditty in fun just to frighten Sammy, especially when it grew dark, the shadows fell heavy, and the wilderness pressed upon us. The song had been carried from farm to farm quite recently. There was a man who had been a soldier in England wandering the countryside, they said, an ogre, a child eater of a man.

"And he had consumed the rest of the child?" Sammy asked, his blue eyes wide with fear.

"Yes—though why he left the hand I do not know—that is the best bit," Cuffee said, and winked.

And Sammy waited in apprehension for the monster to come through the woods and up the soggy path to the cabins. For he would come—in the earliest dawn, before the birds woke; or in the blaze of the midafternoon, when we slogged, taking axes to some trees, burning others, grubbing or breaking up the soil with our hoes; or in the evening, when we cooked the corn mush and the watery gruel that barely filled us. The child-eater would come then and rap on the door, sharply.

"Do not be afeared, Sammy," I said one day as we brought the hog her feed. "He will not come. He would be too frightened of old Ganter."

"You think so, Tony?"

"He would not want to come to this stinking hole," I replied.

That night Sammy, who sometimes slept in the cabin with the rest of us, sometimes in the other one with Ganter, picked up where we had left off: "He might still be tempted, y'know, Tony, if he comes to know there are three lads here for him to eat."

Sometimes, I thought Sammy was a little simple. He certainly looked it now with his round face and popping eyes. But I still felt a tenderness for him.

"He would not count me as a regular lad. I am a moor—my flesh would taste different. And Bristol and Cuffee are black *and* grown, so he will not be interested in them either. So that leaves only you and Dick—and you both have gotten so wasted working day and night that it would not be worth his while."

Sammy contemplated my reply.

"You know what, Sammy?" I said after a short silence that spread out and filled the dark corners of the tiny cabin. I was fatigued suddenly. Very, very tired. "The child eater is already here—he is this hard, grinding life, this hunger, these beatings, this savage place. This place and this life are consuming us. There is no other child eater riding up from Banbury, or anyplace else."

Little Sam nodded. He understood—he was not so simple after all.

"Shut up, you two," Dick muttered from his corner in the straw.

So, we went to sleep. And I was so exhausted that I dreamt of nothing.

I was alone at the far edge of Ganter's lands—he had asked me to clear more land there, while he kept Dick and Sammy busy near the cabins. I sometimes believed that he did not like those lads spending all that much time with me. I was the only one of my kind, old Ganter thought, so it was fitting I spend time alone. The river, partly lost in mist, was to my left and I remembered other rivers—the big, slow Thames in London, the monsoon-filled Coovam near São Tomé. They all flowed to the sea and became one, and then all the seas merged into the oceans of the world. But did they? Perhaps even in the oceans the waters did not mingle into one undistinguishable saltiness but remained distinct, each one holding on to its own memory of its source, its own particular journey.

So lost in my musings, I did not notice the stranger at first, and when I did, I wondered if I was seeing things: if that was a man or a tree, growing slightly apart from the others at the edge of the forest. And then I saw he was an Indian man, an Indian of Virginia. By another trick of the light he looked like he had wings. And I remembered hearing tales of the Powhatan warrior the English called Jack-o'-the-Feathers, who did not wear the red and black paint that other warriors did but went into combat covered all over with feathers that served as magical armor and with swan's wings fastened to his shoulders as if he meant to take flight. Like my mother, he had wanted to be a bird.

The man did not move, so I went closer, emboldened by curiosity. In my few months here, this was the first Virginia Indian I had clapped eyes on. He had no wings on him after all. He was dressed in English breeches, a shirt, and a sleeveless leather jerkin. His skin was as brown as mine, and his long hair, neatly bound back, was also black, like mine, although sleek and smooth. He had a knife at his belt and put his hand to it, cautiously. I was close enough for him to see that I was a brown man too. I registered some confusion in his face for an instant, and then he narrowed his eyes and looked at me intently, trying to understand my presence, to decipher how I had been washed up on his shores, along with the white and black peoples of the world outside, adding to the clamor and turmoil. I looked back at him—an Indian who was and was not an Indian. Two men standing on the earth that was of our color, plain brown, with no undertone or moderating hue. Just the earth, plain and simple, in broad daylight. Then he turned around, walked back into the forest he had come out of, and it was like he had never been. And I was once again by myself.

FIVE

One pleasant morning, Dick, Bristol, Cuffee, and I were sent off in the skiff to aid in the construction of the Great Wall. We left Sammy behind, woebegone.

"Cheer up, lad—we are coming back by sundown," Cuffee said, chucking him under the chin. We all had a fondness for Little Sammy. I hoped Ganter would not work him too hard when we were away.

We traveled further upriver. The wealthy men, like Master Menefie and his friends Masters Adam Thoroughgood, William Spencer, Abraham Wood, and others like them, had the best land, the land close to the tidewater, where the soil was fat and rich, where the tobacco ships could come all the way to the farms to collect their bales of harvested and cured crop to transport. Further inland, closer to the outer reaches of the settlement, were the smaller farmers like Ganter. And then there were those who had had dreams of becoming Virginia tobacco farmers, only to learn that what they had been granted was little better than wasteland—too distant from the coast to ship their produce to Jamestown, too infested with wolves and Indians.

We met one such man at the construction site. He was from the Shetland Isles, he told Dick, as Bristol, Cuffee, and I hung about and listened. He had ventured from home with eight and a half pence in currency and three pounds' worth of woolen stockings for sale to make his fortune in London but, having found no success there, had boarded a ship to Virginia.

"And all ends well, does it not, Master Anderson?" Dick said cheerfully. "Here you are in America, with your own land an' all."

The man spat on the ground. "Land that is fuckin' useless. Cannot wrest a thing out of it; and if you do, you cannot sell the stuff you grow; if you sell it, you cannot sleep at night for fear of the wild things—beast and man—outside your cabin when dark falls."

He was going back to Jamestown, he added, to bind himself again to a master—at least he would not starve there. "Fuckin' land!" he swore again, and spat once more on the dusty earth. So, they continued discussing whether it had been worth uprooting their lives and coming across the big waters, whether America rewarded those who had grit and were not afraid of work, whether it favored the wealthy, like the rest of the world did. All along they labored on the Wall: arranging the palisades, nailing them, testing them to make sure that they did not tilt over. They might or might not have faith in the promise of Virginia, but they believed in the Wall.

"To keep them out."

"The Indians."

"The Savages."

"Brutes."

"Wolves."

"Worse."

"Their food stinks."

"They stink."

"Their women stink. Especially down there."

"How do *you* know?"

"Because they look like it."

"You bastard! You *know*!!"

"To keep them out."

"To keep us in."

"To show 'em who we are."

"Who *they* are not."

The Wall.

Bristol, Cuffee, and I held our tongues. Indeed, we were not expected to participate in the conversation. We worked on as the sun rose high in the sky, stayed suspended there, and then began its slow, leisurely descent. The white men were sore and tender at the end of the day and their skin had broken into welts. Bristol, Cuffee, and I stayed smooth and intact. The sun, at least, favored us.

As the men chattered on, I realized, once more, how few of them considered this home. One day they would haul their bundles onto their shoulders, head to the coast, and sail back to England. For home is singular and unique: everywhere else is but a stopping place, a bed in a stranger's house, eating off plates not one's own, an unfamiliar view from a casement. If even these Englishmen plan to go back, so must I, I decided with newfound resolve. I too must find a ship to cross one ocean and then another. And so, I too will be home.

"When the Fairy King and Fairy Queen quarreled, the winds suck'd up fogs from the sea and blew them into the land. So the green corn rotted before it grew its beard, the folds stood empty in the drowning fields, and the ravens grew fat on the bloated corpses of the sheep."

"All this because the King and Queen quarreled?" Sammy asked, wide-eyed.

We had got back from our building expedition. Sammy looked so forlorn that I had started on a tale.

"Yes, the world turned topsy-turvy when the fairy folk were in a rage; streams changed course, the moon turned deathly pale, and the air was awash with disease."

"Disease like the bloody flux?" Sammy breathed steadily by my side. I could not see his face in the dark, but I knew his eyes were wide with wonder.

"Remind me of the name of the entertainment, Tony," he said.

"*A Midsummer Night's Dream,*" I said. "I saw it in London. It was composed by William Shakespeare—"

"Never heard of him," interrupted Dick. "Never been to a play either. Waste of a good penny if you ask me."

Sammy and I ignored him. Dick liked these stories as much as anyone else did. He just feigned he was too grown a man for such childishness.

"Go on, Tony," Sammy pleaded. "Tell me about the changeling boy." He had heard the story before, but he liked it more with every retelling.

"The Fairy King and Queen—Oberon and Titania—quarreled over the little lad. The king wanted him as his servant. The queen refused to give him up because, you see . . ."

I stumbled. I had not ever understood why the queen wanted the boy, the little *Indian* boy. Was it only because the king claimed him? Did she look upon him as a child, as a servant, or simply as a rare *thing*?

"*His mother was a votaress of my order,* she told the king. *And, in the spiced Indian air, by night, Full often hath she gossip'd by my side . . .*"

"For God's sake, how many times have you seen that stupid play, Tony?" Dick asked, astonished.

"Just once," I mumbled, both proud and embarrassed that I could recite the lines. But it really was only that set of lines I remembered. Of course, Dick would not understand my excitement, my bewilderment, when I heard of an Indian boy woven into an English story. But maybe good stories are like that—infused with borrowings, lendings, and crossovers. No confines can keep them apart. Not even the Great Wall could exclude the Indian boy from Master Shakespeare's vision as he wove his tale.

"Was he Indian like you are Indian, Tony?" asked Sammy drowsily.

"Yes, he was."

"And is the Indian air spiced, Tony?"

I could not even begin to describe it—the lotuses like big scented bowls, the frangipani and jasmine that loaded the dusk with perfume, my mother's hair fragrant with frankincense, the foods my grandmother cooked, the perfumed waters the men sprinkled on themselves, the incense smoking before the household deities, smells so intense and varied that they could not be translated into words, and those other odors of color, sound, and memory. They twirled around me in that dark, stuffy Virginia cabin, and I was heady with the *spiced Indian air.* And then the scents wafted away, and I could have wept.

Titania had insisted that the boy was hers because of her love for his dead mother: *For her sake do I rear up the boy, And for her sake I will not part with him.*

I was just at the start of Master Shakespeare's tale, but Sammy and Dick had drifted into slumber.

It was about that time that we heard report of the Man Who Would Not Die. He had been found guilty of a crime in England—a crime that was no crime at all; the unfortunate fellow had probably been wrongfully accused, they said, but no one knew for certain. In any case, when the day of the hanging arrived, the hangman, who had strung up fifty men in his chosen profession and was looking to finish his fifty-first and go home to his bread and cheese breakfast, had trussed him up. But the convicted man could not be hanged—his neck had been bruised from the rope and he had been slightly dizzy, but not dead. They had tried again, thinking that his neck needed a fatter rope. But this time too his neck had not snapped. They had brought another hangman, one who had hanged a hundred men in his career, but he too had failed.

"How can that be?" I asked skeptically. "How can a hanged man not die? The witch hanged on the ship died right away."

The customer at the Gray Foxe who was telling us the tale shrugged. The second hangman volunteered to try yet again, but the law ruled that no man could be hanged more than three times. So, the accused was put on a ship to Virginia—where exactly he was no one knew, in Jamestown perhaps, or perhaps somewhere upriver, closer to us.

I moved between doubting and believing the tale, but it fascinated me, this story of a man who refused to perish, who had crossed the ocean and now lived in Virginia, alive and, by all accounts, faring well.

So, the days rolled by hastening towards the cold weather. Leaf fall was all gold and yellow and the light was shifting and muted. Ganter kept us busy pulling the weeds that sprang up on the cleared land, putting up fences, building a curing shed for the tobacco once it was harvested next summer. In sum, there was work from morn to night, every morn and night, and so it seemed it would go on to eternity. The only thing we had was each other's companionship, for our bondage to Ganter pulled us even closer together in common suffering, united us in our dislike and fear of the man we had to call master.

Sammy every so often asked me if I had received a reply to his letter. Surely, they had had time enough to peruse it and write back? And I said he had to be patient, it would come. Dick whispered why was I lying to the poor mite, why did I not just tell him the truth and be done with it, while Bristol and Cuffee sighed in sympathy.

We had become acquainted with one Flynn Keough, a fellow about twenty-two years of age, who had been hired by another farmer. Flynn had no intention of staying out his indenture; he hated his master, he was going to run away one of these days, so he said, and he invited us to join him. We would steal away at night, take one of the skiffs and go up the river and deep into the forest till we reached Indian territory. They would offer us shelter for a while.

"And why, pray, would they not slit our throats instead, and display our scalps on their belts?" Dick asked sardonically.

But Flynn was convinced of the Indians' hospitality—to this end he studied (he was among the few servants who could read) a ragged book, which, he said, listed words in the Indian tongue.

"It cannot be called just 'the Indian tongue,'" I insisted, "it must have its own name."

"Do you speak it?" he asked me, eager for a tutor to supplement his book study. When he learned I did not, he sighed and continued to look through the pages of his book whenever he could, braving the other fellows' mockery.

"I maintain that a white man can learn the Indian tongue if he sets his mind to it." He pointed at Bristol, Cuffee, and myself. "Look at how the darkies have learned English."

And he explained, yet again, that he would go to the Indians, impress them with his grasp of their language, and convince them to take him for a bit, before he traveled north to the country which the Dutch had settled. It was better for servants there, and there was better land for the taking too.

"That is what they told us about Virginia," someone said.

But Flynn continued to glow with hope. Some of it infected me, and I thought of what a wonderful thing freedom would be.

We were barely into October when we woke up one day, to everyone's puzzlement, to warm, vaporous weather. People had just about got used to the coolness, the morning dew on the grass, and the mists that ascended like veils along with the sunrise. That evening we heard a howl from the direction of the sea, as though a monster had risen from the waters. We looked at each other, bewildered.

"What's that . . . ?" I started, but the rest of my speech was muted by a wind the likes of which I had not heard since the gusts that had raged into Armagon from the sea. It screeched and roared like it was whipping through a tunnel and it ripped up everything in its path. The dead leaves that blanketed the earth came hurtling towards us in a monstrous wave, the dirt at our feet lifted, and we feared that we would be smothered by it.

A cyclone, I thought.

"Get indoors!" Bristol yelled, and all of us, including Ganter, hurled ourselves towards the nearest cabin, only to see it wrenched up from the ground and dropped about twenty feet away, where it crashed in a pile of rotting logs.

We could see our poor belongings—the pots and pans, a stool, a blanket—flying about before they disappeared. We ran towards the second cabin. It was further away and the wind stood in our path like an invisible, solid wall, so we had to push mightily against it.

We huddled indoors—fearing that this cabin too would fly up in the air at any moment and us with it. All around the gale blew, battered the walls, tore through the trees, and shredded the very sky to rags. *Vayu, the God of the Wind. He carries a white banner and his chariot is drawn by one thousand purple horses. He is virtuous and wise, but he is also prone to abrupt and inexplicable rages. In one such fury, he battered the top of the peak Meru, which was flung through the air, came to rest on the ocean, and became the island of Lanka. The sons of Vayu are Hanuman, the mighty Monkey God, and Bhima, the great warrior, Mountain among Men.*

Through the roar I heard my grandmother's tranquil voice. The one thousand purple horses clattered and crashed through the firmament.

"'Tis a hurricane," Ganter said, and he looked sick. We knew he was thinking that our labors would come to naught.

It was indeed a hurricane, as they call cyclones in America, and it raged on for three days and nights. By some miracle the cabin stood its ground. The wind brought dreadful claps of thunder on its wings, and when the rain came, it fell in torrential sheets. We had no casements to look out of, but we could hear it whipping on the roof and sides of the building.

The cabin, always miserable, was hellish for these few days. It was close and smelt of sweat, the stale food we lived on, and piss (for people had urinated indoors at first when the wind was too wild to risk stepping out). While in England I had got used to people not bathing every day, but in the heat, damp, and closeness, the stink sat like a presence in the room. Besides, nothing was as bad as being with Ganter, seeing his vile face awake and sleeping, for three days at a stretch.

It was with great relief when the rain and wind died away that we stepped out into a flattened and soggy landscape, beneath a blue, birdless sky. The hurricane had brought down several trees and strewn tree trunks, branches, and rocks over the fields we had cleared. Master Ganter instructed me to go check on the hog. She was not in her pen so I squelched through the mud, putting aside broken barrels and other sundry objects, and there I saw, some feet away, a great heap of hog flesh, all battered and broken.

As I stood over the hog's carcass, filled with sorrow for the unfortunate creature, and yet glad that I was out of the cabin and breathing air that was fresh, I heard a noise like that of a scrabbling animal. And then I heard a hoarse voice calling my name: "*Tony . . . ?*"

"Tony . . . ?"

I heard her before she came into sight, rising from behind the tangled branches of a fallen elm. She was covered in mud, and her sodden, filthy skirts were torn in places. Even through the dirt I could see that she was covered in fresh bruises—purple ones that seemed to grow rapidly even as I looked, like some strange flower. One eye was blackened and shut tight. I knew the face, it was the same one that had loomed by my side on the first morning I had gone aboard the *God's Gift.* It had been smiling then—the smile of the wholly innocent. The last time I had seen it was on the boat that brought us to the landing stage in Jamestown.

"Mad Marge!" I cried out in astonishment. "Is that you?"

It was indeed her. Marge came towards me, her gaze expressionless, and I noticed that she limped as she walked as if she had sprained an ankle. I took her by the arm and half-dragged and half-led her to the others.

Dick and Sammy were as astounded as I. We had all thought that Mad Marge had been plucked up and spirited away as we waded towards land. We, frankly, had thought she had perished. And here she was standing with us in this rain-washed world.

"Marge, Marge . . ." Sammy said, and embraced her.

Over the next few days, we were to get her tale in jumbled fragments. She could not tell who had whisked her from our side in Jamestown or where they had taken her, but she knew that she had been bound to a master and mistress whose names she could not recall. She could not tell us anything else about them either, but they must have farmed somewhere near where we lived and it was quite clear that they fed her badly—she had almost no flesh on her bones, her eyes and nose were enormous on her sunken face.

And then her masters died, she said.

"They *both* died?" we asked, unsure how much of this had transpired only in Marge's head.

But she was right. We later found out that the man who had been Marge's master had worked a small, scrubby farm till he was hit by a falling tree the first day of the storm. As for his wife, she was nowhere to be found. The hurricane might have killed her or she might have run away from her husband, tiring of her life of toil with nothing but a grouch and a madwoman for company, although she had picked a bad night, and might have ended up drowned.

"Marge must bide with us," I declared.

When we led her to Ganter he was repelled.

"Is the whole pack of you gone mad?" he asked. "What will I do with a lunatic?"

Marge began to wail, a thin, long yowl, like a frail babe crying, and Ganter stepped up and slapped her. She stopped and stood there, her mouth agape, her eyes large and wet. A fresh blotch appeared on her face.

"She would do no work and be a great feeder—as if you lot do not consume enough of the victuals," Ganter muttered, but I could see that he was thinking hard, he already liked the idea of a free servant, one whose term would never end.

And so, we went back to work and Marge came with us. The river was swollen with the downpour and for some days we could not go anywhere to trade for supplies and had to make do with the small stores we had left in the cabin. Marge was surprisingly strong, eager to please, and very grateful for the small plate of mash we shared with her. I made a salve of the leaves and petals of the flower known as Mary-gold—a recipe I had learnt while at Master Menefie's—and applied it on her skin. I was proud beyond words to see that Marge's wounds covered over and grew new skin.

"Tarry here for now, madam, but we will run away soon enough!" Flynn Keough said, leaning forward to whisper in her ear when he came sloshing through the woods and fields to borrow something for his master. "Once I learn the Indian tongue, we will be on our way to join the tribes."

Marge nodded. She was the only one who ever believed in Flynn's madcap scheme, if she understood it at all. She stuck mostly to Sammy and me. She would stroke the little fellow's hair and murmur soft endearments. She would take me by the hand and smooth my cheek. *Talk,* she'd say, *talk,* and we'd speak to her, tell her about our homes, our families, the lives we'd lost. We could not tell if she understood all of it, but she appeared to enjoy listening, all along nodding and smiling. At mealtimes she'd insist we eat the poor bits of meat in her share of the stew, and once, when I sprained a foot, she took it in her lap and pressed it firmly but gently to soothe the pain. Sam and I were glad she had come back to us. We knew little by way of tenderness and were very grateful for hers, and, soon, we grew to feel great affection for her, our Marge.

After a drink or two at the Gray Foxe, Flynn would sing his favorite ditty: *I'll set my foot in the bottomless ship, / And sail across the sea . . .* he'd croon soulfully. And the other men hanging about would join him: *When are you coming back, my son? / My son, come tell to me.*

And so, they'd lament together. For what they had left behind, for all that was separated from them by an ocean. Their tune was carried on the back of the chilly breeze, through the woods and down the river, to the seashore, where it lingered, waiting.

Dick, however, had little time for song, none at all for lamentation. Yes, he was a Londoner born and bred in the slums of Saint Giles; he missed the crops of men in the street corners and he missed the markets, the alehouses, the gambling dens, the bridges, the river, all of it. But he did not miss the watchmen who patrolled the streets, kicking the vagabonds and ordering them to move on, did not miss his drunken dad beating his mother and breaking her nose, thrashing his sisters and then thrashing him. Above all, he did not miss the hunger that was always there squatting inside the pit of the belly, in the head, and deep in the heart. *Do not talk to me of homesickness,* Dick said. *Hunger is worse; hunger makes you an outcast wherever you are, even in your own home. Hunger exiles from place, family, people. You belong to it alone, and nothing else belongs to you.*

"I do not love any place enough to go back to it penniless," Dick said. "For now, this is home."

"Look at Master Menefie, look at Master Thoroughgood," he added. "Not highborn men, and here they are, masters of servants and lands. How did they get here? Through guts and hard work. Why? Because they wanted to. Who helped them? Only themselves, and the place—*this* place, the newness of it, its size, its wildness, its riches, its beauty . . . Think about it, Tony!"

I did think about it as winter came on, the cold numbing the tips of our fingers, the snow making its way through our work boots and thin wool stockings. There is something about a year divided into seasons that makes one believe in cycles, a pattern of coming and going, departures and returns. Back in my homeland there was only the heat and the rain. Now that it was cold weather in Virginia, the white snow dusted the earth and the silence was so deep that it made our very thoughts audible. Dick dreamt through the long months—first he would work off his indenture and get a few acres like Ganter, he would labor like no man has labored before, and one day he would be *Master Hughes,* owner of fine lands further down the river. He would name his farm . . . Never mind, the name would come later. It would be a good name, like Hughes's Hundred or Richard's Hope. He could already see the bales of tobacco being rolled down to the riverbanks, the tobacco ships sailing up; the wife, who would be a nice girl who had come recently from England (not like the filthy trulls around here, who would raise their petticoats and spread their legs for a penny or a drop of ale); and there would be their children, and then the children of their children—and the future rolled forward, a ribbony river; it spread itself out and wheeled through the sky, like the blue heron, which took off from the marsh and flew up in the air, strong and swift.

Flynn too dreamt, of running away, of mastering the Indian tongue, of moving west and north, where somehow life would be better, life *had* to be better.

I dreamt of my return. Of familiar sights and tastes and sounds, of my mother restored to life, of moving not just back in space, but back in time, to a time that had been before ships sailed and voyages started, when the world stood still, when there was only a salty land, a salty sky, and a sea.

Bristol and Cuffee—surely their dreams were something like mine. They'd be surprised if I asked. They had got used to me being standoffish, not a white boy but less a black man than them—that is what they believed I thought of myself, and, perhaps, that is what they believed of me. They would not share their dreams with me.

Mad Marge. Who can tell what went through her muddled old head? But she was probably the only one of us content to be where she was at that moment, doing what she was doing, with Sammy and me by her side.

And Little Sammy himself—he labored on in silence. I believe that Sammy had ceased dreaming.

When the Christmas season came along, Dick and Marge tried to cheer up the cabins (we had rebuilt the one that fell in the storm) by hanging greenery from the cypress trees. In England, it would be holly, bay, and ivy, Dick and Sammy said. In England, there would be pudding and souse to eat, mulled ale, plum pottage, mince pies, frumenty, custards, marchpanes, apples, nuts, and cheese. I doubt those lads got to eat any of those delicacies even back home, but they liked to talk about them.

Ganter permitted us to go to the Gray Foxe on the twelfth night of Christmas, and there we saw such a carousing and dancing of jigs that we quite forgot the cold. A man played his fiddle and though he was a poor player we thought it was the best music in the world, being played especially for us there under the cold, white stars. A servant from a neighboring farm served as the Lord of Misrule. He kissed the maids and patted their bums; he made faces at the children and said rude things to the men. He then walked up to Ganter, who had come too and was drinking with a couple of the other farmers, and asked him if he was Ralph Ganter.

"Aye," Ganter said with a scowl. "*Master* Ralph Ganter to the likes of you."

"Tobacco farmer, eh?" the man slurred cheekily. "And master to your servants? In Bristol, I heard your father was but a beggar and a drunk."

Ganter turned quite pale at that and put down his cup.

The poor fool, Misrule, emboldened by his drink and his mask with the exaggerated fake nose (where had he got it from? Which ship had brought *that* from England?) went on: "And hearsay is that your mam was a whore who tried to strangle you when you were but a child."

Ganter was up in a flash and had knocked the Misrule down, just a single blow on the face. The man crashed to the ground and lay there, his mouth open and his nose bleeding, a red spatter that looked almost black in the dim light and against the dusting of snow. Ganter sat back down, but I could see that he was still furious. Like all men here, even the grand ones like Menefie, he was sensitive about his origins in England. I stared at him, wondering if his mother was a whore. I remembered too the slight scar around his throat and how I had thought it was just a part of the ugliness he was born with. But maybe his mother had wanted him dead . . . For an instant, I felt something almost akin to sympathy for him.

The fiddler went on scraping on his instrument and a few men and girls got up to dance—there was only one girl for every two or three men, but they got by and did a decent enough jig. I did not join them—was not invited, and, at first, I thought it was because I was but a lad. However, Bristol, Cuffee, and a few of their African friends from other plantations did not dance either, so there must have been another reason. They sat clustered together, smoking their pipes and watching the white folks dancing. It was hard to tell if they were amused, scornful of these drunk Englishmen, or simply indifferent, content in their momentary leisure. Every now and then they turned and whispered a comment in the ear of one of their group. Marge was not with us—Flynn's master and mistress had borrowed her for a few days to help with something that needed doing. I sat by myself huddled in the shadows, fingering the pouch of unicorn-horn medicine powder, which I kept about me these days as a lucky charm, as a reminder of times gone by. Someone—I cannot tell who—handed me a drink and then another. The ground swelled beneath my feet, and rocked gently as I moved. I drank another pot of ale, maybe two more. The world spun and steadied for an instant and then spun again. The snow was silver, my mind was cotton wool. I decided to sing. It was a good song, I thought. The words I had heard a long, long time ago, sung by the peasants tilling the paddy in my homeland—the tune I made up myself on the spot:

The earth believes (e-le-lo) *that the rains will arrive* (ay-ya-sa)
The tree believes (e-le-lo) *that the earth will ever remain* (ay-ya-sa)
So I too believe (e-le-lo) *that you will come* (ay-ya-sa) . . .

I heard laughter around me—*e-le-lo* . . . went the traditional wordless refrain, and *ay-ya-sa* . . . Yes, it was a good tune and I had done an excellent job singing it. They were laughing at something far away, something that I could not hear. And someone was jabbing me in the ribs and telling someone else that I was talking in the tongue of the East Indians. I was puzzled at that; I thought I had sung in English, the tongue of Master Francis Day; the language of Their Royal Majesties King James and King Charles, both of England, Scotland, and Ireland; the tongue I was even beginning to dream in. Why had they not comprehended the words of my song? I staggered forward to interrogate them, a slight boy, drunk out of my poor black-brown senses for the first time in my life, although I did not know it. And then I was lurching over and puking exactly where poor Misrule had bled.

"The stink!" a maiden screeched. "What nasty-strange foods did you eat for your puke to stink like that?"

"I eat what you eat," I might or might not have said. But I fell silent after that, and I suppose I slept. When I came to, I was shivering slightly, my mouth a dry, foul pit. I felt repelled at myself and, at the same time, angry and suddenly desperate. A shadow fell on the ground, and I sat up. A stranger stood over me, a man neither young nor old, both small and strong, his face an outline in the darkness.

"Who are you?" I whispered, suddenly fearful.

"I came over recently," he replied. "I bide close to you now."

I somehow knew who he was even before he completed his utterance. This was he, the Man Who Would Not Die. His face was expressionless; he was less pale than one expects a white man to be—perhaps his complexion had been changed by the Virginia sun. Did he say more? Did I ask him a question? Would he have replied if Dick, Bristol, and Cuffee had not appeared, urging me to pull myself together, to go home with them? I looked back as I stumbled off, but the stranger had vanished.

I did not dare tell my friends what I had seen. Indeed, my mouth was so parched that I could barely say anything at all. We were well on the road before I remembered: Little Sammy! Even in my sodden state I was filled with panic; we had left him behind at the Gray Foxe . . . he had wandered into the woods . . . there really was a child killer on the loose like in the verse we sang.

"*Sammy!*" I cried out, startling my companions. "Where's Sammy?"

Dick drily explained to me that when I was sleeping like a prince after getting drunk on the ale that he and Cuffee had to pay for, Ganter had left with Sammy.

"Why?" I asked.

"What do you mean *why*? Sammy is Ganter's servant. Just as we all are, in case the drink has made you forget."

Of course, Dick was right. Sammy had gone home with Ganter. I wished I had not fallen into my stupor. I could imagine Sammy looking at me pleadingly when Ganter ordered him to go with him. If I had not gone and got drunk, I would have left with them both, stayed by Sammy's side, assured him there was no child eater, no wicked figure with a severed hand bleeding crimson in his pocket, and riding through the dark night to *tidings tell / How Lunsford fell* . . .

I should have been with Sammy, holding his little paw, as he went with Ganter through the dark woods, to where another darkness waited in the cabin. I too was but a boy at that time; however, I felt I would have been, for that wee fellow, an amulet, like one of those that my mother would put around my wrist to ward off evil.

It is now many years since Sammy Mason died. He was nine years old. He is not even a side note in the history of the settling of Virginia—not even a side note to his own life as it could have been, if he had not come, borne by the *God's Gift,* to this precarious edge of the world.

It did not happen till seven days after the twelve-day Christmas festivities ended. He waited, poor lad, for even the memories of the auspicious season to be behind us before he elected to go. When we got back to the cabin after the twelfth night revelries, he had been there and asleep, much to my relief. As soon as I clapped eyes on him lying there covered with his coat and a thin blanket, I crashed on the straw. I slept the sleep of the dead or the drunk. Bristol later—much later—said he did not think that Sammy was asleep.

"He was just lying there—he might have been sobbing a bit, or he might not have." Bristol had assumed the lad was despondent with homesickness again, and because he too was slightly tipsy, Bristol slept.

The next couple of days were dark and bleak. The season's gaieties were over, and winter came to roost in our midst like some giant, dank-feathered bird of prey. A blizzard blew about one night, and the morn after the sky was gray and a pale violet behind the bare, brown-limbed trees, lovely in a way that I never imagined a winter morning could be. During the day we shivered in our thin, inadequate coats, and we huddled around small fires at night—we were always at least a little hungry and a little cold. Ganter told us not to be a set of ninnies, it was colder in England, he said, and far more frigid up north in the Puritan settlements.

"Should get you lot out there," he said. "Should bind you to one of the brethren—you would know me to be a good master then."

He grinned at his own humor. We knew better than to answer.

We were putting up fences, Ganter, Dick, Sammy, Bristol, Cuffee, and I. Marge had been set to salt and preserve the flesh of a deer that had wandered nigh the cabin, which Ganter had shot. I saw out of the corner of my eye that Sammy looked pale and I asked him if he was doing all right. Yes, he said.

"How much longer, Tony?" he asked in a whisper. Ganter was just out of earshot.

"The sun will set early enough in this weather, we can return to the cabins," I assured him, thinking he desired to rest.

"No, how much longer before I get a reply to my letter? The one you wrote my mam and pap for me."

I had almost forgotten about that letter and, anyway, it had not struck me that he was still hopeful for an answer.

I do not know why. I could not get myself to tell a falsehood in response, say something soothing and foolish about the next ship bringing him a packet with a reply in it. 'Haps it was because after the dreary, unrelenting toil of the day, I too was sick at heart.

"Your answer should have come by now, Little Sam," I said. "In truth, I cannot tell why it has not."

It came to the tip of my tongue to tell him that he had best give up hoping, but Dick hailed me to assist him with something, and the words did not leave my mouth. I thank God they did not—that those were not my last words to the lad.

He looked ill enough after that and close to fainting, so Ganter sent him off to the cabin. The rest of us continued to labor. I somehow remember Ganter by our side working away. But I was lost in my own misery, my mind wandering great distances as it often did—and Ganter might not have been with us after all. Cuffee later said that he was not—he had left for a short while around lunchtime and returned, while the rest of us stayed, gnawing at something nearly unpalatable.

Cuffee was the first to see the lad when we filed into the cabin as the sun set. He exclaimed in a tongue I had not heard him use before, and I peered around his bulk and saw Sammy. He was strung up straight as a needle from the rafters, a piece of meat hung out to dry. Dick gasped; someone set up a loud piercing wail and I did not know it was me. Ganter heard the commotion and came in behind us. He held up a lantern, and I saw his ugly face grow uglier. He cursed, a long, low string of oaths.

Sammy must have done it to himself that afternoon while we worked on the seedbeds. The next day we buried him just before sunset, a hasty burial, setting the ground on fire first to thaw it a bit before we could dig a shallow grave. Before that, someone came by boat from the sheriff's office and cursorily examined the body to determine that it was not a murder. That was the extent of the law. The other servants and I dug the hole—Ganter came just for a moment, after we had placed Sammy in it, pale and slight as a child's plaything. I wish now I had killed Ganter then, because he was responsible—he had starved and beaten the boy and I *knew, I knew* better than the others did, that he had done worse. I knew, had always known perhaps, but had pushed the knowledge deep into my mind. *Sammy, Sammy, Sammy . . .* I wept. *I too am at fault.* And for years after that I carried that thought with me, like a canker.

That was in January. Just over six months after I came to America. Later, I wondered if I had been foolish grieving like that for a lost, pale-faced English lad when I myself had other things to feel sorry about. But I did mourn. Long after Sammy died, I would walk over the frost-crusted fields thinking of him. I would even start to address him and then realize that he was not by my side. And then I would feel my chest swell with the pain of his loss.

How much longer, Sammy had asked me. And I asked the same through the bleak nights and slate-gray days of that first Virginia winter: *How much longer? Is it going to be a very long time?*

III

WESTERN PASSAGE

SIX

I went to hear the new preacher sermonize at a chapel downriver, which was really only a good-sized wooden shack. The whispers going around about the treatment of servants (rumor had it that at least two servants in the last year alone had been beaten to death and surreptitiously buried in the lonely farms they had worked on) might have prompted the preacher to speak on servitude: . . . *Servants,* he solemnly instructed, *be obedient to them that are your masters according to the flesh, with fear and trembling, in singleness of your heart, as unto Christ* . . . I snorted under my breath; Ganter, I knew, was no Christ.

A dappled bird flew into the church, causing a stir of interest, before it went out with a rustling and flapping. Imagine, I thought, that angels have come bearing messages, and this is the sound of their wingbeat. The sparse congregation started and then settled back with a sigh. The preacher continued: . . . *And, ye masters, do the same things unto them, forbearing threatening: knowing that your Master also is in heaven* . . .

I wondered if any of the masters in the room were moved by this. I knew Ganter certainly would not have been. I shuffled out of the church into the sunshine, embarrassed that I did not have anything to leave the preacher as the others were doing, not even a pumpkin or a small bag of cornmeal.

Winter gradually turned into spring, the earth thawed, and the daylight lingered a little and then more. I stood under the March sky watching the fowl fly from a southerly direction, chirping and squawking with anticipation.

Marge, who shed tears for weeks after Sam's death, took to wandering

the farm and the woods at night. Sometimes she would halt in the middle of
a field and wail aloud, and I would wake up with a start and stumble out to
fetch her back to the cabin. If Ganter was angry enough to rouse himself, he
would smack her on the head and threaten to put her out. I tried my best to sit
by her in the evenings. The others and I agreed not to bring up Sammy when
Marge was about, but we sometimes talked of him among ourselves.

Remember this about Little Sam? we would ask. *Remember how he used to say
this and do that and the other?*

And we would be quiet for a bit, till Dick, to change the melancholic
mood, would talk about how he would be a big man someday, owner of land,
shipper of tobacco.

"That is the only way to be, Tony," he told me earnestly. "Otherwise, a
fellow ends up like our Sammy, hopeless and dead, or like one of these one-
acre farmers, forever scrabbling on a bit of earth, forever resentful, forever
ill-treating his servants."

Somehow, for Dick, the death of Sammy reinforced the promise of Virginia.

We got into an argument one day—it was about something trivial—some
quarrel over work, who had done more than his fair share, something like that.
Heated words were exchanged and one of us shoved the other. And we were on
the ground, engaged in a fierce, urgent tussle. I heard his soft panting—he was
slender, but taller and stronger than me and stood a better chance. I got on top
of him and gripped his wrists hard so he flinched; he rolled us over and freed
his hands and pinned down my chest. I bit at his arm and he yelped softly, but
did not let go of his hold. Cuffee stood by watching, egging us on—cheering
Dick one moment and me the next. Dick and I, we both knew that the other
was a friend, that we had been on a ship together, made a great crossing, that
we had both loved the boy who had died . . . But in that instant it felt like we
each could have murdered the other. His watery, sandy snot dripped onto my
face, his sweat and mine mingled, and we were covered in dirt. Finally, it was
Bristol who came up and put a stop to it. When he firmly yanked us apart,
we were both bruised and breathless. We did not speak to each other for two
whole days.

To make up for Dick's hostility, I would go out into the fields and have my
imaginary conversations with Sammy: a scrap of a story, a memory of something, the shape of our shadows.

"I know what you did to Sam!" I wanted to shout at Ganter sometimes, when we were gathered in the cabins eating our corn mush and passing around the cup of ale, or when we were in the fields silently laboring together. "I know . . . I have always known!"

But you did not do anything about it, a measured voice in my head reminded me.

And then Ganter summoned me to his cabin, once and once more.

How does one tell that which cannot bear telling? How . . . ?

Let this part of my story go unrecounted. Permit me to leave a gap, not an erasure, but an anguish covered over with silence.

I resolved that the next time I would bash him on the head with a hoe or a boulder, slit his weasand with the knife used to skin the animal carcasses. Never mind if he was bigger than me and stronger, I would do it. But nothing of that kind was to happen, for Ganter lost me soon after. And so began another chapter of my life in Virginia.

By the middle of March, we had sowed the tobacco in seedbeds and covered them with pine boughs to protect the young plants. In April, when the birds were singing as if they had gone mad, we thinned the young seedlings, and, the next month, we hilled the fields and transplanted the young plants. As the tobacco grew, we spent much time squashing the horn worms and flea beetles that came in greedy hordes to destroy it. Black-blue beetle blood stained our fingers and got under our nails, and I began to see the creatures crawling behind my eyes in my sleep.

Ganter rarely left the farm, and I was surprised when one evening he announced that he would accompany me on an errand to the Gray Foxe to trade some turnips. The thought made me uneasy—I did not want to be alone with him, not even in the vessel, but what choice did I have? I was the one who both rowed and navigated, having become familiar with this stretch of the river, the flowing water and the still pools that gathered along it, the shallows and deeps, the creeks and inlets, this cluster of swamp ash trees and that one of weeds where the waterfowl nested. Ganter sat at his end, resting his knees on the sack of turnips he would overcharge Mistress Hodges for, if he could get away with it. The water was green in parts and muddy brown in others.

"Dirty muck, like you, eh, Tony?" Ganter needled. He always thought it was droll to make reference to my tawny skin; a mongrel mix, he would mock, the color of dirt, the color of worse. I did not ever respond to those comments.

I looked up once, noticed him staring at me silently, and trembled. When I looked again, he had dropped off to sleep and I wondered whether to topple the boat so he would drown. But he was a strong swimmer and such dreaming was pointless. We reached our destination, docked the boat, and walked towards the dramshop. I hauled the sack of turnips over my shoulders, and it was heavy enough to make me stagger a little. Ganter strolled by my side, and I could smell his breath, foul as always, and see the hairs on his beard that were beginning to be touched with gray. He inched closer to me, and I felt his muscled arm against mine and flinched.

I huddled on a barrel in the corner while Ganter conducted his business with Mistress Hodges and then sat down with a group of farmers to drink. He drank steadily that night—surprising to me as he was not a big one for it. He grew loud and boastful, talking of the money he knew he would make that year. He talked of saving enough to go back to his family in Bristol, to his wife (this was the first I was hearing of her; I suspected he was lying) and his mam, who was getting on in years and would be glad to see him. I remembered what the Misrule had said about Ganter's mam being a drab who attempted to stifle him at birth. I watched him finger the scar, so faint that it might as well not have been there, and take another sip of the watered-down ale that the Gray Foxe served.

Another man came in shortly after and seated himself with his drink. He was a stranger to these parts: a giant of a white man, with broad, powerful shoulders and arms. His skin was burnt red, and it peeled off his neck and nose, leaving painful-looking blisters. He wore a waistcoat made of patched leather very roughly sewn together, and his hair, long and bleached to a light gold that was almost white, fell well below his shoulders, rough and unkempt as his beard. He drank quickly, tipping his head back and downing the brew in one smooth movement.

Ganter had shut up at last, mainly because the men at his table had started a game of dice. They played loudly and excitedly. This was not the first game I witnessed at the Gray Foxe—the fellows loved dicing. But, for the first time, I saw Ganter join in. He wagered and won and wagered and won again. He was getting loudmouthed and animated. The last of the sunlight seeped in through the window and lit up the center of the room, leaving the corners swathed in shadow. Ganter had called for venison pie and was eating it. He did not care to buy me any food, and I sat there hungry, yet thinking that it was better to be here surrounded by the bustle and jabber of men than alone with the monster.

The big newcomer uncoiled himself from his seat, something of a monster himself, a dragon that the English tell of in their tales, or a lion-man-god of the fables of my grandmother. He strolled across to the table where the gamblers sat and hovered over them. Ganter barely noticed him—he had just gathered up a lot of money and was tallying his winnings. He called for more drink. I would have nodded off if my stomach did not feel so empty.

The stranger addressed himself to Ganter: "I would play with you, master, if you permit me." And Ganter, eager at the thought of a new competitor, waved him to begin.

The stranger won the first round, and Ganter the second. Promissory notes exchanged hands. Ganter wagered a jar of honey that he had been saving to sell; he lost it. He wagered his hat and lost that as well. The stranger wagered his coat and kept it. The crowd was loving the sport—someone pulled up a stool for the stranger. Such a fine player deserved to sit.

In the great epic Mahabharata, King Yudhishthira, who had a weakness for gambling, was set up to play by his cousins. He lost his jewels, his horses, his palaces, his slaves, his very person, his wife, and finally his kingdom. Beggared and humiliated, he prepared to go into exile, mocked by his jubilant adversaries. His beauteous wife, Draupadi, was to stay behind with the victors, since she had become their property, but she refused. "You did not own yourself . . ." she told her husband. "What right did you have to wager me?

Ganter lost many times in a row. He took a great gulp of drink and clenched his fists. His countenance grew even uglier—I could tell that he was angry.

"One more round, Master Ganter . . . ?" the newcomer suggested. He had a calm, collected air about him, which seemed to infuriate Ganter. He had taken off his patched jacket and rolled up his shirtsleeves, and there was a tattoo on his forearm—from where I stood, I could not tell what it was.

"Go for it, Ganter!" someone yelled. "Beat the fuck out of him!"

"I have nothing left to wager," Ganter said, glowering.

"Nothing at all?" the stranger asked.

I hoped that Ganter, like Yudhishthira in the epic story, would wager himself and that we would be rid of him.

Ganter looked around him and his eyes lit on me.

"Wait . . ." he said. "I still have the boy—the Mahometan—whatever he is—East Indian rascal—there he is, perched yonder like some black imp—I'll wager him."

I was not a cockerel, or a pig, or a slave—he could not wager *me*!

I got off the barrel and stepped up to the men. "Please, Master Ganter," I said. "'Tis time to go home."

He ignored me. I was trembling, but I spoke again. "You surely would not play me, sir."

Ganter's face lit up with rage. "I *would not*? Pray, who is master here and who the bondsman?"

I might have said more, but Ganter was no longer paying heed to me. Besides, no one else seemed to think it was a problem if he wagered me. And they cupped the dice in their hands and let it rattle onto the table—Ganter first and then the stranger.

And that is how I switched hands and became servant to Master Archer Walsh—woodsman, trader, and adventurer. Ganter did not so much as glance at me when he left—which he did directly after that last game. I could tell that he was in a rage. He only muttered to the stranger that he should come by the farm the next morn for my papers.

"And watch out for that one," he slurred, still not looking at me. "He is a bad 'un—crafty as the devil. Give me a black man or a white boy any day— these brown ones are the worst. Think they are better than both."

He spat at my feet before he wheeled around and left. And I was by myself cowering in the tavern, which smelt of burnt meat and drink. People began to shuffle out, disappointed that the wager was over. One or two might have peered at me, curious more than pitying.

How did I feel at that moment? How should I have felt? Relief at being rid of Ganter? Fear at having my lot cast with this stranger who had won me and then had casually stepped out to smoke his pipe in the fresh air? Sadness at the thought of not seeing Dick, Bristol, Cuffee, and that lot again? Worry about Marge? I remember feeling a little of each of those things, but above all I recall feeling hungry—a fifteen-year-old lad can endure plenty of things but not hunger. I had nothing on me except my medicinal powder, which I had got into the habit of carrying about me.

I also remember, if I am remembering correctly at all, that someone slid up to me out of the gloom. I thought it was Master Walsh asking me to leave with him, or better still, getting me something to eat. But it was not him. This person stood before me, a gaunt outline.

"So, you are finished with Ganter," he said quietly.

"Yessir. I was lost and won."

Silence. I felt his gaze on me and willed myself to meet it.

"The question is what have *you* lost and gained."

I contemplated that. "I will find out," I replied.

He nodded. "And I will see you again," he said.

"You will?" I asked, but the silence that remained where he had stood was my only answer. And that was the first time I spoke to the Man Who Would Not Die. At least that's how I remember it.

Master Archer Walsh was a man of few words. Whatever I learnt of him, I gathered in fragments, in the time I spent with him. He was one of those traders who went deep into Indian territory to buy furs from the natives. The fur traders were generally considered a desperate, godless lot, who spent so much time with the Indians that they had practically turned Indian themselves. They were fabulously rich, some reports said, while others said that they had little more than the clothes on their backs and the damp smell of the forests that clung to them.

After Master Walsh got my papers from Ganter, we took his boat and went all the way downriver to Jamestown. Men there owed him money, he said, and he meant to collect it. He had been looking for a servant for a while and now had me. He smiled, not unkindly, and I saw that a front tooth was chipped almost in half. He looked the kind of man who had been in many a quarrel.

"East Indian, eh?" he asked, contemplating me.

"Yes, master—from the Coromandel." *As if he would know the difference.*

"First one of your kind I am seeing. Do not know anything about East India."

I shrugged. "Some people mistake me for a Virginia Indian, master."

"You do not look like one of the people native to this place," he said firmly. "That much I can say with certainty."

Master Walsh was one of the first white men I knew who could tell one brown man from another.

We traveled leisurely. From my master, I learnt more about the world we moved through—the names of the fish that we caught, the names of trees. I learnt to identify birds by their songs. With him, I stopped to examine the unusual leaves of plants, the shape and texture of insects' wings. These seem trivial things—but it is the ignorance of them that makes a place alien, and thanks to Master Walsh, I learnt to feel a certain intimacy with the wild things of this new world.

The weather was warm enough for us to sleep outdoors and we would stop every now and then to camp in the woods or on the outside edges of farms.

"My friend Dick Hughes says land is the key to happiness," I told Master Walsh. "Although for myself, I would rather possess the knowledge of things."

"What kind of things, Tony?"

"My father was a medicine man—he knew to cure, and to kill too, I suppose. If I had stayed in my homeland, I would have learnt his trade."

"You would have been a healer?"

"Yes, master. I was even assistant to a physician for a short time in London." An untruth certainly, but how would Master Walsh know?

"Still, do you think Dick is right about land, Master Walsh?" I asked.

He replied after some thought—he was never one for hasty answers. "In England—the landless are dependent, the landed are free. That is the notion we carry with us here."

"And it is a good notion?"

He shrugged.

"Wherefore do you not have land, Master Walsh?" I persisted. "Surely farming is better than trading with Indians?"

"You ask too many questions, Tony," he replied, and shut his eyes. "But the answer to that one is simple enough: land demands that you put down roots in it. The Lord created a wanderer when he fashioned me."

When he slept he looked even greater in size, a bull of a man. His snores almost made the earth beneath him shudder. I imagined that the creatures of the forest came to see, drawn by the sound, that they stood in the shadows studying the man, the dying fire, and the dark boy, sitting up, awake and watchful.

When I first came ashore to Jamestown from England it had looked a poor and bare outpost with its unimpressive houses, public buildings, and warehouses. Now, after being so long in the wilderness upriver, it appeared to be a bustling place, with ships dotting the water, men walking about the streets and gossiping in the taverns, others playing skittles to loud cheering, all sounds and sights accompanied by the city stink of unwashed bodies and piss. In the public house where Master Walsh and I went for our evening meal, we heard that there were more migrants coming in than ever before, they sailed in in droves. We heard other things too, discussed amidst much smoking and drinking: that five beastly sodomites were being returned to England for punishment; that one Goodwife Williams had been subject to the humiliation of a cucking stool for calling a group of men base knaves; that His Majesty the English king had reinstated the ousted governor of Virginia, Sir John Harvey. Everyone seemed disgruntled by this last bit of news—Sir John was a most vile governor, they said, and deserved to be gone. But things were not going well with King Charles either, the gossips said. He was taxing his subjects too heavily and had been long ruling without calling a parliament. It would doubtless lead to trouble, people muttered worriedly. They seemed to care very much for the English king and raised their cups to him in the middle of the conversation. I did not comprehend why—Virginia was an ocean away from England.

"That might be the case," Master Walsh explained to me later. "But for many loyal to the king, Virginia is but the western edge of England—not the first post of an entirely new world, but the last border of an old one."

"Who is the monarch of East India?" he then asked.

I was discomfited that I did not know the answer to that. I was embarrassed too that I did not know if there was even a country of that name, like there was the one called England and the other called Portugal, and such. If there was, I had never heard of it. How foolish Master Walsh must consider me, I thought. That I had lived in a country and knew neither its name nor its king.

"We had a sultan who lived north of Masulipatnam on the Coromandel," I said. "He was the lord of our region. Master Francis Day would travel to get his permission to trade."

"And who might Master Francis Day have been?" Master Walsh asked. In spite of his quiet manners, he was a curious man who liked to know things.

"He was a factor of the Company—the English East India Company," I replied. "He came to trade in Armagon, the place where I was born."

"An Englishman in your town," he mused. "And you here, Tony, in James-town. We indeed live in a world in motion. An unfixed, unsettled place—

every man a journeyman, drifting from land to land, getting and spending, gaining and losing. So it is, and I think that is the way it is going to be for the rest of time."

And I felt the globe spin about me, a whirling place filled with stirring, spiraling people; a world shrunk, defined by movement from one land to another, from one life to the next; oceans and mountains coming to signify only frontiers meant to be crossed—the thought filled me with awe and wonder, and also some fear.

"In my country, we believe that a soul keeps in motion even after death," I informed Master Walsh. "You are born and die and are born again."

"That is what Pythagoras also said," said Master Walsh.

I did not know who Pythagoras was, but I continued. "Therefore you, Master Walsh, after you die will be born again, a cabbage, or a cow, or an African woman, or an Indian chief, or a brother to that gnat settling on our table, the one you are about to kill."

Master Walsh promptly smacked the gnat. It jerked its little legs and died right by the sticky spot it had been exploring.

"Has it already been reborn?" he asked, smiling.

"Probably, yes. Maybe as an East India Company official or a future governor of Virginia." I grinned.

We stayed at an inn that night. I lay next to Master Walsh on the straw mattress thinking that his smell and snores would keep me up. But I slept deep, waking only once, in a panic, thinking that it was Ganter by my side. When I realized where I was, relief washed over me and I slept again, dreaming of Marge, Dick, Cuffee, Bristol, and all the people in motion around the world. And then, Mary Bengal, Peter Mansur, the witch who had been hanged, and many others, they crowded my dream. And also the Indian I had once seen on Ganter's farm, on the edge of the forest, who might not have boarded a ship, but whose life had been forever changed by the vessels that sailed to his shores. And then my mother and Little Sammy, both of whom had crossed the last of frontiers. A warm, salty breeze made the shutters creak, and at dawn I was woken by the rumble of a barrow outside. And just on the other side of the inn was the river, ever moving, yet always there.

During the day, Master Walsh went about his business and I either accompanied him, hauling his furs and skins, or stayed at the inn, earning my meal by washing and cleaning. Sometimes I went to the dock, where there was always some money to be made carrying loads and such. On certain days, due to some illusion of sky and water, the river looked like it was made of vapor or smoke. I watched the ships from Europe appear over the horizon, big-bellied, with their sails puffing in the wind, the pilots by their sides. As they came closer to the shore the sails would be lowered—I could sometimes even hear the sailors' cries. Boats came ashore bearing more migrants from the ships. I had been one of those just about a year ago. One afternoon, I saw two small white boys waiting with their parents on the dock, surrounded by their bundles and wearing the same expression of bewilderment as Sammy, Dick, and I had once worn. Another boat came up bearing a single passenger, a young man of indeterminate race. Unlike some other migrants, he had a group to receive him—finely dressed gentlemen who stepped forward and pressed his hand. He seemed shy and ill at ease with himself and his surroundings, but he was swept away by the gentlefolks and disappeared.

"That is young Master Thomas Rolfe," an African man standing by me said. "Half Englishman and half Indian. The son born of John Rolfe and the Powhatan princess they called Pocahontas. Both his parents are gone, and he has returned to claim his inheritance."

Another boat, the last one before the tide rose, was getting ready to go out to a ship. Five men were being hauled into it and I saw that their hands were lightly bound. They kept their eyes to the ground. A few men hanging around the docks jeered and spat in their direction.

"And those," said the chatty African, who seemed to know everything, "are five sodomites being sent back to London. They will cut their pricks first before cutting off other bits, and then they will burn them at the stake and display all their parts, even the cut-off pricks."

I looked at them curiously. They were very young men, about twenty years of age, much like Master Rolfe. I knew enough to understand what they had done, and I suddenly remembered my uncle and how he'd go to visit other men in the afternoons. The thought crossed my mind that he might have been one like these youths. And I found it in my heart to pity them, to pity also the lads who'd just arrived, even the young man who was both English and Virginian Indian. And then, as the light drained from the sky, there was Master Walsh done with his errands, striding up the wharf, gesturing that I should go with him.

We bided in Jamestown for a couple of months. When our day's work was done, we'd linger in the tavern attached to the inn. Master Walsh would sometimes play dice, and at first I was nervous that he'd decide to wager me. I wanted my situation to stay like it was for a while, till I found my way home to the Coromandel. The men in this Jamestown tavern were sharper, slicker than shallow-pated old Ganter, and next to them my new master appeared rough and unpolished. But Master Walsh mostly bettered them. In any case, he never wagered me. Often, on the evenings he had won a few rounds, women would come up to him, no doubt attracted by his good luck and rough good looks, and he'd draw them down and kiss them on the mouth while the others cheered. And sometimes, at night, after we went up to our chamber, when I was almost asleep, I would hear Master Walsh get up and softly leave, and I would know whither he went.

It was on one such evening after supper in that selfsame tavern that we heard the tale of the little trifling box that had come from the east—the story that spurred Master Walsh and myself on an adventure together.

SEVEN

The moon shone big and lustrous outside the tavern, and a goodly breeze blew in from the sea. I watched the people coming and going. There were a few African men at the tables and three white men, slightly darker than the rest, but not by much, who spoke a tongue that I thought was Portuguese, such as they had spoken in São Tomé, till Master Walsh told me that it was Italian, and that the men were glassmakers who had been brought over when there was a scheme to start a glass foundry in Virginia. These men were masters at their craft. Back in their country they had created wonders at their furnaces—goblets of light and fire, vases of air, plates so iridescent that they had the sea and sun trapped in them. And now, in Virginia, the glassmaking venture had collapsed, and the Italian artisans were forced to turn to working as servants. So, they complained and drank and dreamt of a world made of glass, light and brittle to the touch. More drinkers floated in, everyone got louder and more boisterous, and the stars shone like crystals in the vault of the sky stretched tight across the land and over the Chesapeake Bay.

A group of women came in—five or six of them attired in brightly colored petticoats and blouses that they had somehow pieced together. By daylight they would doubtless have been a hard-faced, exhausted crew, but in the fading light of dusk, with the candles just being lit, they managed to look beauteous. Then the drink was flowing and chatter grew louder. Men reached for the women, grabbing at their arms, the bolder ones going for their bums and thighs. The fiddler played louder and faster, and someone burst into song.

Here was a jovial tinker
Which was a good ale drinker,
And he came from the Weald of Kent
When all his money was gone and spent,
Which made him look like a Jack-a-Lent,
And Joan's ale is new!
And Joan's ale is new, my boys,
And Joan's ale is new . . .

And soon they had pushed aside the table and were dancing zestfully, the women taking turns with the men, screeching with laughter. Someone whistled and hooted, and someone else clapped. I leaned against the wall in a corner where the candlelight did not reach, feeling the whirl and warmth of the dancers' bodies. And suddenly a large woman with a kindly face sidled up to me and pressed her hip against my side. It was the first time I had felt a woman's body so close against my own, and I could feel the heat exuding from her and hear her quick, shallow breathing. I impulsively turned to her and drew her to me. She felt warm and damp, her breasts big and soft against my chest. She smiled and placed her hand on my thigh and I felt a stirring between my legs.

Then came a drunken Dutchman
And he would have a touch man,
But he soon took too much, man,
which made him after rue . . .

But then she was gone, and I was in such a state that I had to leave the tavern and hide in the bushes behind, where I lowered my breeches and pleasured myself till I squirted into the leaves. I then stood there for a bit, feeling light and relieved although my prick was burning a little. When I went back in, the fiddler seemed to have tired, and the singers were finishing up their ballad, promising the Joan of the ballad *again to come when she had brewed anew—*
When she had brewed anew, my boys—when she had brewed anew . . .

I looked for Master Walsh—there he was with two gentlemen, one of whom was talking animatedly, while the second listened with a half-smile on his sleepy countenance. He gestured to me to join them and I did.

"Hearken to this, Tony," he said. "Doctor John Pott and Master Newton here are talking of something interesting—they say one can voyage westwards across this land and find a great sea."

The man named Doctor Pott was rattling on at great speed: "We know well now that the earth is round, gentlemen, a globe that spins around the sun!" he said. "The Portugal seaman Fernando Magellan set out to circle it. He sadly died on the journey, but another sailor, Juan Sebastian Elcano, took over command and completed the voyage. *Primus circumdedisti me—You went around me first* . . . That was the heraldic motto granted to them by their king. Is not that glorious, sirs all? He might have been a bloody Portugal, but is it not glorious? And then our own English hero, Sir Francis Drake . . . My father was in Plymouth when the *Golden Hind* sailed into harbor in '80, from circling the globe, all laden with Spanish treasure."

At the round earth's imagin'd corners, Blow your trumpets, angels . . . murmured the other gentleman, Master Newton.

"Is that from the Bible, sir?" asked Doctor Pott suspiciously, none too pleased at being interrupted.

"No, Doctor, an Englishman and poet penned those lines—John Donne is his name."

"Hmmph . . . no time for poets . . ." Doctor Pott said. "We've got to be practical, sir, in these modern times—*practical*!"

And he launched into a lecture on the great English explorers of yester-year—Frobisher and Hudson and Raleigh—dreamers, men of destiny, men who were also men of action. I wondered what all of this had to do with find-ing a passage to the Indies. I also hoped the doctor would cease his chatter for an instant so I could tell him that I had been a physician's apprentice in London.

Master Walsh intervened, his tone only slightly curious: "Pray, tell us, sir, more about how one can reach Asia and the East Indies from where we stand—here in this colony."

And the gentleman told us about a box that some Englishmen had seen at an Indian chief's home. It had been a small box, but it had impressed with its intricacy and delicateness.

"Whither did this come from?" the Englishmen, who had come to buy beaver skins from the chief, had asked. The object was fashioned in a manner that did not look Virginia Indian. In fact, one of them knew right away that it was from Asia, from the land to the utmost east inhabited by the people of China. The Englishman had seen similar boxes in the possession of Jesuit priests who had traveled to that place.

"The Indian chief," continued our storyteller, "after a great deal of hemming and hawing, which had led the Englishmen to wonder if he had stolen the box, replied that he had obtained it from another chief. 'And who is this other chief?' the Englishmen had asked, still very polite. 'Where does he live?' 'Over those hills,' the Indian had answered, pointing westward."

Our narrator stopped and leaned back, very deliberately and carefully putting his cup down on the table. "'Tis true. 'Twas a thing adorned in the fashion of Cathay and those places. So, there must be a passage to the western ocean, across which is China, Tartary, and Japan, a passage starting not too far from where we stand, sirs!" he announced, quite red in the face now and very excited. The rest of the group raised their cups.

Look, and tomorrow late, tell me . . . Master Newton murmured, in a voice as drowsy as his eyes. He puffed at his pipe languorously. . . . *Whether both th' Indias of spice and mine/ Be where thou leftst them, or lie here with me . . .*

"Another one by your poet, sir?" Doctor Pott asked suspiciously.

"That selfsame man, sir." The second gent smiled. "The verse is addressed to the sun."

And the group dispersed soon after, swaying a little as they walked, heading to their numerous lodgings, some with the strumpets, slightly tipsy themselves, on their arms. And we retired too, my master and I. And I dreamt that night of naked women, Indian chiefs, English poets, and oriental boxes, till I woke up, a little ashamed and very bewildered.

It was daylight when I opened my eyes. I left the chamber and went out to piss against the back of the inn. I then strolled around to the front of the building. It was going to be a fine day—the sun was a disk of gold. Last night, the gentleman had mentioned the spherical world, a world that spun around the sun, which was the true center of everything. Did the brahmins back home know that? That could perhaps be why they immersed themselves in the rivers at dawn, bowing before *Surya, the most brilliant of the gods, he who traverses the sky in a chariot drawn by seven horses. The eye of the universe, the all-pervasive one. The god who goes by many names—Aditya, Bhanu, Ravi, Savitr, Martanda, Bhaskara.*

For the next few days, Master Walsh made it his business to find out more

about this western passage, and several men—shipmen, planters, traders—
were willing to oblige. We learned that several colonists were convinced of
the importance of making further discovery of the country west and south, to
the source of the James, and over the western hills. They were confident, from
what they had learned from the Indians, that there was a way to a great sea
that lay west, that it could be reached by land or rivers, and across that sea lay
Cathay and the East Indies.

We walked out to the river one evening. It stretched broad-backed and a
greenish brown, like some giant reptile lounging in the sun.

"I do not know about you, Tony. But this is the biggest river I have
clapped eyes on."

I too had seen none bigger, I said.

"I always thought that was the only way out of here, master," I added,
pointing eastwards. "And now they say there is another way too, that lies the
other direction."

"And you'd like to find it, boy?"

"Yes, sir."

"Why would you?" he asked.

*Because I want to go home. I am grateful you won me from Master Ganter, sir, but
still, you see, I would go home.*

But I did not utter those last words aloud. I knew too well that in spite of
his kindness and his general good treatment of me, he was still the master and
I only a servant, and no master would brook his servant taking off like that.

"I like adventure, sir," I said simply.

"So do I, lad," he replied, and we watched a bird glide lazily over the waters, till, with a sudden burst of vigor, it rose towards the sun.

All these years later that voyage I made with Master Walsh is like a dream, a
fevered one, in which sights and sounds are heightened, in which colors ex-
pand and explode, where the land speaks in strange tongues, where mountains
loom up right before your face where they were not there an instant before.

The arrangements took some weeks. Master Walsh purchased a new boat,
collected more information, and bought a map. I packed some food that would
keep, a cooking utensil or two, and blankets; I checked to see if I had a store of
Mary-gold salve and the powder from the London apothecary. And when Master Walsh decided we were ready, we sailed upriver past the newly established

counties of Charles City and Henrico, past the places where the farms grew smaller, the houses squatter, and the people even tougher and more desperate. We carried two muskets, several knives, some food, and the crudely drawn map made by some earlier traveler. We crossed the Great Wall. Construction on it was complete but a couple of palisades were already crooked, and cracks appeared in the ones that stood straight. It was a crude monstrosity standing in the midst of the forest. The Wall was meant to keep out the Indians; I wondered where my place was—this side of it or the other, inside or out.

"They will never finish it," Master Walsh commented.

"Why do you say that, sir?"

"Because that is the way of walls—one has to keep at them forever—expanding them this direction and then the other, till they girdle the world. And then one finds they are not tall enough. And so, one has to build higher still."

"It seems high enough to me," I said.

"People who want to cross will learn to scale it. They will learn themselves to fly across it, if needed," he said.

Soon we were in Indian territory, land that Master Walsh was familiar with from his trading ventures. But this was my first time outside the boundaries of the English settlement. The trees got thicker, although there were also clearings in unexpected places, where the greenery was getting back to its feet—these, I guessed, must be the parts the Indians slashed and burned to grow their corn. I was nervous—I felt that people were following us, men so soft-footed that the twigs barely crackled, shadows watching from behind the trees.

"Do you remember the massacre of 1622, Master Walsh?"

"I was not here to witness it, but I am told it was horrific. At times like that there is so much hate and terror on all sides, that almost no one goes untouched—English or Indian."

"Do you hate anyone, Master Walsh?"

He laughed. "I dislike some men. But I don't know about hating them; that seems a great waste of energy. Do you hate anyone?"

"Mostly Master Ganter."

"And when you lived in East India?"

"I had no occasion to hate anyone. I was surrounded by an abundance of love—they made much of me, my mother and grandmother."

"What of your father, lad?"

I imagined a man who could be my father coming to the house, walking between the peacock paths. Coming to claim my mother and me; sometimes coming after Amma left this world, through the trees, seeking me, the rain on his face, coming to stop me from leaving on the ship . . .

Master Walsh's cough startled me from my wonderings. We were walking side by side and I saw him glancing at me curiously. I remembered what I had told him once before.

"My father was a medicine man, sir," I said. "A famous practitioner of physic. He would have liked me to take on his trade."

As we penetrated further west, Master Walsh bartered our boat for a flat-bottomed bateau, which he thought would serve us better. We reached the fall line of the great river and encountered thunderous rapids. The land grew craggy, and the oak, hemlock, and hickory trees looked thicker-leaved and -branched. When we saw smoke coming from a distance, Master Walsh said that it was a Monacan Indian village and that we must stop to rest and replenish our food supplies. The Monacans were an aloof people and kept to themselves. Master Walsh was one of the very few white men whom they traded with. We walked towards the smoke and soon saw the homes and smelt cooking venison. The tribe apparently cultivated sunflowers, and the land outside the houses was all green and gold with hundreds of blooms standing up like sentinels. And then, suddenly, it was a world populated by brown-skinned people. Some of the women working outside appeared to know Master Walsh and called out greetings, and he replied in their own tongue. Children tumbled about and their nakedness and fat, dark bodies reminded me of babes back home. We stayed at the home of one of Master Walsh's trading partners and the people of the family looked at me inquiringly, no doubt wondering where I was from. I think they thought it curious that I was of their complexion but that my hair was in curls—they touched it and exclaimed laughingly.

We were two days with the Indians. They gave Master Walsh copper coins and tobacco for some wool cloth and tools he had carried from Jamestown. Some of the Indians spoke the English tongue well, and I discovered that one or two spoke Catalan too, apart from several other Indian tongues that were not their own. They were indeed worldly for an aloof people. Two of the elders had long, low discussions with Master Walsh through the first night—I heard them talking each time I woke up—and the next morning Master Walsh informed me that they would send two of their young men with us, as our guides.

So, I was introduced to Shurenough and Amoroleck. Shurenough, whom we addressed as Shuren, was a slender and muscled youth, about twenty years of age, with glossy long locks, very popular with the young maidens, I could tell. They giggled and looked coyly at him as they went about their chores. Amoroleck—Amoro to us—was small and plump-faced, but no less strong. He was a little younger than Shuren. They both spoke English.

We left the Indian settlement at dawn. Shuren and Amoro stopped to look back at the village, as if in farewell, and for an instant I wished we could all return down the pathway to where the women washed their linen and the fires for the day's cooking were already being lit. Maybe I should just live with the Indians, I thought, an Indian among Indians, and all would be well. But I remembered that it could not be, that I had a voyage ahead of me, a journey west and a journey east.

The days were still warm, but in the mornings strands of mist hovered softly over the trees. We went by boat mostly, and then, when that was no longer possible, we traveled by foot. The forest was heavy with silence at first, but I realized soon enough that it spoke incessantly—the snorting of a wild boar, the call of a bird, the response of the other, the sudden rush of flapping wings as a family of grouse rose together out of a tree. We let Shuren and Amoro lead, with Master Walsh following, and me at the tail, my mind sometimes alert to the life around me, sometimes taking its usual circuit, dreaming of the place I hoped was my destination: my home, where the salt flats baked in the sun, where the sunsets were swift, with the light gone in a matter of minutes, where clay lamps flickered on the front porches of houses decorated with auspicious designs in red and white. And then I was drawn back by Master Walsh addressing me.

There were more rapids than I had ever imagined. They rushed by us, white, as if composed of pearls. The land was verdant and lush and dotted with cool, clear lakes and streams. It was indeed a place blessed with water. We stopped to catch a blue-gray-colored fish that glinted in the sun. I knew it from my days on the farm as a chucklehead fish, but Master Walsh called it a fork-tailed cat.

"Look at its face," he instructed, and I knew why it was called by the name he used. It made for a delicious meal when cooked over a fire we made up. I told Master Walsh how some foods were forbidden to me in the old country— beef, pork, on certain days any kind of meat, even onion and garlic. Master Walsh, Shuren, and Amoro said that they did not understand. Where they came from one ate what one found and considered oneself fortunate.

"I too have become like that," I told them, a little sadly.

One afternoon we entered the dark mouth of a cavern and found that cave led to another cave, which led to still others. My master lit a lantern and held it high, and we saw that we were in a large cavern with tall ceilings, almost as tall as those of a cathedral in London. The rock chamber smelt musty and we could hear the high-pitched squeals of bats, disturbed by our light. Pillars of pale yellow mineral formations were suspended from the ceiling like men hanging from the gallows, and other such pillars grew from the floor and reached up with grasping, skeletal hands. Other rocks formed delicate, lace-like draperies that hung before our faces. I had never seen anything like it, and neither had Master Walsh. Our echoing whispers circled about our heads.

Tony! Master Walsh called out, and another voice, his and yet not his, called back. *To—nee . . . To-nee, nee—nee . . . nee . . .*

And a whole ensemble of voices hailed me then, called out, urging me to go on, to find what I was seeking.

We were now truly in the mountains. They were dense with forest and occasionally there were craggy rock faces. We heard the howls of wolves at night and the high, yelping barks of coyotes. Giant cats' eyes glinted behind the trees and then vanished. The Indians told us of other explorers of their tribes; Master Walsh talked about the Englishman, Martin Frobisher, who'd looked for the Northwest Passage and brought back a pile of what turned out to be fool's gold to England. I, in my turn, told them of the Chola kings of my land, who were great sailors and had gone all the way to the Spice Islands in olden times. And I then narrated the tale *of the two brothers charged with circling the world—the victor would be awarded the fruit of wisdom. Murgugan, the older brother, leapt on his favored mount, the peacock, and raced off. Sometimes, he thought he saw his younger brother ahead, sometimes he felt him laboring behind, breathless, the portly Ganesha, who preferred not to move too much.*

"Who won?" Shuren asked me.

The truth is, Ganesha had not troubled himself to leave home. He only circled his parents, the great god Shiva and his wife, Parvati. "You are the world," he said simply, palms folded in obeisance. "When I go around you, I circle all creation."

"Clever fellow!" Master Walsh grinned.

"Cheat!" exclaimed Shuren.

"Who got the prize?" Amoro wanted to know. "The son who traveled? Or the one who stayed?"

The story is not clear on that. It does not say who was victorious.

As we went on, we saw signs of men, most likely Indian hunters or white trappers, who had passed on the same paths we were taking, although we did not meet them. Shuren and Amoro said that there were hostile tribes in the region and it was best to keep away from them. There was a blue haze about the mountains, and I felt like I was walking in a dream. We had been traveling for two weeks now; I had lost count of sunrises and sunsets.

"We must get to the top," said Master Walsh, "and on the other side we must travel till we come to the river or rivers which will take us to the salt water, to the western sea."

"The one which will circle one-half of the world and take us east?" I asked anxiously, desiring confirmation.

"Yes," he replied.

Shuren and Amoro only shrugged. I sensed that they were getting tired of the journey, of pursuing the mad dreams of a white man and a brown boy who was not one of theirs. Sometimes I could hear them muttering to each other, and my fear was that they would abandon us.

EIGHT

Rapids slowed our progress, forests resisted us, the dark reached out, trying to retain us. We pressed on.

Master Walsh, Shuren, and Amoro were better hunters than I. I could only kill squirrels and coneys, but they brought back young deer, geese, and raccoons. I had learnt to smoke meat well and season it with the salt and dried sage I carried in my bundle. We never went hungry. Why then were we starting to look sunken-eyed and weary?

On the twentieth day, we stumbled upon a valley of flowers. Red, violet, pink, yellow, white, purple blooms grew all around us, thrusting from the earth, bursting from bushes in unimaginable profusion. Even Master Walsh, who knew about such things, was astounded at the abundance. I asked him for their names and he recited: *clover, anemone, green adder's mouth, thimbleweed, liverwort, angelica, aster, arrowhead, doll's eyes, beardtongue, bee balm, blanketflower, turkey corn, crimson clover* . . . We stood there in silence, gazing at this wonder in the wilderness. A spectacle that existed solely so it could be, with no beholder in mind. A breeze ran through the valley and the thousands of blooms moved with it, so we were surrounded by rippling color. I carry the vision in my mind's eye to this day—the hidden Valley of Flowers. I sometimes even wonder if it was real, or if I visited it in a dream.

It might have been the plenitude of colorful life about me that prompted me to turn to my master with a question: "Master Walsh, have you encountered the Man Who Would Not Die?"

"No, who is he?" Master Walsh was never surprised, always curious.

I told him about the man they had tried to hang many times in England and failed. "He is now in Virginia," I said. "I am surprised you have not seen him—he appears to be in many places."

Master Walsh shook his head and smiled. "Somehow I have not had the pleasure of his acquaintance."

"I—I have seen him several times." Suddenly, I felt very foolish.

"No mortal cannot be killed, lad."

"This man is an exception," I insisted. "He simply could not be hanged."

"Is he born again and yet again, like one of your Indian souls—condemned to birth and rebirth for eternity?"

He was teasing me now.

"No, no, Master Walsh. He simply cannot die."

All mountains surely have a descent. One clambers down, whether recklessly or cautiously, relieved that the worst is over. We did not even reach the summit of ours.

The blue light surrounded and then swallowed us. The rock faces defied climbing and looked like they would shrug us off their backs. The very birds called to us jeeringly from the trees. Master Walsh and I tried to ignore the hostility the landscape spewed. Shuren and Amoro, who had been looking scornful and impatient, started looking sorrowful.

Was there a river on the other side? A river that led to a salt sea? A sea that led to the sunrise?

One morning, four weeks into our journey, Shuren, Amoro, and I shed our clothes and leapt into a mountain stream. The chilliness of the water made us shudder before it zipped through our blood and into our heads. Master Walsh sat on the bank smoking—he did not believe in bathing every day.

"Come on in, Master Walsh—the water is wet!" I called to him teasingly. He shook his head and moved a little into the bushes.

The two youths and I splashed each other, watched the sun setting the eastern sky on fire. I should have felt joy, just being there with them, in that place, at that moment, being young in their company but, as always, my contentment was marred by my anxiety to hurry onwards, to be elsewhere.

That same urgency made me the first to get out of the water. I had washed my apparel and left it in the sun—the shirt would dry rapidly, the breeches would take longer. They would be damp when I donned them. I clambered

onto the grassy bank, shook the water off me, and walked towards the undergrowth in search of my master. In days past I would have been bashful at being
totally naked like that, but I had forgotten that feeling a long time ago.

I could not find him right away, and when I did, he was reclining against a
tree as if asleep, except that an arrow had got him about the heart. The strong
odor told me that he had just defecated, perhaps just pulled up his breeches
at the moment. At least he had not been killed shitting, I thought numbly. I
should run, I also thought, I should conceal myself. I glanced this way and that,
scanning the woods, listening, like an animal would, one who knew that hunters were about. I could neither see nor hear anything. And though the sensible
thing would have been to retreat for the moment, I went forward. There might
yet be life in Archer Walsh, perhaps I could do something to help him. But
when I drew close, I knew. He was quite, quite dead. I pulled the arrow out,
and a clean, crimson fountain of blood spurted from the site—it reddened his
clothes, some of it splattered on the leaves and on my bare legs and feet. I stood
there, stark naked, my hair still dripping water, my limbs bloodied, knowing
that my only friend in this world had left me without a word of farewell.

*Yama, the God of Death, is also the son of the sun. Four-eyed dogs lead the dead
to him; Agni, the God of Fire, lights their path. Yama has royal status; he is always
addressed as "raja"—a king; he is also known as Sirnapada or "he of the shriveled
foot" because he was cursed by another god and his foot was consumed by maggots. He
has green skin and is clad in red robes; he rides a great black buffalo and carries a mace
or a noose or a sword. He is neither Just nor Unjust. He just is.*

I felt I was alone with Master Walsh for a long time, although it must have
been but a few minutes before Amoro and Shuren came up to us. We moved
around swiftly, cautiously, muskets and knives drawn, looking for whoever did
this. We searched in the undergrowth; we looked for footprints, straining our
ears for a cough, an exhaled breath. But there was nothing. Amoro guessed
that the killer might have been a Shawnee—the Shawnee were fierce, lonely
hunters who sometimes wandered this part of the land, he said. Shuren, however, wondered if it was a white man, one of the Catholics who had settled
in Terra Maria—the place to the north. They were often to be seen here, and
they killed Virginians, just as warnings. The killer had taken the only thing
Master Walsh had on him—a leather pouch in which he carried his pipe, a
bit of tobacco, and a coin or two perhaps. My master had left his jacket on the
riverbank and so it was untouched.

We stared silently at Master Walsh, so alive till this morning, and suddenly not. He had won me in a game of dice, he had taken me from Ganter. I remembered his rough kindness, his strength. He had been that rare thing: master and almost a friend. With him, I was supposed to discover a passage home. I sat by his side and wept.

Shuren and Amoro consoled me as best as they could. *"Brother . . ."* is how they addressed me then. "Stay strong . . . our brother." When the sun began to set Amoro sensibly suggested that we bury Master Walsh.

Once that sad task was done, we sat about quietly. Amoro and Shuren informed me of their decision gently, solemnly: they were returning home.

I nodded in agreement. In any case, what else could I do?

"I am grateful to you for bringing us this distance," I told them humbly. "From here I will venture it alone."

They sighed and looked at me helplessly. It was desperate, foolish to go on, they said, there was no route, no passage, no western sea.

But I was obstinate. "I will find it," I insisted. "Tomorrow I will carry on."

That night I lay wide awake looking out at the night, waiting for Master Walsh's killer to return, waiting for Master Walsh to come back too, and stand over me. The world is an immense place. The gentleman in Jamestown had quoted a verse, something about *the round earth's imagin'd corners . . .* Its great expanse pressed down on me in the dark and made my breath catch.

The object that the Englishmen had brought back reports about, the one they had seen in the possession of the Indian chief had been a small box, a finely carved one. It might have been adorned with a crane, or a dragon, or a fabulous sea serpent coiled around the earth. It was proof that the world was round and that a western route from Virginia would lead to a river, which would lead to a sea, which would lead to Cathay, which would lead to a place on the other side of the world where the night air was *spiced,* as Master Shakespeare wrote in that play, where a beautiful woman had lived with her child.

But that boy had lived a long time ago. I realized it was now another lifetime, another boy. I swore to forget that child, his previous life, those other places and people, the dream of return. He would hereafter be known only as *Tony, the East Indian; Tony, the Virginian.* His original name was lost even to himself.

At dawn, I went to Master Walsh's grave to bid him one last farewell. He would now become one with the mountains. It occurred to me that I too would be buried in the soil of this New World. But before that, I resolved, I would flourish in this selfsame soil, this place where I had been scattered.

So, with Shuren and Amoro, I turned back.

It was a long way through the valleys and forests, over the rocks and under the sky. Everything was undisturbed as if it had never been troubled by the presence of man, although we had walked through it with Master Walsh just weeks before. I could swear the Man Who Would Not Die visited me frequently then, that phantom, that presence. He came in the dark, the slightest of sounds, a passing shadow. Wordlessly, he reminded me to stand up when the morning came, to face the sun.

Amoro told me that Shuren was to be wedded to a beautiful maiden when the leaf fall season came along. He told me of the damsels his family was considering for him, Amoro, to wed. Shuren told me how good a cook his grandmother was, how his aunt was known to be a wise medicine woman. They both told me about the spirits who had to be appeased with gifts of tobacco, beads, and fur. They told me of their dealings with the Powhatan people; how their ancestors had heard that the Powhatan priests had prophesied that an enemy would come over the sea, and how the arrogant Powhatans had foolishly ignored it. They saw that I was sorrowful and tried to cheer me with their kindly chatter. They told me about their ritual where boys were secluded, subjected to great privation, and experienced hallucinations and madness induced by a specially prepared potion. At the end of it they would have lost all memory of their early life and would rejoin the tribe as warriors.

"Sometimes such oblivion is necessary, even good," Amoro said, sounding like a wise old shaman himself. "All boys must shed their boyhood, like a snake its skin."

"It is necessary," Shuren added.

They were telling me for a reason. I too had to understand that previous lives are no longer accessible. That they are, in fact, quite gone. That one can learn, *must* learn, to live anew.

In the distance we saw wisps of smoke—we were nearing the settlement. We had been away for over eight weeks.

The fairy king and queen in the *Midsummer Night* play by Master William Shakespeare settled their quarrel and the story drew to a close with a feast and the beginning of lives infused with love and happiness.

"What happened to the Indian lad the Fairy King and Queen quarreled over, Tony?" Sammy had asked.

"I suppose he was sent to the Fairy King."

"But what *really* happened to the Indian boy?"

It remains to be seen, Little Sam.

IV

APPRENTICE

NINE

I stayed with Shuren and Amoro's kinsmen. We came to be known as the young men who traveled out west to the mountains looking for another salty sea, and the elders liked to ask us questions of what we had seen. We saw much, we said: mountains as blue as smoke, land that touched the sky, flowers in such profusion that we believed we had stumbled into heaven. But we had found very little else. Nothing, in fact. Except for Master Walsh, who had unexpectedly encountered death. The old men shook their heads regretfully, the women sighed, the children played with my curls, happy in their ignorance of dying, happy also because they did not yet share the bitterness the elders felt when they remembered the days before the strangers' arrivals from the sea. The past hung, a tainted shadow, over the older men and women, and the future remained an unnamed fear.

Two small silver pieces that I had found in Master Walsh's coat were taken from me by a man who I gathered was an uncle of Shuren, as were Master Walsh's gun and hunting knife. I was allowed to keep the coat, made of leather and trimmed with fur. It was twice too big for one of my size, but it served well enough as a blanket during the cold nights. I also retained the pouch of unicorn-horn powder—certainly no one was interested in that.

When it turned warmer, the women planted their pumpkins and corn, and in those long days suffused with light, I floated in some dream state, even as I worked hard for my keep, assisting my hosts with sundry tasks. I did not let myself think of where I would go next or what I would do. I only knew that I had buried, along with Master Walsh, any hope of returning to the Coromandel. I envied the Virginia Indians, people for whom this was so clearly and indisputably home. But then I reprimanded myself for being foolish: these people were being pushed further and further inland, having long since bade farewell to their ancestral lands around the mouth of the river.

Shuren's aunt, the wise woman he had talked about, took me with her when she gathered roots and berries that would enhance the taste of food and also cure disease. She tutored me on the virtues of sarsaparilla, snakeroot, and the three-lobed leaves of the sassafras plant, which were shipped in vast quantities to Europe by the white men because it was said to cure the syphilis. I asked her if she was a medicine woman. She said no, the tribe's witch doctor was a man, an esteemed elder, but sometimes the women came to her for assistance.

And I then told her about the unicorn-horn powder that I still carried on my person. I even offered it to her to use.

"I will take a little, but you must keep the rest," she replied. "You might find some use for it."

On days like that one, I felt a sense of comfort and belonging. I would think that I would just dwell with the Indians, live like them, learning to hunt with the men and grow things with the women, eating their food, worshipping their gods, some of whom reminded me of my own, hoping that one day they would wholly accept me, having forgotten that I was a different kind of brown man. Other times, I would think that I was a stranger here as well, that I should depart someday, bid farewell to Amoro, Shuren, and their families, gather my possessions, and go back to Jamestown. There, it would be like I had died out in the mountains and had come back, born again and learning to live anew.

But the decision was not mine to make. A young man of the tribe, wandering far from home, trespassed onto English land. Apparently, he had been hunting wolves. He had heard that the English rewarded wolf hunters, and there was good money to be made by handing over the heads of dead beasts. But an English farmer apprehended him and turned him over to the sheriff for trespassing. He languished in the sheriff's gaol for over a month, still stained with wolf blood, smelling of fur, homesickness, and fear. The tribal chiefs busied themselves with negotiations—one of yours for one of our own, they told the English—we will release an English servant we have held captive, if you let go of our man.

That is how, one morning, as the light crept up from behind the trees, I was taken by two of the Indians down the river in a canoe. Shuren and Amoro had been asked to escort me, but they had refused, and would not meet my eyes when the time came to bid farewell. The two Indian men rowed swiftly—they knew the rhythms of this river better than those of their own bodies—they did not say a word. I knew that the Indians owed me no loyalty or love, that they had to do what they could to take care of their own in this new regime. But I still could not help feeling wounded.

With our destination in sight, the canoe slid towards the bank, and we clambered out. Two white men who had been sitting on the ground smoking got up to receive us. Just behind them, his arms lightly bound, was a young Indian, who I guessed was the prisoner being exchanged for me.

One of the Englishmen spoke first. "Where is the white man?" he asked roughly. "You promised us a white man in exchange for the prisoner."

One of the Indians shrugged. "This is he," he said, pointing towards me. "This is the boy our chiefs release."

"He is not one of ours!" the Englishman exclaimed in disgust.

"He comes from your side. He is Archer Walsh's servant."

The white man looked doubtful. An Indian for an Indian—that was not his idea of a good trade.

But I did depart with the two men that day, and the Monacan youth did return to his people. I was taken all the way to Jamestown, where, after months surrounded by tawny-skinned people, I found myself once more surrounded by white men. It was a strange feeling. Suddenly, I felt that my skin looked black, my hair the color of jet.

I was handed over to Parson Blair, the same Parson Blair who had taken in me and my companions when we first arrived on the *God's Gift.* This time, I was to dwell with him for close to six months. I found that since our parting the parson had grown even more fond of his drink, and when he was not drinking, he spent his time in his bedchamber with Maria, a tall, wiry, sharp-faced black woman who came in to cook for him. All of Jamestown knew of their activity, and the men on the street would snigger and comment on the parson's negro wench. *Does he do her every day,* they'd ask me, *can he even do it, the old soak?* The parson was oblivious of or ignored this jeering commentary, but he still looked melancholy all the time, and more so when he was in his cups, and I wondered why a man would drink, if not for happiness.

"This land will refuse us," he would tell me, nodding gloomily over his ale, "it will force us back into the sea."

And then his mood would inexplicably lighten and he'd say that America was the Promised Land: *O let the nations be glad and sing for joy: for thou shalt judge the people righteously, and govern the nations upon earth . . .* And he'd call for more drink.

I spent my time working the patch of tobacco in the parson's half acre, helping him with other tasks, or lifting loads on the docks. It was when I was running an errand that I saw a finely dressed black man coming out of the house where the burgesses of the colony assembled. He carried a sheaf of papers and had two servants with him—one black and one white—carrying his loads. He was clearly a man of some fortune. I was curious, so I inquired at the tavern and found that he was Master Anthony Johnson, a free black who had arrived some seventeen years ago on the ship named the *James* and had worked his way up to owning over two hundred acres of land in the Northern Neck, land that he had acquired through headrights. He had named his plantation Angola.

I was filled with awe and asked Parson Blair about Master Johnson.

The parson seemed to know of him. He said that there were a few other landowning Africans too, men who might have arrived bonded, but who had become landed men over time.

"They came as slaves or as servants, sir?" I asked. Only recently had I fully understood the distinction.

The parson did not know. "I cannot recall rightly if some of these men are from the group of twenty and odd negroes who came in the *White Lion*—the first Africans to set foot in Virginia in 1619," he then said. "They were paid for in victuals."

"I knew two Africans named Bristol and Cuffee, sir," I said. "They were my dearest friends," I added, although that was not entirely true. "And they were Christians."

I then took the opportunity to inform Parson Blair that I too wished to be instructed in the Bible and baptized as Bristol and Cuffee had been, as my friend from long ago, George Bishop, also had. I remembered how George's black countenance would shine as he recalled his famous baptism in London and how King James himself had selected his name. How his voice would tremble in ecstasy as he read from the Christian Scripture: *They that wait upon the LORD . . . shall mount up with wings as eagles . . .*

The parson brushed me aside saying that he had a bloody headache and could not worry about saving heathens, which confused me because I thought that was the very purpose of his coming to the New World. But I pestered him again the next day, when he appeared less poorly from the drink, and he seemed interested.

"You might even be the first Christian from the East Indies," he said, and his countenance lit up at the thought.

I wanted to tell him about Saint Thomas and how he had come to East India shortly after Christ's death and had converted some of my people, and also about George Bishop and the other East Indians who'd been baptized in London, but I decided against it. If Parson Blair liked the idea of making the first East Indian Christian, so be it. And the parson took on my catechism, to the extent that he gave me a copy of his Bible and ordered me to study it (he knew I could read) and to ask him if I had questions.

Ganesha, the Elephant-headed god of Auspicious Beginnings. He of the mighty body and curved trunk. Remover of Obstacles, the deity of Intelligence, Learning, and simple Good Sense. His form created from sandalwood, from the God Shiva's laughter; his head that of a tusker; his four arms bearing weapons and flowers and food. He is known as Ekadanta—the single-tusked one, Lambodara—the potbellied one. He rides on a mouse, because he, like that little creature, penetrates the most secret of places, and also because the greatest is often reliant on the diminutive.

So, I called on the deity Ganesha and began my Bible study, not always diligently or regularly, because I was kept busy working by the river, tending to the tobacco, cleaning and cooking for Parson Blair (Maria increasingly made it clear she could not and would not be servant, cook, and mistress to the priest), scraping the Jamestown silt off his boots, fetching his drink, and holding his head in the mornings before cleaning the rancid puke, tending to his garden, and, whenever I could, hiring myself out to other people to work their vegetables and small cornfields. In my spare time, I read about how God created Heaven and Earth, and how His spirit hovered over the waters, about Adam and Eve and the serpent, about the sea parting, about the great flood, the child born in a manger, the water turned to wine, and the god who chose to die (this last I had already learnt, a long time ago, when Master Day introduced me to his religion).

Parson Blair would on occasion question me on what I had read. He was sharper than I thought, in spite of his habitual inebriation, and nearly always caught me when I gave him an erroneous response. He would begin an explanation of a verse now and then, but would lose interest less than halfway through and drop off to sleep, breathing heavily through his mouth. I knew I would be an ill-informed Christian, one knowing all the tales because they were good ones and pleased me, and remembering the lines because I had a good memory for words, but not acquainted with the meaning behind them. But I did not think any of the rough, ignorant Englishmen around me were any better; most of them could not read the Scripture for themselves and knew little to nothing of it although they had been born into their faith. I kept pressing Parson Blair to baptize me, but he was too lazy, too distracted, or both. So, one day I grew impatient and told him that I would have to run away if he did not make me a Christian.

"Run where, pray?" he muttered. "Towards the sea to drown or towards the woods to be murdered by Indians?"

I scowled. "I was with them, sir, and they did not murder me."

Parson Blair only grunted at that. "Why do you want to be baptized, boy?" he asked after a brief silence, and I was surprised to note that his voice was filled with curiosity and something like gentleness.

What could I say to that? Could I tell him that I fiercely yearned to be akin to other men here, to belong to this land in a way that the white people belonged because, although it was not their place, they had come here and made it their own, wrested from the earth a sense of belonging by sheer, unrelenting will? It is true that the Africans did not belong in the same way as the English, although they were Christian, but even they, I felt, were less alien than me. Other than the Virginia Indians, I was the sole pagan on this side of the world, an idol worshipper, one who carried a multitude of gods who were not God in his head and heart.

"I wish to receive the Holy Spirit," I mumbled unconvincingly.

"Bide your time," the parson replied, and might or might not have said more, but Maria came in that minute and bustled about the room, scolding us for conversing in the dark.

I thought I would have to study for months more like the scholars do, but Parson Blair was suddenly moved to baptize me a few days later. I had been in his house several months then. He sprinkled water on my head and made the sign of the cross about my face and muttered in one long breathless rush:

Receyve the signe of the holy Crosse, both in thy forehead, and in thy breste, in token
that thou . . . To continewe his faythfull soldour andservauntuntothylyfesendeAmen.

So, I became a Christian.

Maria, who had been baptized by her Spanish masters many years ago, said
that it was not really a baptism at all, that Parson Blair had got the words wrong,
that the ceremony had not been in a chapel or church, that there were no wit-
nesses, that the priest was piss drunk, that I still was a heathen and condemned to
be one forevermore. But I did not believe her, thinking that her harsh words arose
from her slight jealousy because she saw me as a rival for the parson's attention.

Parson Blair named me Tony. He pronounced it with such aplomb that
I did not have the heart to remind him that it had been my name for many
years now.

There were books other than the Bible in Parson Blair's trunk. Indeed, he
loved books, and Maria was of the opinion that 'twas all that excessive reading
that pushed him to drink. I was excited to see that he had two quartos of plays
by Master William Shakespeare. *An Excellent Conceited Tragedie of Romeo and*
Juliet was a very ridiculous story in my opinion, and I could not bring myself
to read much of it. The other play, quite incredibly, was a copy of *A Midsomer*
Night's Dreame, which I devoured right away and then read repeatedly, moved
by its evocations of woods, love, dreams, and madness, and still wondered, as
before, about the Indian boy.

The parson also had a volume titled *De humani corporis fabrica Epitome,*
which he said was an anatomical textbook he got off a ship's surgeon. It was
in the Italian tongue, but I liked gazing at the drawings of human bodies
stripped of their covering of skin and flesh, leaving skeleton, muscle, and
viscera exposed for study. At the center of the frontispiece was a corpse with
its abdomen cut open, exposing all to the view of a crowd which stared and
reached out with eager hands, excited to gaze on the inner world the anato-
mist was putting before their eyes. A dog sat amidst it all, eager and panting,
perhaps sensing well before the men the first stench of putrefaction. The scene
too reminded me of the theater, the spectacular nature of it, the curious audience, their horror, their applause. And Parson Blair told me that these public
dissections were indeed called anatomical theaters in Europe and many members of the public went to witness them. I looked repeatedly at the pictures,
and I marveled.

And so, my life proceeded. I had abandoned all hope of going home, but I was over sixteen years of age and I did not wish to be a menial forever. Perhaps I could be a tobacco farmer, I thought, perhaps I could learn a trade. As luck would have it, I ran into Master Johnson, the African landowner, once again, this time accompanied only by his servant, also a black man. I ran towards him, raised my hat, and bowed low.

"Good morrow, master," I said. He inclined his head graciously, but he looked puzzled. He did not know what to make of me.

"Yes, boy?" he said a trifle brusquely, and I wondered if he was naturally a stern man or forced to assume that demeanor. It was surely easier being a black landowner than a black servant, but it was still not as elevated as being one of the propertied white men. I wondered if he had to wrest from the world the honor and regard due to him.

I told him in one long breathless rush that I wished to join his service, that I had no master, was a freeman, a good worker, as diligent as any, and strong in spite of my slight build, that I was also eager to learn new skills. He listened attentively enough.

"I would take you on," he said. "But I cannot agree that you be an entirely unbound servant. Will you sign a bond of indenture for seven years?"

My heart sank a little at that; I was hoping to work for him as an unbonded servant, or at least for a shorter term. But I saw that there was no choice—I would either work for him or languish in Jamestown. So, I said yes, I would, and he instructed me to come to him in a month, when he returned. He had other business to attend to at the present, but next month we could draw up the indenture papers and I could leave with him for the Northern Neck. I bowed and made my departure. I could see the black servant's eyes on me, suspicious.

It was with mixed feelings that I went to tell Parson Blair of the impending change in my fortune: I had found a position, but I was to be bound once more. As I entered the house, I saw that the parson had a visitor. Standing there, his shoulders slightly more stooped, his hair a little more gray, his ugly face even less wholesome, was Ralph Ganter. My heart beat faster and my throat turned dry. In my travels among the mountains, he would sometimes intrude into my thoughts and I would hope that he had died—that a horse had kicked him in the belly, that he had caught the plague, that he had been struck by a thunderbolt, killed by an Indian. But here he was, a little more worn, but still in good health.

"Here he is, sir," Parson Blair told the stranger, huffing a little. "Tony, the youth you are seeking."

Ganter smiled, displaying his decaying teeth. "And I thought the East Indian was dead," he said. "I thought he would have perished on his adventures with the fur trader."

I was provoked to speak: "No, sir, here I am alive and well."

Ganter scowled at what he surely saw as cheek. "And whose servant are you now?"

No man's servant, I wanted to say, but thought it would be safer not to divulge that detail to Ganter. "Master Anthony Johnson's, sir. I am to join his service anon."

Ganter looked like he would have spat if he had not been standing in Parson Blair's house. "'Tis come to a fine state when we have blackmoors who own land," he snarled.

Neither the parson nor I responded. I wondered what Ganter's business was with me.

"I hear that you were the only one there when Walsh was killed?" he asked, looking at me contemplatively.

"No, sir, the killer was not to be found, but . . ."

Ganter raised his hand. "How do we know that you did not murder him?"

I was dumbstruck. Why would I want to murder Master Walsh, who had been nothing but good to me?

"Archer Walsh sets forth with an East Indian on some fool's errand, and . . ."

"We were looking for . . ."

"Hold your tongue, boy," Ganter said. "Have you forgotten that I was your master?" Parson Blair gestured to me anxiously to be silent.

"And then he does not come back," Ganter continued. "What does a man make of that?"

I stood in silence, refusing to turn my eyes away from his face.

"Walsh was a knucklehead. Just because he had voyaged to rough places and traded with Indians, he thought he knew barbarians."

Parson Blair and I waited for him to say more. I felt my heart thudding.

Ask Shuren and Amoro, I could have said, *they will back my story.* But he would have scoffed at that. Which man in his right mind trusts the word of Indians?

Why would I have wanted to kill Master Walsh, I could have asked, *for his moth-eaten jacket and gun?*

But the retort would have been yes, to me, poor wretch that I was, those things might have been worth it and, more to the point, the three of us, brown men, were natural brutes. Besides, Ganter would say that he, better than any other man, knew me, knew the full extent of my insubordination.

I expected him to drag me to the sheriff right then and there, and to be hanged, tomorrow or the day after. But he swept out of the room without another word and I was left alone with Parson Blair.

"Should I worry, Parson?" I asked.

Parson Blair huffed a bit again and then said no, there was no occasion to fret. Ralph Ganter was just trying to harass me for his own pleasure.

The parson's words comforted me, but I was seized with anxiety once more that night after the parson and Maria retired. It was my word against Rumor, and my word meant nothing. What did they do to foreigners who broke the law, to dark-complexioned men who killed Englishmen? Did they burn them at the stake, hang and quarter them, disembowel them while they yet lived? Sleep evaded me, and I stepped out into the Jamestown night, slipping on Master Walsh's jacket because a chilly breeze was blowing from the river. A group of men bathed in the ghostly moonlight barged by, singing a bawdy song. I walked on and would have walked further when I heard a hiss and felt a dagger pressed to my side.

"Giving someone the slip, eh?" the man said, and I noticed that his mouth reeked of decay. For a minute I thought it was Ganter, till I saw it was a much younger man. He held his weapon in one hand and a cup of drink in the other.

I trembled where I stood. He raised the knife and pressed its point to my cheek. He wanted to mark me before he left.

"Turk, eh?"

Was it wiser to say yes to that? Or to deny it? Or to keep mum? Before I could speak, the most peculiar thing happened. The stranger dropped both his knife and cup to the ground with a clatter and began to wring his hands as if they were on fire. I would have picked up the weapon, but he placed his foot on it quickly, although he continued flapping his hands. And he then fell to scratching one palm with the nails of the other, and even retrieved his knife and scratched with its tip till his skin began to break and bleed. I should have run then, but he was a sight to behold, this man in a torment of itching, with his bleeding palms and expression of agony. I found myself rooted to the spot. He saw me gaping.

"You know what it is, this affliction?" he groaned.

I nodded because he seemed to expect me to know, although I had no notion.

"Yes, 'tis exactly what you think—the clap, the French disease, call it what the fuck you will. I got these everywhere, sores on my hands, in my mouth, on my back, even on my bloody shithole. And the itch comes on all of a sudden and takes over my body it seems—and then it goes, till it comes again."

The itching seemed to have abated a little. I cursed myself for not fleeing when I had the chance. He would rob me of my coin now and of my coat too, and then he would knife me. I thought quickly.

"I possess something that might help you, master," I said, my voice trembling just a little. To this day I cannot say where those words came from.

"What is it?" he asked, holding his knife with one hand and reaching behind to scratch his back with the other.

"It is the best physic for your condition. It is unicorn-horn powder from India."

"And what are you? A moor who is master of physic?"

"The son of a physician and formerly an apprentice to a London doctor," I said. "This cure is used in East India and was also vouched for by my English master, who knew much about these things." And I reached into my pocket and took out the little pouch.

"East India, eh? This looks like commonplace flour to me," he said suspiciously as I tapped some of the powder into his outstretched palm, which I saw was marked with darkened spots that I was to learn later were palmar lesions, the result of advanced syphilis.

"It is physic meant to heal the clap. I assure you it will aid you," I said with all the conviction I could muster.

"Give me the whole lot then," he demanded, aggressive once more. Yet again, I thought quickly. If I gave him all of the powder, he might rob me, and then murder me just to round it up.

"This will last you all of two days, sir. And then where would you be? You need to take this every day between one full moon and the next to feel better. Let me go home now, and you return to me in the morrow for more."

He looked uncertain, but tipped the powder into his mouth and quaffed what little ale was left in his cup to send it down.

"Where do you bide?" he asked.

I told him. There was no point in lying—he would find me easily enough.

"I will come by tomorrow. And mind you, I will kill you for the piece of filth you are if this proves of no avail."

"I assure you it will give you relief," I said, and turned around hurriedly to go to my pallet on the parson's floor. I could feel the stranger's eyes on my back as I retreated. I could almost feel the very air about him moldering with his disease.

TEN

He returned a few days later as the sun came down and the dwellings and warehouses turned to sharp silhouettes against the Jamestown sky. He returned to claim what I had promised him—a new lease of his sorry life.

After my encounter with the pox-struck sailor, I had crept into Parson Blair's house and fallen into a restless slumber. I had dreamt of Ganter covered in leaking sores, of Ganter covered in gray scales that flaked off his body and fell about him, of Little Sam afflicted with ulcers in the mouth when at sea, hoping to be cured by the salt spray, and I then dreamt of Ganter again, and yet again of Ganter.

But I had felt more at ease in the morn. Parson Blair reassured me that too many fur traders died out on the mountains for them to lay Master Walsh's death at my feet. Even Maria, surprisingly, had been comforting. She had already found out that Ganter had been forced to return to Jamestown, an embittered man because his farming venture upriver had failed. His harvests had been meager and the tobacco ships would not sail that far in to collect his crop. He had sought work from Master George Menefie—for a short time, he had said, to tide him over. The master had asked him to serve as overseer of the land belonging to his wife's nephew, one Master Joshua Adams. That gentleman himself had gone to England to seek out a wife. And my friends Dick, Bristol, and Cuffee—they too were now back at Master Menefie's.

I resolved to seek them out, and as chance would have it, I found them easily enough. A few days after my meeting with the stranger, I went to the tavern to fetch the parson his supper. There was the customary smell of stale drink and food, there was the closed, smoky air, and, suddenly, there was Dick. Dick Hughes walking up like we had never been parted, like I had not been lost and won in a game of dice, like a year and more had not passed since we laid eyes on each other.

"Tony!" he exclaimed. Though he was still slender, his shoulders had acquired more breadth and his skin had turned ruddier than before. He looked quite a man now, tall and strong. I was the one who stiffened and hesitated before the clapping of hands and the slap on the back. He seemed glad enough to see me.

"Tell me all that happened, you old dog!" he cried. "You left without a word—all we were informed was that old Ganter had gambled you off!"

But Dick, I discovered soon, was too full of his dreams to concern himself with my doings. He had a few years to go before his term of indenture ended, but he was planning for that day. Master Menefie had now hired him and the others out to his nephew, the absent landowner, Master Adams; so they worked under Ganter's supervision in the plantation called Adams's Grove. When the time came, Master Menefie would give Dick freedom dues that were generous. Ganter was good to him too—he had already promised him a musket that he said Dick could consider his own.

"A musket is a grand thing," Dick said with a touch of pride in his voice. "Especially in this country, where guns are the levelers. They make a gentleman and a poor fellow one."

He was right about that. Guns were a necessity here to fight wolves, intruders, and Indians. They were always in great demand and ever in short supply. I had even heard tell of a law that was soon to be passed that required every man sixteen years of age and over to own a gun. "I will get you one, Tony," Dick promised. "See if I don't." And I could already imagine a fine English musket, a good flintlock that I would heave over my shoulder, the possession of which would truly make me a Virginian, something like a white man. And we talked little of other things, not of my travels, not of my present life, and barely of Sammy, although he was in both of our hearts, I am sure, the little lad, and also present in the selfsame tavern with us, sitting on a stool, wide-eyed and listening.

And here was Cuffee loping in, smiling, and clapping me on the back and saying that I had become a man, that I had grown handsome and tall but not tall enough. And here was Bristol, still tranquil, still imposing, smiling as well. When are you going to be as tall as me, he asked, he, who was the tallest man I had laid eyes on. And we laughed together, and I asked eagerly, "And what of Mad Marge? Where is she?"

I gathered that she had been abandoned by Ganter upriver. Bristol and the others had protested, but to no avail, and the morn they left for Jamestown, she had vanished from sight.

"Must have perished by now," Cuffee said with a sigh, and I shed a silent tear for my old friend who had crossed the water with me and later had mourned with me for Little Sam.

Dick told me that many other servants were returning as well, all moving back to Jamestown as farming ventures failed upriver. Flynn Keough's master was one of them, and Flynn now worked on Master Adams's lands. Flynn joined us then and was also happy to see me. He still had a bad digestion, he said, which left him feeling queasy after meals, and he still talked of learning the language of the Indians and running away to them and then further north, to Dutch country.

"We'll get away, my boy," he said. "Just wait and see—we'll get away yet."

The stranger who'd stepped up from the dark, the pox-ridden man, turned out to be a sailor named Noah Giles. He accosted me on Parson Blair's doorstep as I returned from my reunion with my friends.

"You the moor with the corn powder stuff?"

"Yes, the unicorn-horn powder from India," I said calmly enough, although I was dismayed. Had he returned to knife me for deceiving him?

"I have come for the second dose you promised me," he said. "It was potent, although it is but moorish medicine. I have had attacks of the itches every hour it seems since this thing I caught from a whore in Spain took me, but since I took this stuff I've barely felt yeuky. And look!"

He stuck out his palms to me. The sores did not look any different than they had looked in the moonlight. In truth, they appeared worse in the glare cast by the lantern I shone straight on them. But I was not the one to tell Noah Giles that. I fetched a two-day supply of the powder from my little store, and he took it gladly.

"I was in the mind to kill you last night," he said cheerfully as he left. "I cannot bide tawny moors and such—the whore in Spain was one, from Algiers, methinks. But 'tis good I let you be!"

I thanked him for his clemency, and after he left, I went in to tell Parson Blair, who had already sent Maria to the door to see what the chatter was about.

They were much taken up by my tale and wanted to inspect the medicinal powder for themselves. Maria declared she had heard say of people being cured of things worse than the French disease, and she told us of a maiden in Santo Domingo who had vomited a green thing long and thick as a grown man's finger, which had wings, a great many feet, and a turned-up tail, and had taken off in flight after it emerged from the maiden's insides, and how she had been administered handfuls of chalk to flush out the parts of the creature that had remained inside her. Parson Blair was inclined to dismiss Maria's medical miracle, but he had a story of one Thomas Parr, Englishman, who had lived to the great age of 152 and even kept as mistress a woman aged five and thirty when he himself turned a hundred. His extraordinary health was attributed to his lifelong diet of subrancid cheese, coarse bread, and sour whey.

"Does he still live?" I asked interestedly.

"Sadly not. The good King Charles wanted to meet this ancient subject of his and summoned him to London. Master Parr, it appeared, gave up the ghost the day after the royal audience on account of the rich viands and strong drink he feasted on at the palace kitchen."

Maria did not see how the parson's tale was about the wonders of modern physic; the parson retorted that it was about the wonders of diet, the wonders of rancid cheese in particular; I deliberated on how much of the powder I had left to keep Noah the sailor satisfied. If he kept returning every day until I left for my new post at Master Johnson's, I would be forced to seek out a unicorn, slaughter it, and grind down its horn.

After four or five visits by Noah, I reckoned that it was time I started charging him a fee for the physic. After all, I had gone to the trouble of stealing it, and I had safeguarded it for all these years. So, the next time he came by, I told him he would have to give me a bit of tobacco in exchange—just two pounds would do. I had long paid off what I owed him for sparing my life, and he now owed me. He grumbled a little, but the powder was aiding him greatly. His itching was much abated and he fancied that even the sores were drying out. He asked me to examine them, and I agreed, not only because I had told him I had been apprenticed to a physician and I needed to keep up the pretense, but also because I was genuinely curious to see what syphilis sores looked like. Noah stripped himself of his attire right there in Master Blair's presence and I saw the parson shudder at the small, firm boils that covered the sailor's back like a mantle and the ones that spotted his tongue. But at least the parson did not have to see, as I did, the ones clustered on the poor fellow's prick and around his lower orifice. I felt a wave of revulsion and then another of sympathy, which almost made me offer him the physic gratis. I did not believe at all that Noah was improving in health, but he thought he was, and who was I to argue with him?

The powder was almost depleted—after all, I had only stolen a pouchful of it and even a spoonful a day is not nothing. I bound Maria to secrecy, and she assisted me in making a powder of white alum and chamomile. If nothing else, the latter had soothing properties, so Shuren's aunt had told me, and it might help calm poor Noah's skin. I considered grinding in deer horn as a substitute for unicorn, but I abandoned the idea. I knew very well that no unicorn had come near the original powder, that unicorns did not exist in India or elsewhere, that they, like the medicinal powder that was supposedly derived from them, were projections of men's desires and dreams.

In any case, Noah was happy with the substitution, and things would have gone on that way till I left for Angola plantation with Master Johnson if Doctor Joseph Herman had not paid me a visit.

One evening after the candle was lit, there was a firm, self-assured knock on the parson's door. I thought it was Ganter and my throat went dry. But the visitor was a stranger, a short, slight man with a face so pale that it was startling in the dark. His almost black hair streaked with gray was tied back with a ribbon, and his breeches, waistcoat, and shoes were finer than those of laborers and servants. His brown eyes were grim and his mouth set in a straight line. He clearly had no time for ceremony.

"So, you are the charlatan moor," he remarked grimly in an accent I could not place. "The one selling an elixir that can cure the clap."

I thought quickly. "I do not claim it is an elixir, sir," I said. "But it is indeed physic from a London shop."

And that was my first conversation with Doctor Joseph Herman, who lived in the settlement of Pasbyhayes, just north of Jamestown, where Ganter and my friends now farmed Master Joshua Adams's land—Doctor Herman, who had lived in Virginia since his thirtieth year, was a man of medicine.

He had more questions about my powder. How had I laid hands on it? What was its composition? The answer to the second question I could not divulge, I said. But I had got it simply enough—I had apprenticed for a physician-apothecary in London and he had given it to me when I set sail to Virginia.

"A moorish apprentice, eh?" Doctor Herman said doubtfully.

"Yessir—an East Indian."

"And you know something about physic yourself?"

I felt it would be unwise to tell an absolute falsehood. "Just a little, sire. My London master closed shop soon, and I left to seek a living in America."

The doctor remained unsmiling to the end of our brief conversation. He warned me to heed him and stop selling fraudulent physic—it is unwise and dangerous to do so, he said, although God knows I was not the only quack and fraud in Virginia. I assured him that I had no regular medical practice; the powder was my only product; I meant to close operations in ten days, when I would head to the Northern Neck to be bound to Master Anthony Johnson; no, I would close operations right away. I was courteous and deferential to the doctor, and I believe he was pleased by my manner. He grew a little less stiff and bade me good night before he left. Fortunately, Noah did not arrive till after to claim his daily dose of physic. He said he had a fever and a swelling on his neck, but the itching was almost gone. Overall, he felt strong and hopeful.

Doctor Herman visited again in two days.

"I have an offer to make, sirrah," he said, again without preliminaries. That was how Doctor Herman was always to be, in all my acquaintance with him, a blunt man, with no bent for ceremony and often lacking social graces. "I am looking for an apprentice—I am a busy man and could do with some assistance. I attend to the sick, I perform surgeries, I also prepare and sell physic. Unlike in England, physicians, apothecaries, and chirurgeons are one and the same in this godforsaken land."

I was so surprised that I could not utter a word.

"I also grow some corn on my few acres, raise bees, and keep a dovecote," Doctor Herman continued. "I thought you would be a reasonable choice in the light of your previous experience in London. Bind yourself to me and you will learn a great deal about the art and mystery of physic."

Was he truly telling me this? A dream I did not even fully know I had nurtured had come true—I would be a physician's apprentice . . . I would cease being a laborer, and become a man learning a trade. Besides, I would dwell close to where my friends, Dick, Bristol, and Cuffee, lived. It was true I would have to see Ganter occasionally, but what harm could he do now? All in all, it was a good sight better than moving to the Northern Neck. However, I remembered the ship doctor's demand for fees, which was precisely what Doctor Herman next brought up. He clarified that he would expect an annual payment for taking me on. It was but the custom for apprentices to pay masters.

"I am grateful for the opportunity, but I cannot pay you a fee to learn, sir," I said, trying not to let my despondency show.

"Nothing at all?" He sounded a trifle disappointed.

When I said I owned almost nothing in the world, the doctor sighed and seemed to consider it.

"I assume you can read?" he asked.

"Yes, sir."

"Write a tolerable hand?"

I proudly replied that I could, and replied in the affirmative to his other questions: I would help him gather and grow herbs, was not averse to traveling bad roads at night to see sick men, was willing to start by learning the most basic of tasks, that I was not put off by the sight of blood and the human body in various states of decay and disrepair.

"You will do," he said at the end of the interview. "Come to me on Monday."

And that is how I became an apprentice to Doctor Joseph Herman, Virginia physician.

A few days later, I thanked Parson Blair for his many kindnesses, I reminded Maria that she should be glad that she was being rid of me, I promised them both to treat them gratis should they fall ill, and left with them some medication to be given to Noah, my first patient. I then went out to the quay to look at the river. It was still that morning and the sky was serene. I prayed to the many gods of water and air and to the One God for good fortune in my new trade. A ship had come in the day before. I had heard the usual hollering that accompanied the arrival of a vessel. Soon a boat bearing a fresh batch of servants—all Africans—sailed towards the quay. I remembered how Bristol and Cuffee had appeared to me when I first set eyes on them—urbane, well-traveled men of the world, Christian, versatile in many tongues. I wondered if I was like them now, I, who had been till very recently an East Indian peasant working in the mud in one of the world's backwaters.

A wagon was setting out midmorn and going most of the way to Pasby-hayes. I would walk the last few leagues to Doctor Herman's property. We rode past the abandoned glassmaking building up the new main road, and past the point where the road split in four, one fork leading to the new settlement of Middle Plantation. The land there was divided into fifty-acre parcels all held by the governor and leased out to farmers. It was in two such parcels, planted by Master Menefie's nephew, that Dick, Bristol, and Cuffee worked the fields, supervised by Ganter. It was beautiful country though, far more pleasing to me than Jamestown. Although the trees were still skeletal, the sap in them would flow soon enough and the quick buds would thrust through, making the land verdant.

As I walked the last stretch through the tree-lined path, sometimes stumbling over stumps and fallen logs, I remembered the doctor telling me that I would have to travel these roads often in the dark with him. Still better than sowing and hilling tobacco, I reckoned, an improvement over sweating in the fields. A fair-sized rivulet, the Powhatan Creek, flowed on the other side. I stopped to look at it, at the roving clouds reflected in its waters. A boat passed—a small one with a single man in it rowing leisurely. I squinted out at it and saw him, the Man Who Would Not Die. I had not seen him for a while now. I raised my hand to him, but he did not nod or raise his oar and went on, leaving behind ripples like delicate tracings on the surface of the river. He had grown quite dark-skinned now. I wondered at that, but it was important not to be late, so I got out of the water and proceeded hurriedly.

From the outside, Doctor Herman's cabin, built under a cluster of poplar trees, was only a little better than that of a small farmer. By the side of it was what seemed to be a small vegetable garden. As I hesitated, an African maiden hurried out of the house. Her thick hair was pinned back and her eyes were large and luminous. She had a grave demeanor, although she smiled at me briefly when I wished her good day, and I saw that her teeth were strong and straight and her cheek dimpled.

"Go on in," she said softly, gesturing towards the house. "The doctor awaits you." And she hurried off between the trees.

There was no one in the cabin. The room had more furnishings than the cabins in Ganter's Hope, including a chair, a table, and a low bed with a feather mattress. I noticed a ladder leading to a loft, and alongside the pewter utensils scattered by the fireplace were vials and bottles and containers of sundry shapes. I guessed that was where the doctor brewed his concoctions. I felt anew the excitement of the adventure I was embarking on. Physic was an art and a craft, Doctor Herman had said, and also a mystery. And I was to be admitted into it. And suddenly there was the doctor, standing at the door.

Over the years I spent with Doctor Herman, I was to learn that he was born in Bavaria but had lived in England since he turned sixteen. It was in London that he was inducted into the study of medicine. The doctor was also to hint that his father, a physician too, had been born a Jew but joined the Church of England simply because people were inclined not to trust a Jewish physician with their health; that some four decades before, Doctor Roderigo Lopez, Jewish *converso,* physician to the late Queen Elizabeth, had been accused of plotting to poison the queen and been hanged for *the most dangerous and desperate treason.*

All that came later. On that first day, he put me to work in the fields almost right away. He planned to grow a little tobacco, so the fields had to be prepared for sowing. Vegetables had to be planted in the kitchen garden. The two and twenty inhabitants of the dovecote had to be fed and watered and the neck of one of the birds wrung for supper (Doctor Herman had a great fondness for pigeon meat). And then the bees kept in the bee gums and box hives needed to be inspected and a box or two constructed with wood.

"Will they sting, sir?" I asked.

"Of course, they will," he said in his bland voice, which I was still getting accustomed to. "It is not unusual for bees to sting. It is for you to handle the boxes tenderly."

I learned that he abhorred the taste of both honey and mead himself but used them for his medicine and took the rest to market in Jamestown. In any case, he found the enterprise of beekeeping entertaining.

It was a day filled with hard work and much learning and I was ready to go to bed in the pile of hay in the loft. I heard Doctor Herman moving about below, and I do not know how long he meant to stay awake in the dim light of his candle. In Jamestown there had always been some noise to interrupt the night—mostly drunks reeling their way home, sometimes a cry from the direction of the great river. Here the silence was heavy. The loft was windowless so I could not see the sky or the stars, but I could imagine them and the empty fields stretching around the cabin, bordered by thickets of trees. I thought about the pretty black maiden and wondered when she would return.

I felt alone and yearned to be back at Parson Blair's, falling asleep to his sozzled mutterings. I wondered if I should have gone to Master Johnson: at Angola farm there would have been other moorish servants I could have befriended.

Soon there was no sound from below. The doctor must have blown out his candle and gone to bed. I sensed dead people crowding in the shadows. Little Sammy, Master Walsh, Mad Marge—all who had lost their lives in this land. Their shadows overlapped, their heads hung heavy, their shoulders slumped, their limbs were squat. What did they wait for, I wondered, what did the dead have to look to? As sleep came over me, they slouched out, soundlessly.

ELEVEN

In the light of the morn, Doctor Herman talked of the dead. How death had walked in the wake of the English settlement of Virginia—how the Indians had perished in shockingly large numbers of new and unexplained diseases at every village the English stopped at and began to believe that the white men shot *invisible bullets* into them; how the English had fallen prey to the gross and vaporous air of Jamestown, its brackish water, and died of agues, fluxes, and distempers; how the settlers had despaired because, as one of them wrote in a missive to England: *in the health of the People, consisteth the very life, strength, increase, and prosperity of the whole general colony.*

And that is where the physician comes in, the doctor said. His business is life and health, although he knows too well that death comes at the end.

But such things momentarily slipped from my mind when the same maiden I had seen the day before came later that morning. Doctor Herman had stepped out and I was sweeping the cabin and cleaning the table of the sticky residue he had left on it from whatever he had been concocting last night. The girl came in and, apart from a quick nod, took no notice of me. She went swiftly about her business, going outside to scour a pot, bringing it back in to set on the hearth. All this without saying a word. I wanted to address her, but I was all of a sudden struck mute. The silence between us grew and took up the space of the cabin. She was remarkably unfriendly, I thought.

"I am Tony," I offered, and I sounded like a boy, and a sulky one too. And I had so fervently wished to impress her by sounding elegant and gentlemanly.

"Lydia," she said. I hoped the announcement would be accompanied by a smile, but it was not. She was a little stern of demeanor, but still very beautiful. She might have been a year or two older than me. She reminded me of someone—the stillness of her, the gravity. At that moment I could not recollect whom.

"You work for the doctor?" I asked.

It was a foolish question. Why else would she be here scouring his dishes?

"I come in every other day to cook his meals," she replied. "I work at the Pooles' farm otherwise. I expect Doctor Herman will not require me now that you are here."

"I am his apprentice," I said quickly. "I will aid him in his medicinal practice."

She stared at me. "An apprentice," she said slowly. "So, you will not cook. Cooking is women's work, I suppose, and you would not do it."

I shrugged. "I have cooked before for other masters."

She continued with her tasks. She was brisk and efficient, and quite strong in spite of her slightness. Her petticoats were of plain stuff as was her blouse. Her shoes were those of a man. I suddenly wondered how she would look with strands of flowers on her hair like the ones the women in my homeland wore.

I stood at Doctor Herman's shelves and studied his bottles and boxes. Every single one of them was labeled: *gentian root, white vitriol, turpentine, ginseng, ginger, lavender, valerian, goldrod tincture, wormwood, antinomy, rattlesnake root, mercury.* Names like incantations. I hesitated and then unplugged the top of a bottle, and sniffed. The pungent odor tickled my nostrils and I sneezed, once, once more, and a third time. My eyes were watering as I hastily put back the container, and through my tears I saw Lydia glancing at me, with half a smile on her face. As I wiped my nose I wondered if she was to Doctor Herman what Maria was to Parson Blair. I felt a pang.

The doctor himself came in at that moment. "Ah, Tony," he said. "The sun is high and you should be outside seeing to the doves."

I wondered if seeing to the doves was part of a physician's apprentice's duties. But I held my tongue. And the doctor then turned to the young woman. "And, Lydia, you can tell Master Poole that I will not be requiring your services any longer. I have Tony here now to prepare my meals."

She nodded at that and glided out without a word, expressionless, not looking my way.

To say that there was no study those first few weeks would be untrue. Late that evening, after I had cleared away his supper and eaten my own, Doctor Herman launched into a discourse without introduction or preliminary. The small fire towards which he stretched his feet crackled, and the only other sound was the doctor's own speech, low and steady, his tone touched slightly by the accents of the German tongue he must have spoken in his early years:

Mixtures are blends of qualities. Each person has their particular mixture that Galen termed temperamentum, *which is their individual nature or constitution. These mixtures are comprised of the humors of blood, phlegm, yellow bile, and black bile, the bodily equivalents of air, water, fire, and earth. Blood is held to be moist and warm; phlegm is held to be moist and cool; yellow bile, dry and warm; and black bile, dry and cold. When one of the four humors is very much out of balance, sickness results.*

I realized that I was to embark on a journey of discovery. A journey different from but akin to those undertaken by explorers looking for new lands. I too would voyage, inwards, and uncover mysteries.

"And the physician attempts to restore the balance, master?" I asked.

He nodded briefly, and continued:

Treatment thus consists of removing or diminishing the offending humor by purging, bleeding, vomiting, blistering, urinating, sweating, or salivating; on the other hand, a deficient humor is to be restored by diet and drugs. Galen classes drugs according to their warm, cold, moist, or dry qualities . . .

That good start filled me with hope and the desire to learn more. Which is why I was sorely disappointed at the shape of the days that followed. I spent them cleaning the droppings of pigeons, hauling bags of feed into the cote, making more boxes for the bees, planting cucumber and beans. Doctor Herman asked me to make a sign. "Doctor Joseph Herman, Physician and Apothecary. Licensed and Examined." Following the notice, I wrote out to the doctor's dictation: *Well-known for care of flux and gives notice he can cure following disorders: bad coughs, scurvy, running Humors. The Yaws, the French disease, sore legs, dropsy, scurvy in the Gums. Apprentice to the physician will also geld pigs for 2 p.*

The last items startled me. "Will I, sir? Geld pigs?"

"You will, my boy."

"But I have never gelded a pig," I said.

"You will learn with practice. That is what physic is about."

He was probably right, and there had certainly been barber-surgeons in London and back in my homeland as well: men who had the sharpest of instruments and could use them to cut beards as well as boils, to sew split flesh, and I supposed, if necessary, could turn them to the gelding of pigs.

I was not sent to geld a pig, but I continued to labor as I had done in Ganter's Hope. And since it was too much work for one man to prepare the fields for sowing, Doctor Herman hired men from the largest holding in Pasbyhayes, which turned out to be Adams's Grove, where my old friends worked. The servants sent were Dick, Bristol, and Cuffee. I knew they worked close by and I had been longing to see them.

"I thought you were a physician's apprentice, Tony," Dick mocked gently. "That you had left behind the laboring life."

I shrugged and laughed it off, but his words rankled.

"Tony will start on the learning soon," Cuffee said consolingly. Bristol, as always, stayed silent, but his gaze was pitying. Maybe he thought I had been foolish to hope, to have forgotten that dark bodies are made for field labor; they plod at it till they blend with the ground, the earth, which is of their color. I aspired to rise above that inevitable lot, and Bristol was already sorry for my impending disappointment.

I swore that night and every night that I would complain to Doctor Herman, who was out most days visiting the sick, or in Jamestown taking care of business, or, when home, was at his shelves and table sorting through his powders and liquids, or ordering me to cook his meals, clean his house, wash his clothes. He was very keen on the orderly life, on what he called civilized living, which included tidy apparel, meals at tables, and books to read. Without these, he maintained, a man would descend into savagery in this place, this ragged periphery of the world. Apart from the household and field tasks, he had already ordered me to commence on the construction of a second small cabin where we could carry out compounding and distilling of physic, away from where we ate and slept. He would hire Master Adams's men to help me.

It was just as Cuffee, Dick, and I were starting on the cabin that Ganter came by. He watched us work, leaning against a tree, chewing a bit of straw.

"You have business with the doctor, Master Ganter?" I asked.

Ganter spat leisurely. "Never seen a doctor in my life. Never trusted them, never will. Fear the physician more than the disease, that's what *I* say."

He waited for me to respond to that. I would not oblige.

"I heard you were on your way to learning physic," he then jeered. "*A moor doctor?* I thought to meself. Who in his senses would trust a moor with his body?"

I turned away. I was in no mood to pick a fight with Ganter.

He continued: "But it looks like I need not worry—you look like no physician's apprentice to me. More like a physician's slave."

I loathed Ganter, but he was correct in his assessment of my situation.

A week or two passed, and my routine in my new post had not changed. I was standing outside the cabin one evening, discontented and bored, when I heard the bushes rustle. I saw the flash of a petticoat and my first thought was of Lydia. But it was a white woman, about thirty years of age.

"What is your business, mistress? Doctor Herman is not at home," I said.

She hesitated. I wondered if she had an illness that she was ashamed to talk about—a problem with her monthly courses, or a blockage that left her unable to defecate, or a boil in a delicate part. I had already read about those problems in *The Booke of Physicke,* a volume on Doctor Herman's shelf that I glanced at when I had the time.

"I have come for a bit of a love potion," she said.

I laughed. "This is a physician's house, mistress. Do you not see the sign?" I pointed to the wooden board I had created. "Doctor Herman is no countryside crone dealing in magic potions."

"You talk too much for an Indian," she said sourly.

I shrugged at that.

"But I have heard that your kind knows a lot about love potions and such," she said slyly. When she took a step forward, I could feel her eager breath on my face and see the despair in her eyes. "You seem like a knowledgeable fellow—go on, give me something."

I was not unmoved by her flattery, but I hesitated.

"I will pay you for it," she added hurriedly.

I was glad that someone saw me as knowledgeable, even as my master had hired me as an apprentice and decided to treat me as a mere servant. I was glad, too, at the opportunity to dabble with the substances in Doctor Herman's cabin, to disobey the doctor, who had promised me much and given me little. It did not matter that she thought I was the other kind of Indian.

I asked her name and she told me it was Sisley Patton and that the potion was for her husband, who had ceased loving her. I swiftly considered it and then asked her to return the next day.

There is a recipe for everything under the sun. I did not even have to spend too much time among the doctor's books before finding *Love Potions for Men, Cold and Impotent; and Women, Prudish and Overmodest.* The concoctions could be delivered in cakes, syrups, plasters, pomades, pills. They could be rubbed in, poured over, smoked, or swallowed. I was dismayed at some of the recipes: they required the use of assorted ingredients such as a deer's heart, human bone, spleen, pubic hair, rose petals, and consecrated host—of all these only the deer's heart and pubic hair seemed remotely attainable. And then I came upon an *Aphrodisiac Pill Following an Old English Recipe,* which required nothing more than asafoetida or stinking gum (also from India, Doctor Herman was in possession of a little), extracted opium, the woman's menstrual blood, and something called castoreum, which I assumed was castor oil, till it turned out to be an odoriferous oily secretion found in two sacs between the anus and external genitals of beavers. I decided to substitute the last with something simple, like hog's lard. The woman, I would request for the menstrual blood. If she could not deliver that in sufficient time, she could give me her spittle.

It might have been because of my concoction that the unfortunate Master Patton lost his wife. I could administer love potions, but I had no way of telling if those who requested them told me the truth. Mistress Sisley slipped the potion, not into the ale of her wedded husband, but into that of their servant, Adam Gray. It was Flynn and Cuffee who told me of how Gray, who had just completed his indenture, had taken off with his master's horse, bed, and gun, and also his master's wife, Mistress Sisley, whom he had suddenly grown besotted with.

When another woman, Fanny Moore, came to me for a potion, I followed the same recipe. Her husband was at sea, and she needed to administer the potion to another fellow only so she could be assured of that man's love if her spouse should not return. Fanny was a pretty, vivacious woman. It seemed only natural that she kept a man as a backup.

And so it went. The Indian lad in the Shakespeare play was denied a full role, so I took on the role of that other boy, Puck, the spirit-like creature who assisted the fairy king. Puck had wreaked havoc with the juice of the *little western flower, Before milk-white, now purple with love's wound,* willing and withdrawing desire, causing men and women to fall in love and out of it at dizzying speeds, leaving them elated, confused, and hapless. I sold a potion to a woman who intended it for a man, and then to her sister, who intended it for the same

man; I sold one to one maiden but mistakenly put the spittle of another female customer in the mixture. I was very busy indeed. Doctor Herman was in
Jamestown for days at a stretch and did not know what was going on. I felt no
regret nor guilt. In the play, Puck did not rue his actions. Indeed, he reveled in
the mayhem and madness he had created: *this their jangling I esteem a sport . . .*
he declared triumphantly.

There were times I refused my services: I would not serve a woman who
intended it for my friend Bristol, because I knew there was another woman he
had a fondness for; I turned away a maiden who asked me to sell her a dose of
poison along with the potion, so she could administer the venom to the man,
in case the potion did not work. And it was my rule never to sell potions to
men who intended them for women, even those supposedly *prudish or overmodest*. Over the weeks, I found more efficient ways to distill and compound; I
learned to substitute and alter ingredients so that Doctor Herman would not
notice particular goods in his store depleting. And all this even as I worked
around the house and garden and sometimes even went to work in Master
Adams's lands, when my master hired me out. My old friends were generally
glad to see me when I was at their farm, or when we met on Sunday afternoons
at the Crossed Keyes, the local tavern. Cuffee was amused by tales of the love
potion, but Bristol warned me to take heed.

"Oh, they are harmless enough," I said. "They may not be of any help, but
they do not hurt either."

"Tony, Tony, moors do not play tricks on white folks without inviting
trouble."

"You make too much of it, my friend." I laughed. But inside me I was still
resentful, disappointed at Doctor Herman's betrayal of me. I had counted on
the apprenticeship to him to help me start anew in Virginia, and here was I,
up to entertaining, but foolish tricks.

It was some months since I had arrived to work for Doctor Herman. Hands
were needed at Adams's Grove, and Doctor Herman had hired me out, promising that I could keep a percentage of the payment he received for my services. Ganter was away for the day, so we were supervised by Dick. We also
had several other people working with us. One was Lydia, the pretty African
maid, whom I had seen at the Crossed Keyes every now and then, but with
whom I had not exchanged more than a few words after our early meeting at

my master's. She had come with a black lad of eight or ten years called Sancho, who came from the Spanish isles and who also worked for the Pooles. And then there was a woman new to me, one named Annie, who had also been hired out for the day by her master.

Annie was red in the face, with messy hair the color of straw, a loud, jolly lass. Just two nights ago, I thought I had seen one servant named Martin, also bound to Master Adams, coming out of a bush all flushed and sweaty, with Annie following, straightening her petticoats. I envied him, because I had never known a woman myself, but I also did not. Annie winked as she passed by me, and she smelt of the sharp tang of perspiration and something else.

That morning I attempted to work closer to Lydia.

"Are you from around here?" I asked, hoping to strike up a conversation.

"Ay. I was born on a farm in Charles River Shire or thereabouts."

"You are not from Africa then—like my friends there?" I nodded towards Bristol and Cuffee.

She shook her head. "No 'twas my parents who came from over the sea. My mam said I am among the first blackmoors to be born in Virginia."

"And I believe I am the first East Indian in this land. At least I have heard of no other."

"Is East India a long way off?"

"I have seen a map of the world and 'tis bang on the other side."

A butterfly settled on my nose and then on Lydia's cheek. She smiled as she flicked it away gently. Her smile was indeed very pretty. I heard the woman named Annie laughing aloud in the distance.

"I wonder why these butterflies here are spotted like leopards, Miss Lydia."

She seemed lighthearted that morning, inclined to be more friendly than before. "And pray what are leopards, Master Tony?"

She had just mentioned that she was born in Virginia. How would she know of leopards, elephants, and keen-eyed vultures? How would she know of gods who were animals, animals who were gods? The bestial and the divine undifferentiated (How ridiculous was that? How infinitely wise?). For her, dark-skinned though she was, Virginia was home. Maybe she was slightly embarrassed by her parents and people like them, who have traveled further than she could dream of, who speak English with strange lilts, who can speak other tongues, who secretly worship other gods. Lydia's heart did not ache for another place beyond the sea.

"Your mind has gone a-roaming, Tony?" I saw that her large, serious eyes were fixed on me inquiringly and I was pleased that she seemed to want to continue our conversation. We came from different ends of the earth, but here we were together, with the same sky above us, sharing this place, this time. I had just opened my mouth to say something when Sancho called to her and she left my side, a little reluctantly, I thought.

We did what task we had been assigned in the fields and repaired to the small peach orchard that Master Adams had planted. Someone—it might have been Martin—had carried a small barrel of cider from somewhere, and we drank the sweet and cool beverage cup for cup. The sky was blue, and more butterflies, the selfsame color as the cider, flew plentifully around us.

Soon the cider barrel was half-empty—I had drunk little and felt not the need for more.

I lay under the trees and looked up, feeling the sun warm on my face. Lydia sat some distance away with Sancho. All the other men lounged likewise, glad to rest in the tiresome heat. Flynn told me he had heard that Adam Gray regretted running away with his master's wife, who had turned out to be a loathsome shrew.

"Perhaps your love potion has worn off, Tony," he murmured. "Perhaps you should sell the lady another dose."

I laughed and shook my head. The woman named Annie then asked me to fetch her a drink, and I obliged. She took the cup, sipped of it, and pulled me down by her side. In addition to her other scents, she smelled of the sharp, fruity scent of the cider.

"Come on, Tony—talk to me, will you not?" she said, laughing. She laughed a lot, did Annie.

"I have nothing to say, Annie," I said, slightly annoyed because I wanted to go sit by Lydia.

"But you had much to tell little black Lydia, did you not?" Annie pouted, leaning over to whisper into my ear. At least she thought it a whisper, but it was loud enough for the others to hear. What was worse, Lydia might have heard it, because I saw her get up and leave, Sancho following her. I was dismayed, and would have hurried after them, but Annie put her hand on my arm. Her breath was hot and damp on my face.

"C'mon, Tony . . ." she murmured, and pressed against my side. Her hips were round and soft, and I could see the outlines of her thighs where her skirts clung. Perhaps because I had been thinking of Lydia or, more likely, because I was merely a man, I felt a little throb of desire. It took even me by surprise and I crossed my legs hastily. Annie issued a warm, husky laugh and pressed herself to me again, and because she had turned her body slightly, I felt her billowy breast against my arm. Her face was close to mine and she flicked her tongue against the lobe of my ear.

I got up, maybe a little too abruptly, and pretended to stretch. I must admit that I was also slightly flattered, at least till it occurred to me that she was probably mocking me because I was the most youthful there and a moor and foreigner at that. And, also, importantly, she was tipsy with the drink.

She got to her feet and yawned. She was a little taller than me when we stood. She looked aggravated at my moving away from her, although she chucked me under the chin and smiled a tight little smile. Cuffee was grinning now, like a fool. He too had clearly had too much to drink and swayed slightly as he walked to rest his back on the tree. Dick and Flynn had gone off to piss, and Martin stayed unmoving and unmoved, prone on the grass, his eyes shut. I wanted to nudge him awake, to tell him to get this woman away from me. After all, he had fucked her; if she was anyone's woman, she was his. But I knew that she really was not—he had taken her into the bushes because she was around and he was in the mood for it. He might have given her something in return, a bit of tobacco, or a piece of cloth, or he might not have either, may not have bothered himself to pay her for her services.

I went to lean against the tree trunk. Annie followed. I chewed at a blade of grass nervously. She playfully took it from my mouth and threw it away. And then she leaned her weight against me and kissed me full on the mouth. It was the first real kiss I had received from a woman, and, to tell the truth, it felt very good. Her lips were warm and full and had the smell of overripe fruit—her thick, fleshy tongue swiped over my own lips, and I might have responded to her, for an instant forgetting everything: the ground below, the blue sky above, Lydia, and certainly myself.

Later, Annie would say that I put my arms around her waist and pulled her towards me, that I rubbed against her mightily, that I was horny as a young black bull and all ready to get going. The way I remember it, she raised my shirt and placed her right hand on my crotch, and said, laughingly, that she thought I would have a good prick. I stood still, hoping that my body, in spite of me, would not respond to her touching and kneading.

"All black men have good pillicocks and I reckon brown fellows such as yourself have too." She then leant her forehead on my shoulder, and nuzzled against me, like some giant, sozzled kitten. I hoped she would collapse from the drink, right there in one big, fleshy heap.

"Wilt thou hear some music?" she mumbled. "I will have them play a tune for you."

Over Annie's shoulder, I saw Dick coming out of the underbrush, whistling lightly, without a care in the world. The sight of him propelled me to push Annie with all my might and, tripping over a protruding rock, she fell on the ground. I walked, almost ran, back through the fields and towards Doctor Herman's. It might have been more manly to stay with the others and have a good laugh at Annie as she lay there, sloshed and mumbling, her skirts lifted to her knees, but I was in no mood for that.

Later that evening I was to hear that Annie had hit the back of her head on the rock and had a slight swelling on it. Even later, Annie was to admit that she had flirted with me a little, but that was only because I had slipped some of the love potion I was selling about the countryside into her cider. Why would she flirt with a moor otherwise, with some kind of *Indian*? She said that I had taken advantage of the state the potion had put her in and had pulled out my yard and attempted to ravish her, right there under the poplar; that she had tried to push me away, but I had become enraged and shoved her backwards and caused her to fall. Fortunately for her, she said, she was able to pick herself up and run.

All this Annie said at the Crossed Keyes. Some of the men, regulars at the place, a shiftless lot, former servants without land or money or hope, had been ready to come and find me, *to thrash him, to show him, to spoil his knavish black face, to show him, to show him . . .* Annie swept up a storm and made people feel the swelling on her head. And the men who till the day before were just the kind to call her whore and pull her down for a quick one in the dirt and then spit on her as they hitched up their breeches, suddenly turned into knights gallant, quickening in anger, ready to defend her honor against a moor.

It might have gone very badly for me if Dick, Martin, and Flynn had not come to my rescue. Bristol and Cuffee had spoken up in my defense too, but their words would have been to no avail if the white servants had not raised their voices for me, saying that I was innocent, Annie had been piss drunk, that she was anyway a loose-tailed harlot, as any man could testify; that those who had known her back in England knew that by sixteen she had a husband in Warwick, and another in Kenilworth, and a third in Coventry.

"Tony is a good lad though he is a moor," they said.

"What about the love potion?" the enraged men asked. "Did he not give her something to drink?"

It was Doctor Herman who stepped in then. He put the word out that he could say on authority that there was no love potion. His apprentice, Tony, did not know chamomile from camphor. How would he concoct a love potion? And even if, somehow, he had, Annie would have not just flirted with him, she would have done more. And because Doctor Herman was respected, a little feared, his words were heeded. Although some men still muttered that the doctor was foolish to *trust a moor,* the others turned from me and called names after Annie; and the women, with whom she had never been popular, spat at her.

"Annie the moll who'll jump over hedges to lie with a negro!" they would say loud enough for all to hear.

I found it in my heart to feel sorry for her—she had not done much more than get tipsy that afternoon and the men who called her hussy and jade would not hesitate to sleep with her, in truth, were still doing so. People talked about the episode long after, and I heard the story traveled to Jamestown, where it transformed itself as such tales do, and men sniggered over their cups about a slummy strumpet and a young mulatto.

Doctor Herman was furious. He had made a mistake hiring me, he said. I had appeared quick-witted, and indeed I was—but why was I turning my wit to all manner of ridiculous things? Unicorn powders and now love potions! It was perhaps best if we parted ways. I begged him to reconsider his decision, but he would not hear me and insisted that I depart his service at the month's end.

I sought out Dick, Bristol, and Cuffee for companionship, for consolation. But it did not seem the moment to share my troubles because Dick was excited over a new musket that Ganter had bought and let him use. He gathered us around him to demonstrate. We watched as he heaved it up and fired into the distance. It put a burning hole in the air and set the very ground beneath our feet rocking. It could also kill neatly, unlike an ax, pike, or sword. I believe every one of us there longed for one of those guns.

I brooded over that and other things on my way back to the doctor's that evening. The truth is that I would never own a musket. Whatever weapon

I wielded to make my way in Virginia would have to be of another kind—I remembered the invisible bullets the Indians had believed the English to have discharged. I must get hold of one of those. I also remembered how I was meant to start over, to live anew upon my return from the Indians. Virginia was a new creation, at least for us who came to it from outside; indeed, for the Englishmen who came earlier, now all passed on, it had been a vision. But somewhere in their journey the vision had been transformed into an actuality, verily a place, a home, a land to live in. The New World was, for these men, both a departure from their homeland and also a restoration of it. Ganter and Dick certainly no longer thought of any other home. That was what I had wanted too: I would *thrive wherever the wind laid me,* I had resolved. The yearning continued to stir me, but here I was, and nothing in my present circumstances held promise.

I was out of favor with Lydia too. I saw her at the Crossed Keyes a few days after the Annie incident. She was with little Sancho again but ignored me so completely I might as well have been made of air. I went to sit by her. She looked straight ahead.

"I did not encourage Annie," I blurted.

"But you gave out *love potions*? I thought better of you."

I felt my face turn hot. Lydia, so reserved, so dignified, so quiet, so beautiful—she thought me a rogue and, even worse, a clowning dolt.

"I am sorry for that," I said earnestly.

But she got up and left, taking Sancho by the hand, and I was quite alone.

I realized then who she reminded me of—with her large eyes and smooth, dark skin, her quietness and her grace. It was Mary Bengal, the last person from my part of the world I had laid eyes on, the maid who had been taken from my side in London, so many years ago. Shortly after, I heard that Lydia was sent away to the Northern Neck for a short while to see to her mistress's sister's childbirth. Any reconciliation between us, even if possible, would have to wait.

Walking home to the doctor's one evening a few days later, I was in no mood for bed, so I went to the dovecote to check on the birds. They had all returned home for the day and huddled in their nesting places. They set up a mild cooing when I entered, and I, who always had a fondness for creatures of all kinds, found the sound comforting. I caught a glimpse of a small heap of feathers on the ground and went closer. An injured fowl. I went to fetch a lantern to examine it, and the birds set up an even louder gurgling, excited by my light. The bird had broken a wing—the injured limb hung awkwardly low and there was a little bleeding at the joint. My impulse was to strangle it, as one does with wounded things. It looked at me as if it knew the fate that awaited it: its crimson eyes were sorrowful—it wanted to live. I picked it up and bore it into the cabin and up into the loft. It struggled a little, but I held it firmly. It was soft and warm in my arms, its small heart beating like a wild drum against my flesh.

Tending to that creature—so unimportant, so dispensable, but yet also a miraculous work of Nature—took my mind off my own sorrows and failings. I used the ointment of Mary-gold after mixing it with corn flour and a paste of the woundwort flower, whose merits Shuren's aunt had told me about, and bound the wing to the body with a clean rag. The bird seemed to be stronger the next day, although it would be weeks before he could be put back with his fellows. I reapplied the mixture every day and replaced the rag every few. There was a satisfaction in my handiwork that even exceeded the enjoyment that came from the spectacles caused by the love potion.

When Doctor Herman returned from Jamestown, where he had gone for a few days, he naturally wanted to know what the dove was doing in a box in the house, and I showed him my work. He peered at the creature and examined it with the sure touch of one used to handling broken bodies. He then looked up at me and nodded.

"This is fine work—very good indeed. You doubtless have a steady hand."

The doctor somehow looked even paler and more withdrawn. The silence between us was heavy and uncomfortable as I prepared his stew of greens and meat. He sighed loudly before he spoke up:

"The so-called love potions—I did not expect that manner of foolishness from you."

I was going to say nothing, but after a moment's thought I decided to speak. "Respectfully, sir, I engaged in the trickery only to divert myself and to forget."

"Forget? Forget what?" he asked sharply.

"My hopes of learning from you. I must confess, sir, that I told you an untruth when I said that I was bound to a physician in London, but still, I expected to be your apprentice, not merely a cook or a beekeeper or a field hand."

He did not say a word to that, only turned to his book, probably further disappointed that I had lied about my London experience. In the corner, the bird rustled and cooed.

The heart is the beginning of life, 'Tis the Sun of the Microcosm, as proportionally the sun deserves to be called the heart of the world, by whose virtue and pulsation, the blood is mov'd, perfected, made vegetable, and is defended from corruption and mattering; and this familiar household god doth his duty to the whole body by nourishing, cherishing, and vegetating, being the founder of life and author of all.

—so Doctor Herman read to me from the writings of the great English physician William Harvey, who had quite recently made the revolutionary discovery that the blood flows around the human body, pumped by the heart, through a single system of arteries and veins. And so, my training was renewed. To this day I do not know if my protestations convinced the doctor, or if my handiwork on the dove impressed, or if he simply decided that it would be too much effort to seek out a new apprentice. In any case, he began to introduce me to his art in full measure. And because he was a physician and also an apothecary and a chirurgeon, I began to learn the secrets of those trades as well. I read the books on his shelves, listened to Doctor Herman's brief lectures, and accompanied him to visit the ailing. Very gradually and over the course of months, I acquainted myself with the methods of bloodletting, purging, and cupping. As my master read his patients' urine, he told me about what one should look for in water casting—what pale or dark or frothy urines said about the state of the body. He taught me to place my hand on men's wrists to interpret the rhythm of the mysterious palpitation there, and also that of the most sovereign of organs, the heart.

I learnt that tobacco leaves could be used as a compress, mixture ingredient, or inhalant for treating cancerous growths, headaches, stomach cramps, head colds, intestinal worms, and somnolence; that wine and other strong beverages preserved the stomach, strengthened the natural heat, aided digestion, defended the body from corruption, and concocted food till it turned to blood. I learnt the distinctions between salves, poultices, tinctures, infusions, cordials, and decoctions, and when it was best to prescribe which. I learnt that men and women suffered bladder stones, apoplexy, the falling sickness, syphilis, pleurisy, eruptions, and swellings; that there were other minor ailments too that plagued every day: fevers, putrid sore throats, fluxes, blockages, toothaches. I learnt that the human body was frail, but also wondrously robust; that its workings were mysterious, that the job of the physician was to map it and decipher it; that death always comes at the end, that all men desire to live.

And then one day Cuffee carried the news from Jamestown that Noah the sailor had died. Cuffee knew him as the man who suffered from the clap, the man to whom I had given my magical powder. At the very end, Cuffee heard, Noah had turned blind, suffered raging agues and agonies in his head, which was inflamed with gross matter. He had apoplectic fits for two days—one fit following the next—and then had given up the ghost in an agony of suffering. Noah the sailor, who had come on me from the Jamestown night; Noah, bearing a knife; Noah, hissing threats in the dark; Noah, who said he had got the clap from a whore in Spain, a whore in Hispaniola, a whore in Virginia; poor Noah, who had unknowingly changed the course of things for me.

Doctor Herman said that, based on my description, the man was already in the last stage of the disease, which was more correctly termed lues venera or syphilis. Nothing could have remedied him, no sassafras powder or mercury, which were the customary methods, and no unicorn-horn mix from India or anywhere in the world.

V

INVISIBLE BULLETS

TWELVE

So, I attempted to give rebirth to myself, yet once more. Tony East Indian—laborer, adventurer, and now physician's apprentice. I was both the parent and the babe, and I was resolved to make a success of it. I felt I had found my calling, but I still struggled to fully shed my old self, to grow a different person under the same-colored skin. The pangs of rebirth, too, are real and enduring.

There were not too many physicians in Virginia, so Doctor Herman's services were sought out frequently. His reputation was enhanced by a couple of cases some months after I began my training with him. A female patient he treated for the falling sickness with a mixture of iron and copper filings dissolved in vinegar was cured, and soon after that Master Thomas Rolfe, the half-English half-Powhatan-Indian gentleman, the son of the princess Pocahontas and Sir John Rolfe, who lived as an English gentleman upon his return to Virginia, was cured of rabies caused by a raccoon bite. While my master administered the cure, he let me visit the patient on my own afterwards to administer further medication. Subsequently, I was told that Master Rolfe spoke highly of his physician's moorish assistant.

But not all men had equal faith in me. Master Poole, Lydia's master, was always sending for syrups and powders. He came himself every other week to be treated for pains of the head, or eruptions of the skin, or other ailments. The doctor informed me that our good neighbor suffered from hypochondriasis, which was the result of an excess of black bile, gross melancholic humors that rose up from the abdomen and corrupted the brain. But we discovered, to both my amusement and my annoyance, that Master Poole would be healed hastily

on the days when the doctor was absent and he had to instead subject himself
to treatment from me.

My master and I talked of these cases and other matters related to our
profession. I was always interrogating him:

"Doctor Herman, why are men of different races and complexions?"

"It is a matter of breeding and generation."

"Or is it a matter of creed and custom?"

"It could be that too."

"Are differences of complexion and countenance, or of custom, linked to
other kinds of difference, like goodness and civilization and intelligence, and
such?"

"It is hard to tell. There could be a connection. An old English emblem
says blackmoors cannot be washed white—that signifies that color is more
than skin deep. But I do not think it is true."

"Do the scholars believe that nature crafts differences?"

"Yes. And that nurture magnifies them. The Spanish physician Juan
Huarte writes that the varieties of men—both in composition of the body and
in the constitution of the soul—spring from humankind inhabiting countries of different temperatures, drinking diverse waters, and eating a variety
of foods."

"But the churchmen sometimes say that all men are God's children. Does
that signify God fathered sons of not only different hues, but different consti-
tutions?"

I would talk to Doctor Herman and try to understand the reason behind
white skin and black and brown and, more important, what greater distinctions of wit, sensibility, and soul the differences in hue signified. I read and was
taught by my master the new ideas put forth by men of learning in England
and Europe on the workings of the bowels, the brain, the blood; the causes of
migraines, melancholy, and madness. But I never got closer to understanding
the real meaning behind what they called the different races of men, and if
such difference exists in any profound sense that really matters.

The July days were long and things grew abundantly due to the unseasonable
rains. I labored in the damp earth of my herb garden, which was filled with
yarrow, angelica, valerian, and pennyroyal, among other plants, from all of
which we would compound sundry powders and decoctions. Doctor Herman

had been in Jamestown for two days. I wondered what he did there. Conversed with other physicians? Visited whores? Or did he minister to sick patients without me at his side? The last thought made me a little anxious. I wished for every opportunity to practice and observe. I was lost in my speculations when a stranger walked up to the garden.

"Your master calls for you," he said. "He says 'tis urgent." And he gave me directions to the place where I would find Doctor Herman.

I found him in a timbered house in Jamestown, not too far from the river, a house that was slightly bigger than the cabins around it. He himself opened the door for me, and I saw that his pale skin had taken on a red cast, as if he was in his cups. But I also noted his swollen eyes and knew that the redness was a result of weeping. A figure lay on the low bed in the darkness behind. As I drew nearer, the doctor lit a candle and I saw that it was a very sick man. His face was withered and shrunk, and his lips so dry that they cracked and bled. At Doctor Herman's direction, I wet a sponge and applied it to his mouth.

"He cannot drink," the doctor whispered. "There is a swelling in his throat."

And he explained to me that Master Thomas Greene, tobacco trader, had developed in his throat a year ago an *oncos* or swelling. Doctor Herman had first assumed it to be a cantankerous sore, but it had grown further.

I remembered a passage that my master had shown me in a volume by the great barber-surgeon of France Ambroise Paré: *if a hard and localized tumor begins to suppurate, it turns into cancer. There were sarcomas soft and fleshy in the place where they originated. There were sarcomas of the uterus, rectum, bones, breasts, and throat. Surgeries could only be performed on patients with nonulcerated cancers. The best treatment for ulcerating cancers was to wash them with vinegar, oil, and milk.*

"The tumor is hard to examine because of the location," Doctor Herman was telling me gravely, "but I can see enough to see that it is of unequal shape with a rough surface."

Thus he went on, describing the growth and the symptoms in an even voice. The darkened blood vessels that extended outward indicated the spread of malignant matter into the surrounding flesh, causing the corrosive and cruel pain the sick man felt. I listened carefully, wondering all along why my master had been weeping. It is the physician's lot to witness pain, he had often told me. The good physician feels compassion, but he does not shed tears. If you weep for every patient, you will run dry and, more important, you will not be able, through the water in your eyes, to see the ailment for what it is. But I was certain that he had broken his own rule in the case of Master Greene.

I learnt much over the next few days. I understood that physicians sometimes fail, sometimes when they most want to succeed; that Doctor Herman had tried his utmost, administering every herb and hybrid he could think of; that love and hope are important ingredients in physic. I also understood why Doctor Herman visited Jamestown so often, stayed there days and nights, why he had no wife, why he did not seek out the company of women. I understood too—or rather, I remembered once more with full force—the depth of human grief, the raw edge of it.

It took Master Greene a week to die. My master stayed by his side almost every moment—my responsibility was to go back and forth, carrying out my duties at home and, when back at Master Greene's, cooking for my master and preparing a mixture of opium and other substances to ease the sick man's passage. In between, I would walk to the river and watch the boats coming in. I would overhear traders hopefully discuss the rising rates of tobacco, the expanding markets. On Master Greene's table was a piece of paper which contained his last wishes: *to Joseph Herman the four hundred hogsheads of tobacco ready to be put on ship, my house in Jamestown, my furniture, my turquoise ring, and the gold.*

Master Greene's habitation smelt like sickrooms always do: of bodily fluids mixed with the pungent odor of sulfur and boiled herbs. My master hung over the dying man, holding his hand in his own. Master Greene's breath came quick and shallow; occasionally he called weakly, and I would hurry over to wet his lips.

"It is the grip of cancer—the crab. Whatever it grasps with its claws, it holds," my master whispered, his voice hoarse.

Master Greene went early one morning as the rain drummed on the roof and beat against the casement. Doctor Herman laid his forehead on the dead man's bony chest and wept. I think that he was my master's last and greatest love. For the rest of the time I was to know Joseph Herman he carried his grief in him. Like the very crab that had taken grip of his friend's throat, it held on to my master, tenaciously.

The physician treats the wounds; it is God who heals, Monsieur Paré also wrote.

And, at times, He decides not to.

The seasons turned, and nearly a year passed since my arrival at Doctor Herman's. A physician and his apprentice are kept busy in Virginia, where disease and pain are ubiquitous. It was always the season for something—fevers and fluxes, colds and colics, distemper, sore legs, the yaws. And men and women also needed boils abscised, broken bones set, growths removed, and teeth pulled. Master Herman went about his tasks expertly but I could not help but think that the passing of Master Greene had caused a darkness to settle over his soul that he could not budge. I wished I could purge him of his grief, make him vomit it, sweat it, or otherwise draw it out of him, like one draws out bad blood from an ailing man. But I knew not how to *minister to a mind diseased . . . Pluck from the memory a rooted sorrow . . .*

Ralph Ganter had his troubles too, though of a different kind. The horse he had been provided by Master Adams shied and bucked at something one day, and threw Ganter off. It was Doctor Herman who set his shoulder—the arm hung out of the socket like a puppet's and Ganter clenched his teeth and grimaced as my master slipped it back in. Because Ganter's back was also hurt, the doctor instructed me to supply our patient with a juice made of the *Datura stramonium,* sometimes known hereabouts as the Jamestown weed or jimsonweed, in order to take the edge off the pain. The medicine was sometimes smoked through a pipe, but the juice was easier to administer, and we used it to treat convulsive and spasmodic disorders and to ease pains caused by scaldings, broken bones, and such.

A week later, I was in the cabin cleaning out equipment—the mortars and pestles, the weighing scales, and the gallipots—when a shadow fell over the threshold. It was Ganter. I felt the old familiar unease. I knew he could do me no harm, but fear sprang up in me unbidden whenever he appeared. And there he was squinting at the door, as revolting as he ever was.

"The young moor doctor is busy, eh?"

"I am only an apprentice, Master Ganter."

"Well, fellow, this shoulder kept me up the night and I will need some of the jimson."

I explained to him that it would be best if he waited for Doctor Herman to return. He would know what to do.

"God damn you—what is there to *do?* All I need is something for this shoulder."

I could see that he *was* in some agony. His jaw was tightly clenched and a bead of sweat rolled down the side of his face, which had grown grayer and slightly more withered of late. I had a mind to not help allay his pain but dismissed the thought. He was already having a difficult time, sorely dis-appointed at not having succeeded yet as an independent tobacco farmer. I understood how it felt to have broken dreams.

"Tarry awhile then, sir," I said, and set down to fetching and preparing the leaf juice and other ingredients. Ganter watched me all along, his eyes following me twitchily, still perspiring.

"So, you think you got away, eh? From the real work, the dirty stuff?" He gestured towards the fields.

I did not reply to that.

Ganter continued: "I warrant you that the doctor will tire of you and send you back someday—set you to the work you are meant to be doing. And I too might still get you for the murder of Archer Walsh."

His jeering tone provoked me. "Do you or do you not want the jimson, Master Ganter?" I asked. "Mind that, for now, I am the only one to give it to you."

He would not brook my insolence, he replied, he had only come to get what he had already paid my master for.

And he settled back and waited, still following my every movement with his eyes. In less than an hour, I gave him the anodyne mixture and was glad to see his retreating back.

I also knew that Bristol, Cuffee, and the others were aweary of Ganter's brutal control. Work on Adams's Grove was hard and unrelenting. Master Adams was still in London. Master Menefie visited occasionally to see if all was going well at his nephew's farm, and although he too was a taskmaster, he mostly left Ganter to rule the roost.

At the Crossed Keyes, Bristol told us he was tired of being man to master.

"Let's run away," Flynn eagerly interrupted. "I have been telling you boys for a long time that we should . . ."

"Hold your tongue, Flynn Keough," Bristol cut in. "I have other notions—better than your half-baked scheme. Remember how I told you fellows about the men in the Northern Neck protesting because of the bad victuals they were supplied by their master? We will do the same—we will protest against Ralph Ganter's treatment of us—the bad food, the overwork, all of it."

"Yes, we will protest," Cuffee spoke up unexpectedly. "It will signal to the masters that they cannot do to their servants as they wish."

And we fell silent, contemplating his words. Above us, the western sky was red as if a spark from a musket had set it on fire. I too was momentarily touched by its glow, before it flickered and died.

"How is the curing trade going?" Cuffee asked, turning to me.

"It is good," I said eagerly.

"In England, some people say there is no need of physic to cure certain conditions—they say that the king's hand placed on a disease can heal well enough," Flynn said, his pipe in hand, watching the smoke delicately coil up and outward.

"I know—I have read about it," I replied. "'Tis called the Royal Touch. It is supposed to be a reliable method to cure scrofula or the King's Evil. Some even say it can cure rheumatism, fevers, blindness, convulsions, and goiter."

"You have certainly studied your books, Tony," Cuffee teased.

"But a king—even a king of England—is no miracle healer. The King's Touch is blind superstition!" I said, suddenly very indignant. "Only physic can cure illness—and some ailments cannot be cured even with physic!"

I noticed some men looking at me, and murmuring amongst themselves. Some of them were strangers and did not know that I was Doctor Herman's assistant. They must have wondered what I knew to talk about physic.

Doctor John Pott, the man who had first told Master Walsh and me about the western passage, was among the first physicians to settle in the colony. He had arrived in the year 1620 or thereabouts, and because there was such a great need for medical men, he was awarded great quantities of land. Over the years, he had grown to become an important personage in Jamestown and among the first to farm in Middle Plantation. My master did not harbor much affection for him. He told me that Doctor Pott had used his knowledge to poison a number of Indians during a ceremony held to sign a treaty with the English. This was in retaliation for the 1622 Indian massacre of the settlers.

"Did he really do that?" I asked.

Doctor Herman shrugged. "Pott was cleared of charges, but who else present at that meeting knew enough of toxins and their efficacy? Surely not the other members of the English party, who cannot tell piss from poison."

He paused. "It was an abhorrent act. Yes, they were Indians, and men hold the Indians to be baser than them. But a doctor's paramount and only charge is to heal. Injury, even negligence—he should never be guilty of those wrongs."

Doctor Herman had already told me about the solemn oaths of physicians—that of the Jewish doctor Moses Maimonides, who wrote that Providence had appointed doctors to *watch over the life and health of all of God's creatures*, and also of the oath in the Hippocratic Corpus: *I will do no harm . . . Neither will I administer a poison to anybody when asked to do so, nor will I suggest such a course.*

One evening we were walking about in Jamestown after visiting a man suffering from grievous pains in the belly. Our patient was in agony, and we had given him physic to soothe his pains. Doctor Herman was of the opinion that the caecum attached to his entrails had probably burst and was flooding his stomach with blood and pus.

The streets of Jamestown were getting more crowded by the day, it seemed, with migrants arriving by the shipload and new homes and warehouses being erected. They were calling it James Cittie these days. But the ground was still muddy and damp, and, just beyond, the wilderness still pressed in, as if it would, even after decades of settlement, drive the colonists into the sea. As my master and I walked, darkness fell and the stars appeared like little fires in the firmament.

A tall, imposing gentleman on a horse stopped alongside us. I recognized him as Doctor Pott. He took off his hat to my master. "Good day, Doctor Herman," he said.

My master bowed to him.

"I hear you are working wondrous cures these days, sir," Doctor Pott continued. "And with a moor for an apprentice too. Is this the fellow?" He gestured towards me. He clearly did not remember his previous encounter with Master Walsh and myself.

Doctor Herman did not say a word.

"And I hear you are spreading it about that purgings are not always desirable. How can that be when the authorities from Galen onwards have maintained that the health of the body is based on the balance of the humors, and that balance is best achieved by purging?"

My master replied courteously. "We can only suggest lighter purges and at greater intervals. We are not against purging itself. In fact, we recently saved a man's life through purging alone."

Doctor Pott opened his mouth as if he would continue the argument but appeared to change his mind. "Well, a Jamestown street is no place for a philosophical debate. But . . ." He looked directly at me before turning to the doctor again. "A moor for an apprentice . . . ?" he said wonderingly. "In my opinion, such men are best suited for the fields."

With that he bowed and went his way, and my master launched into a description of an anatomical theater he had witnessed in Paris where a cadaver was opened, revealing a ruptured caecum resulting in acid and corroding material blocking the abdominal cavity, much like what he believed had happened to the patient whose side we had just left. And so forth.

When the unfortunate Jamestown patient with the burst caecum died soon after, we were not surprised to hear the news. But apparently some folks were. A day or two later, I was at the Crossed Keyes with Cuffee and Flynn when a group of men came in, some white men and two Africans. Soon there was heavy drinking, and one particularly loudmouthed man they called Joe Miller lurched about pouring ale into strangers' cups. He stopped by a group near where I sat.

"Do not think I am drunk, my friends," he slurred.

"We do not say a word, Joe," a man replied, grinning.

"I mourn for my friend—Will Carter. He died yesterday. A grievous death!"

The group of men murmured assent.

Will Carter was the man with the burst organ, Doctor Herman's patient and mine.

"I have heard that he need not have perished," someone spoke up. "That he could be alive now sitting here drinking with us."

"Poor fellow dreamt of returning soon to London, where he had a wife and young 'uns waiting."

I wondered who the woman I'd seen weeping by the deathbed had been. Will Carter had apparently found another wife in Virginia.

"The physicians killed him," Joe declared, a sudden fury in his voice.

"That they did."

And there was a murmur of assent from the group. I suppose that is when I should have quietly left.

"The physicians in Virginia are charlatans and cheats," Joe continued. "And I heard that the bastard Joseph Herman took for his fees all that Will had left."

"The German dog and his moorish assistant!"

"The moor is a slimy one," another man added. "He sold a powder to the sailor Noah Giles, who was in perfect health, and killed him as well."

And suddenly, someone was pointing at me and saying, loudly and angrily, "There he is—the selfsame apprentice—bold as can be, drinking as if his was a clear conscience."

And although I had my gaze fixed on my cup, I felt a half dozen pairs of eyes looking at me.

Joe came up to me. "Sirrah, you are the one, are you not? The doctor's servant?"

I nodded and continued to sip my drink.

"Is it true that you refused to purge my sick friend, Will Carter? A purge would have saved poor Will—even Doctor Pott thinks so. C'mon, deny it now!"

"We followed the proper course," I said shortly. "Will Carter was very sick and there was no saving him."

"*Proper course*—he says." I felt the spittle fly out of Joe's lips and land on my face. "What would you know of the *proper course*?"

"And the other day I heard him speak ill of the king himself," someone said. "He denied the divinity of the monarch and said that the Royal Touch cannot heal!"

More murmurs. "His Majesty cannot heal, but *you* can?"

I don't believe Joe Miller cared about the Royal Touch or even for the dead man as much as he claimed. He might have even gone his way after a few more rumblings, if Ganter had not strolled up that very instance. I saw him surveying the scene swiftly.

"What has my Tony done now?" he drawled, sitting himself down on a bench. "I was his master, lads, till I got rid of him for spite and impertinence. And to this day I am of the suspicion that he murdered his next master." And Ganter proceeded to pick at his teeth.

"I knew he was a bad 'un before I even knew him," Joe said. "Master Ganter further confirms it."

Ganter sighed and nodded.

Joe put a hand on my shoulder. "I could never abide Turks," he announced, bending towards me, and I could feel his hot stale breath.

I did not bother to tell him that I was no Turk. There was no point. I sipped my drink and kept mum.

"Nor could I abide Persians, or Moriscos, or Mahometans," he went on.

And then he shot his arm out and hit me full on the nose. I felt the blood, sticky and metallic, on my upper lip. My cup toppled over and the ale spilt across the crude wood of the table. I bunched my hands in fists and contemplated my next move.

The blow I received from Joe was all it took. The other men came over to where I sat:

"I hate Saracens."

"And Mahometans."

"I hate moors."

"And orientals."

"I hate Powhatans."

"And gypsies."

Arabs and Asiatics . . . Berbers and Mullatoes and Jews.

All the world's races coalesced in me. The hue of my skin, my race, both of them in-between and indeterminate, made me every person these men despised, feared, or knew nothing about. I was the monumental other, the stranger.

They came slowly first, and then moved faster, some four or five of them. A blow took me on the chest, winding me. I fell on my knees struggling for breath, while they laughed drunkenly. I staggered up and hit out at someone. He flew backwards, which seemed to infuriate his mates. One of them grabbed me by my coat and slammed me against the wall. I felt the impact of the wood on the back of my head and the blood rushing upwards.

"Never trust a tawny moor!" someone snarled.

"Never trust an Indian!"

"Don't trust a moor who can read!" someone else added.

"*Can* he read?"

And one of them laughed, a slightly maniacal chortle, and others joined him. Someone tugged at my hair, and I grabbed for his, and we were like a pair of hoydens scrabbling by a village well. All along Ganter stayed where he was, sipping the ale someone had brought him, studying the scene, his face expressionless. The men dealt me punches on the face, shoulders, and back. Where were Flynn and Cuffee? Why were they not stepping in on my behalf?

Soon one of the African men joined—and then another. One of them jabbed me lightly in the gut and another stamped my foot.

"Thinks he's better than us!" said a black man I did not recall meeting before.

"Villainous toad . . ."

"Heathen prick . . ."

"Idolator . . ."

"Devil worshipper . . ."

"Barbarian . . ."

I later wondered why they had picked on me. Because I had been involved in the treatment of the dead man? Or because I was the only one of my kind: a freak, a monster, from a land no one even fully believed in? Because they had no one else to beat up—these men, black and white, who found themselves here in this place, led here by want, force, or deception? Men crushed and neglected themselves, who felt, as they came down on me with their fists and feet, fully alive for once: the red blood coursing through their veins, the clean breath in and out of their lungs, the agility and lightness of their limbs. Had they felt, at last, some small flush of success?

"Kill the Mahometan bastard!"

That was Joe Miller again and that was still him dealing me a mighty kick. At that moment I wanted to kill him, I cared not if I ended up hanged—I would kill him. I hated this man I barely knew. I lunged forward. Someone else stepped in the way and I dealt him a blow on the nose and felt the crunch and wetness. It was very gratifying. And then someone else smashed my eye and pushed me backwards so I fell to the ground. And they were kicking my ribs with their heavy-booted feet.

Even Cuffee and Flynn have joined these louts in beating me, I thought, and that thought hurt more than the damage to my body.

And that was the last I remembered till I woke up to see a dark face and a light one hovering over mine. I had been moved outside the tavern and was shivering violently.

"You were beaten up, man," Cuffee said, quite needlessly.

"Thought you had given up the ghost, in truth," Flynn added.

"Nonsense! He was not beaten *that* bad," Cuffee retorted.

And they tried to sit me up and were thrusting a cup of ale at my lips.

"Where were you two?" I asked after shooting out the spittle mixed with blood and feeling my teeth with my tongue to see if any of them had fallen out.

"I just stepped out to piss," Cuffee said apologetically. "And then I began to feel a bit dizzy with the drink and sat down to clear my head. And Flynn here had disappeared behind the trees with some tipsy tart," he added accusingly.

Flynn looked sheepish. "I came back right after. We tried telling them you were not a Mahometan, nor a devil worshipper either."

"That you were a heathen of the East Indian faith . . . or something like that," Cuffee added.

They hauled me up and we began the walk home. They were on either side propping me up as I hobbled, my legs shuddering, snot and blood flowing from my nose in one watery mix, my heart sore. They fell into silence.

"You forget I am baptized," I mumbled through stiff lips. "I am as Christian as you bastards."

They did not reply to that. They aided me all the way back, murmuring words of consolation. I was grateful to them, for their breath close to my shoulders, their warmth against my sides, the steady plodding of their boots. However, I had never felt this alone.

The pain kept me up that night, and the next morn I left the cabin at dawn to breathe the more wholesome open air. Indeed, it was not daybreak yet—the darkness sat over the world like a shroud. I crossed the field, a slight figure in the gloom. Someone could well catch sight of me, mistake me for a thief, and fire. And I would die right there amidst the tobacco. I brooded over the incidents of the night before, and thought that in spite of my name, my new religion, my new learning, I would remain a perpetual stranger in this land.

Behind a thicket of trees, I caught a glimpse of a cabin. It was lopsided—one half of it sinking into the earth. A candle shone in the window and I was invited by the comforting glow. There would be someone inside and there would be a fire, perhaps, and warmth and friendship too. I could not imagine how I had not seen a cabin in that particular spot before. I hurried towards it, curious. I imagined a fire crackling, a leaf or two blown in by the wind. I knew he would be waiting there—the Man Who Would Not Die. Biding his time, patiently. That was his way; he appeared in unexpected places. I hurried my steps, not knowing if I felt fear, anticipation, or grief. But when I neared the cabin there was just a hole in the dark, an emptiness.

I shook my head in exasperation. Too often, I felt myself surrounded by apparitions. I wondered if I had an illness. Surely such a man should not be a physician. *Lovers and madmen have such seething brains . . .* Master Shakespeare had written in that same play, which was perhaps the only play I would ever see or read. After a long time, I thought of the little Indian boy when he grew to be a man, no longer as lovely as he had been as a child. *What happened to the Indian lad, Tony?* That was Little Sammy asking again, concerned, curious. Standing there, alone, I was suddenly terrified by the unbounded world of the playwright, the one in which the fairy and the human merged, in which an Indian boy found himself in English woods, a vastness in which one is forever adrift, where echoes travel long distances.

My face and head still hurt as the day wore on, and my face was covered with bruises. Master Herman was away, and I had to treat my own wounds. I remembered the syrup of the jimsonweed that Ganter took—it would help soothe the poundings and it would take the edge off my humiliation and anger. The doctor had got a fresh supply of the smooth, toothed leaves and the prickly fruit, and I boiled them in water and extracted the dark green juice, which was bitter but still somehow pleasant, like the gourds cooked and eaten with rice in my homeland. I sipped some and then sipped more, and more.

The next few hours. I remember them and do not remember. The trees stretched towards the firmament, and the river reared up like a bucking horse and overflowed its banks. In the world of purple sky and violet earth I was visited by my previous lives—young East Indian in Virginia, wandering fields of loneliness, a lad in London, a child in Armagon and Mylapore, Place of Peacocks. And preceding that . . . an emperor, a knave, a slayer, the slayed, a sinner, a saint . . . and even earlier, a fish, a flower, a boar, a bee . . . Life before life before life, and all of them I had lived. The cycle persisted; there was no escaping it. The *God's Gift* was a womb—it had sucked me in and then heaved me out into this life, the one I was struggling to learn to live.

A distant rumble, like a drumbeat. It grew closer. I had been so wrapped in my vision I had failed to notice that the sky had grown ominous. Then the clouds opened and the downpour was torrential. I did not run for cover, nor did I flinch at the next thunderclap, which broke directly above me, and the lightning that covered the sky. I was soaked to the skin and I could feel my feet squelching in my tattered boots. I pulled them off. I tugged off my shirt too and stood there half-naked, my slight body the color of the mud that was now swirling around me in rivulets. The blood and tears of yesterday, the grime of centuries, ran off my limbs.

And, behold, I, even I, do bring a flood of waters upon the earth, to destroy all flesh, wherein is the breath of life, from under heaven . . . That was in Parson Blair's Bible.

Little, hard pellets of ice had started to fall, and they stung on my bruised skin. I reveled in the pain.

I cannot tell after how long I opened my heavy eyelids, and found myself prone beneath a tree. The air was still, there was no sign of it having rained, and a small, stony moon sailed aloft in the sky. There had been no storm, no soaking. In fact, I had not moved. By my side was the cup with the dregs of the weed at the very bottom, green and sludge-like. A line from the *Midsummer* play came to me unsummoned: *I have had a dream, past the wit of man to say what dream it was . . .*

"Tony!"

Someone was calling. I was in no mood to answer.

Once again: "Where are you, lad? Are you home?"

It was my master. He must have returned. He called for me again and yet again, his voice growing more impatient. I heard him moving towards the dovecote and the beehives, circling the herb garden. But I stayed where I was, not calling back, not wanting to be found.

"*Tony . . . !*"

THIRTEEN

When Doctor Herman asked about my injuries, I told him a little of what had occurred: how some men had been distraught at Will Carter's death and how they had set upon me. I omitted some of the details, such as the names I had been called. I could not brook sharing with the doctor the full extent of my humiliation.

"Benighted oafs . . ." he fumed, and might have taken it to the sheriff if I had not convinced him that little would come of it.

One evening well after my bruises had healed, I was out by Adams's Grove when I saw the child Sancho walking along a path. The scratches on his arms indicated that he had squeezed himself through trees and undergrowth.

"Where are you going, lad?" I asked.

He looked down, tongue-tied with shyness. He was always a quiet boy, wary and reserved, although he had learned to speak English well.

"It will be dark soon," I said. "You ought to be home." And indeed, the night was coming down hastily.

"I ain't afraid of the dark, Tony," he said. "The woods do not frighten me. I am afeared only when I have to cross Taylor's Bridge. I worry then that the headless toll keeper will come out and chase me."

I remembered Little Sam's nightmares. "There is no headless toll keeper, Sancho," I said. "Don't you go filling your mind with such things."

He did not respond to that. "They say you are an East India Indian," he then said. "I do not know what that means. Does that signify you are a black man? I asked Bristol that, and I could not comprehend what he said." He grinned shyly.

"What did Bristol say?" I asked curiously.

"He said that mostly you are black and then sometimes you are less black."

"That is a confusing answer," I agreed. And, indeed, it was.

He stood there looking at me, with his big eyes, like a doe's. The luminosity of them reminded me of the girl Lydia, the sweetness of his gaze of Sam.

"See how my hair is wet, Tony," he said.

I looked closely and indeed it was, the tight coils of it covered with water droplets.

"Did you slip and fall in a pond?" I asked.

"No," he said simply, "Master Ganter dunked my head in the wooden trough filled with water for the hog and held me down till I was a-choking."

"Did not Bristol and the others try to stop him?"

"Bristol and them were not by. The master never hurts me when they are by."

Cold fingers wrapped themselves around my heart. "How else does he hurt you, Sancho? You can tell me."

"He beats me sometimes, Tony."

"And nothing else? He does nothing else to you?"

I knelt down and looked into his eyes. He stared back, wordless.

"You will tell me, lad? You will come to me and tell me if he hurts you?" I could hear the urgency in my voice; I could not tell if he did.

He nodded shyly.

I took his small, sweaty hand and walked him back to the cabins. A flock of lapwings flew over us, so low that we could hear the rustle of their wings.

"When I first saw you, I mistook you for a half blood or something," he said. "There were many such on my island."

I smiled. "I have been mistaken for many things," I said. "Sometimes people think I am a toad, a toad who has miraculously grown a lot of hair, or an owl with long legs, or maybe a strange kind of monkey."

I was glad to have made him laugh. He was too grave for so young a lad.

Ganter's pain kept him up at nights, he said, it gnawed deep into his bones. He came to see Doctor Herman on a Sunday morning, bearing a small bag of tobacco. Before he left with the syrup of jimson, my master advised him to take less of it in the future. Ganter must find other ways to deal with the pain, he said.

After Ganter's departure, I left for the chapel. Doctor Herman was no churchgoer himself, but Bristol, Cuffee, Flynn, Martin, and Dick joined me along the way. The chapel was a new one, although still not more than a slightly expansive cabin. The farmers occupied the seats up front and the white servants sat behind them. The Africans and I huddled at the back.

Give peace in our time, O Lord, the parson read out from his book. And then, perhaps because some agues and fluxes were being reported around the farms, and several cases of extreme drunkenness, he prayed for sound bodies and minds: *Know ye not that your body is the temple of the Holy Ghost . . . and ye are not your own? For ye are bought with a price: therefore glorify God in your body, and in your spirit, which are God's.* Except for a few intent listeners, the congregation sat unmoved.

We closed our eyes in prayer. Dick, I knew, was praying that his Virginia dream would come true, that the lanky lad from London would one day be the owner of lands and guns; Flynn surely pleaded that he would succeed in getting away to the Dutch settlement; Bristol was not even pretending to pray; Cuffee was praying hard. I squeezed my eyes shut and cast around for what I most wanted. As always, older prayers from another life came to me unbidden:

God of the curved tusk and mighty body . . . He whose glory is that of a thousand suns . . .

. . . God of the leaf-shaped spear, long and trembling . . .

. . . Goddess, daughter of the mountain, destroyer of the demon . . .

And the old deities pressed around me, grotesque and grand, blue- and red-skinned, six-headed and four-armed, fires ablaze in their mouths, stars embedded in their eyes, planets in the palms of their hands, bearing weapons, lotuses, conch shells, overflowing pots of gold. They whispered and demanded to know if I had forgotten them.

"Leave me alone, you lot," I said to them. "I have become Christian— I worship a single god, who is God."

But they laughed and murmured; they reached out to touch me, urgent and insistent. The martyred Saint Thomas joined them, still bleeding gently from his side, and then the One God too, white and glowing: *For thine is the kingdom, the power, and the glory, forever and forever . . .* I realized then that they were all—every single one—mine to worship as I pleased. There was a new freedom in that . . . And perhaps, truly, I worshipped none of them any longer. I believed only in the rhythms and volitions of Nature, which perhaps occurred regardless of any higher will. I opened my eyes and was relieved that

I was still seated in the plain wooden chapel, with Bristol to my left, just starting to snore softly.

As was the habit of many Virginians, we proceeded from prayerhouse to tavern. It would have been sensible of me to avoid the place, but where else did one go hereabouts for leisure? There were a fair number of people at the Crossed Keyes, many of them new fellows, lean-faced, shiftless, drinking more than they should. I asked Bristol about them. He told me that more and more men were not being given their freedom dues at the end of their terms of service, or were given pieces of land so close to Indian territory that farming was far too perilous to keep at, forcing them to return to Jamestown to seek service, much like Ganter had done.

"The landed men are uneasy about all these other fellows hanging about," Bristol said. "These men, who are neither landed nor servants, too many of them carrying guns."

"Why are they uneasy?" I asked. "They are white men after all—they are not foes like Indians." Bristol only shrugged at that.

"And did some servants really rebel in the northern peninsula because they were not given adequate food?" I pressed him.

"Yes, servants work hard and must eat well. We are but men," he said.

"These men were not frightened of their masters' wrath?"

"Masters too are but men," Bristol said, and got up to refill his cup.

The morning wore on. Drinkers spilled outside the tavern. It was a fine, warm day and it was even more pleasant outside. The groups of men were getting a little boisterous, and I did not feel easy joining them, especially after the previous time. Slightly disgruntled, I sat by myself on the stump of a tree nursing my pot of watered-down ale. The sun rose high in the firmament and I felt the sweat start on my face and back. I had become Virginian enough that the heat, although not nearly as searing as that of my homeland, made me perspire.

I saw a small shape come out of the blackhaw bushes and then pop back in, as if startled. And then a dark head peeped out from the leaves and looked around, like a cautious, little wild creature checking its surroundings. It was Sancho. I took my cup and went to see what he wanted.

"Sancho!" I called into the undergrowth. "I see you! It is me, Tony!"

He came out and I saw that he was shivering as if it were frigid cold. "What is the matter, lad?" I asked. "Are you ailing?"

He did not say anything and I extended my drink to him. "Take a sip. It might warm you up."

He simply bent his head low before me, and I saw a red and bloodied spot just about the crown. The coils of his hair stuck to the wound.

"Who did that to you, Sancho?" I asked, although I already knew.

Sancho did not weep as he told his tale. Master Ganter had been in a foul mood because of his painful shoulder and back; he had cursed a bit, cuffed Sancho a few times. And when the lad had tried to run, Ganter had suddenly exploded in rage and picked up a stone and flung it at him, striking him on the head, all along screaming terrible oaths.

"And then?" I asked, breathless. "And what did Ganter do next?" *Many years ago, a small boy lit a candle in the dark. Ganter had similarly erupted, and then—*

"He went back to sleep, and I came to find you."

"Come along," I said. "I will dress your wounds."

Doctor Herman came in just as I was cleaning Sancho up.

"New patient, eh?" he asked.

"Yes, sir. This is Sancho. He was beaten by the overseer. I will now take him back to his friends."

"And is young Sancho paying us for this service?"

Sancho stood there, so small, blinking.

"He cannot pay, sir."

"We expect those we treat to pay us, Tony," my master said wearily. "We are in a trade."

He was right, but I could not abandon the boy for that.

"Sancho looked to me for help, sir. I have to aid him."

The doctor did not say anything to that. Later, he might lecture me on my foolishness—do not give your services gratis, lad; what is more, do not interfere between masters and servants.

I told Bristol and Cuffee that they needed to take care of Sancho and come between him and Ganter when they could. The overseer had grown unpredictable, they said. He moaned incessantly about his pain. If he did not have the syrup at hand, he was irritable and so agitated that he could not sleep even in the nights and wandered about the farm restlessly. When he had his medicine he sat in a blissful stupor, oblivious to all around him.

"Watch over Sancho," I repeated. "Watch over him."

They assured me they would, but I was troubled at the thought of what could happen to the boy, what had possibly already happened.

Other servants—both black and white—occasionally sought me out after that. While some masters sent ailing servants to doctors because servants were valuable and good money had been paid to bring them over, others were reluctant to pay the physician's fee only to cure a menial and preferred to leave the cure to nature and time. So, I furtively treated sick men and women for coughs, toothaches, dysenteries, and other things which visited rich and poor alike, and often strike the poor with greater force. Sometimes Doctor Herman found out, especially when a good quantity of medicine was used up. At times he was annoyed; at other times it did not seem to trouble him too much.

I was the first to wake up in the morn, the first to bound out of the cabin, to splash my face with water in the pail. The moon was still in the sky even as the mild sun rose in the horizon. The light felt soft and liquid. I stopped to look at my herbs, picked and crushed a leaf or two between my fingers—the minty catnip with its feathery foliage, the pungent pennyroyal or squaw mint, the hyssop with its pink and blue flowers: *purge me with hyssop, and I shall be clean* . . . Where had I heard that line . . . ? It was still, so quiet that I could almost hear my heart's steady beat. And then I heard footsteps—and there she was standing at the edge of the garden. I had not known she had returned from the home of her mistress's sister in the Northern Neck. She looked like she had hurried; her thick, dark hair was down to midback; her linen blouse had slipped off one shoulder, revealing the top of a soft, brown arm. I had not seen her for well-nigh a year, and the last time we had spoken, she had been vexed with me. Lydia.

She halted and looked towards the house, her face luminous, so lovely that it passed all description, and I knelt by the plants, unobserved, breathless. It was merely an instant but it remained with me, and the next day, and the next, and even later, I carried with me its radiance.

Then a bird, some eager warbler, shrieked loudly from a tree, and broke the silence. I moved, to indicate that I was there, so she would not be startled, and she, seeing me, permitted a smile to tug at her lips and adjusted her blouse, though she let her hair be.

"Tony," she said simply. And I was grateful for her smile, for coming.

She was back at the Pooles'. And because they needed the money, they had requested Doctor Herman to let her come over two or three days a week to do household chores. I was grateful to the doctor because it freed me of some of my duties, but above all I was simply glad that she had returned. Sancho had told her of my care of him, she said. And I supposed that was what made her set my past idiocies aside and feel kindly towards me.

"I am well on my way to learning the curing trade," I told her, so she would know that I had not been spending my time in folly.

"That is good. You are fortunate to be able to assist those in pain," she said.

"I am just learning," I replied.

"I wish I could learn too."

"I hear you already help women in childbirth. They said that's why you went to assist Mistress Poole's sister."

She nodded.

"I once knew another maid who was a midwife though she had never borne children herself," I said wonderingly.

It was a little later that Lydia told me she too had borne a child once. Four years ago—when she was fourteen or fifteen—when she still lived on the farm where she had been born, the one her parents had been brought to from across the sea.

"My parents had died, and I saw the servant men on the farm as my own people. How could I not? I had no other. Besides, I was born in Virginia and set myself as apart from the Africans who had come over the ocean. Later, when the mistress found out what had happened, she said I had been too friendly with the fellow, my behavior had been unseemly even, that every sensible maid or woman knew better."

It was true, she said, that the servant in question had been taken to court for forcing himself on her, but the judges determined that it was not really a rape. After all, they said, others were about when it happened, in the adjoining chamber, and no one else had heard Lydia cry out. Therefore, it could not have been against her will.

"We were sent to stand at the church door in white sheets, to do penance as all fornicators do. I was filled with shame, but he stood there with a smirk on his face, and when some of the passersby jeered, he laughed and told the men not to pretend they would have done any differently with a black hussy."

All this she told me in a low, expressionless voice.

She had discovered that she was with child soon after, had concealed her condition, denied it even to herself, even as her belly swelled. She had not known then that pennyroyal flowers would have cleared her womb. "Is that correct?" she asked me.

Yes, she was right. A mix of pennyroyal and wine could induce an abortment, or a mix of bloodwort and the bark of the red cedar.

She had been four months with child and still keeping her secret when she felt a sharp pain as she worked in the field. She had delivered it in the midst of the tobacco. It was born dead, of course. And after it was all over, her mistress had sent her away to the Pooles' farm. Before Lydia got into trouble again, she said.

"So here I am," she said. "Having learnt that a girl does not trust anyone but herself, does not laugh with men, even those who are not strangers."

"I am sorry," I said, feeling so wretched that I did not know what to say.

She smiled one of her rare, precious smiles and touched my arm, as if I was the one who needed comforting. "It is over now, Tony. I carried it inside me for a long time, my anger. But I rid myself of it, I purged myself—like you physicians do for ailing men. Do you not draw out what is inside, drive it out even, through your bloodlettings and vomitings and sweatings and clysters and such?" And she smiled once more.

"Yes," I said, smiling back. "Some of us have to cleanse ourselves out and start over. I thought it was only those who crossed the ocean, but it seems others such as you too must."

And then she appeared to want to talk of other things, for she asked me more questions of what I had learnt lately from Doctor Herman and his books.

Ganter came once more, bearing more tobacco and some corn.

"You cannot have more of the syrup, sir," I said with as much politeness as I could muster. "The doctor said so."

I stood at the door, and he peered over my shoulder. "Is your master at home?"

I shook my head and he stepped up to me, as if he would force his way in. Lydia, who was standing by, looked startled.

But Ganter did not push past me. Instead, he scowled and said in a voice raspier than usual, "When I first had the misfortune to lay eyes on you, you were a mere boy, a tadpole the color of the muck you had crawled out of." He thrust his chin towards me and I saw his jaw was clenched and a muscle above it twitching. "And now you think to deny me what I can pay for. Look here . . ." He thrust the bundle of tobacco at me. "I can bring more later."

"But, Master Ganter . . ."

His tone altered unexpectedly from enraged to wheedling: "Look at you now, Tony. Grown up and on your way to learning the curing trade. I knew you would make me proud. I was your first master, was not I? I cared for you—you surely remember, do you not?" I found him so repugnant that I gave him the syrup just to be rid of him. He clutched the container and hurried off. Lydia gazed at his retreating back, puzzled.

The next time I saw Ganter was when I was working with the other lads in Adams's Grove. Bristol and Martin, the white man who also worked on Adams's Grove, chose that morning to steal one of the three new piglets born on the farm. Ganter had talked of selling the young weaners and keeping just one for consumption. Bristol and Martin said that they were tired of their poor meals, they went to bed hungry too often, they said, and after a hard day's labor too. So, they took one of the young piglets into the copse of trees bordering the farm and slaughtered it. They brought pieces of roasted piglet to share with us.

"Where did that come from, man?" Cuffee asked, though we could guess.

"Do not ask questions—just eat!" urged Bristol, always the generous sort.

We refused at first, but then we could not resist and ate some, all along fearful of Ganter.

He emerged from his cabin, blinking in the morning light, looking as if he had woken from the dead. It was not till later in the day, when he was more himself, that he found out about the piglet. He was furious. He lashed out at Bristol and Martin, calling them lubberworts, turd eaters, sow fuckers, and whatnot. He first threatened to have them put in stocks in front of the chapel, after which he would keep them on bread and water.

He turned on Martin. "I should have known this was coming!" he said. "Do not think I have forgotten, sirrah, that you got your pox-ridden ass onto a ship straight out of Bridewell!"

It was surprising that none of us had known Martin had been in gaol—usually news of the old life follows a man to the New World. I looked at him with new interest and wondered what he had done. Killed a man perhaps. He seemed capable of it—I had always sensed a hidden violence behind that pale-faced blandness.

Martin satisfied my curiosity right away. "I was no murderer or assaulter of innocence," he told Ganter stiffly, his mouth pinched. "I was in gaol because of seizing a cart of grain to feed the hungry in the village—grain that was rightfully ours."

So, Martin had been a food rioter of the kind I had heard about in London. Not a major crime in my eyes. Ganter did not like Martin talking back to him like that. He looked ready to explode. The rest of us stood around, uneasy, thinking that somehow it would be our turn next. And then Bristol put his hand in his pocket and pulled out two little piglet ears, all bloody flesh and soft bristles, and flung them at the overseer's feet. He looked straight at Ganter, and when he spoke his voice was cool and steady. "Sir, you had promised us fresh meat a fortnight ago. And seeing it was not coming . . ."

It was too much for Ganter. He reached out and hit Bristol on the face, a quick, sharp blow dealt with a fist, strong enough to make Bristol bleed just below his eye. He then picked up a stick and lashed out at the two men, who raised their hands to cover their faces, but did not run. I could not help but notice that the stick fell on Bristol's shoulders more often. The lashing lasted only a minute or two. I stepped forward to help Bristol and Martin up, and Ganter turned to me as if he would lash me next, but then dropped the stick with an oath and turned away, wiping his sweaty palms on his breeches. Flies gathered thickly around the bloody piglet's ears.

Bristol was worse off, the skin on his shoulders raw and inflamed. But Martin seemed to be even angrier. Maybe he was irate that Ganter had revealed that he had been in gaol, or perhaps simply because Martin was also an Englishman and thought himself equal to the overseer, and so would not brook a beating.

I prepared quantities of my special salve to apply on their wounds, and even then they continued to fester.

Wildflowers grew in abundance in the open spaces where we did not plant tobacco and in clearings in the woods. That summer was ablaze with color: turtleheads, black-eyed Susans, butterfly weeds, and goldenrods. I remembered that valley of flowers hidden in the mountains, and how we had walked into that profusion. I then remembered Master Walsh and felt a pang, but it was a sweet sadness, like for a childhood friend whose life has simply taken a different road than my own. And because thought leads to thought, I remembered Little Sammy, and how he too would be close to being a man now, if he had lived. And Marge, how she had been so gentle with us, and Mary Bengal, how she must have, surely *should* have, escaped and gone back to her home by the Ganges. I remembered my amma, and for the first time the memory was not touched by grief. One must hold the departed in one's heart, I thought, but surely one must also bind oneself to the living . . . ? For a long time, I had lived vigilant, taut, in a state of hankering for what was not, foreseeing what lay ahead, fearfully wondering where I would slip, and how I would fall. But at that moment, I was content, glad to be strolling amidst the blooms, under the clear sky. I knew the names of these plants and of the trees, and I felt I had made them my own, part of some new interior landscape. I gazed at myself in a still pond and I thought that the countenance that gazed back at me was that of a good-looking youth, with thick black curls, and large, dark eyes, and skin that was akin to the color of gold, a countenance that was neither lean nor round. I could imagine a young woman finding me attractive . . . a woman like Lydia.

I picked a bunch of flowers. They were of different colors, shapes, and sizes, and although I intended an elegant posy, it ended up being a very large bouquet. Blood-red and sunlight-yellow blossoms filled my arms in profusion. I added, from my medicinal herb garden, purple lavender, violet rosemary, and bright pink bee balm—all of which promised good health and happiness. They tickled my lips; their fragrance was both heavy and sharp in my nostrils. I stumbled back to the farm carrying my treasure. I did not think about Doctor Herman seeing me and asking what I thought I was doing, or of someone else stopping by and jeering at me for being such a knucklehead. Lydia was by herself, washing our master's clothes in a trough and hanging them out to dry. I came and stood by her, and could not say a word.

She looked up and pushed away a damp curl with the back of a hand. She had been working hard, but her skin, like mine, would not flush with exertion; it would not display on its surface the motion of the blood, the state of the head and the heart; it was designed to conceal rather than to lay bare, to keep secrets. But her lovely eyes looked my way, and I thought they lit up. She had tucked her skirt up slightly so it would not get soaked. I caught a glimpse of an ankle, and that was all it took for my heart to be pounding.

"That's a lot of flowers you got!" she laughed.

I had nothing witty to say to that, as lovers do in the plays and such stories. I stood there like a fool, half smothered by the blossoms and foliage I carried.

"Are they for a sweetheart, Tony?" she said in a gently teasing voice. She was the kind of maid who rarely teased.

"Will you take them?" I asked, and was surprised at how steady my voice was.

The world paused. Around us, the trees heavy with their summer growth; the clouds languidly wandering above; the waters burbling in the nearby brook; the squawking, screeching, singing birds that had suddenly gone quite, quite still; the spirits of my friends, Little Sammy and Mad Marge, that hovered around kindly and curiously.

"Yes," she said quietly. "I will."

FOURTEEN

I was on the way back from cutting a swelling from a man's palm when I ran into Bristol. He was walking towards the woods and beckoned me to follow. It had been the first time performing an operation of that type on my own, and I was filled with triumph. I gave Bristol an account of how it had gone: how the cabin had been dark and how the single candle would not stand upright on the table; how the patient had to hold it up with one hand, all along gritting his teeth and looking away, while I sawed at the ulcer on the other; how I had got the swelling off satisfactorily and dressed the wound.

In spite of my excitement, I sensed that Bristol was preoccupied and listening with but half an ear. We had reached a clearing, and I was surprised to see servants from other nearby farms gathered. Martin stood in their midst addressing them. Most of the group was white men, but there were a few Africans as well. There was Cuffee, of course, another Tony, one Caesar, and one Bernard.

I learned that the gathering was mainly Bristol's idea. Bristol, who had long been seething about the servants' lot, the relentless round of punishing labor, the bad diet. But he needed a white man by his side to garner the support of the other white men, and who better than Martin, who had been humiliated by Ganter's recent thrashing?

"How many of you lot have firearms?" Martin asked in his usual brusque fashion.

No man present did. Muskets were not to be picked off trees, and working ones were even rarer.

"We need to get hold of weapons," Martin said. And he repeated what was commonplace knowledge in Virginia: muskets are the great equalizers; the man at the end of your muzzle might have all the land in the world, his grandfather might be the Duke of Norfolk himself, but a musket made him no better than a quivering rabbit.

"Except I would not get the noose for shooting a coney, but a duke would be another matter!" a wag shouted out, and some of the men laughed.

"This is no time for clowning, man!" Martin remarked testily. "We have grave business at hand."

I noticed that Dick had not been invited. Martin had once told me that Dick was a despicable knave who thought that the sun rose in the master's shithole, who only waited for the day *he* would wake up to find himself lord of the manor with servants of his own to work to death.

Bristol then spoke up: complaints and petitions had been sent to England by other servants across the colony, but little had come of those. Hence the proposal at hand was to gather in the clearing and march together, first to raid the cabin at the edge of Adams's Grove where food stores were kept and, they suspected, muskets as well. And then on to the Pooles' farm, where they would hold the master and mistress hostage till their demands for a better diet and more humane treatment were met.

"Are we going to slay them—the masters?" someone else asked.

"No," replied Martin. No blood was to be shed. We were not barbarians— we would be moved by higher things—our cry would be *Liberty and Freedom*.

"Do we cry out the slogan as we march through the fields?" the same wag asked, or it could have been another one.

"No, you fools—we must be silent as we march!"

That was Bristol, tense with purpose, outraged at their levity, exasperated that he had to turn to this group of homespun country bumpkins to lead his uprising. I looked around: the white men's faces were pale in the moonlight, with a bluish tinge to them, the Africans and I grew perfectly black—we could have stepped into the trees and vanished.

"You must keep the cry in your hearts. We are Englishmen. We were promised much and we have endured more, and we have made but a poor living with our hard labor in this terrible wilderness," Martin said, his tone low and passionate.

He seemed to have forgotten that not everyone was English in the gathering and that even some of the Englishmen had not been promised anything, just lifted and brought here. They were simply necessary parts of a grander project, a dream that had not been theirs—not when they had set out from London or Bristol or whichever port their ships had sailed from. But by the end of the night, something about Martin's and Bristol's tone and serious demeanor made clear the fire that burned in their bellies—and no one laughed again. They decided to meet next midweek—once more before the big night of the march.

The men split into small groups to go homewards. I felt that I would rather be left alone, but Bristol, Cuffee, and Martin seemed to expect me to walk back with them.

"I am glad you are with us, Tony," Martin said.

I did not reply. My confused thoughts got in the way of speech. Even in the gloom, I knew that Bristol was looking at me inquiringly.

The next day Cuffee, Bristol, and I were returning from the Crossed Keyes together when we heard the click-clock of hoofs. When the horse and rider approached closer, I saw that it was Dick. Ganter sometimes lent him the horse to ride. He slowed the beast down to a walk and looked at us—three moors and he, the only white man in this lonely place. He hesitated, and only because I knew him so well and for so long, I saw a pinch of fear in his eyes, a barely perceptible shadow, and it shocked me that he felt that way.

Our small group parted, pressing ourselves against the hedges to let him pass. I saw him relax at that, and he went by murmuring greetings to us. I was not about to let him pass us that way—I stepped up and laid a hand on his horse's back. The others walked ahead.

"'Tis a long time since we talked, Dick."

He nodded. "That it is," he replied.

"'Tis many years since we climbed onto that ship."

"Years flown by, Tony," he said, and halted his horse to get off and walk with me. I was glad at that—I did not enjoy looking up to him as he sat astride the tall mare.

"Remember the sights we saw?" he continued. "The lights dancing up on the masts? How we gaped and wondered, us lads!"

"Yes, we did indeed. And do you remember the witch?"

He looked puzzled for a minute, as if he did not, before he nodded. When he spoke, he said, "In close to three years I will be done with my service, Tony."

"So what will come next?" I asked.

"I am not going to hire myself out. I have asked Master Menefie to give me my dues, and since land don't seem to come with that anymore, I have asked him to give me a loan to purchase some acres."

"And will he?"

"He has promised. He understands ambition. As does Ganter."

"Ganter . . . 'haps he does. You have had him for an overseer for many years now. Would you say he is a good man to work for?"

"He is as good an overseer as any, man. We cannot expect anything more."

And I wondered then, as I'd wondered many times before, if Ganter had spared Dick what he had inflicted on Sammy and me. Surely he must have—Dick would abhor him otherwise, just as I did. I almost asked Dick then, but could not brook the thought, even after all this while, of telling another what I had experienced. So I only said: "He beats the men—he is especially harsh to Bristol and Cuffee. I cannot help but notice that. He hates me too, but I am fortunate that I am no longer his. And there is young Sancho . . ."

"Ganter is not faultless, Tony. But 'tis no easy task keeping discipline among these wastrels. As for the men, they should keep their eyes to what is to come."

And he shared with me again his hopes—of land, of harvests of his own, of making it good. Dick's face was alight with the setting sun and with the fiery glow of his longings.

"And you too, Tony. Once you complete your apprenticeship you will be set up in the curing trade. I have already heard from many that you are skilled at your work."

I felt a touch of pride at that. There was nothing I wanted more than to be known for my work. I felt hope too, the golden glow of things to come. Then I remembered why I was talking to him.

"Some of the others do not feel they have such good prospects, Dick."

He shrugged at that. The men should work hard and look to the future, he repeated.

"And if things do not work out for you, Tony, if men will not accept you as a physician, you being a moor and all, know that I always will have a place for you in my farm when I have it."

I did not know what to say to that. And we walked on, talking of this and that. Sammy walked with us for a while, completing the trio—Sammy, as he had been, a small, smooth-cheeked lad; Sammy as he would be if he had lived and grown, as I saw him in my mind's eye, a young man with golden beard and blue eyes. And then he went his way, taking the road only the dead know of. Dick proceeded his own way, and I went on to the doctor's.

I wanted to confide in Lydia, to ask her if I should throw my lot in with Bristol, Martin, and the others. Or if I should stay away, quietly? If a rebellion against the masters was also a rebellion against my own, the man to whom I owed a debt of gratitude? I wanted to ask Lydia this and more, but when the time came I did not. We talked instead of other things. Just because she was born a woman, she said, people expected her to do what female servants did—cooking, fetching water, mending clothes, taking care of other people's children, and also working in the fields (because women were called upon to do it all). But she was not in the mind for that alone. She could read and write, and her first mistress, who taught her, had said that she was quick in learning. She too could and would study aspects of physic, especially compounding. And, indeed, of late, Lydia had used every opportunity to observe me mix and distill using the methods I had learnt from Doctor Herman, and together we pored over the doctor's tomes that described the properties of substances. It was a strange way to get close to a woman's heart, through talk of mercury and alum and sarsaparilla and such, but that was our way.

A farmer's daughter was brought to see the doctor once when Lydia was by. Her father said that she ate next to nothing—she seemed to be determined to wear herself down to the bone. Doctor Herman looked at the maiden sitting there, her gaze vacuous, the skin around her eyes dark on her pallid face, and diagnosed it as the green sickness, the virgin's disease, best cured by drinking metals mixed in white wine with sugar and spices.

"She also needs to marry," he whispered to the anxious father. "Relations with a man will cure her of it." The girl heard him, and I saw a look of rage pass over her face.

Later, I discussed the green sickness with Lydia. I had also read that it could be caused by the menstrual blood flowing backwards and building up in the womb in a festering swamp.

"Nonsense," she said firmly. "And relations with a man is no cure for any disease. The lass is melancholic because she lost her mother. Sometimes sickness is just caused by an aching heart."

And so, we disagreed sometimes and other times agreed. I told her about the Christian saint in my homeland—Saint Thomas—who had hovered between doubt and belief. "The doctor says that having respect for the authorities and also questioning them—that is the way to make progress in learning. I too doubt and I believe. I believe in physic; but I do not believe, as some do, that medicines have to be given at full moon or no moon, or that Jupiter on the ascendant causes disorders of the liver."

"And ailing men too," Lydia said. "They doubt physicians even as they believe."

"Yes, at times they wonder if they should get a doctor to their bedside, or if they would be better served by a priest, or a witch."

Lydia scoffed at that. She had no time for old wives' tales and country customs—she did not believe that a cat turning its back to the fire signaled ill weather or that a cricket in the house brought good luck. Hers was a crystal-clear mind that arrived at conclusions through observation and thought. Mine, in spite of my calling, was the one more overwrought. I believed, however, that she possessed beauty, grace, goodness, and strength in full measure, that she had labored to cultivate them even in the soil of that obscure Virginia farm she was reared in.

"I believe in you," I said, and reached out to touch her cheek. And I would have told her of what Bristol and the others wanted of me, of how I did not know whether to believe in the course of action they had chosen for themselves. I opened my mouth to speak, but someone rattled at the door of the cabin, and it was Ganter come again for another dose of his jimsonweed.

Bristol asked me what Dick had had to tell me the day we walked together.

"Oh, we talked of this and that," I replied. "Mostly of our voyage, the days before we got onto that ship. Dick had a hard time of it, you know, back in London."

"You think that white man is still your friend?" he asked brusquely.

"Martin is yours," I pointed out.

He shrugged. "We are working together."

There was a pause.

"Are you joining us next week?" he asked.

The rebellion consumed Bristol these days. He barely spared anything else a thought.

He must have seen the hesitation in my face. *Yes . . . no . . . I am not certain.* I felt his eyes on me.

"Do you see your face in the water when you go to wash in it, Tony?" he asked. "Or perhaps your master has a looking glass he lets you use, since you are an apprentice and all."

I waited for him to continue.

"If you look, you will see what I see only too well—your countenance is only slightly less black than mine."

That is true, that is true. Bristol, my friend, I know only too well that that is true. But I am the only one of my kind here, you see. I am an East Indian, a moor from that faraway place. The only one, the first. I have to make my own way. In the only manner I know how to.

Bristol studied me closely, trying to read my thoughts, I suppose.

My father might or might not have been a medicine man. It does not matter. I was not a physician's apprentice in London. That was a falsehood. But this is what I do best—heal broken bodies. This is all I want to do. This is the way for me. For this, I came to Virginia.

Somewhere a mock bird called. The creature excelled in imitation. It could mime the calls of other birds, the sounds of insects and other things. This one began a high clicking sound.

You see, Bristol, my friend, I strive to give rebirth to myself. It is a hard labor.

Bristol spoke. "Listen, my lad. You are never going to be a physician like Doctor Herman. No one will bring you their sick and dying. Who would trust a moor? They let you attend to them now because they see you as the white doctor's man. But later . . . it will be different."

I looked down at the leaves at my feet. I felt tired in a way I had not felt for a long time. A bird started from the bushes and took wing. It could have been the mock bird taking off to try its hand at being something else. When I looked up at Bristol, I was surprised to see that his countenance was pitying. He reached out and put his hand on my shoulder.

"When I first saw you, you were but a lad," he said, smiling now, just a little. "'Tis a long time we have been friends to each other." He paused again. "Think about what I have to say."

When I got home there was Ganter at the door once more, begging for his syrup. *Just a little bit more to get through the night. Tony, Tony . . .*

All of this transpired sometime in September. Golden asters bloomed by every wayside, and for those who cared to look for it, the tall, delicate flower called the crippled cranefly grew in the woods. I wished I could have lost myself in the loveliness. But my mind was weighed down.

One morning I had left open the door of my cabin, which was also the dispensary, and the day's first light that peered through the entry was the yellow-gold hue of the season. All around me sundry utensils and containers filled with herbs and compounds glistened.

The door creaked open and Lydia came in, standing in the light, her arms folded at her breast. She saw me and smiled. I went towards her.

"You are early today," I said.

"Yes, I could not sleep. I thought I would come and start on the doctor's meal." She hesitated. "I saw little Sancho on the way. He was weeping. I think Ganter thrashed him again."

I wish Bristol and Cuffee would keep an eye on the lad instead of plotting their grand rebellion, I thought.

"Does he need me to attend to him?" I asked.

"No, I think he is all right. Ganter has not marked him this time."

As before, I worried about what else Ganter was doing to him.

"I am glad you are Sancho's friend," I said.

She placed a hand on my arm. "I saw you and Bristol talking last evening. You looked very grave indeed."

I stood very still, looking into her lovely eyes.

"What was he saying?" she persisted. "Or is it a secret between you?"

"It was not important."

"You look anxious, Tony. As if you are burdened by weighty thoughts."

And she stepped forward and took my face in her hands. They were small hands, the skin slightly chapped, the nails jagged and uneven, but they were firm on my cheeks. She drew a finger along my jawline. I became conscious of my awake and pulsing skin, my warm breath, the fine hairs on my neck standing on end, and then, only of her body, its living warmth, its proximity. She came closer and pulled my face down to hers, her hand firm behind my head, as I pressed my mouth on hers. I put my arms around her and pulled her close. I could feel her breasts round against my chest. I realized how strong she was, from years and years of work in the fields and at the hearth—the firmness of her arms, the straightness of her back, the toughness of her body, which pushed against mine, her slender thighs, her hips. I stepped back slightly and, bending down, reached for the ties fastening her blouse. She waited patiently as I undressed her. She wore so many layers of clothing . . . I could feel her body tremble slightly. She then took off my worn garments—there was a deliberateness to our actions, which, looking back, was unusual. How many people make love fully naked and in a cabin surrounded by medicinal compounds?

The yearning we both felt then was strong and urgent, but it was also languid, weighty. The time we spent together felt like a moment, even as it seemed an eternity. The sun left a splash at the door but discreetly cast the rest of the room in eclipse. Birds might have sung outside in chorus and flowers bloomed, seasons might have changed—I do not know. We sank down together on the wooden floor scattered with straw. I smelt only the scent of her, which was the smell of sweat and lust and labor, of the voyage her people had made across the ocean, of the *round earth's imagin'd corners*, of this land we had come to; and it was my scent as well. And all around us the salts and seeds and minerals and herbs, crushed, dissolved, steeped, in water, in spirits, in wine. They glistened and stirred, and silently acted as their natures dictated. After, she and I lay together, lips aching, her head on my shoulder, her hair about her shoulders. I reached down and felt the inside of her thighs and she was wet with both of us. All my life I will hold this to me, I thought, this moment, this place, this woman.

"The master will soon be astir," she whispered damply into my ear. "I must be going."

I looked at her anxiously. Many men said that women regretted it after it was done. She reached out and kissed me, once again full on the mouth, and I knew she did not.

"Say something, Tony," she said softly, smoothing my hair. Her fingers got entangled in the curls. Perhaps she was feeling the same concern that I had.

"I love you, Lydia," I said. And I realized, even as I said it, that it had been years since I felt love, such deep and strong feeling for any living person. And because I did not have the words for it then, I did not add that to me she was wondrous, like this new land with its mysteries and riches and promise, and that she was also warmth, intimacy, and comfort, like home.

FIFTEEN

Dick was to be in Jamestown on the night of the planned uprising, so he was safely out of the way. The men were invigorated when they gathered in the clearing for the second time—there were fewer jokes, and an air of gravity prevailed.

"We are in this together—each man for everyone else," Martin said. I noticed that the white men regarded him as a leader. Although Bristol had hatched this plot, the white servants were in it because of the Englishman.

"What of the servants who have not joined us?" I asked. "Either because they do not know yet of this or because they do not want to?" I was thinking of Lydia.

"All servants are servants. Even if they are not among us, they will be treated with mercy," Martin declared.

"Lydia knows of our plan. I just told her," Bristol said as if reading my mind. "She had to be informed. She lives at the Pooles', and we do not want to startle her. Besides, we need someone to let us in."

He was right—Lydia had had to be told. But I had planned to request the doctor to ask the Pooles if she could come over to our home the night before to help with some task. She could have the compounding cabin to herself, so it could not be said she spent the night under the same roof as two men. However, it appeared now that she would remain at the Pooles' farm to aid the uprising.

"She wants to be part of this. Especially because you are with us," Bristol told me.

I do not know at what point I had made my decision, but I too was part of Bristol's scheme. Flynn, Bristol, and Cuffee stayed close to me as we made our way back. Cuffee remarked that he was glad I was there with them. *My own lad, Tony,* is what he said, and squeezed my arm. Bristol did not say a word. But when the moon lit up his sculpted face, I saw that he was smiling ever so slightly, caught up in his dreams.

The next morning I asked Lydia if she was certain that she wanted to remain at the Pooles' when the men marched up there. "Yes, of course," she answered. "What do I have to fear? The men leading the march are my friends. And you will be there among them."

"I will," I said.

And then Lydia wanted to talk about a particular treatment for rashes that Doctor Herman had recently concocted. That was Lydia's nature—ever calm and unshaken. Later, as she walked back to the Pooles' through the maze of sunlight and shadow cast by the trees, I watched her retreating back. I felt I had known her all my life, and I felt that she was a complete stranger. I wondered: does any man ever fully know any woman? He thinks he does—she is the girl living down the lane, the girl fetching water from the communal well, the girl who speaks in accents familiar, and suddenly one day, he finds out that she has been a stranger all along, a dreamer of dreams he never suspected, a poet of verses better than his, or a more effective physician, or a saint, ultimately unavailable to him or any man.

The week flew by and the Wednesday of the uprising arrived. My first thought was of Doctor Herman. I did not believe he would come to harm, because the plan was to skirt his land and head to the Poole farm. But he might choose to stay up at night reading or compounding and keep me by him, making it impossible for me to slip out and join Bristol and the other men. It would be better if he were away. Fortunately, the doctor announced that he would be going to Jamestown—to meet friends, he said, although it was more likely that he would go to Master Greene's empty house, which was now his, and stay for the night, keeping his old friend's shadow company.

"Look to the house, Tony," he said, pausing at the threshold, and in my nervous state I wondered at his words. Did he suspect something? But after delivering a quick instruction or two, he departed, his old mare ambling along the road leisurely. I occupied myself preparing the potions and ointments he had directed me to, but my mind was on the plans for tonight and my own role in it. What would transpire if things failed? What lay ahead if we succeeded? I gazed out of the window lost in thought. The first signs of the coming season were now apparent. Sneezeweed and fishmouth blossoms grew in profusion on the edges of the field even as some trees started exhibiting their autumn colors. I stepped outside to momentarily escape the strong smell of boiling condiments. The chokeberry plant at the door of the cabin looked like the burning bush from which God had spoken in the Bible story. *Here I am . . .* Moses had replied when he was addressed, simply offering himself to whatever was asked of him. Surely, that is the best any man can do.

When darkness fell, I made my way to the clearing. It was a good two-league walk for me. My heart beat faster. It was to be a big night. I would not think of what the morrow would bring for me, of what the doctor would say when he found out. I heard a scrabbling sound coming from the thicket that grew on one side of the path. I stopped. And I fancied that whatever was in there paused too, holding its breath, watching me. I went on, and it proceeded too. And when I halted again, it hesitated, before it stepped out into the path. A small, dusty figure—Sancho.

"Tony, Tony!"

"What is the matter, Sancho? Are you hurt? Did someone send you to me? Was it Lydia?"

He looked confused at my barrage of questions. No, he said, he was not hurt. And he had not seen Lydia that day. He was coming to say that Master Ganter . . .

"What about him?"

"Master Ganter is restless tonight. He is going to step out to walk through the land, he says. I fear he will have his musket when he finds Bristol, Cuffee, and the other men. He will shoot them, Tony!"

Old Ganter. We had reckoned that Ganter would stay safe in his cabin till our mission was completed. But we should have anticipated this; we all knew that he was often agitated at night these days. I thought for an instant before I took Sancho by the hand, and we hurried back to Doctor Herman's. The lad stood outside by the chokeberry as I went into the darkness and lit a candle. The odor left by my day's labor still hung heavy. I found what I wanted, stepped outside, and gestured to Sancho to follow me. It was a warm night; late fireflies gleamed in midair.

"Look, Tony . . ." Sancho breathed, reaching out to the bouncing lights.

We sped through the darkness—time was of the essence. *Let Ganter not have left, let him be home . . .* When we reached Adams's Grove and approached the cabins, I bade Sancho remain in the one he shared with Bristol and Cuffee, and I went towards Ganter's cabin, a shadowy bulk, appearing bigger than it actually was. As I stood, hesitating for an instant, I got the strong stink of excrement and wrinkled my nose. Ganter need not shit at his own threshold, surely. The door was ajar and I wondered if he had left already, was already walking through the fields. Should I look for him outside? But what could I do even if I encountered him? He was the man with the gun. My breath quickening, I entered the cabin—a candle was lit in the corner and by its glow I saw Ganter. He clutched his shoulder and, what is more, I saw that there was a little blood trickling down the side of his face, about his ear.

"Master Ganter . . . ?"

He only groaned in reply and I stepped closer.

"Is that you, shit-face?" he asked and cursed. "And why does every moor and madman think they can barge into my house tonight?"

"You are hurt, Master Ganter?"

"The bitch did it. And I am glad to say I have clobbered her." He pointed to the corner of the room where a pile of ragged petticoats lay prone in the shadows. It smelled foul. I could hear its long, ragged breaths.

It was Flynn who told me what transpired later: how the men huddled in the clearing, waiting for Martin and Bristol to give the signal to start. They talked in low voices, and then did not speak at all. It had all been planned; there was nothing to say. They had just one lantern between them. The fireflies would light their way to freedom.

I made my way to the figure prone on Ganter's floor, crouched down, and raised the candle. Her hair, now grown longer and ragged, was fallen about her face, and her shoulders were thin and bony. When I pushed back the gray strands, the countenance below resembled a death's-head more than a living face. She had found her way to us once more. She, whom I had last seen at Ganter's plantation. She, who had been abandoned there by Ganter when he moved back to Jamestown. Mad Marge.

I called her name and she stirred and opened her eyes. She had a dark bruise on her head—she had been hit with something heavy.

"I struck her," Ganter said. "Who asked the mad bitch to creep in on me in the dark?"

Marge groaned. I could see now that her face and arms were covered in scratches—she had lost her shoes. She had been walking through the woods. But surely, she could not have walked here from upriver. How did she find her way? How did Marge find her way anywhere?

Ganter spoke up again: "Is she dead? About time the lunatic died. And about time I got up and out. I am in no mind to sleep tonight."

I turned to him quickly. "You are hurt, sir. Your arm, your back . . . now your face too. Let me see what I can do."

Ganter's scowl turned to a leer. "Have you . . . have you brought it, lad?" he asked in a strangled voice.

I measured and poured him what he desired. It smelled pungent-sweet— an odor that was its very own. He watched me, his mouth agape, strings of spittle stretching between his lips, his eyes, his very body yearning. He took the syrup and gulped it down in one quick movement.

"I should be fine in a bit. She has never not worked for me," he gasped.

"Aye, you should feel better, Master Ganter."

A groan from Marge. I turned to her again.

Marge . . . Marge . . . it is Tony here . . . your friend.

She raised a withered hand towards the gash on her head, but it fell back wearily. She was exhausted and injured, clearly in pain. I would clean her wound later, I would apply my salve on it, I would nurse her back to health. *Marge . . . Marge.* Could she hear me? I gave her a spoonful of the jimson to ease her pain, to help her sleep. Ganter looked on, resentful, envious.

"She set upon me all of a sudden, just as I was venturing out," he volunteered. "Thought I'd seen the last of her when I dumped her upriver—but here she is uglier than ever and even more mad." And he described how Marge had been standing at his front door, grinning and grimacing, jerking about till Ganter could verily hear the bones crackle. He had got the shock of his life, he, Ganter, who was never disturbed by sight of man or beast. He had grabbed her by her skinny shoulders but she had ducked, and the next thing he knew, she had squatted by his doorstep, hauled up her skirts, and defecated. It had splattered all over, copious amounts of it, hot and reeking.

"And then she sprang up and pushed her way in, gabbling and hooting all along. She is strong for a mad cunt. It was she who gave me this with that hoe." He felt the swelling on his cheek and ear, fast growing to a fierce purple. "So, I gave her a smack in the nozzle with an ax handle—knocked her out, it did. Killed her, I hoped, but I suppose not." He chortled and leaned back.

She had come seeking; seeking Cuffee, Bristol, Dick, Sam, and me. Instead, she had found Ganter in his hovel and had inadvertently delayed his departure, at least till I appeared. I glanced around at the straw mattress, the single stool, the pewter plate and mug, the coat piled in a heap, the iron chest, the candle, the windowless walls—in spaces akin to this I had lived, slept, dreamt, experienced the unspeakable, and once, not too many years ago, had found a boy hanging from the rafters.

Ganter groaned once more. And suddenly, before I could stop him, he bounded forward and grabbed the bottle of syrup I had left on the floor. He plucked the rag stuffed into its mouth and drank a draft, then two. He then stood up and felt for his musket.

"Master Ganter . . ." I said. "Sir . . ."

"Shut your hole up and help me haul her out and then get going yourself," he said. "Time I made a move. Must go check on the land, on those dunghill villains—Bristol and that motley crew."

And Ganter stood up. He was not a large man, but he grew in the shadows cast by the candle. And he had a gun.

"Master Ganter," I said, my voice steady. "You are in no state to go out."

He sat down again and leaned against the wall, his eyes shut. "Y're right I am not. This wound . . . this shoulder . . ."

I had placed the second bottle on the floor, just within his reach. He jerked forward and took it.

The men started to march. Cuffee and Bristol might have looked for me. *That fucking Tony.* Their hearts were bitter. Curse him. *The traitor. The turncoat. The milksop. The East Indian.*

They walked softly through the woods, keeping to the cover of the trees, skirting the open clearings. It was a breezy night, and the moon scurried behind clouds, the fallen leaves whirled around their feet in small eddies. The men stayed silent, only a muted cough here, or a clearing of the throat there.

Except for a commonness of purpose and a sense of expectation, they might have simply been walking back to their cabins after an evening at the Crossed Keyes.

Ganter's hands were shaking. He spoke rapidly, and even in the light of the candle I saw the perspiration starting on his face. All doctors were frauds and cheats, he said, glaring at me balefully. Had it not been ruled in Jamestown, just last year, that the physicians overcharged and fleeced their patients and could be taken to court? He had a mind to do that—to take me, to take Doctor Herman, to have us put in prison. In England, his old mam had given birth to a monster child, and a fool of a doctor had said that she must have thought of a beast or ogre when she lay with her husband, that maternal impression was the reason behind monstrous births.

"The simple fact of it," Ganter said, leaning forward, "is that she was an ugly whore and the babe favored her in looks. She strangled him shortly after he came out of her and said that he had died of the plague."

I remembered the story of Ganter's mam trying to kill him. I had seen, or fancied I had seen, a scar about his neck.

Marge slept deep in the corner. The syrup had taken its effect. How glad she would be to see all of us tomorrow. I would take her to Doctor Herman's. I would ask Lydia to tend to her, to tidy her up, put her in clean apparel. Ganter, on the other hand, was yet wide awake. The truth is, his body had grown habituated to the jimsonweed. He was still talking, saying that Master Menefie's nephew, Joshua Adams, the one still not returned from England, was a great dolt and ne'er-do-well, that he, Ganter, would have preferred to stay in Master Menefie's employ, that that bastard Adams was supposedly looking for a wife, but spent more time with the whores in Covent Garden, and was unlikely to return to his muddy farm till he ran out of money. And he, Ganter, his own plans had come to naught. Ganter's Pride, his own farm, he had wanted so much of it. But it had failed; *he* had failed. Menefie claimed to have Ganter's welfare at heart, but all he really desired was for Ganter to be his servant, a brutal one who knew how to extract work from the baser servants, so Menefie and masters like him could heap up their riches. And here he was, once more landless, penniless, with no man but a fucking moor for company. For this, he had come, all those years ago . . . to Virginia? And so Ganter went on.

"What brought you here?" he demanded suddenly. "Did I bid you come? I do not think I bade you come."

"The doctor bade me come and check on you, Master Ganter, because of your pains."

He looked at me suspiciously and heaved himself up. He was only slightly unsteady on his feet.

"Damn my pains. I want to go check on my villainous crew," he muttered. "The rascally group of jackanapes foisted on me." He glowered at me balefully. "And you were one of them, till you sucked Archer Walsh's cock and he took you with him. I heard you served him well."

I would have struck him, but it was not the time.

He took a faltering step towards the door and paused to raise his hand towards his face. The wound must have caused a twinge.

"Master Ganter . . . Master Ganter . . . let me help you, sir," I said.

The men broke into the warehouse on the margin of the Pooles' farm. It was crammed with sacks of cornmeal, dried meats, and turnips. The intent was not to carry away all or even some of it—that would hinder their progress. Instead, the objective was to haul the victuals outside the cabin, to conceal some of it in the bushes, to ransack the warehouse a bit, and to march on. It was to make a point, said Bristol, which was that the servants were not fed enough, that they were malnourished. So, the men did as they were instructed—Cuffee, Flynn, Caesar, working quickly in the dark, feeling the soft, loamy earth below their feet, the night about their shoulders and backs, and the hunger within, as well as the warm touch of triumph, only slightly tempered by the fact that they had not found muskets. At last, they were doing *something*. Bristol and Martin kept a lookout, urging the men to hurry because there were still things to accomplish before dawn. And then it was time to keep moving, on to the Pooles', where Lydia was waiting.

"They are here tonight." Ganter was tense and quivering.

"Who, sir?"

Had he heard something? Was he talking about the plotters?

"I believe it might be your people, the Indians."

And he sat up and cocked his head. "Hark . . . !" he whispered.

I listened, and I heard nothing.

And shortly after, Ganter too ceased to hear noises, ceased even to think. He lay on his side, his knees drawn up to his chest. His eyes and mouth were greedy, pleading. I had carried it with me, three containers of it, this thing that could humble Ganter. I watched as he slurped eagerly and then when he no longer could do that, the liquid just slid into his maw and down his throat. He did not choke on it—his body opened up and embraced it. It became part of him, with his blood, his black bile, his yellow bile, his phlegm—a fifth humor, the one that dominated.

For the body is mutable. Not merely in that it ages, breaks down, perishes, and then decomposes further after death, turning itself to ashes and dust. When alive, it is also open to influences, opens itself up to them—influences of the wind and weather, of food and physic. And of all the substances I knew, the thorn apple or the devil's snare or *Datura stramonium,* the selfsame jimsonweed of which Ganter had grown so fond, had the greatest transformative effect. I do not know about the powder of the unicorn horn, but the datura, like me, has its origins in East India, so some natural philosophers assert. In that land it is said that it is a favorite of *Shiva, the God of Destruction: blue-skinned, ash-smeared, a serpent wound around his neck, the crescent moon in his hair, the river Ganga captive in his matted locks,* Shiva imbibes the juice of the datura, and he dances.

As Flynn recounted it, having completed their mission with the food warehouse, the men marched on once again. *To the Pooles'. . . To the Pooles'.* Things had gone well so far. This would be a rebellion to remember, it would go down in the chronicles and record books. It would learn their masters to treat their men as men.

They paused about twenty feet from the Pooles' cabin. Two of them— Caesar and Flynn—were to go ahead and knock softly, not loud enough to wake the master and mistress, but enough for Lydia to rouse herself. An owl hooted, startling the men as they crouched in the dark. Caesar and Flynn proceeded, two silent shadows. When Lydia opened the door, they would all barge in and would overpower Poole, who was anyway a scrawny fellow; they would seize what muskets he had and bind the mistress to some piece of furniture. It seemed simple enough. It *should* have been simple enough.

To render Ganter immobile and then to leave, that had been my intent when I entered the cabin. And tomorrow Ganter would wake up with a throbbing head and dry mouth, cursing as he attempted to piss and his cock stayed in his hand, dry as a twig; as he tried to push out his morning stool, which would have turned to rock, because that is what the syrup does, once its effects on the mind have worn.

But even as Ganter lay prone, I stayed. I crouched by his side and watched over him as I would over any ailing patient. The candle dimmed, and I lit another. Marge was still unconscious. Ganter's face had swollen and turned a bluish black. Indeed, it seemed like it would burst into fragments of flesh, tatters of skin. His breathing grew labored and rapid—the gasp and rattle of it filled the cabin. I could go get something that might allay the effects of the jimson. I thought quickly—of hurrying through the night, hearing only the sound of my footsteps and Ganter's breathing still loud in my ear, arriving at Doctor Herman's cabin, fetching something, and then running back to administer it to Ganter. But to what purpose? I knew of no concoction that would help; there was none such. Besides, it was too late, too, too late for Ganter. His breathing slowed for a few moments and then picked up pace again.

I heard a rustle from the corner. I thought it was Marge stirring, and turned around. But no, it was a little, golden waif. Sammy sat there, his face a perfect moon in the shadows. He leaned against the wall, pulled his knees, clothed in their worn breeches, close to his chest, and watched. *You were always my friend, were you not—?*

—*Tony, Tony.*

I placed my ear to Ganter's chest to listen to the drumming within: a wild, unsteady beat. His skin was clammy now, but I knew he felt neither warm nor cold. His eyes were open, but I could not tell what he saw.

And so it went. There was nothing in his sorry life Ganter loved as much as what I had brought with me. *Give us some of it, will you not, Doctor . . .* His eyes wet and yearning, his teeth bared in the beggar's pathetic grin. *I've got what it takes to pay for it . . .*

Someone had joined Sammy in the corner. Another little lad, the hue of his skin the brown of the earth, no more, no less. He had stepped out of the play by Master Shakespeare. A *lovely boy,* one with *the spiced Indian air* still wafting about him. He was not well versed in love potions, like Puck, the Fairy King's little sprite. But in another version of the play never written, he knew to gather other stuff from the wild, things that also grew in the dark woods of the mind . . . *Fetch me that flower, that herb I shew'd thee once . . .* He knew what he could do with things of that nature; he felt the power of knowing them, a power that was a dormant, slumbering thing, biding its time until, one day, it ignites. He carried no guns, but he knew about *invisible bullets*.

I think Ganter might have looked at me. He might have even spoken, asked me to do something.

Into whatsoever houses I enter, I will enter to help the sick, and I will abstain from all intentional wrongdoing and harm . . .

All evening I remembered that oath. I remembered, I remembered:

May I see in a sick man only a fellow-creature in pain . . .

The candle had sunk low but I did not care to light another one. I instead got up and opened the front door and let the moon peer in. The two little lads whispered and laughed softly together in the corner, their heads, golden and dark, drawn close. Ganter's face fell slack, his pupils became pinpoints, he whimpered. Somewhere else in Jamestown the ships pushed out into the sea, a man lay sleepless in an empty house by the docks, a sailor staggered down a street, burghers drank to the health of a king on a distant shore, people gathered in the rustling dark. All of this somewhere else in Jamestown—as Ganter spasmed and grew still, and a gust of wind blew the door shut.

SIXTEEN

Flynn told me later how it had unfolded at the Pooles'. Just as the men approached the cabin, there was a mighty rustle in the bushes and they were laid upon by what seemed like a horde. It had been a strangely silent struggle—except for grunts, labored breathing, a softly uttered curse or two. Till the butt end of a musket clobbered Flynn, and it was all darkness, he said, and an endless falling.

When he had come to, his head had been throbbing and he was with some eight others, all trussed up in a strange barn. He had looked around the gloomy space—all of the rebels were there except for Martin and Bristol. "And you, Tony," Flynn added.

In the later servant rebellions—the bigger ones that made history—the rebels were hanged for treason, or imprisoned at best. These men were more fortunate, I suppose: perhaps because no great harm was done—a food store had been ransacked, but that was it. They were taken to the council house in Jamestown and whipped. Cuffee was whipped first and hardest—either because they believed that the black men were behind it, or because he could serve as a lesson for the others. They insisted that he knew Bristol's whereabouts, although, truly, neither Cuffee nor the others had any notion; in fact, they had thought that Bristol and Martin had been killed in the dark.

After that, the masters were told to have a special care of their servants. An idle, drunken lot, the judges proclaimed, with spirits turbulent and unquiet. They needed to be ruled with a firmer hand. With that, the men were let go and ordered to return to their farms and not permitted to venture out for some weeks, not even to the Crossed Keyes or the chapel.

Dick Hughes was the hero. It was Dick who had somehow caught wind of the plot and come racing back from Jamestown to rouse the masters, not caring to involve Ganter, who he knew was probably foolish with the syrup which he took so much of these days to ease his aches. It was Dick who organized the ambush in the dark. He stood tall and upright before the Jamestown officials, giving his story.

That whoreson Dick Hughes, the other plotters muttered. How did he ever find out about this? How indeed?

Of course, I had not known what was to come or even what had transpired at the Poole farm when I stepped out of Ganter's cabin into the subdued light of dawn. I looked into the other cabin to check on the boy, Sancho. He was deep in the fast slumber of the very young. I shook him awake. I needed him to keep watch in case Marge woke up and decided to leave, although I suspected that she would sleep for some hours more.

"Is Master Ganter inside?" Sancho asked.

"Yes, but he is dead."

Sancho's expression did not change. "I thought he would die soon," he said.

I looked at him sharply. I wondered if he had been standing at the door and peeking in—the third little lad to bear witness, along with those other two crouched in the shadows. But he merely blinked sleepily. "Why am I watching over a cabin with a dead man?" he asked.

"Because there is someone else in there—a woman."

He looked terrified this time. "Is she dead too?"

"She is sleeping."

I left Sancho and sped through the fields and pathways to the Pooles'. It had turned chillier overnight. I had to see what had happened. When I reached the farm, I saw a small group of men standing about and talking animatedly. Dick was among them. Lydia stood by herself under a tree. I hurried over to her, and in a low voice she told me that the plot had failed. That the men had been set upon before they entered the Pooles' cabin, that they were locked up in the curing shed, that Bristol and Martin had disappeared. She had tears in her eyes, but she would not let them spill.

"They do not suspect I knew of the plan, that I was to open the door," she whispered. "That is why I am out here, and not barred with Cuffee and the others."

I knew she felt guilty about that. I reached for her hand.

"And where were you, Tony?" she asked, looking straight at me. "I expected you to be among the marchers."

"'Tis a long tale. I will tell you later."

Mistress Poole called sharply to Lydia, and I turned away to go home.

"What is the East Indian moor doing here?" one of the farmers called. "And at this early hour?"

"Oh, I suspect he has come to see our girl Lydia," Mistress Poole replied over her shoulder.

"He is sweet on her? Will we have a young 'un soon? Black and a little less black makes what? I am of the mind it somehow makes even blacker!"

While some men laughed, others were too agitated by their servants' behavior for such frivolity. Master Poole asked me regarding Doctor Herman's whereabouts. The night had ruined his health, he declared frantically. He had palpitations of the heart and felt a new kind of pain in his head which he had never sensed before, not to mention the usual ache in his belly.

"Is not the boy the physician's apprentice? He will give you something," someone said, probably just to shut up Master Poole.

Mistress Poole spoke up. "Do not trust a moor, I say. I cannot understand why our good doctor keeps the fellow."

I would usually have felt resentful at that. But at that moment—what right did I have? *Do not present to me with your ailing bodies . . . Do not bring your sick . . .*

I turned to leave. I saw Dick looking at me curiously.

As I walked away, I caught the odor of my own sweat, sharp and strong. I had not realized that I had been perspiring through the night, along with Ganter. I stopped at a pond to wash my face and neck. The water was cool and still. I saw my reflection. It did not seem right that I looked exactly as I did the night before—the very same countenance, the selfsame expression on it. I should have changed. After last night, after what I did, after what I did not do.

Doctor Herman heard of the ill-conceived rebellion the first thing in the morning and rode back from Jamestown right away. He was relieved, I suppose, to find his house intact and to find me waiting for him, having completed all the compounding tasks he had assigned before he left.

I informed him of Ganter's death, but it was not till later, after Dick came to see him, that he interrogated me more closely. Had Ganter summoned me to his cabin? Had he been ailing? Had I given him the jimson?

Yes, sir, yes.

"And why did you remain in Ganter's cabin, lad? Was Ganter's state such that you were required to watch over him?"

"Marge was hurt, sir. She is my old friend and I was loath to leave her. And Master Ganter was badly off too."

"Was he in pain?"

"Yes, Doctor. Because of his usual aches and also because of the injury Marge inflicted on him."

"Did you give him the jimson in the proper dose?"

"Yes, sir."

"But he seems to have died of poisoning from it. Surely you can see that as well."

"I can, master."

"Why, Tony, would Ganter have died, if you gave him the appropriate draft?"

"In faith, I gave him only what he needed, Doctor, no more nor less. He must have quaffed more when I was tending to Marge. When I looked, the bottle was nigh empty."

"He took so much that he was poisoned?"

"I suspect he had had a good amount of it before I came."

"And you could not tell?"

"No, sir."

Doctor Herman sighed in exasperation. "Ganter is well known among the farmers and their overseers. And you were by his side last night. 'Wherefore?' they will demand to know—'What was your man doing there?'"

"He summoned me, sir."

And so, we were back where we started. My master was right. Ganter's death caused something of a stir. Of course, people knew that he had been drawn to the jimson for some months now. But why would he die all of a sudden, they asked. And why was the East Indian by his side? And what of the madwoman? What was she doing with Ganter?

Marge had been removed to Bristol and Cuffee's cabin. I went to look in on her. The wound inflicted by Ganter, along with malnourishment, had made her frail beyond belief.

And Cuffee and Flynn also questioned me. They were sore and heart-broken at the outcome of the rebellion. They had hoped to bring their masters to their knees and instead were back on the fields.

"Where were you, Tony?" asked Cuffee.

"Where were you, lad?" echoed Flynn.

And Bristol, wherever he was, Bristol surely demanded to know the same.

I had to tell them about Ganter, how I went to his side, how it was Sancho who had summoned me.

They looked at me doubtfully, their eyes hard and suspicious. *While we, the rest of us, gathered in the dark, ready to press on, to fight. We had sworn an oath together, had we not? No man his own; each man for all.*

I told of how I found Ganter and Marge, both wounded, and how Ganter had been getting ready to go out, to look for them.

Lydia spoke up for me. "If not for Tony, Ganter would have stopped you lot before you even got started," she said, her voice firm and insistent. "If not for Tony . . . if he had not gone to Ganter . . ."

They heard her, but I found it hard to read their countenances and could not tell if they truly believed her, if they truly thought I had really done them a service.

After they left Lydia took me in her arms and held me close, I felt her heart beating steady against my own and was filled with gratitude for her trust, her love, even as the burden of the knowledge weighed heavily on me, the terrible awareness that I had betrayed quite something else, my profession, my calling, something which I had made my own.

Ganter's passing was a suspicious death. No, it was not—the man had been poi-soning himself for weeks. *But, no question, it was.* And so, the arguments went back and forth the whole day and the next. In spite of the stir caused by the servant uprising, the decision was made to carry the body to Jamestown for an inquest. It had to be done soon, before the remains began to decay. The jurors were to be landowners, tradesmen, a ship doctor who happened to be on land (because Doctor Pott was away in England), and, to my surprise, Parson Blair. Doctor Herman and I were required to be present. The doctor was cold and silent on the journey up. He was most vexed that I had got him into this. Love potions were one thing, but a dead man was quite another. Yes, men died all the time, death, as he himself had told me before, stalks among us. Especially here in this land, where it crouches behind every bush, waits holding its breath in the waters, hangs in the very air, and stands in attendance behind a man's chair as he sits to his dinner. Bides its time silently, till it is the apt moment. The doctor saw it all the time, as I did. But he knew, as everyone else did, that a healer should never be thought of as an ally of death—he was to be the one who countered it, who warded it off with every tool at his disposal. And here I was being suspected of having a hand in the death of a man.

Master Herman did not say any of this. In fact, he did not say a word. But I could almost hear his thoughts and feel his ire directed my way. My heart sank, for what transpired at court depended in large measure on his support.

In the courthouse one of the jurors announced the task at hand. We had been called *to inquire into the cause of the death of Ralph Ganter whether by the hand of man or by a fall onto the earth or the kick of a horse or by the infirmity of disease . . . if by the hand of man, then with what weapon and whether the wounds or blows of the said weapon were the immediate cause of death or not.* And there he was, Ganter. I felt the old loathing for him, he who was now a cold slab of flesh, and also the old fear. But now added to them was a touch of something else—not grief, but compassion, or something like it. The dead, simply by passing into death, somehow become innocent of all charges; it is we, the living, who bear the burden of guilt.

Before the questioning, before anything at all, there was to be the ordeal of touch, the *stroking of the corpse* as they called it in Virginia. The suspected killer was to handle the corpse, and if he was indeed the killer, the blood would begin to flow through the body, momentarily. Lydia had told me that I should be prepared for it. It is a load of rubbish, I had said, another foolish superstition.

"They don't see it that way in Jamestown," she had replied. "It is still used to judge a man."

Under other circumstances, Doctor Herman would have snorted dismissively when the jury called for the procedure, but that day he took care to remain expressionless. I was instructed to go up to the body and put my hands on it, on the thing that was once Ganter. The jurors gathered around to watch. Doctor Herman stayed where he was. I did as directed, placing my hands on the waxy forehead, the bare chest, the arms, the abdomen, the legs, down to the feet. Ganter was even paler in death than in life and the skin of my hands was the color of pitch on him. I am never as dark as when I am touching a white man. My hands moved as instructed, up and then down the cold flesh, in gestures so mechanical, so terribly intimate. Five minutes passed, ten. The jurors looked on, expectant, not daring to breathe almost. I did not raise my eyes to look at them or at my master.

And then Ganter's blood rose up in sympathetic motion at my touch. It flowed again through the veins and arteries, those networks akin to byways through the body that the esteemed Doctor William Harvey of England describes in the revolutionary new theory I had read about, the roads that led to the single throne of the heart. It brought color to the dead man's face, air to his lungs, and before my very eyes Ganter sat up naked as he was, the scar around his throat red and raw. He smiled a vile grin, and pointed a finger at me.

Tony, once again, he croaked. *The East Indian.*

I closed my own eyes and waited for the first blow to fall.

But the jurors were now shuffling back to their seats, Doctor Herman was clearing his throat, a horse neighed, and a man called out to someone else on the street outside. I opened my eyes, and Ganter lay on the table, unaltered.

"Since the ordeal of touch has not revealed the truth in this instance, we must proceed by interrogating the youth—Tony, East Indian, apprentice to Doctor Joseph Herman of Pasbyhayes and James Cittie," one of the jurors announced. I was put the same questions my master had asked me. I gave the same responses. The farmers on the jury looked at me with hard eyes and spoke in hostile tones. Ganter was only an overseer, but still one of their own. The ship doctor appeared to be tired—his eyes grew more heavy-lidded by the minute. Parson Blair, my old friend, was surprisingly sober. When they appointed him to the jury, they had probably mistakenly overlooked that I had lived with him for a good while before I came to be apprenticed to my present master.

Doctor Herman was called up then. There was silence before he spoke— he had established his reputation as a good healer. Perhaps the one thing that cast a blemish on him was his East Indian assistant. I felt quite calm at that moment, my body as still and cold as Ganter's corpse. The doctor was questioned as the doctor who had been attending to the dead man. Yes, he said, Ganter had grown addicted to the juice of the *Datura stramonium* plant, commonly known as jimsonweed; yes, it was he who first prescribed it to him; yes, it was common practice to give it for aches such as the one Ganter had been experiencing. And yes, it could turn men frantic or into fools, often for days at a stretch, and when the influence passed, they could remember nothing of it. It was toxic if consumed in large quantities, death was a rare consequence, but there were several instances where it was known to have happened. Such cases were reported in the books and occurred even here in Virginia, where the herb was to be found in the wild and also cultivated by men who were not physicians, who took jimson for the pleasure it gave and often did not know of its ill effects or, even if they did, could not get themselves to stop consuming it.

When my master finished, the ship doctor grunted and spoke for the first time: "Aye, I witness it at sea too—men turned to drooling idiots by the jimson and a few of them dead by it."

And the jurors conferred in low voices, glancing at me sideways every now and then. My master went to gaze out of the door, a dog wandered into the courthouse, sat down to scratch its fleas, and was shooed out. And then it was over, and I was free to go home. Two of the jurors spoke to the doctor in grave, low tones. From what I could hear, they were urging him to at least expel me from his service. No one particularly looked like they wanted to address me except Parson Blair, who pressed my hand and told my master and the ship doctor that I was the first East Indian Christian, and that he believed that a heathen who saw the light was as good as a man born into the faith. And Doctor Herman ushered me out, and we were on our way.

I wanted to say something but my master enfolded himself in silence. It was only when we reached home that he said, "Ganter's blood did not respond to your touch—that is what convinced them. That is the sort of evidence that is persuasive to ignorant Jamestown fools." And then he would not talk any more of the matter. I never found out if he had done other things to shape the outcome of the trial of that morning.

Ganter was brought back to Adams's Grove by some of Master Menefie's men and buried under a poplar tree. Flynn said he would go spit on the grave when he had some leisure. Cuffee only sighed. He was thinking about Bristol, as we were all.

And after that, as I walked the fields, I would occasionally catch a glimpse of Ganter, a hoary figure lurking behind a tree. He appeared, too, in other unexpected places—by the water, in a clearing, at a casement. I would return to the cabin and see that he had been there too, moving about familiarly, having touched my possessions, having toppled some of the bottles of medicine. Was he seeking more of the syrup? And, at night, he would be waiting, jaw slack, eyes pleading and accusing, both. Waiting with the patience of one who had an eternity of time at his disposal.

Marge was dying. Hearsay was that she had come to Jamestown with some other servants to look for her old friends. With their help she had made it to Adams's Grove, only to stumble upon Ganter in his cabin. There was not much I could do now but go see her every day in Bristol and Cuffee's cabin. She had developed a raging fever and barely swallowed the gruel we spooned down her throat.

"It is a matter of time," I said, and the others nodded sorrowfully.

Two days later, Sancho summoned me, just as he had a week or so ago.

"I am afeared she is going, Tony," he sobbed.

And he was right. Marge's forehead was blazing and her skin dry and chappy. She tossed and muttered and then lay quite still, staring ahead. She saw a village in Lincolnshire, a cottage, a river with a mill, a cart drawn by a favorite pony, a long bumpy road, the sea. And she saw the ship. The ship, the ship, always the ship . . . the *God's Gift,* into which she had been slipped by someone who had known her. Their grief, their burden, their Marge. She saw the turbulent waters, the burning sky, she saw a woman they had called a witch, she saw three boys, one darker than his friends, she saw . . . And she opened her eyes and saw me, and her gaze was clear and unwavering.

"You know me, Marge?"

"Aye," she whispered. "Tony."

I wondered if she would ask for Sam. I would tell her that he had stepped out for a little.

"Little Sammy is dead," she said simply and sadly. "He hanged himself many years ago."

I nodded, unable to speak.

I remembered how Sam would hold her by the hand and lead her about; how she would take his face in her hands and kiss his golden head. He had overlooked that she was a lunatic and taken her for the mam he was always seeking. For her, he had been her little beloved child, her dearest friend. Well, it would not be too long now before she saw him once more.

I sat by her as she faded. Cuffee and little Sancho huddled behind her, silent. Marge, attended at the end by us, three moors.

She opened her eyes and weakly asked me to open the cabin door. I did so, and the stars, brilliant that night against a blank slate of a sky, grouped themselves together for her. Marge turned her gaze to take in the night, the crisp breeze, the last moths lingering, the scent of the trees. She took them all into herself, and she was abundant.

Bristol's and Martin's bodies were found by a willow that grew aslant a rivulet that ran broad and deep off the James. They lay in the midst of the thick weeds along the bank. The trees grew dense there and no sunlight penetrated. Fish darted in the water, so close to the bank that one could almost reach out and grab them with one's bare hands. It was a young Indian lad out fishing far from his settlement who had seen them and gone home to tell his elders, who, in turn, informed the sheriff of the county.

There was a whirlpool and they had drowned. Bristol and Martin, revolutionary leaders, black and white, caught in a watery embrace. Their bodies were bloated, smelling of rot and river. It was a wonder they had not been scavenged yet. When the two of them were laid side by side on the bank, bruises were visible on their heads and faces, as if they had been hit against rocks and stones.

The men speculated on what might have happened: when they had been surprised by the Pooles' cabin, Martin and Bristol had escaped; they had floundered through the trees till they reached this bend in the river; they had fallen in, or attempted to swim across, and the current had sucked them under. And the two corpses had lain in the mud, half-submerged in the water, till the little Indian had been drawn there by the cry of a catbird and the promise of fish for dinner.

It was the season for dying, it seemed.

We buried them in a clearing in the forest because neither Master Menefie nor the new overseer Master Menefie had temporarily appointed in Ganter's stead would have them on Adams's Grove. It was just Flynn, Cuffee, Lydia, and I that gathered. They asked me if I would recite from the burial service.

"Being a better reader than me and all," Flynn said, only slightly sardonically. But all my Bible study had not taught me what to say on this occasion. *The wages of sin is death,* Pastor Blair had said, quaffing away at his drink—but those words were not fitting, not for these two men, exhausted with labor, who had died strange, sad deaths along a river they had never heard of for much of their lives. *Behold, I shew you a mystery; We shall not all sleep, but we shall all be changed . . .* The lines floated into my head, wonderful and quite incomprehensible.

"I do not recall a reading like that at me granddad's funeral back home," Flynn objected. And so, we decided not to recite anything at all.

Cuffee wept like a child as we shoveled earth over them. He and Bristol had walked many long roads together from Angola to Lisbon to England to Barbados to Virginia, and now their ways had parted. I stayed by his side as we returned to the farm. He lay down right away and slept, first like one dead, until he began to mutter in another tongue, one I had never heard him use with Bristol in all those years.

Other reports swirled like dust almost the day after the burial: that it had not been an accident, that the two men had quarreled about whose fault it was that the conspiracy had failed, that Bristol had killed Martin by striking his head with a stone and flung him in the water. And then, so they speculated, Bristol had killed himself knowing that he would certainly be hanged. And soon enough it became a matter of common belief—Bristol had killed Martin. Bristol had killed a white servant. A black man had killed a white one. There was a feeling in the air, a different kind of strain than we had felt before.

"Why are they spreading such tales?" I asked Cuffee. "We all know Bristol would not have killed Martin, nor would Martin have Bristol!"

"We do not know anything," he said angrily. "I told you, and I told Bristol as well: do not be so foolish as to claim a white man as a friend."

In the shortening evenings of the leaf fall season, I thought about Bristol's spirit moving swiftly across land and across the boundless sea, orbiting with the stars, which flowed in the sky creating their own deluge, Bristol's spirit among them, flying, like spirits do, with an uncanny sense of direction, gaze fixed ahead, till the green coast of the land he had left behind came into sight. Bristol, at long last, completing his journey.

VI

CONTAGIOUS FOGS

SEVENTEEN

The summer of 1641. Nearly two years since Bristol and Martin had died, and Mad Marge, and he—the one whose name sits heavy on my tongue—Ralph Ganter; the summer when Cuffee said, all of a sudden one day, *let us go, my friend,* just like that. But much transpired before that.

Some things had changed. For instance, there were several other Africans working in the local farms, two of them on Adams's Grove. The two newcomers, Solomon and Gumby, had tribal markings by way of filed teeth and scars on their cheeks. I had not seen them when they first arrived, but I heard they had been almost frozen with terror and that Harry Jones, the new overseer, had given them a good lashing to get them to shake off their fear. They spoke two distinct tongues, we gathered, neither of which Cuffee could understand. But they both learned English quickly, and in six months they were speaking it, haltingly, but well enough, and I could not understand why the English called the African arrivals stupid.

"Such a long journey," Solomon told Cuffee and me. And though we nodded, we could not fully imagine when they described the African captives packed to choking in the holds of ships.

"Five men thrown into water," said Gumby. "Because they were sick and no use for selling."

These recent voyages were different from the ones we had endured—far worse, far more brutal. Once, on a visit to Jamestown, I noticed the odor that hung heavy over the harbor and was told that it was a slave-bearing ship from

Africa that had arrived the day before. The stench lingered for days, and penetrated the warehouses, taverns, and dwelling places.

Gumby and Solomon did not get along.

"You good for nothing," one would tell the other, and spit.

"*You* good for nothing," the other would reply. "You Iba, Iba are great rascal."

And we gathered that they were from enemy tribes in their native lands, and that there had been a bloody war going on there for a long while.

"Gumby, will you fight Solomon if you get back home?" Cuffee would ask teasingly.

"Fight him worse than ever," Gumby replied, and Solomon would gnash his filed-down teeth.

But in a couple more months, they were inseparable. They labored together in the fields and were exhausted together, they both drank at the Crossed Keyes, and walked back after, with their arms slung around each other's shoulders.

One day they confided that they planned to get a canoe and sail down the river till they reached their homeland.

"Your homeland is too far, man, the river does not go there," I said. "You will perish."

They looked at me skeptically. They too did not quite know what to make of me. They only knew I was Cuffee's friend.

"Yes, too far, too far," Cuffee said. "Do not attempt it, lads."

"I once went west looking for the east," I said, feeling chatty.

"And . . . ?" Gumby urged.

"Oh, I turned around and came back."

"And we thought you were mighty brainy—that you were a medicine man," Solomon remarked, rolling his eyes.

Some months ago Lydia and I had been wed. She had been having a hard time of it at the Pooles' because they might have suspected that she had known about the servants' plot, so I had pleaded with Doctor Herman to take her in.

"Please, sir. She already comes in two times a week to cook and clean. You can request Master Poole to transfer her bond of indenture to you." I hesitated before I added, "She has been learning to compound physic too—she would be of great help to us."

"A woman playing apothecary?" he asked, his brow raised.

"She is very good at it, sir. Most people do not know it, but she can read and write almost as well as any white man."

"It is well known that learning breeds arrogance and sedition," he said, and I did not know if he meant it or not.

I continued pressing the doctor. "Besides, she has assisted as a midwife, sir. It would be good to have a midwife attached to us in our practice."

"You seem very eager to have her here, Tony," he said with a ghost of a smile.

"I am, sir." There was no point saying it any other way.

"As if I do not have fingers enough pointed at me for keeping an East Indian apprentice," he said wryly. And there was no getting anything out of him, till finally he spoke to Master Poole, who was ready to hire Lydia out full-time to my master. For some reason, however, her bond was never formally transferred to him.

She dwelt with me in the compounding cabin and we made love every spare moment. Our bodies were new countries we both discovered, without lodestone or compass. And surrounding us, stacked against the walls: crude antimony, æther, verdigrease, succotrine aloe, common alum, rock alum, ambergris, compound waters, quicksilver, balsams of capri and amber, borax, calomel, turpentine, pearls . . .

Lydia—*my America! My Newfoundland . . .*

. . . camphor, *Camella alba,* cantharides, cloves, castors, lunar caustick, antimony, potash, cochineal, colcothar, vitriol, colocynth, confecto cardiaca, wormwood, orange peel, cinnamon, cascarilla, creme of tartar, saffron, essence of lemons, bergamot, chamomile, flower of brimstone, fenna, grains of paradise . . .

All of them, potent, rare, mysterious, acting as their natures dictated. And, furthermore, inside the two of us, pulsing through our young blood, the unnamed humors that bring about desire, love, bliss. For who is to say what causes those human yearnings and emotions, what mighty mixture of compounds and essences, placed in us and stirred? The body, which was our study and preoccupation, the instrument of life, the vessel for being, still always a mystery. Our longing and our pleasure, sensations in and of the body, yet exceeding it. And we would pore over the doctor's books, dark heads pressed together. With her, I stumbled across the piece of advice I had last heard from the medicine man in the Coromandel: *If you would be at all times merry, eat saf-*

Brinda Charry

fron in meat or drink, and you will never be sad: but beware of eating over much, lest you should die of excessive joy.

"I must have eaten a surfeit of saffron," I would whisper in her ear, and for a while we would again forget the books. Till one day, Doctor Herman advised us to marry in haste so there would not be further scandal. So, we went to Jamestown and Parson Blair proclaimed us man and wife.

"In my country, the wedding ceremony would have lasted five days," I said, hardly able to believe it had happened. "And at the end of it, I would have placed a slender cord dipped in turmeric paste around your neck to signify that we are wed." And I promised myself to one day find her such a thing.

Lydia was an excellent addition to the doctor's household. Apart from her regular duties, she helped prepare the physic, and was preoccupied with trying to make a more potent version of a cure for rattlesnake bite that her mother had brought from Africa, a cure which involved shaved bezoar and a decoction of dittany root. With her joining us, we could also add midwifery to our list of services. Lydia asked for one hundred pounds of tobacco for every birth she assisted, and she gave the doctor half of it. More and more children were being born in and around Jamestown—children of the New World, like Lydia herself. There was a share of bastard births too, and Lydia was charged with getting the woman in question to confess to the child's father, because it was believed a woman would admit the truth in the throes of labor. Lydia would not insist they tell her. "Because sometimes a woman wants to forget," she said. "She wants the child to simply be her own."

We got notice one day that Mistress Poole was ailing. One of the Pooles' servants, a small black girl brought to replace Lydia, came to tell the doctor that he was needed right away. The mistress had a great fever and the sweats, she reported.

"Are you sure it is not your master?" I asked. Master Pooles' ghostly aches and ailments were still near-daily occurrences, and it was surprising to hear that the mistress was the one who was ill.

"I think I know my master from my mistress, sir," said the child tartly, and had to be reprimanded for her cheek by Lydia.

So we went, the doctor and I, to attend to Mistress Poole. Master Poole would complain when he saw me. He still could not bear the thought of a moor at a sickbed, but he knew by then if he wanted Doctor Herman, he should take Tony too.

As we neared the Poole farm, I could not help but notice that the house, recently rebuilt, was made to last, unlike the cabins that had dotted the landscape when I first came. For more and more people now, America was not only the place to go to and return from; it was where lives were built, families were made. It was home. I remembered, too, what I had been told: how the men had congregated outside the Pooles' cabin on the night of the revolt, hushed, expectant, how at that very spot, they had seen their plans crushed. And I was visited once more by the memory of myself, sitting by Ganter. Setting that last thought aside, I followed the doctor, murmuring good morrow to Master Poole, who was standing at the door. As expected, his face clouded upon seeing me, though he held his tongue.

The mistress was ill, though it did not seem anything too grave. She had the ague and pains all along her body, she said, and a headache that blinded her. The doctor bled her, recommended cold compresses, and asked that the servant girl return with us to collect a tea of elderflowers and yarrow. For the rest of the day, we devoted ourselves to other things. Till it was dusk, and Doctor Herman began to feel chilled and feverish too and took to his bed early, saying he might have caught something from Mistress Poole.

So two days passed, and on the third Lydia and I woke to a knock on our door, and there was the Pooles' lass once again, saying that the mistress was somewhat recovered now, it was the master who was ill. I went to report it to the doctor, who was still in bed and shivering in spite of the heat.

"Mistress Poole is much improved, but it looks like her husband is ill now, sir!"

And the doctor, who never missed an opportunity to give me a lesson, said that women's humors were different; their bodies were colder and spongier than those of men, who were hotter and drier and therefore more prone to ailments. Besides, he said, the hard life in Virginia thinned out women's blood and therefore drew out vitious matter.

"Do they not say that only hogs and women thrive in this clime, sir?" I asked, grinning. Lydia sniffed at that. *Nonsense,* she said later, when we were out of the doctor's earshot, *that is only an excuse that men use to make women labor.*

I agreed, I said. Mistress Poole's sex was not what saved her. "It is probably the drink she is so fond of. Did you not once say that if all the ocean was sherry sack, Mistress Poole would drink it up?" I chuckled. "Some of the scholars say that liquor is a good medicine that aids digestion and hastens the transformation of food to blood."

"Nonsense," Lydia said once more. "All it does is turn men and women into fools."

Lovely and young as she was, she had a way of speaking directly, just like that. She was my wife, but she made it clear I owned neither her nor her thoughts and opinions. I once told her about how on the night of the rebellion, Ganter had begged for jimsonweed and how I had given it to him, at first only to prevent him from going out. How things had unfolded, how I had watched and waited.

I looked at her as I spoke. I expected her to tell me to halt, to say that some secrets are not for divulging, some burdens not meant to be shared, to keep silent, she did not want to know. But she listened intently till I reached the end of my account.

"So that is what happened," I said. "That night. When I came to find you at daybreak, Ganter was dead."

I heard her draw a sharp breath. She looked at me carefully and when she spoke it was in a measured voice. "And what of it? He would have died soon enough anyway. And besides, he deserved death."

That was Lydia's way. She said that she did not believe in overcomplicating things, was not interested in fine philosophical distinctions, unless they had to do with medicine and disease. But the truth is that Lydia believed that right and wrong were thorny in this complicated place, as were truth, justice, and mercy. The one thing you can do is walk onward. There is a reason, she said, why nature did not give us eyes on the backs of our heads. What is done is done.

But as for me, Ganter continued to haunt me and was to haunt me for the rest of my days. He was to visit me at unexpected moments and in unexpected places. To squat stubbornly inside my head—never quite letting go, never wholly allowing me to forget. In some sense, I was to be bound to him forevermore.

Master Poole, like his wife, appeared to recover, and so did my master, but many others were swept up and away by the mysterious malady that spread across the colony that year. The doctor, once he was improved, and I were called day and night to come to the beds of those ailing with the fever, vomit, and aches that were the first symptoms of the disease. Many believed that it was like the pestilence that took people in England, that it was a contagion that spread through breath and touch. When Doctor Herman and other physicians said it was the miasma that brought the sickness—either the damp air rising from the swamps or the ill vapors of the slave ships that wafted out onto shore, I remembered the *contagious fogs* the playwright had described in the *Midsummer* play. We told our patients to burn tobacco to clear the air, to have regular mud baths as a preventive measure, and administered mercury pills to strengthen men from the onslaught of the disease. And we went home every night, our legs weak with fatigue, the warm air redolent around us with the scent of summer blossoms, the creeks and streams filled with darting, shimmering life, knowing all along that the fever too hung thickly in the air, water, and land—all so menacing, so beautiful.

I ran into Solomon, Gumby, and Flynn when I was walking back from a sickbed and was glad of a moment of leisure. We lingered by the river and watched a heron stand on one leg and then the other. Gumby leaned back on the tree and sang a song that was both melancholy and pleasing. I did not understand a word, but it made my throat catch. Even Flynn kept mum and listened.

"He is singing of home," Solomon said, resplendent with his scars and tattoos in the red light of the setting sun. "He is hoping the wind will catch the words and take them back to his land."

I had thought Solomon could not understand Gumby's tongue. But perhaps he was talking about the kind of song *he* would want to sing. Gumby continued his melody.

"Damn fool song, sung by Gumby's rascal tribe," Solomon proclaimed, suddenly remembering that he and Gumby were foes. But he did not sound convinced, and I could see that he was moved by that quaint, sad tune.

The four of us sat there for a moment, all washed up in this spot from different corners of the world, each man holding the song close. As I got up to leave, Flynn said that Dick was ailing too, with the same ague that had struck so many others.

"Hope he die," Solomon said simply. "Hope the fever takes him."

I had once wanted a man to die . . . Now I was done with such wishing. And, besides, the sick man was Dick Hughes. They stared at me in puzzlement when I started up and said I would have to go to see him.

"He did not even call for a doctor, man," Flynn said. "I do not see why you are in such haste."

Never popular with the other servants, Dick was even less liked after his role in aborting the revolt. But they did not understand. I had to go to his side.

He was poorly as they said. His forehead was hot to the touch, and he grimaced with the pain that he said afflicted his back and limbs. He barely seemed to know who I was. I wiped him down with damp cloths and administered him the draft made of hypericum, wormwood, and foxglove that was Doctor Herman's standard treatment for the ailment.

"Thank you, Doctor," Dick murmured. It seemed he thought I was my master.

I was back again the first thing in the morning, before I went to other patients. Dick appeared to be much improved, but I knew that that was the nature of the illness—it seemed to dissipate, giving the illusion of recovery, only to reappear with renewed malice.

"Oh, 'tis you, Tony," he said in a weak voice.

"Yes. And I have brought you something to hasten your cure."

I had mustard plaster with me and more of the draft, as well as some broth. I sat by his side to give him the physic but sensed something in him, a stiffening of the limbs and a shrinking away. He does not want the medicine, I thought. *He does not want anything from my hands.* He thinks I will harm him . . . He has always suspected, he *knows,* I thought, about that night with Ganter. I did not know what I felt—some mix of hurt and guilt, and a sudden fury. How could he not trust *me?* I was his oldest friend, the only person he had left from the crossing. But he closed his eyes and turned away, and I had no choice but to leave.

When wheat is green, when hawthorn buds appear, sickness is catching—so Master Shakespeare had written. Understanding, perhaps, that death and beauty go hand in hand, that death undoes love and friendship, hope and longing. I dreamt that Dick died on a perfect July night. He went where Little Sam went and Mad Marge too, into the place where the land meets the sea, where the sunsets we had watched together from the *God's Gift* finish, where the fantastical sea creatures sing. And I was the only one left in America. I, who had made the longest journey of all, I would have to press on.

When I woke up from my troubled sleep, it was still dark and I could barely wait for daybreak to wake my master and beg him to go with me to Dick Hughes. He complained that we do not go to sickbeds unless summoned, and I said that although we had not been called to attend to Dick, we would surely be paid later—Dick was a trusted servant, his master would want his health to improve. He then asked why I could not go by myself, I knew perfectly well what to do. I had nothing to say to that, but pleaded so urgently that he accompanied me. I saw Solomon and Gumby stare stony-faced at us as we entered the cabin Dick occupied. Dick's skin had turned yellow—a signal that the fever had got into his liver and kidneys. He appeared a stranger in his illness, as if he had already traveled a distance I could not cross. But he was awake, and took the physic my master administered him and even thanked him for coming.

"'Twas Tony," Doctor Herman said briefly. "He insisted that I see you."

Dick turned his gaze to me then and smiled wanly. The master had to leave soon after but told me I could stay for a bit. I applied the mustard plaster on Dick's chest and arms to ease his pain. As I watched, his stomach heaved mightily and he vomited a thick black sludge. He then fell back, covered in perspiration, and was so weary he could barely speak.

"I am much afeared, Tony," he whispered, so low that I had to bend down to catch what he said. "I think I will die and everything will come to naught."

Everything—for Dick the promise held out by America. It was this promise that gave him purpose to live from one day to the other. And as a hardworking, ambitious Englishman, he expected America to give him his due.

"It will be all right. Good things will still come to pass," I said, pressing his hand. He shook his head and drifted off into what seemed a stupor rather than sleep.

I had many patients to see that day and could not tarry longer. I stepped out and told the men to take turns watching him. Solomon and Gumby grumbled—they had much to do in the fields without being nursemaids, but Cuffee, who had joined them when I was indoors, said I was not to fret, he would keep an eye on Dick.

"You are wasting your time with him, Tony," Gumby solemnly pronounced. "You said he made black vomit, did you not?"

I nodded, and Gumby said that for seven days now he had been dreaming of a man drowning in a black river and also of a horse running wild, with black mane afloat. And then Solomon wanted to know why Gumby had not shared his dream till I told him about the vomit and, anyway, what had horses to do with anything. And so, they bickered, having quite dismissed Dick and his illness.

The fever of that summer took many men, women, and children. Death wafted from the swamps, out of the ships, neither manacled nor chained; it hung about the air, invisible and unknown, till it was time. It came to many, but each person met it with the surprise reserved for the stranger who presents himself unforeseen. Almost nothing we did seemed to help the dying. Those who lived might have done so only because of the natural resources their bodies drew on, the living being's simple, single-minded impulse to live, an impulse beyond thought, feeling, and knowledge. Masters watched in dismay as servants died, leaving the fields unmanned at a crucial time of the year, as the harvest got ready to be gathered. As always, the poor died in larger numbers than the rich. I fretted that Lydia would take sick, that Doctor Herman too would, once more, and they also worried for me. For the few hours we were at home, we would sit swathed in tobacco smoke, which my master believed neutralized the contagion. Occasionally, especially on the evenings when I was exhausted and disheartened, I saw him, the Man Who Would Not Die, veiled in fumes himself, waiting for I knew not what. I also caught glimpses of him trudging through the fields, head down, back straight, gradually turning into a smudge against the sky. And once I saw him by a deathbed, a shadowy presence who I assumed was a mourning family member, till someone lit a candle. Always, always, he went as suddenly as he came.

And there were the usual tales of the wailing phantoms of the dead, of black vomit seen on paths no man had trodden on, of sick men dissolving into liquids, burning to cinders.

"I heard of one fellow stricken with the ague who was so heated up that he turned to smoke," Flynn informed me one day. "A gray wisp—that is all that was left of him finally."

"Black man or white man?" I asked. I was skeptical of the tale.

"Tawny moor like you."

"A Powhatan man or a Pamunkey?"

"No, man. I said 'twas an East Indian, just like you," Flynn replied knowledgeably.

Someone else confirmed that an unfortunate man who identified as East

Indian had died of the yellow fever in Charles River County. Some said he was lighter than me, almost like a Turk or Persian, others said he was darker, like an African. Any of them could have been right—they are of practically every complexion known to humanity, my people. So, the first East Indian I had heard of in Virginia in six years was a dead one, one who might have spontaneously combusted. I did not know whether to laugh or weep.

It was Lydia who said that Master Poole would die of the fever. The Pooles had taken turns being ill of it, but both of them had come through this far. Then Lydia saw Master Poole one evening, once again afflicted, and said that this was it.

"Oh, that man is as strong as a horse," I said dismissively. "He merely suffers from hypochondriasis and is the most robust sick man I have seen."

"No, Tony, he is very badly this time. I do not think he has hope. He has the look of a dying man."

And she was proved to be right because Master Poole perished after two days of fever and pains. Barely four and twenty hours later Mistress Poole was knocking at our door. Her sharp, small face was wan with grief, and her skirts and hair were in disarray.

"Can I help you, mistress?" asked my master gently. After all, our visitor had been a widow less than a day.

She answered without ceremony or greeting. "It is the girl, the black girl, who is to blame . . ."

"Lydia . . . ?"

"Who else could I be on about? She said my husband would die and not a day later he did."

Lydia stepped forward. "Mistress, all I said was that the master was poorly."

"You lying, lying . . . black bitch and whore. My girl heard you telling that moor of yours that Master Poole would be gone soon enough." She sobbed and then spat fiercely on the ground at Lydia's feet.

She was right, of course, but Lydia had been telling what she judged to be the truth.

"You are a witch, you are a *witch*!" Mistress Poole said, still whispering hoarsely, her eyes burning like fire, her heart breaking with grief.

Lydia stayed calm after Mistress Poole left, and Doctor Herman too appeared undisturbed. I was the one who was troubled.

The next morning Lydia and I went to the dovecote to lay out water and feed before we set out on our sickbed duties. Even before I stepped through the entryway, Lydia, who was before me, called out softly. Eight birds lay on the ground, crimson legs up in the air, their feathers ruffled. Two of them appeared to have been strangled and two were headless.

Lydia knelt by them, too shocked to weep. "Who did this?" she asked. And I could only imagine Mistress Poole coming through the night, intent and secret, armed with a kitchen knife, thinking that killing the birds Lydia tended to would somehow allay her grief.

Over the next few days, Mistress Poole let it be known to all who would listen that Lydia could foretell death, and soon enough loose tongues murmured that it was my wife who had caused Master Poole to die. She had been in sympathy with the rebels, many suspected that. Perhaps she was seeking vengeance on those who curtailed the rebellion. She had probably caused Dick to fall ill too. And so it went. A woman, the same Mistress Fanny Moore who had purchased my love potion some years ago, who had delivered a child recently, said that Lydia had offered her midwife's services but she, Mistress Moore, had refused because Lydia was left-handed and it was well known that left-handed midwives could harm the child. And she said that Lydia had been angry at being refused and caused Mistress Moore's milk to congeal in her breasts.

"I was a little annoyed, yes," Lydia told me. "But that was because she did not want a black midwife and used my left-handedness as an excuse. I certainly cast no spell."

We went to the Crossed Keyes, and we saw some of the men, the same ones who had joined the rebellion, edge away from us, and look fearfully, as if Lydia's mere presence would bring ill fortune upon them.

"Even a white woman who knows medicines and such opens herself to accusations of witchcraft," said Cuffee. "And your little Lydia is black."

"There are medicine women in my country," Gumby said. "And they get plenty regard."

Lydia was silent on the way back. "Do not worry," I said. "The rumor will die away, as rumors do. Doctor Herman will see to it."

She sighed. "But some things will stay unchanged. A black witch and a fraudulent East Indian moor. That is what we will always be to them. No less and no more."

I took her in my arms. She placed her head briefly on my chest and then looked up. In the moonlight, her large eyes were even more beautiful.

"We have endured much before, apart from each other," I said. "We will do more, we will triumph together now."

We walked back to our cabin hand in hand.

I went to see Dick the next morning. I had been visiting him throughout, bringing him medicine. Harry Jones, the overseer, might make arrangements with his master to pay for it, but there was a chance he would not. Dick was clearly much stronger that morning. In fact, his condition had been improving for days now.

"I would not be alive but for you, Tony," he said. "You were good to me."

I felt embarrassed at the sudden expression of sentiment. "I only did what any man would," I said. As any man would, who is true to his friend, true to his calling, who wishes, more than anything, to atone for another death. Dick talked then of how he had heard that Master Adams had at last picked out his English wife, how he would return, how Dick meant to impress him with his hard work. I could see that my friend was indeed better. Filled with the same aspirations as before, not particularly interested in other men's hopes or fears. And when it was time for me to leave, Dick pressed my hand warmly and I was indeed glad he was so cheerful and well. Three boys had got off the ship. Surely, at least two must live.

I went back to the cabin to find Lydia anxious and fearful. She had found, in a small heap at the door, a bit of some unidentifiable root and two dead spiders.

"Someone is trying to cast a spell on me because they think I am a witch," Lydia said, torn between scorn and fear.

"Or more likely someone is trying to cast blame on you as a practitioner of black magic," I said.

Doctor Herman too looked troubled. He drew me aside and wondered if Lydia should go away for a bit.

"But the problem is that she is still bound to Mistress Poole, and it is Mistress Poole who started all of this," he said. "The people here are ignorant peasants. There is no telling what fear will make them do."

He was right—all the sickness and death around us had made people fearful. They were looking for someone to blame or to sacrifice. And whom better to blame than a young black woman, a witch? And I thought of the other woman who had been hanged from the yardarm of the ship on the fourth week of our voyage to America. She had been kind to me on the one occasion we had spoken. But at her trial, I too had had no doubt of her guilt. I felt ashamed for the boy I had been, and I also felt fear for what was to come.

EIGHTEEN

That is why, when Cuffee said, *Let's go, Tony, let's get away from here,* I took heed. Flynn Keough had been talking forever of running away, Flynn, who had the madcap dreams. But it was Cuffee who said it this time. One day that week, even as the ague reigned, even as the summer was still about us, it was Cuffee who stood up and gingerly felt his aching arms, Cuffee who said, "Let us go," as if he were suggesting the obvious: "Let us go, my friend." Just like that.

He was tired of his bondage, he said, and we were all better off running away: Lydia might be in trouble; I was not only her husband but the only one of my kind, so the easiest to target, the easiest to dislike. I could see that Cuffee was right, but I was still hesitant. Should I go, aborting my apprenticeship? Would staying lead to all manner of dreadful things? What was there for me here? What was there for me elsewhere? When I told Lydia of Cuffee's proposal, it was as if something new stirred in her. *Let us go,* she too said, her eyes shining. And I could tell that it was not fear alone that drove her. She yearned to see whatever lay beyond these farms and woods, to discover whatever was outside and ahead.

So, it was decided. It was also decided that I would tell the doctor, so that it would not be a running away but a mutually agreed upon termination of an apprentice's term. We were uncertain if he would permit me to go—I was still bound to him for a few more years. And what would he say about Lydia leaving when she was still in Mistress Poole's service?

When I informed Doctor Herman of our plans, I emphasized how anxious I was for Lydia's safety. He was silent for a bit. "You are still bound to me,

Tony," he said. "If you go without my permission, it will mean you are running away from a master."

He paused. "And I cannot condone Lydia leaving either. She is bound to
Mistress Poole."

We were both uncomfortably silent for a bit.

"Sir," I asked, "do you think I could someday be an independent physician
hereabouts?"

"I do not see why you could not."

"People say no man or woman would trust their body to a dark foreigner.
I am acceptable only as long as I am associated with you."

He shrugged at that. He agreed; he did not. I could not tell, and he would
not enlighten me.

No further word passed between us on the matter, and he said nothing a
week later when I told him that Cuffee had sent word that the following night
would be the night. A night when the overseer would be in Jamestown and
Cuffee could get away easily. I wanted the doctor to know. I did not want to
slip away from his house like a thief; I would have liked him to give me his
blessing, to bid me goodbye, but neither a benediction nor a farewell seemed
to be forthcoming.

"Please know I am grateful to you, sir," I said, because those words could
not go unsaid.

He turned away wordlessly, and with a heavy heart I slipped out to join
Lydia in our cabin.

We were to meet Cuffee two hours before midnight. It was oppressively warm,
and although we lay down, neither Lydia nor I could sleep. I knew she was
gazing into the dark in silence. I listened to the familiar scratching sound
of insects in the walls. The room was close, and desiring fresh air, I stepped
towards the door and pushed at it. It resisted opening—someone was standing
on the other side, pressing his weight against it. *Ganter,* I thought, *Ganter is
here again, and he hinders my going.* I halted where I was, and he waited noise-
lessly on the other side. But when I pushed it once more, the door opened
easily enough, and I felt foolish. There was nothing there but crooked night
shadows. And, just at the door, a small package. I brought it in, and there was
in it an apothecary's mortar and pestle, a scalpel, a probe, and a few pouches of
powders and herbs. Doctor Herman had left me a farewell gift.

Lydia and I departed, softly shutting the door behind us, carrying our small bundles. She also had a few coins sewn into the waist of her skirt. Cuffee would wait for us at the edge of Master Adams's lands. It was dark within and without, but a half-moon flitted from behind a gauze of cloud and looked down upon us wonderingly. My doubts and anxieties were allayed all of a sudden as I inhaled the scent of the woods and the fields, and heard the rise and fall of a cricket's chirrup. I took Lydia's hand and felt the warm flesh in my own and the pulse throbbing on her wrist. Now, so many years later, the moment lingers: that particular memory of fear and freedom, anxiety and anticipation, Lydia by my side, the shadowy world, the promise of light.

Cuffee was awaiting us as planned. *Ready to go? Yes? Let's go then. Let's . . .*

We had barely walked twenty yards when we saw a movement in the bushes. A rustle and a high sound that could only be one thing—a man farting. Followed by a mighty stink. The three of us froze. Who could it be, out shitting in the bushes? The overseer? Dick? They would want to know what we were doing there.

The leaves parted and Flynn Keough came out, wiping his filthy hand on his breeches. In the faint light of the moon he saw us standing there, like three statues.

"Gave me the start of my life," he was to say later, repeatedly. "Thought you was bloody Indians!" At that time, standing in the dark, surrounded by the undergrowth and the smell of Flynn's excrement, none of us said a word. Till Cuffee cursed softly: "Fuck you, Flynn."

And that is how Flynn Keough ended up running away with us.

We reached the creek—the four of us walking single file through the woods, Cuffee leading the way, his body taut; Flynn behind him, fairly shaking with excitement, hardly believing that his long-standing dream of escape was coming true; Lydia, slender and strong, holding up her skirts a little; and I, at the tail end, the blood beating about my ears: *Let us go . . .* steady and staunch: *let us go . . . let's go . . . letsgo . . . letsgo . . . lessgo . . .*

We found the skiffs that Dick kept concealed in the bushes and pushed them into the water. Tomorrow, someone sent to find us would see the marks on the sand and would guess how they were made. They would say that we were runaways and thieves to boot. But we cared not—*lessgo, lessgo, lessgo . . .*

We rowed towards the James—the plan was to go across the river and then to abandon the vessels and make the long journey north, across the York, Rappahannock, and the Potomac rivers or, if a vessel would take us, across the Chesapeake to the Province of Maryland. That was the place to go, Cuffee said. It had smaller, newer settlements than Virginia, but there was plenty of work to be found in Saint Mary's Cittie and the farms surrounding. Also, the Catholics' hostility to Virginians meant that we would not be looked for or returned. That is where some Virginia servants fled to, that is where they lived. We would avoid the farms and plantations and work our way through the woods; only the beasts of the wild would see us. We'd find a boat to take us across the bay.

We went till daybreak—the splash of our oars quiet and steady, Flynn and I at them, Cuffee and Lydia, holding the bundles on their laps. The woods stirred, and the birds were soon creating a mighty cacophony, twittering, whirring, clucking, and clacking as the sun rose, a red glow streaming through the dense foliage. Herds of deer standing along the bank took off into the woods as we approached, and a bear stared, stolid and unmoved. The river widened and narrowed, as was its way.

As day broke, we rowed to the shore, to some spot that seemed remote from human habitation. We left behind the boats in a thicket, and ventured into the dense woods. We were glad to eat and get some sleep. Flynn rattled on: Maryland was a terrible idea, still too new, too wild and desolate, he had heard. We should have gone to the Indians first and with their help gone even further north to the Dutch country, as he had been suggesting for years . . . He had long worked out his scheme.

"And the Indians would have helped you because you have mastered their tongue," I remarked quietly, and Cuffee laughed. We never tired of that jest. But when we woke up, Flynn had killed two rabbits and had them skinned and ready for roasting. We were very glad he was with us, Flynn. Four was more company than three.

We began walking. Did I visualize what it would be like once we reached our destination? Only vaguely—Lydia and I would be free of fear, we would work for ourselves. *Somehow,* it would be better; a blessed future awaited although I could not fully envision it. I, Tony, was to be born yet once more. I suppose that such visions sustained the others too. Even Flynn stopped talking about how his was the better plan.

The next afternoon we heard the undergrowth rustle and the soft murmur of voices. We swiftly concealed ourselves in the bushes.

They are seeking us . . . I thought, my heart pounding in my chest. But they were only loggers—three men, probably servants themselves. They passed within feet of us and I could smell the strong odor from their boots as they trampled the grass. I could have reached out and touched them. It was surprising they did not smell us too—our clothes were foul and noisome. We stayed in the undergrowth long after they passed, our limbs strained and wakeful.

So, we went on for two days. Always walking northwards, resting for a few hours and moving on. The food we had carried was long gone, and we relied on our ability to trap small animals. Our limbs were bruised by the foliage, and my boots were practically in shreds. Lydia looked exhausted. But we never thought of turning back—forward was the only way to go. To the north, to Maryland, to somewhere, to freedom. *Lessgo . . . lessgo . . . lessgo . . .* Even the birds took up the refrain, and the chirping insects: *Lessgo, lessgo.*

On the third day, it started to rain, light and steady till it picked up all of a sudden and grew torrential. We raced to find shelter under the trees for what it was worth. I ran, wet mud squelching through my wretched shoes, the droplets hitting my face like gravel. When we reached a clump of trees, I saw that Lydia was not with us. I ran about looking for her, the water cascading down my face—she could not have gone far. But when the rain stalled and grew to a fine drizzle, she was still not in sight. All around me the soaking woods, suddenly swathed in silence, the sun coming out halfheartedly from behind the clouds, and mud everywhere it seemed—on my clothes, below me, splattered on the tree trunks. I called out:

"Lydia . . . !"

And again: *"Lydia . . . ! Where are you?"*

There was no response, except from a bedraggled bird that called out mournfully from a branch overhead.

"Lydia . . ." I cried yet again, hoarsely, suddenly in a panic. *I will never find her.* I was walking faster, I thought I was walking in circles till I saw that the woods were moving. The trees closed in, snarling, and the scraggly path between them whipped itself tight around my feet, rooting me to where I stood before it swiftly unwound itself with a hiss and was sucked into the earth. The wooded maze with neither start nor finish to it swirled and spun under and around me. And then I was stumbling wildly through it. I could hear my breath coming in gasps and the forest was filled with sounds and shadows—they were all there: Mad Marge, her hair flying, head thrown back, shrieking soundlessly; Little Sammy, pale and shorn, looking like a death's-head; Martin and Bristol, staggering through the trees, grotesquely long-limbed; Old Ganter naked, his turgid red member swinging between his legs, his breath coming fast and shallow. And up above, beyond the trees, so I could catch only glimpses of their leaning shadows, were the gods—Murugan, Shiva, Ganesha, Varuna Agni, Kali, Durga, God, Christ, Saint Thomas—all of them watching stony-eyed and still as I thrashed around.

I stumbled onto her in a clearing. She was kneeling on the ground, bent over, her skirts sodden, her wet hair loose about her.

"Lydia! What is the matter? Are you ill?"

She shook her head and got to her feet.

"Why did you leave us?" I asked.

"I don't know. The rain . . . the trees . . ." She looked confused for an instant, and then pulled herself together. "Come," she said, taking my arm. "Come, let us go to our friends."

We found Flynn and Cuffee easily enough. But things did not look good in that quarter. Flynn was on the ground with Cuffee crouched by his side. Flynn had been stung by a snake, Cuffee told us, probably one of the pit vipers that one sometimes saw in the fields and woods. I knelt down and took Flynn's foot in my hands. The creature's fangs had left two needle points on his ankle and the blood trickled thin and red out of one of them. I soaked a rag and wrapped the foot with it.

"He will need your mother's cure for snakebite, Lydia," I said. "Shavings of oriental bezoar and dittany."

There was no way we could lay our hands on the bezoar, so we used the volatile oils of dittany in the package my master had left me. But the swelling grew alarmingly big and the skin around it black. Poor Flynn was in an agony of pain, although he would not admit to it. His stomach, always delicate, also could not hold down the scraps of game meat which was all we had. He complained of a burning in the pit of his belly.

"He needs bread," I said. "Or cornmeal—those would allay him."

"Let me be," Flynn said. "Let me be, and you go on, all of you."

"We cannot do that, lad!" I think all three of us said that together. And we decided that I would go seek some human habitation and request help—food and some herbs I could use to make up a poultice for Flynn.

"You go, Tony," Cuffee instructed. "A tawny man might be mistaken for a Virginia Indian, or something, and they might not get too suspicious."

I trudged for about two leagues till I came to a makeshift cabin in a clearing. Until this morning we would have skirted around it, not daring to breathe. But now I was glad of the sight. A child played outside—a boy not yet ten, with a white, wizened visage and gray eyes. I had not expected to see a child here, in the middle of the wilderness. I approached him, trying not to rush.

"Do not be afeared, lad," I said.

He stared at me, stony-faced; he did not look the least apprehensive.

"Anyone inside?" I gestured towards the cabin. "Your pa, maybe?"

He chortled quietly at that.

"Who are you?" he asked, and his voice was as dry and ancient as his face. "Come any nearer and I will shoot."

I could not see a gun on him, but I was not taking the chance. We stood there staring at each other, man and boy. A man came out of the cabin. He was as unkempt as I was, with his wild beard, unwashed face, and filthy clothes.

"Who you talking to, you filthy sod?" he asked, not raising his voice. I hoped he was addressing the boy.

"Him here—the black rascal," the boy said, crooking his thumb at me, and he turned his aged man's face away and squatted on the ground and proceeded to spit on an unfortunate beetle at his feet, whose wings he had already wrenched off.

The man beckoned me towards him, his hand on his musket all along, and I had no choice but to go to him. I explained how things stood—my companions, a snakebite, a man needing food. He gestured me into the cabin and there was another man there, who resembled the first. I noticed that his face was slightly swollen on one side. They seemed to be hunters. Their trophies cluttered the cabin—a musty bearskin, which clearly served as a bed, the antlers of a buck, sundry hoofs, hides, and paws. The first man asked me to repeat my tale. They both listened, expressionless.

"Take us to your companions," the first man said at the end of my breathless account. And without further ado, we stepped out together. The second fellow had not said a word all along. The boy had disappeared.

We walked back into the woods—one of the Fentons (I learned that that was their surname) ahead of me and one behind; they were being cautious. We had to walk well over an hour to get to where I had left the others.

"Damn long way off! What you fellows doing here?" the first one asked.

"We have completed our indentures and are going north looking for work," I said.

He nodded. The second Fenton stayed silent. Every now and then, he felt his jaw gingerly.

Flynn still looked in a bad way when we came upon them, and between us we hauled him back to the clearing. The first thing we did was get him some cornmeal mush provided by our hosts, and then Lydia got to preparing a fresh poultice to apply on him.

We meant to bide with the Fentons just a day or two at the very most; we meant to stay vigilant while we were there; we meant never to step into the cabin and make ourselves vulnerable; we meant, above all, to move on, to get going—to *less go, lessgo, lessgo* . . .

The first night was a fine one. We stayed outside, taking turns to sit up on watch for wild beasts or other dangers of the dark. We hoped the fresh air would do Flynn some good. Lydia was tired too, and I hoped that the break from tramping through the woods would help her recover her strength a little. Early next morning, the Fenton brother who had not said a word gestured to me.

He looked like he was in some pain and spoke with difficulty. "You seem to know something about physic?"

"Yes, master. A little."

He pondered that for a bit. "Got a god-awful toothache, I have," he then said.

I had already guessed that he was afflicted by a sore tooth and nodded, eager to help in return for the aid they were rendering us. I made him an herbal compress and pressed it against the offending molar, which was indeed in poor condition.

"This should make the worm burrowing in the cavity fall out," I said. "If not, I will extract the tooth for you."

He grunted in reply. An hour or two later, the boy came up to me.

"Give me something too," he said, looking at me steadily with his old man's eyes.

"Are you ill?"

He shrugged. "No, but I want something. Anything."

And he sat against a bush and whittled a stick.

"Funny little bastard," whispered Cuffee.

The man with the toothache came out in a short while and proceeded to scrape at a deerskin. He seemed less wan than before.

"How do you fare now, sir?" I asked, but he paid no attention to me, did not look up even when I heard a rustle behind us and felt a musket pressed against my neck.

"You boys come with me now," the other Fenton said. "Just come quiet."

We turned around to protest.

"I know you are no freed servants. Hold your tongues and haul your black asses up."

"My husband and I are free," Lydia said, her voice filled with fury. "Our master is aware we left . . ."

"We will find out direct from him" was the reply. Flynn moaned quietly. All along the other Fenton worked on the skin of the dead beast, looking up at us every now and then. I might have eased his tooth affliction, but he clearly felt he owed me naught. The boy watched us unflinchingly, from his position crouched in the dust.

We stood up and, prodded by the musket, stumbled into the cabin. "Be gentle with my mistress," I said sharply. Once we were inside, the door was barred on us.

Cuffee and I refused to tell them whom we had run away from. But they got it out of poor Flynn, who was half in a stupor still. The more talkative Fenton left for Pasbyhayes on a horse he borrowed from somewhere to inform our masters, and we were transferred to two cramped cabins near the edge of the clearing, Lydia and I in one, and Cuffee and Flynn in the other. Lydia sat leaning against the wall, her eyes shut tight, and I could see that, once again, she felt sick. It was then that I asked her what I had suspected for the past two days. Yes, she said, yes.

We stayed confined for three whole days, being let out only for short intervals.

"Your master is in a hurry to have you back; it seems his men will arrive to fetch you either today or tomorrow." So the Fenton who had stayed behind informed us. I would have succumbed to despair if Lydia had not been by my side. And one morning, as I splashed my face with the dusty water standing in a trough, I saw my reflection and just behind me that of another, nut-brown, earth-hued. It was he again, the Man Who Would Not Die. To this place too he had accompanied me. He was looking down at my reflection in the water, expressionless yet somehow expectant, as if he wanted something. I did not look around, because I knew he would be gone.

Later that day we heard the gallop of horses and men in conversation outside—the younger Fenton saying what a crew of blackguards we were, how we had fought him fierce when he locked us in the room, how . . . and then other voices, lower than Fenton's and then Fenton's again, this time churlish and complaining, and I knew he was vexed about how little reward they were offering him for his pains. And then the door was pushed open, and I did not have to look at the man standing outlined against the light to know it was Dick who had come for us.

Once he had confirmed our identities, Dick stepped out again, shutting the door behind him. He had brought from one of the other farms a black servant, who looked at us expressionlessly. We guessed that Dick and his companion were eating and drinking, probably renewing themselves before the journey back. An hour passed before I pressed against the door and called out softly: "Dick! It is me, Tony. I would speak with you."

I had to plead a few more times before he let me out. The Fentons were nowhere to be seen and the black man lurked by himself in the shadows, listening.

"What would you have with me, Tony?" Dick said. His voice was hard and he would not look me in the eye.

"You must let us go, Dick. Both Lydia and me, all of us," I said urgently. "The doctor knows I left."

"Cuffee and Flynn are still bound. And where are the papers to prove your master released you?"

"Doctor Herman knows," I insisted. "I informed him."

"And what of Lydia? She is still bound to Mistress Poole, who is in a fury and wants her servant back. The doctor had no authority to let Lydia go, even if he released you. And, although I do not believe in such nonsense myself, some say that your woman is a witch—they call for her to be tried."

"She is no witch, and you must let us go. Also, she is with child." And I would have reminded him, if I had had the time, of how we had been children ourselves when we climbed aboard that vessel, of the woman whose death we had witnessed, of the lad we had both loved so well.

Dick would not look at me as I spoke. His countenance, so familiar yet suddenly that of a stranger, remained blank. I could see that he had fully re-covered from the yellow fever.

"You appear in good health now," I said. "I am glad you are rid of the ague."

He nodded.

I hesitated. I did not wish to remind him. He should have known without reminding. "I did what I could to aid you when you were ill. Surely you know that," I said.

The black man in the background shifted. Dick stayed silent, continuing to look straight ahead, fingering his musket. His fever might or might not have responded to my treatment; he might or might not be alive and well because of me, but surely, I had done my part for him. I wondered what would have happened, who would they have sent to look for us if Dick had perished. Which servant more loyal to those to whom he was bound than Dick?

It was about midnight. We had been tersely instructed to get what rest we could before the journey back. Lydia was restless, but did not utter a word. I did not know how to console her, what to say. Tomorrow we would be back in Jamestown—they would try us for running away. And when they were done whipping us and rebuking us for not being faithful servants, they would try Lydia. Mistress Poole would repeat her accusations, and other men and women would come forward with their tales of illness and misfortune, and somehow Lydia, my Lydia, would be inserted into every one of those stories. And then—and then as on the *God's Gift*—a jostling, jeering crowd; a woman, her dark hair undone.

I stood up distraught. It was not meant to end this way. Lydia huddled in the corner, very still. I do not know what thoughts passed through her head, or what the child she was carrying, our child, was to expect as it bided its time in the enriching fluids of the womb awaiting a birth that was a rebirth, one in a long line of arrivals and departures. It was a child of the New World, but it would carry in its being knowledges of other places, other times, a mighty crossing.

Lydia sighed and moved. I went to her and we sat side by side, very still. We did not speak—what could we say after all? This is my punishment, I thought numbly, for once failing in my duty.

A slight raspy sound from outside. Lydia did not raise her head, as if it had not reached her ears. I hesitated, and then went to the door and nudged at it. It was not barred. Someone had unfastened it for us.

The cool air flowed in, a mere touch, but it prompted Lydia to raise her head. She hastened to her feet. We did not tarry. There was little to take other than our two selves. The other cabin, where Cuffee and Flynn lay, had a lock fastened on the door, and I thought of both of them within, waiting to be taken back to Adams's Grove. I hesitated, my heart heavy. How could I desert them, my friends? Was there a way to get them out? The lock was strong and not to be easily broken. Besides, Dick was probably nigh, or his companion, the poker-faced black man.

"'Tis best to leave it," Lydia whispered. "Whatever we do now will not do anyone good."

And I felt her hand on my arm, urging me to make haste. To neither stop nor fumble, not then, not there, to look ahead even through the gloom. And so, we moved on, the warm night about us, and above us, a vastness both vacant and expectant.

VII

THE MAN WHO WOULD NOT DIE

NINETEEN

When Master Shakespeare's play draws to its close, the Indian boy has been quietly erased from it, and it is like he's never been. For their part, the young lovers are freed from the spell cast on them but are still confounded: *How came these things to pass . . . ?* That truly should have been the boy's question. He should have stayed on to ask it.

Lydia and I were the fortunate ones who got away. We have lived here in this Maryland settlement for many years now and are respected for our knowledge of the healing arts. The unnamed fever, which had ravaged this faraway place as well, abated, returned, abated again. And there were the other ailments men and women suffer from as well: dropsies, dysenteries, eruptions of the skin, aches of the joints, weariness of the heart. And like all people everywhere, these people long to live and flourish. The art and science of the physician is founded on the body's facility to triumph over affliction and also in the abiding belief that life is indeed worth living.

That is our daughter. She is my conclusion, the destination towards which this story was headed. But she also takes us back to the beginning. Her face is my mother's—it has the same unreal loveliness. Her skin is flawless and her eyes large, like those of *her* mother. She is nearing womanhood now, and she will be strong and beautiful—there is no doubt about that. She fills me with joy, and when I see this place anew through her eyes, I feel again the wonder of it.

At times, I ponder going further on—taking Lydia and the girl and traveling to the land to the north that Flynn would have gone to if he had had his way, a white place, with stars like icy stones. Or of carrying our collection of physic and the tools of our trade and taking a ship back to London, and eventually to Africa or the Coromandel. Or of finding at last the passage to the western sea, circling the globe, seeing all of *the round earth's imagin'd corners.* We would be as the wind that moves the vessels, wanderers with no home port. But, at other times, I know that we will simply remain where we are now. The Portuguese fortune-teller in São Tomé might have been both wrong and right when she said that I would come back home: I may never return to the place I started from, but I will be my own shelter, my landing place. Like a snail, I will carry home on my back, find it where I happen to be, make it from what I bear inside me.

News from Jamestown and the farms around it occasionally finds us, brought by other runaways, by men coming to this new colony looking for land to settle. We hear of Flynn's and Cuffee's fate and feel both grief and guilt. When Dick took my friends back, they were tried at a court in Jamestown. It was ruled that four years be added to Flynn's bond. As for Cuffee, he was bound to Master Menefie for the rest of his natural life. We were not the only mixed group of servants who ran away around that time; Flynn and Cuffee were not the only ones taken back and similarly punished. You can read in the chronicles of how in the year 1640, John Punch, an African indentured servant to Master Hugh Gwyn, ran away with two white servants. On being caught, Punch was punished as Cuffee was, with a sentence of labor that would not end till death. The white men had to labor for some more years, and some had to pay back their masters the expense of tracing and locating the runaways. The same year, another group of six white men ran away with a black man. Once more, the white men's terms were extended by two to seven years. The black man Emanuel's time of service was not extended because he was already a servant for life.

And so, men who came in as indentured servants suddenly found themselves slaves. It was the start of something entirely new. Besides, with fewer servants coming from England every year, both to Virginia and here, to Maryland, the planters increasingly rely on Africans; shiploads of them arrive every month and they have already outnumbered the white servants. Many black people maintain that all servants were not just servants in the same way even earlier: the color of the skin always mattered; black servants were black and white servants were white. It is true the latter too had been brought here and were treated like dogs, but they were still white men, and that, quite simply, made all the difference. That is why they—and I—are not entirely surprised at the way things have turned out.

Following this, we hear that the white servants will not do the harder, dirtier jobs—that is *slave work,* they say, and in their minds, a slave is a black man. There is a growing solidarity among the whites, rich and poor ones, a solidarity based on one truth and one truth only—they are not dark of complexion. It could be pointed out to some of them that the only thing they have in common with the rich planters in Jamestown is the hue of their skin, that they would be cast out once their service was done, to live the remnant of their lives landless and dirt poor, but it would make no difference. *At least we are not black,* they would say, *and that is enough.*

What will my daughter's future be? Two bloods—East Indian and African—run in her veins. Her children and their children too will bear both within them, although they may not know it. She is a daughter of this soil, and as a daughter of an African mother she is simply perceived as black. I worry when we hear of black people being declared slaves, and of new laws that dictate that children will inherit the status of their mother. A cruel new order has come to prevail and we are still to find our place in it.

We hear too that Dick has come far. Master Joshua Adams returned from London, and Dick Hughes became a fast favorite. The master gave him land as part of his freedom dues and Dick has added to it. He dreams of becoming a Master Adams, a Master Menefie. He has married a rich widow, as sensible men do, and is now owner of her properties. His tobacco harvests are plentiful. He has children. But I suspect that when Dick wakes up at night and is unable to fall into slumber, he feels the old fears of slipping back and slipping down, of turning into a destitute boy yet once more, of returning to Saint Giles, a slum rat, with dirty face, empty belly, and nails chewed down to the skin. I know that he resolves then that he will do all it takes to keep the wheel from turning full circle.

When my daughter asks about the voyage that brought me here, I tell her that one Dick Hughes, landowner, and I were ship brothers once, friends long after, that both carry in us the same memories of the heave and roll of the sea, the rain-washed decks, the ringed moon, the woman hanged, the third boy we lost, those first years in Virginia, those last years of boyhood, and how we had clung to each other for a long time till our ways parted—white boy and brown, orphans cast adrift. She can barely believe me.

We also heard when my first master, Master Menefie, died in 1646, a very wealthy man. Doctor Herman died too, of drowning in the river when his boat turned over one fine day in late spring. I often think of him, a talented healer, who taught me that within the very confines of skin and bone and flesh lies the living image of the entire universe waiting to be explored.

In 1649 the colonies were shaken by the execution of the English King Charles. A crowd had gathered around the blackened and sanded site in London to watch. Afterwards, some people dipped their handkerchiefs in the king's blood to make relics, while others rejoiced. And thereafter, we heard, Virginia was flooded with fleeing royalists—there was no place in England as loyal to the dead king, no people who grieved him as deeply as Virginians did.

I sometimes think of my friends Shuren and Amoro. In the year 1644 a federation of Powhatan Indians led by Chief Opechancanough attacked the English settlements in one last, desperate bid to reclaim their lands. Even we, who live so far north of the James, feared that the fury would spread to local tribes in our vicinity. And we cowered in our homes, weapons ready, waiting for the Indians to arrive. Because they would certainly come . . . today, or tomorrow, or the day after. But the Indians never came to where we are, although we heard that many colonists settled about the James were slaughtered and several taken prisoner. The English led retaliatory assaults, and two years later Chief Opechancanough was captured and shot dead by an English guard. There is a report that there was a man attending the chief who said that he once knew an Indian of another tribe who had traveled westward with a white man and another looking for a great western sea. After the treaty Chief Opechancanough's successor signed with Governor Berkeley, the Indians have withdrawn from the peninsulas of the James and York and have gone further inland. Occasionally you see an Indian trader or wolf hunter wearing the mandatory coat of striped stuff that identifies him as an ally and friend.

"We've successfully tamed the savages," the masters gloat when at their drinks, but even now, at night, when there is a rustle in the bushes, they reach for their muskets and the first thought in their heads is of the Indians. The Indians are part of the white men's ancestral memory here. They are the others, those who got here first, to whom this place was not new at all. And meanwhile, America is born and reborn, emerging each time from its previous self, bearing each time the weight of its past, yet transfigured, each time, exultant, hopeful, breathing anew . . .

This too I tell my daughter.

There are other things I do not tell the girl, which I have told her mother. About the Man Who Would Not Die, for instance. I can imagine the look of concern on my daughter's face if I were to recount my tale of that man; I can guess at her thoughts: *was my poor father in the habit of seeing things . . . ?* But I know better now who he was, that man.

Some years ago, I met a sailor who had been on an East India Company vessel that had sailed to the Coromandel. He talked of the heat of the food the natives consumed, a two-headed sea monster he had once seen in the cyclone-stirred waters of the Indian Ocean, the spices and muslins that made up the cargo of the ships he had served on. He then told me about Sir Francis Day's city by the sea, the one that was called Madrasapatnam by the locals and simply Madras by the English. How it was on its way to becoming a flourishing factory and a great city, and how the English trade was booming on the Coromandel and, indeed, in all of East India, and how the English were fast becoming more powerful than even the local kings. The man had drunk a little too much, and I could not tell how much of what he reported was the truth.

I remember that long-gone day in Mylapore. I was standing outside, in the shade of some squat tree. Someone had hailed me; it must have been Master Day: "'Tis time to go, boy . . ." I had picked up my bundle and hoisted it on my shoulder. At the door of the house, a peacock dragging its tail in the dust, the sacred basil plant in its earthen pot, the idol of the elephant-headed deity, the remover of obstacles. Surely, there had been another voice, also calling out to me, urging me to remain, a voice barely audible, a half-completed utterance. But I had not stopped to investigate and hurried on. The ship would sail soon and I must go to it.

And so, every once in a while, I am visited by past possibilities, by roving thoughts of what could have been if there had been no crossing, no voyage, if I had remained in that place where I had started. Then, sometimes, I cannot help but think that he is still there, that boy sitting on the shore in that self-same town on the Coromandel, in the shadow of the East India Company fort, looking out at the salt flats and the ships, the sun on his face, having never left, a solitary, large-eyed boy, waiting for a different life to unfold.

Whatever or whoever he had been at first—the Man Who Would Not Die had become myself, a man who defies destruction, wards off an absolute end. One who is delivered into birth after birth after birth in a single life: persistent, enduring, making something of the very things that constrain and confine, insistently striving for the self that is wholly free. Tony, the first East Indian in this land that sits at the end and the beginning of the world. Others of my kind will come here, and still others, and they will tell their stories, tales filled with loss, doubt, wonder, and hope. But mine, such as it is, is a first story.

   I will go home now—the western sky is flush with light and my wife and child are waiting.

AUTHOR'S NOTE

While this is a work of fiction, it is inspired by the "East Indian" presence in colonial North America. Many of the very first East Indians (i.e., natives of the Indian subcontinent) in America probably arrived as indentured servants. They came via London, where they were most likely either servants to East India Company officials or sailors on East India Company ships. Most of them were brought over to America by agents scouting for cheap labor. "Tony" is the earliest known mention of such an East Indian worker. In 1635, he was used as headright by a prosperous Virginia landowner, George Menefie. Under the headright system any individual who paid for the transportation of other people into the colony was awarded fifty acres of land for every "head" brought over. Many of those so transported were indentured servants, although family members and friends could also be claimed as headright.

Although they are now barely a footnote to American colonial history, a number of other East Indians appear hereafter in the records, right up to the American Revolution and beyond. Most of them lived and worked in Virginia and Maryland, with a small number present in the Carolinas, and perhaps elsewhere. Evidence of their existence is to be found in lists of headrights appended to land patents, estate inventories, court records, notices for runaway servants and slaves, and listings of freed servants and slaves. Early East Indians appear to have merged with the African-American population—the children born of their unions with African-Americans were eventually identified as "black."

One young East Indian man is recorded as having served as an apprentice to a London apothecary before he was transported to America. He, and that very first South Asian in America, the long-forgotten "Tony," moved me to write this novel.

Although I used a novelist's creative license and imagined much of what I recount here, the labors of many historians informed and inspired me. While any attempt at a full listing will only result in inadvertent omissions, the sources I consulted include Francis Assisi's "South Asians in Colonial America" (*Span,* May–June 2007, and similar articles on various websites); Roberta Estes's post on East Indians in Early Colonial Records (nativeheritageproject .com); Paul Heinegg's *Free African Americans of Virginia, North Carolina, South Carolina, Maryland and Delaware,* particularly his listing of East Indians; Martha W. McCartney's *A Study of the Africans and African Americans on James-town Island and at Green Spring, 1620–1803;* Nell Nugent's *Cavaliers and Pioneers—Abstracts of Virginia Land Patents and Grants, 1623–1800*; and the Virginia Land Office Patents and Grants Index. Also, *Tales of Old and New Madras* by S. Muthiah; *Black Lives in the English Archives, 1500–1677* and "Indians in Shakespeare's England as 'The First-Fruits of India': Colonial Effacement and Postcolonial Reinscription" (*Journal of Narrative Theory* 36, no. 1, Winter 2006) by Imtiaz Habib; *Black Tudors* by Miranda Kaufmann; *Transatlantic Encounters—American Indians in Britain, 1500–1776,* by Alden T. Vaughan; *Albions' Seed: Four British Folkways in America* by David H. Fischer; *American Slavery, American Freedom* and *Virginians at Home* by Edmund Morgan; *Slave Counterpoint* by Philip D. Morgan; *The Barbarous Years* and *The Peopling of British North America* by Bernard Bailyn; *Jamestown Brides* by Jennifer Porter; "Surviving the Gallows" by Elizabeth Hurren (*BBC History* 20, no. 2, February 2019); *Why We Left—Untold Stories and Songs of America's First Immigrants* by Joanna Brooks; *American Colonies—The Settling of North America* by Alan Taylor; *White over Black—American Attitudes Toward the Negro, 1550–1812,* by Winthrop Jordan; *Good Wives, Nasty Wenches, and Anxious Patriarchs: Gender, Race, and Power in Colonial Virginia* by Kathleen M. Brown; *The Old Dominion in the 17th Century* by Warren Billings; *Myne Owne Ground—Race and Freedom on Virginia's Eastern Shore, 1640–1676,* by T. H. Breen and Stephen Innes; *Many Thousands Gone—The First Two Centuries of Slavery in North America* by Ira Berlin; *Virginia Immigrants and Adventurers—A Biographical Dictionary, 1607–1635,* and *Jamestown People to 1800* by Martha W. McCartney; *The Mystery of the Exploding Teeth and Other Curiosities from the History of Medicine* by

Thomas Morris; *Medicine in Virginia, 1607–1699,* by Thomas P. Hughes; *Medicine in Virginia in the Seventeenth Century* by Wyndham Blanton; *The Apothecary in Colonial Virginia* by Harold B. Gill, Jr.; *The Apothecary in Eighteenth-Century Williamsburg* by Thomas Ford; *Humoring the Body* by Gail Kern Paster; and "Ordeal of Touch in Colonial Virginia" from *The Virginia Magazine of History and Biography* (4, no. 2, 1896).

From *A Briefe and True Reporte of the New found land of Virginia* by Thomas Hariot (1588), I borrowed language advertising tobacco and the reference to "invisible bullets"; *Nova Britannia: Offering most excellent fruits by planting in Virginia* by Robert Johnson (1609) gave me language used for advertising the settlement of Virginia; "Letter from Virginia" by Richard Frethorne (1623) provided some of the phrasing for Sam and Tony's letter; the language used in Doctor Herman's notice is from an advertisement in *The Virginia Gazette* (1771); Martin's address to the other servants is a version of what appears in *Complaint from Heaven with a Huy and Crye and a Petition out of Virginia and Maryland* (1676); part of an exchange between Solomon and Gumby is from *The Voyages and Travels of James Barclay, 1777,* and *Journal of a Tour to North Carolina, 1787,* by William Attmore (cited in *Slave Counterpoint* by Philip D. Morgan); the jurors' charge read at the Jamestown courthouse is from Surry County Records, volume 1 (cited in *Medicine in Virginia in the Seventeenth Century* by Wyndham Blanton); *Prisoners of Hope—A Tale of Colonial Virginia,* an 1898 romance by Mary Johnson, gave me a character called "Margery," whom I further developed into my own "Marge."

ACKNOWLEDGMENTS

I have been given so much by so many, and *I can no other answer make but thanks . . . and ever thanks . . .* My terrific agent, Eric Simonoff, not only launched this into the world but offered valuable suggestions that prompted my re-visioning of the novel, as well as the encouragement that made me persist; Fiona Baird represented this book overseas and has also been its great champion; my editors, Kathryn Belden of Scribner, USA, and Molly Slight of Scribe, UK, have both been staunch supporters of this book and their astute and thoughtful guidance has made it so much better—it has been a wonderful collaboration; Nan Graham of Scribner has been so very gracious and encouraging right from the start; so many people working behind the scenes have done so much to help bring this to final form.

Jeff Friedman, Chris Parsons, and my colleagues (current and retired) in the English Department, Keene State College, have been very supportive of my dual academic identity; Greg Knouff directed me to the books I read when I first began; Jennifer Stemp's talents and efficiency have been indispensable. The folks at the New Hampshire Writer's Project, the staff at Mason Library, KSC, and the Faculty Development Grant Committee, KSC, have all extended their support in numerous ways; Robin Dizard shared with me an article on East Indians in colonial America and so planted the seed of this novel; my much-admired mentor in all things Shakespearean, Dympna Callaghan, has been equally interested in my academic and my creative work and sees no reason why I should not do both.

And my family has always been there, so many of them immigrants and

wanderers, following in the footsteps of "Tony": Premi Shankavaram hero-
ically read this, typos and all, and offered her sound advice and encouragement; Ashok Charry and the late P. V. Shantha have reminded me to get back
to writing fiction; P. V. Madhavi, Ravi Shankavaram, and Rashmi Jagadish
Charry have cheered me on; Varun Shankavaram, Ved Shankavaram, and
Aadith Charry have all grown up asking me to tell them stories (this one is
also for you, dear boys); Magic sat right next to me for almost every word I
wrote; Venkat Sadasivan has been by my side as I conceived and created this
novel—I am ever thankful for his generosity and forbearance while I spent
many long hours writing and for his steadfast faith in this project even when
my own wavered—as in the sonnet, he is the star to my wandering bark. And,
as always, my parents, V. Shankar Charry and Malathy Charry—they set me
off on the journey and it is to them I still return—*The East Indian* is dedicated
to them.